Ring of Fire
PHOEBE CONN
WRITING AS CINNAMON BURKE!
Bestselling Author Of *Lady Rogue*

LOVE'S SWEET TORMENT

"Just hold me a minute," Haven said.

Ian muffled an anguished moan against her throat. "It's not nearly enough."

Haven took a deep breath, but it didn't help. "I know, but anything more will be too much, and I won't be able to stop you."

"Do you even want to stop me?"

Haven closed her eyes, but saw his face clearly in her mind. She knew his features as well as her own and could have sculpted the angle of his cheek and jaw. The sweetness of his mouth lingered in her memory. She could feel the tension in his muscles through her robe. If only she could feel his bare skin against hers for just a moment, but neither of them would be able to stop then....

Cinnamon Burke

Ring of Fire

LOVE SPELL ◆ **NEW YORK CITY**

LOVE SPELL®

December 1995

Published by

Dorchester Publishing Co., Inc.
276 Fifth Avenue
New York, NY 10001

Printed in the United States of America.

Ring Of Fire is dedicated to the memory of the extraordinary master of the maze, M.C. Escher.

Ring of Fire

Chapter One

Summer, 2261

Ian St. Ives sprang from the snow-covered rocks, spread his arms wide, and for an instant seemed to hang suspended in the crisp morning air. Then, with a champion's grace he completed the elegant swan dive and sliced through the blanket of steam hovering above the ice-ringed pool. His hands split the water as he surged deep before surfacing to begin swimming with long, powerful strokes. Warmed by volcanic heat, the bubbling water coaxed the tension from his lean, muscular body more skillfully than the most talented masseuse, but his mind churned with torments the water's soothing temperature would never touch.

A superbly conditioned athlete, he found num-

bers simply an annoying distraction and had
ceased counting laps in his teens. Instead he relied on his senses alone as an indication of his
endurance, and swam with a dolphin's joy. He
heard the low drone of the shuttle engine when
it was still miles away, cursed the intrusion in a
fiery stream of bubbles, and swam until his daily
ritual was complete. When he finally hauled himself out of the magnificent natural pool he had
accepted the fact that his vacation was at an end
and managed a smile as Control handed him a
plush white robe.

A small man who habitually dressed in black,
Control shivered against Iceland's perpetual
chill. "I would have waited for you inside, but I
didn't wish to risk alarming whatever guests you
might be entertaining."

At six feet three inches, Ian towered above his
superior, but he nodded slightly to accord him
the respect he deserved. "You know me better
than that," he chided. "This is a sanctuary as
much as a home, and I never invite guests—or
women, which is what you really meant—to join
me here."

Squinting against the sun's glare off the snow,
Control watched Ian loop the robe's belt around
his narrow hips. Ian St. Ives was one of the Alado
Corporation's most efficient intelligence agents,
and Control never wasted his considerable talents on frivolous missions. Ian apparently
thrived in this splendid isolation, and Control
knew Ian did not enjoy his company any more
than he enjoyed Ian's.

He shrank back as Ian shook a sparkling spray of water from his long blond hair. Anxious to complete his errand, Control shifted his weight from foot to foot in a nervous dance. "I would not have disturbed your solitude, but time is of the essence," he murmured, his breath rising in a spiraling curl of steam.

Ian gestured toward his ski lodge. A light dusting of snow did not even begin to soften the angular lines of his fortress home. "You're always welcome here, Control. Come inside. Your skin is turning a most unbecoming shade of blue."

By contrast, Ian's strenuous swim had given his deeply tanned complexion a healthy glow. His amber eyes sparkled with a teasing light, and as they walked the short distance to the house, he moved barefoot over the snow with a long, sure stride. "Do you have time to stay for breakfast?"

As they came through the back door, Control cast a furtive glance over the immaculately kept kitchen. All polished chrome and steel, it was a chef's paradise, but he could not imagine Ian donning an apron and preparing a meal. "Unfortunately no," he replied.

Control paused at the steps leading down into the spacious living room. A fire burned brightly in the massive fireplace carved out of the stone wall on the east, while on the north a wall of glass afforded a stunning view of the Blue Mountains in the distance. A nubby white rug with an irregular shape spread over the stone floor like spilled milk, and the furniture, which had been custom-built to Ian's impressive size, was upholstered in pale natural hides. The only touch of color in the stark room was provided by the tastefully displayed medals Ian had won in the Artic Warrior competitions. They were more than ten years old, but his record times as a cross-country skier and his scores as a marksman still stood.

The room was warm, but the snowy panorama prevented Control from shaking the chill of the outdoors. He crossed to the fireplace and held out his gloved hands. "Get dressed. Then we'll talk."

"Yes, sir," Ian responded in a lazy drawl. He turned toward the wing housing the bedrooms, den, and gym, and swung into the first door on the right. A snow leopard, his dark spots pale against his thick white fur, was stretched out across the foot of the massive bed. Awakened from his morning nap, the beast greeted Ian with a deep growl that slid into a noisy purr.

"We've company, Samson, but he's a gentle soul and you must try not to frighten him."

Samson remained in a relaxed sprawl while he yawned widely and displayed an impressive set of long, sharp teeth. Ian scratched the big cat's tufted ears, then moved on to the closet. The whole house was decorated in neutral shades, and in the master bedroom the walls, bedspread, and rug were the color of rich cream. Ian's wardrobe was equally severe, for when he was not wearing whatever disguise his assignment required he preferred black. He grabbed a pair of pants and a shirt made of a soft fabric that allowed the complete freedom of movement his profession required. He had never enjoyed kicking an adversary in the face, but when necessary he had the agility and strength to deal a deadly blow.

He sat down beside Samson to pull on black suede boots, then raked his still damp hair off his forehead. Thick and straight, it held the deep tracks of his fingers even after he stood. "Come on, boy," he coaxed. "You want to meet the boss?"

Samson bounded off the bed and followed Ian into the living room but eyed Control with little curiosity. He waited for Ian to sink down into his favorite chair by the fire, then curled himself around his master's feet. Uninterested in human conversation, he licked his paws with deep concentration and began his morning grooming.

"My God," Control gasped. "Is that monster tame?"

"As long as he's well fed," Ian replied. "Which he is today, so you're in no danger from him."

Control did not imbibe spirits of any kind, so Ian did not offer the Icelandic schnapps known as "Black Death," but his superior also refused his offer of coffee or tea. "It isn't refreshments but your full attention I require," Control said, assuming his usual brusque tone, but his eyes remained on the leopard. Clearly, he wasn't pleased to find Ian possessed such a large and potentially lethal pet. He chose the chair on the opposite side of the fire, but that distance from

15

the leopard wasn't nearly great enough for him to feel secure.

"You have it," Ian assured him. "What's the assignment this time: pirates, counterfeiters, industrial espionage?"

Control pursed his lips and frowned darkly as he yanked off his gloves. He reached inside the overcoat he had yet to remove and pulled out a manila envelope. "I have something a bit more unusual. My time as well as yours is too valuable to waste on conjecture, so please listen without interrupting."

A slow smile tugged at the corner of Ian's mouth, but he suppressed it before it widened into an insolent grin. No one had ever accused him of being given to idle chatter, but Control regarded a single extraneous word as an unfortunate digression. Ian could not resist teasing him. "The weather has been extremely mild. This is a good day for your visit."

Not understanding Ian's attempt at humor, Control brushed the comment aside. "Yes, indeed, but the weather will soon change and I don't want your departure delayed. There's been a series of disappearances from mining colony 317, and—"

Ian gave a derisive laugh. "You're joking."

Control's dark eyes narrowed. "I would have sworn you knew I do not regard the work of the Intelligence Branch as a fit source for humor."

Ian leaned down to scratch Samson's broad head. "Sorry, Control, but I fail to understand why an intelligence operative would be sent on a missing persons assignment."

"Must I repeat myself? This is a mining colony. Access to the mine and all its facilities is strictly controlled. Miners cannot simply wander off, nor vanish into thin air, and yet more than a dozen appear to have done just that. My preliminary research into the mine's history convinced me that the most recent disappearances are merely new evidence of a recurrent problem. For the first four years of its operation the mine was an independent enterprise. Then the original owners wished to found additional colonies, and they sold 317 to the Alado Corporation for the necessary capital for expansion.

"That was three years ago. At the time of the sale documentation was provided of the mine's excellent safety record, and the experts conducting our inspections failed to turn up any undisclosed hazards. Production is high and everything appears to be satisfactory, but miners have continued to disappear. I expect you to put a stop to the disappearances, and recover the missing men, or their bodies. It's a simple assignment but one that must be brought to a swift conclusion before the women's Rocketball tournament is held there."

Control was shuffling the notes he had withdrawn from the envelope, but Ian found his supervisor's averted glance far more revealing than his words. He rose, stepped over Samson, and walked up to the fireplace. He leaned back against the mantel, slid his hands into his pockets, and regarded Control with a steady stare.

"Why didn't you mention the Rocketball tournament in the first place? I doubt Alado cares much about a few missing miners, when the only men who will take such dangerous work are either desperate for money to cover their debts or seeking a place to hide from the authorities.

"Rocketball, on the other hand, is one of Alado's most profitable leisure activities. I've never followed the sport. How much has been wagered this year?"

Control mumbled an exorbitant figure under his breath. "The amount is irrelevant, Ian. The work in the mines is exactly what you describe: exhausting and hazardous. You're right about the miners, too; their backgrounds are anything but commendable, but they do necessary work and they look forward to the tournaments with the same joyful anticipation with which a child awaits Christmas."

Ian wasn't impressed. "Without the games the miners would be even more short-tempered and unruly than they already are. Then there's the fortune Alado earns from the gambling on the outcome. That Rocketball is in itself a deadly sport isn't even considered, is it?"

"I refuse to be drawn into that tiresome debate," Control stressed firmly. "You may have decided against making the transition from amateur to professional sports, but that does not mean others should not have that right."

Ian raised his hands. His fingers were long and slim, his palms uncallused despite a vigorous lifestyle. "I'll concede the point. I just don't want any misunderstanding. Am I being sent to protect the miners, or the profits from the tournament?"

Deeply offended, Control puffed out his cheeks. "Forgive me if I've failed to convey the gravity the case deserves. Something or someone with evil intentions is operating at 317. It must be stopped. The tournament has absolutely no bearing on the case. It's merely a coincidence that it will be taking place there this year. As you know, the site was chosen in a random drawing, but it will provide an excellent distraction."

"Not for me it won't."

"I was referring to the miners!"

Ian's glance was decidedly skeptical. "Of course. What's my cover?"

Control reached into his overcoat a second time and removed an identification badge. "You're to be John Hyatt, an insurance investigator. The mine security detail is not above suspicion. In fact, no one at the mine is in the clear at present, but a man from the insurance division won't alarm them, as someone from central security, or intelligence, surely would."

Feeling trapped in an assignment he would never have chosen on his own, Ian sighed unhappily, prompting Samson to rise and come to him. He knelt to give the leopard a playful hug, then glanced toward Control. "I understand. This is a routine undercover job."

Bristling with indignation, Control straightened his narrow shoulders. "The first thing I taught you was never to regard any assignment as routine, or it will surely be your last."

Ian knew Control was referring to an untimely death rather than the threat of an early retirement. "Yes, I remember. Would you like me to repeat all your sage advice verbatim?"

"No; just put a stop to the mischief at the mine before the tournament begins." Control left his chair, but rather than approach Ian and Samson, he extended his hand and waved the information packet.

Ian reached out to take it. Internal security wasn't much of a challenge compared to battling the lawless elements of the galaxy, but he had learned long ago not to complain about assignments when any change Control made would only land him in a far worse situation. "I'll give this my best, sir. I'll have your serial killer, or whatever is menacing the miners, taken care of quickly."

"Good. Use the activity surrounding the upcoming tournament to every advantage. If you appear to be more interested in the games than finding the lost miners, the culprits, if there are any, will lower their guard and be that much easier to catch."

"Of course." Ian walked Control to the door. The shuttle, emblazoned with Alado's double triangle and lightning bolt crest, had landed nearby, but there was no sign of the crew. They had obviously chosen to remain in the warmth of the cockpit rather than enjoy Iceland's beauty. Ian thought it a pity they had not believed the opportunity to appreciate the vast snowy grandeur worth the chill. His own ship was hidden in a hangar buried beneath ten feet of snow, and he provided the sole crew.

"I'll leave within the hour," Ian promised. Samson pushed by him and bounded out into the snow.

"Who tends that beast when you're away?" Control gauged the distance to his shuttle with a fearful gaze.

"There's a man who raises shaggy little Icelandic ponies who lives just over the rise. He and his wife stay here when I'm away."

Swinging wide of Samson's antics, Control began to back away. "They don't suspect your occupation?"

"I've told them I do special projects for the Alado Corporation. It's the truth, if not all of it. Now turn and walk back to your shuttle. If you run, Samson will think you want to play tag."

Control spun on his heel, sending up a small shower of snow, and then carefully retraced his steps to the shuttle. When he reached the ramp he turned back and gave an awkward wave; then, greatly relieved to have escaped Samson's jaws, he quickly ducked inside. A member of the crew withdrew the ramp and closed the hatch. In a matter of seconds the shuttle was airborne.

Even by Control's precise standards the visit had been brief, but as Ian watched the shuttle fade into the distance he felt as though the whole morning had been wasted. He called to Samson, who shook off the snow clinging to his thick fur before following him inside. The big cat had already been fed, and now, having no appetite himself, Ian carried the envelope Control had given him into his den. He removed the disk and switched on the computer.

A soft feminine voice greeted him. "Good morning, Ian. How are you today?"

Ian dropped into the chair opposite the screen. "I felt a lot better before Control arrived."

"Did he offer a disagreeable assignment?"

"No, just one that promises to be tedious." Ian slipped the disk into the slot. "Run the first of the files, please."

Ian crossed his arms over his chest as he reviewed the diagrams of the mine. Located on a distant asteroid valued solely for its mineral wealth, 317 produced astronium, a rare element used as an alloy in the fabrication of the strong but lightweight metal from which spaceships were built. The main shaft was deep and sprouted tunnels creating a labyrinth more fit for an ant colony than human endeavor.

Samson nudged Ian's knee, and he leaned over to give his pet's ears an affectionate tickle before requesting the next file. He reviewed the names of the missing miners and the dates of their disappearances, which had occurred over sporadic intervals. The first had happened six years earlier, while the most recent was just three weeks ago. There was no pattern to the dates.

No men had been lost the first year of the mine's operation, but three had vanished in the second. Four had been lost the third, then only two the next year. Alado had reported one disappearance the year they had taken over. Two miners had been lost last year, and in the first half of this year three men were missing. In all, there were fifteen lost miners.

The only similarity was that all the men had been reported missing not at the end of their shifts, when they might have been expected to have tumbled down an uncharted crevice, but during off-duty hours when their safety was supposedly assured.

"Damn odd," Ian murmured. "Give me the last file," he prompted, and a review of the women's Rocketball standings scrolled up the screen. There were four teams in the finals: the Flames, the Zephyrs, the Satin Spikes, and the Pagans. A modern derivation of the twentieth-century game of jai alai, Rocketball was a wild and dangerous sport in which teams of four players used racquets to slam a small ball off the high walls of a long, narrow court. There were few rules, and the men's games frequently deteriorated into brawls both on and off the court.

The women's teams played with more flair than brutality, however, and their contests were the most popular. Wagers ran into the millions of dollars per game, and fans were fiercely loyal to their favorite teams. That the women were young, fit, usually quite beautiful, and wore skintight uniforms was never cited as the real reason for the games' popularity, but Ian was positive far more than an appreciation of the sport accounted for the male fans' devotion to their idols.

The Flames had the best record going into the

tournament, and although Ian had never attended a game he recognized several names as he read the player roster. The team captain was Haven Wray, who at twenty-seven was already a legend in the sport. A product of the amateur leagues that nurtured athletically talented children almost from the day they could walk, she had turned professional at seventeen when there had been no more amateur medals left to win. Unlike many star athletes, she had accomplished the transition from singles to team play smoothly and had made the Flames the dominant force in the women's division.

"Give me the profile on Haven Wray," Ian asked, and he found himself gazing into a pair of clear green eyes that reflected not merely keen intelligence but the same poignant sorrow he saw so often in his own. Struck by that unexpected kinship, Ian could only whisper, "Freeze it right there."

It took several seconds for his glance to move past the eyes with their seductive sweep of thick lashes, but then he found Haven possessed a fashion model's cool beauty. Her hair was a glorious golden blond she wore pulled back in a long braid. She had a delicate nose that he knew would be perfection in profile and a sensitive mouth with a full lower lip that begged for kisses.

"Print that for me," Ian ordered in the same husky tone. He reached out to take the copy of the photograph. While it confirmed his initial impression, he craved still more.

"Run the Flames' last game." He reached down

to stroke the sleeping Samson with a distracted caress as he watched Haven and three of her teammates enter the court. Their colorful uniforms were dyed to create the stunning effect of a living flame. The boots and legs of their bodysuits were a bright blue that bled into purple to hug the thighs, then lightened to red at the hips. A band of brilliant orange circled the midriff, then burst into a vibrant yellow that stretched over the bustline, shoulders, and down the sleeves. The team's helmets were a glossy red streaked with jagged flashes of yellow and orange flame.

Even with three other women dressed in the same spectacular uniform, Ian identified Haven easily by the grace of her stride. Then she turned, and he saw the number one in gold on her back. In this contest the Flames were playing a team that hadn't made the finals, and Haven quickly ran up the score, then left the court to give a substitute, Elida Rivard, a chance to play. Ian had not seen nearly enough of Haven, and he replayed the opening minutes of the game three times before he recalled his promise to be on his way within the hour.

Reluctantly, he rose and shut off the computer, but he withdrew the informative and surprisingly entertaining disk Control had provided and took it with him. The computer screen was smaller on board his ship, but he was positive Haven Wray would be every bit as dazzling an entertainment in miniature.

* * *

Haven Wray climbed onto the team physician's padded table, stretched out on her stomach, and, with a languid sigh, closed her eyes. She covered a yawn, and then moaned contentedly as Dr. Aren Manzari began rubbing the ball of her right foot. "Better make it fast today, Aren. I'm falling asleep."

"Good. You don't get nearly enough rest."

"I'll rest after I retire."

Aren worked his thumbs into the sole of her foot. "You can't continue playing as hard as you have been, Haven, or you'll not make it through the finals. It would be tragic if a needless injury cut short a career as remarkable as yours."

Haven's voice was a hushed whisper. "You can't scare me. There's more than one pro playing with a bionic knee, and you know it."

Aren gave her right foot a fond squeeze before releasing it, then stepped to the opposite side of the table and picked up her left. She had just left the shower, and her skin was warm and damp. The perfumed soap she preferred gave her supple body the lingering fragrance of ancient spices. As always, he had a difficult time paying attention to his task when his patient's creamy smooth body was so enticing.

"Bionic knees, elbows, wrists, ankles," he complained, "are mechanical parts and won't create a superb athlete, nor keep one playing indefinitely."

"Is this your famous your-time-is-over speech? I didn't expect to hear it before I reached thirty-five."

Aren slid his hands up her leg and gently massaged the calf muscle. "No, this is my conserve-your-resources speech, and you ought to take it seriously. Bodies aren't the only thing that grow weary, Haven. Your spirit could do with a long rest too."

"Aren," Haven begged softly, "don't start."

Aren moved his hands up her thigh. He knew Haven to be a warm, caring woman, but she was maddeningly distant at times. He loved her with a desperation that had made a fool of him, but she treated him with tender consideration rather than the complete indifference she showed to so many other men. It was what gave him hope that she might one day accept his marriage proposal, but the wait suddenly seemed interminable. He dropped his hands to his sides.

The lengthy pause in Aren's attentions caused Haven to raise herself up slightly and glance over her shoulder. "What's wrong?"

"I can't do this anymore." Aren backed away from the table, hit the edge of the counter, and was jarred to a halt. "Touching you, when you don't want to touch me, is the worst kind of torture. I can't do it another day. I'll have one of the other trainers finish your massage."

Haven gripped her bright yellow towel, then tucked it over her breasts as she sat up. Knowing the padded table would make a convenient barrier, she rolled off on the opposite side from Aren and turned to face him squarely. He was a handsome man in his thirties, with glossy black hair, deep brown eyes, and an endearing grin, but his

27

comment was true. He did not arouse the slightest bit of desire in her—but then, few men did.

"There are eight other women on the team, and every single one is in love with you. Why don't you give one of them a chance?"

Aren shook his head. "It wouldn't work. I like them all, just as you like me, but that's not enough, and we both know it." He hesitated, but now that he had begun this painful conversation he couldn't stifle his need to reach her.

"I've watched you with other men, Haven, and your pattern is always the same. You meet someone new and if you're interested, you date him a few times. But then you refuse to move past a casual friendship. You've left a great many men not merely badly frustrated but angry. There's got to be a reason you can't care deeply for anyone."

Haven couldn't dispute Aren's insightful observation, but she wouldn't confirm it either. "I don't believe this is a discussion we ought to be having while I'm wearing no more than a towel," she argued. "In fact, the subject is way out of your area of expertise, which is physical fitness, not matters of the heart."

Aren rested his hands on the table. "I've only been the team physician for two years, but I have access to your complete medical records. It doesn't take any great leap of logic to piece together what happened and why you're so reluctant to fall in love again."

Instantly wary, Haven began to back away toward the door. "You're not making any sense."

"Oh, but I am, and probably for the first time. You were only nineteen when you married Blake Ellis, who was the Flames' lead trainer at the time. He must have known you were pregnant when you played in the finals that year." Aren watched the color drain from Haven's face, but his intention was to be kind, not cruel.

"The Flames won the tournament, but you miscarried the next day, and Blake filed for divorce. He forced you to choose between him and the game, didn't he? But you couldn't desert your teammates in the finals, and it cost you both your husband and your child. You've been punishing yourself, and every man you meet, ever since."

Hot tears of shame welled up in Haven's eyes, and she had to swallow hard to force away the painful knot that filled her throat. She had trusted Aren, and that had obviously been a mistake she wouldn't repeat. "You are never, *ever* to mention your imaginative interpretation of my medical history—not to me, or to anyone else. If you so much as breathe a word of your speculation, or even hint at it, I'll not only have you fired from the Flames, I'll have your medical license suspended for gross misconduct."

Aren knew the risk he was taking, but she meant too much to him to back down. "You're angry because I'm speaking the truth, not conjecture. But please, Haven, for your own sake, if you won't confide in me, then find someone else who can help you resolve your feelings of guilt before they destroy you."

Haven came around the table. Even in her bare feet she stood six feet tall, and she and Aren were equals in height. "Does the word *betrayal* mean anything to you?" she asked in a threatening whisper. "I won't have my most private emotions dissected and analyzed by anyone, least of all you. Now I'm taking the first flight to 317. I'll train there for the finals, and I won't need you or anyone else there to help me."

"You're wrong," Aren warned. "You need me more than you know."

Haven's eyes took on a feral gleam. "No, you're the one who's wrong. I don't need you or anyone else to survive, and I never will."

She turned away and sprinted from the room before Aren could find a reply, but her bitter farewell rang in his ears long after she had gone, and he feared he had lost the only chance he, or any other man, would ever have to touch her heart.

Haven dashed into the locker room, threw her towel down the laundry chute, and grabbed an electric blue robe. She knotted the belt tightly around her waist and left before any of her teammates had time to notice her furious expression. She strode past the team dining hall and went straight to her quarters. She had the most spacious suite, but as the door slid closed it seemed no larger than a cell.

Unable to push her mind past Aren's ridiculous advice, she paced with her hands curled tightly at her sides. She could talk to counselors until she grew hoarse and nothing would change. The past could not be altered. She simply had to live with it, but she had vowed not to repeat it.

Swiftly exhausted by the rage Aren's comments had inspired, she slid into the thickly padded lounger that filled the center of the main room. Once comfortably seated, she called to the computer that controlled the suite's environment. "Max, give me the Dreamer's channel."

Instantly the whole room was flooded with a luminous azure glow that played over the pale yellow walls, ceiling, and floor, enveloping Haven in flickering shadows. She inhaled deeply, then slowed the rhythm of her breathing to match the Dreamer's.

Prized for the richness of her dreams, the Dreamer shared her inner visions with whomever wished to join her, and Haven was a frequent visitor. It was only in another's dreams, rather than her own inner nightmares, that she found the peace to sustain her. Some believed the Dreamer's channel, coming as it did from the subconscious, was addictive, but Haven had never heeded those warnings. She sighed with true contentment as she sank deeper under the Dreamer's magical spell.

Chapter Two

Ian spent the flight to 317 studying the operations of Alado's mines, and by the time he arrived he had become an expert on the industry. A typical mining colony, 317 was constructed of triangular cells welded into a vast modular network that provided the expertly controlled environment human beings require to thrive. The docking bays from which the astronium ore was transported made up the first quarter of interwoven structures, and the aboveground level of the mines the next. The third provided housing, hydroponic gardens, storage of supplies, and living areas for miners, administrators, support personnel, and guests. At the end of the sprawling chain were the sports facilities and the arena where the women's Rocketball finals would take place.

As Ian approached from space, he was struck by 317's resemblance to a gigantic fish. The docking bays formed the mouth, the mines and living quarters the body and fins. The arena created the huge fantail. The triangular components were lit from inside, giving the exterior of the glowing complex the appearance of silvery scales. Having never cared for the taste of fish, Ian hoped the fanciful image wouldn't prove to be a bad omen.

Intending to stow away his gear before he introduced himself to Egon Rascon, the mine superintendent, he rode the tram that ran the length of the complex from the docking bay to the guest quarters, heaved his flight bag over his shoulder, and headed down the long hall to his room. The beige walls absorbed his shadow, and the rust-colored carpet muffled the sounds of his steps. He was still several doors away from his unit when Haven Wray appeared in the corridor. She was looking down as she knotted her hair atop her head and walked straight toward him.

Dressed in a figure-hugging sleeveless red leotard and matching tights, she was clearly on her way to the gym. Ian could have stepped aside to avoid a collision but, surprised to find Haven already there, he chose not to waste such an excellent opportunity to meet her. He timed his approach perfectly and reached out to catch her shoulders a brief instant before she ran smack into his chest. His palms slid over her bare skin, and he felt the resulting jolt as deeply as she did, but as his fingers encircled her upper arms, his reaction was one of pure pleasure rather than fright.

Haven's head came up with a startled jerk. Knocked off balance, she grabbed his arms for support and took another quick step to regain a secure footing. Then, ready to flee, she shifted her weight to the balls of her feet. She was wearing a pair of lightweight training shoes and flexed the soles to gain maximum traction.

A slow smile crept over Ian's lips as he enjoyed his first opportunity to appraise Haven's beauty in the flesh. Framed by long, black lashes, her gaze held the exquisite mystery of priceless emeralds. He noted the pale aqua frost to her lids and the lush coral tint to her lips. She scarcely needed the delicate tattooing to enhance features of such rare perfection, but he was amused to discover the charming blush on her cheeks was completely natural.

"You must be more careful, Ms. Wray," he chided in a teasing tone. "It would be a shame if you were injured before the Rocketball finals have even begun."

Haven quickly eluded his grasp, sending her long hair tumbling over her shoulders and into her eyes. "I'm so sorry. Except for me, this wing's been unoccupied all week." She swept her hair away from her face and stepped back to a more comfortable distance into which to converse. "I didn't expect to—" She fell silent as their glances locked for the second time. It wasn't just the unusual clear amber of Ian's eyes that mesmerized her, however, or his appealing grin. It was the fact that she had never expected to meet him, and most especially not at a mining colony on the edge of the frontier.

"Ian St. Ives," she whispered with an awe-struck reverence. Her smile widened, revealing dimples few men ever glimpsed. "This is such a thrill. I had no idea you were attending the games. I was one of your most enthusiastic fans. In fact, I had photographs of you taped inside my locker when I was—" she paused for a moment to reflect but didn't glance away—"no more than twelve or thirteen. I thought I'd die when you retired from the Artic Warrior competition and just disappeared."

Amazed to come upon her idol so unexpectedly, Haven leaned back against the wall in a casual pose and crossed her arms over her chest. "Where have you been the last eleven years?"

When Ian had been competing in the Artic Warrior games, action shots of him were frequently flashed across popular sports programs. He had even been featured on wall-sized posters, but he had been clothed from head to toe and had worn a helmet with a smoked visor. Virtually unrecognizable in his warrior days, he had never done more than change his name when he began working undercover for Alado. There had always been the off chance he might meet a former acquaintance while on assignment, but in the past he had always seen them first and avoided all contact.

Now he stood not two feet away from the most gorgeous woman he had ever hoped to meet, and her effect upon him was even more stirring than he had imagined from her spectacular photograph and thrilling Rocketball play. The only problem was that he had to complete his assignment before he could devote his energies to pleasing her. That she had once had a crush on him was gratifying in the extreme, but he couldn't admit that yet.

"I'm sorry to disappoint you," he replied regretfully, "but I'm John Hyatt, an insurance investigator for Alado, and I've no idea who Ian St. Ives even is."

Struck by the absurdity of the lie, Haven straightened up, opened her mouth to challenge him, and then thought better of it. He was Ian St. Ives all right. She had absolutely no doubt about it, but if he wished to assume another identity, she would play along for the time being.

"Now I feel even more foolish than I did when I nearly walked right into you," she apologized. "I've always wanted to meet Ian so badly, I was completely fooled when I noticed the unusual color of your eyes. It was a natural mistake, but he's several inches taller than you, a good deal more lean, and probably a few years younger."

That Ian was on the wrong end of her comparison stung. He was taller than most men, and as lean as a whip. As for his age, if anything he looked younger than his thirty-six years, which was by no means old. Ian was too well trained to allow his dismay to show in his expression, however. His flight bag was growing increasingly heavy, and he nodded toward his room. "Let me drop off my things; then I'll walk you wherever you're going. Who knows, after you get to know me you might even find that you like me better than Ian."

Haven's laugh sparkled with a teasing effervescence. "Sorry, but I don't need company when I train." She gave his left biceps a squeeze as she passed by, and even through the soft folds of his gray tunic she was convinced he had Ian St. Ives's hard-muscled body. She jogged the length of the corridor, then turned back to wave before she disappeared around the corner. It wasn't until she reached the gym that she realized she did not need any distractions before the finals, not even one as enticing as Ian St. Ives. Later, perhaps, but certainly not before, nor, God forbid, during.

Ian was still preoccupied with thoughts of Haven as he entered Egon Rascon's office. Life had a way of playing cruel tricks on people, and he was afraid this might be one of them. As he had informed Control, he never invited women to his home, but that did not mean that he did not have a healthy interest in them, or pursue them whenever he had sufficient time. Unfortunately, right now he didn't.

There was no one seated in the mine superintendent's outer office. A sterile waiting room with a padded bench and a chart detailing the mine's production for decoration, it was painted the same soothing beige as the guest quarters. A scanner beam passed over him, and a metallic voice greeted him from the communications panel in the wall opposite the door. "If you have an appointment, state your name. If not, state your problem, and an appointment will be made."

Ian had no use for electronic secretaries. They were more efficient than any human being, required no salary or benefits, but were absolutely no fun to tease. "John Hyatt," he replied. "Mr. Rascon is expecting me."

The door to the inner office slid open with a rasping hiss, and Ian adjusted his posture from proud to a slight slump. As he moved forward, he blurred his usual forceful stride into a hesitant shuffle. When he had retired from sports he had discovered a previously unsuspected talent for undercover work. Now, after eleven years in the field, he possessed a chameleon's ability to affect whatever colorful identity his assignment required. For this investigation he would be a timid, unassuming soul whose methods would not threaten the complacency of any guilty parties until the moment he placed them under arrest.

As part of his investigation, Alado had given him access to the mine's personnel files, and he knew all about Egon Rascon. A handsome gray-haired, brown-eyed man in his forties, Egon had been divorced three times and had sired five offspring: three girls and two boys. Heavily in debt as a result of his marital difficulties and large family, he had become the superintendent at 317 three years ago when Alado had taken over. An experienced geologist, he managed the mine with a dedication Alado had rewarded with extravagant bonuses each year.

Egon was dressed in a rust-colored uniform that complemented his dark complexion. Before landing, Ian had changed into the charcoal gray tunic and pants worn by Alado's central administrative staff. Striving for the anonymity of his shadowlike clothing, he responded to Rascon's greeting in the rapid, high-pitched voice of a petty bureaucrat obssessed with detail.

"I am happy to meet you, Mr. Rascon. I do hope to clear up the problems here quickly. I fail to understand why our branch hasn't conducted a complete investigation long before this."

Egon's office was four times the size of the anteroom, providing the ample space a man of his importance deserved. His massive ebony desk had computer screens embedded in the top, allowing him to monitor the mine's operation without ever having to leave his comfortable chair. The walls were covered with complex maps of the main shaft and the maze of side branches, providing a clear display of the mine's continuous expansion. Due to their frequent use, the corners of the meticulously detailed drawings were curled and frayed.

Egon had risen to greet Ian, and now he gestured toward the row of deeply padded chairs facing his desk. Covered in a nubby rust-colored fabric, they were an example of the expensive furnishings Alado's designers selected for offices in an effort to constantly affirm its image as the premier interstellar corporation.

"Please, make yourself comfortable, Mr. Hyatt. May I offer you something to eat or drink? Our food here is superb, and after your trip you must be very tired of prepackaged rations."

Ian chose the middle chair but sat forward on the edge rather than sinking back into the thick cushions. "Thank you for your hospitality, but no. I would prefer to discuss the reason for my visit rather than be entertained."

Rascon appeared surprised but then nodded and resumed his seat. "May I assume that you're familiar with our operation here?"

"Yes, of course," Ian replied with obvious impatience.

"Good; then you know that mining is a dangerous enterprise." He began what was obviously a carefully rehearsed speech. "But under my management we stay well within the boundaries of safety. We use laser cannon to cut through the rock, which is far safer than explosives, but we still have problems with an occasional rock burst that lets fly with splinters of jagged stone shrapnel. As can be expected, there's considerable seismic activity, but we reinforce the tunnels as we go to avoid cave-ins. We rely upon an extensive use of robotic equipment to minimize the risk to the men and deploy a multitude of sensors to warn of any contamination from seeping gases to prevent fires.

"You are aware of our exemplary safety record?" Rascon asked proudly.

Ian nodded. "You're to be congratulated, but

despite your enviable safety precautions, fifteen miners have vanished from this site in the last seven years."

Leaning forward, Egon Rascon rested his arms on the desk. "Surely we can't be held responsible for the men who disappeared before Alado took over 317."

"No, of course not, but it would be a mistake not to recognize the pattern. What can you tell me about the missing men you knew? Did they share some common trait?"

Egon responded with a rumbling chuckle. "Of course. All miners are the same to some degree. They were either eager to accept dangerous work in exchange for high wages, or simply the thrill, or they needed a place where their enemies, ex-wives, or creditors were unlikely to find them. Interview every man at this installation if you like. You'll hear a tiresome repetition of similar stories.

"We have several women working here as well, but they are all assigned to the medical unit. We maintain a superb emergency hospital to provide immediate care in the unlikely event of an accident. Our female employees tend to serve here only on a short-term basis, however, and soon rotate out."

Ian appeared to relax slightly, leaning forward another couple of inches and softening his tone. "You must have a theory."

Egon glanced toward the door as though he was expecting another visitor. After a brief pause he seemed to be reassured that their privacy would not be disturbed. He shrugged, but also lowered his voice to a slyly conspiratorial whisper.

"I don't believe anyone has actually disappeared," he confided. "I think it's more likely that men who just didn't fit in took a shuttle flight out without bothering to notify the personnel office. After all, they signed a contract to remain six months in order to be eligible to come here. If they quit, they would have had to forfeit a portion of the wages they had already been paid. No one has been willing to do that."

Hoping to appear intrigued, Ian raised his brows dramatically. While his hair was very blond, his brows and lashes were dark, making the gesture effective. "Doesn't the shuttle transmit a passenger list before departing?"

"Yes, of course, but men can always use assumed names."

Ian rounded his mouth in mock horror. "Really?"

"Yes," Egon stressed wearily. "Surely you must have encountered numerous cases of fraud in your work."

"Often, which is what makes my job so satisfying," Ian replied smugly. "But there doesn't appear to be any evidence of fraud in this case." Blessed with a photographic memory, he did not need copies of the files he had studied on his journey here to make his point. "Your theory is easily disproven, Mr. Rascon. Alado keeps logs of all personnel transferred to, and out of, its mining colonies. If a traveler used an assumed name upon leaving here, he would have been greeted at his destination by one of our transit police and his true identity immediately ascertained.

"No one has ever left here who has not been assigned here, and served the agreed-upon term of his or her employment. Another explanation for the disappearances must be found." Ian frowned, as though deep concentration actually pained him. "This is merely conjecture, of course, but is it possible the missing men were killed in rock bursts, or cave-ins that weren't reported so as not to ruin 317's safety record?" Rascon's face began to swell with astonishment, prompting Ian to amend his remark.

"I'm not accusing you of a cover-up, sir. No, indeed. If such a thing happened, it's far more likely it would have been done at the accident site by the other miners in the victims' crews."

Rascon pushed his chair back but did not rise. He gestured toward the array of computer screens on his desk. "If a man so much as drops a coin, it registers on our seismic equipment. There is no way any fatal accident, no matter how quick or contained, could be hidden." He pushed himself to his feet. "I believe a tour will relieve you of any more imaginative speculation. Unless, of course, you'd rather not subject yourself to the possible peril. I warn each shift that just because the last was incident-free doesn't mean theirs will be as well."

Delighted that the superintendent had offered a tour before he had had to demand one, Ian nevertheless appeared reluctant. "My investigations are usually confined to a search of pertinent records," he mused absently, "but in this case I probably should make some personal observations. Is there time for me to change my clothes?"

"Of course," Egon assured him. "We'll provide coveralls, but there's no point in your doing anything so strenuous in your uniform. Take whatever time you need, and then meet me back here and I'll escort you on the tour myself."

Ian pushed himself to his feet. "I shall look forward to it," he murmured without enthusiasm and left.

Ian had intended to go straight to his room, but after leaving Rascon's office he found himself veering toward the gym. In preparation for the arrival of the Rocketball teams, one of the training rooms had already been reserved for their use. Ignoring the sign barring other personnel from using the facility, he walked right in.

Mirrored panels lined the walls, and a variety of fitness equipment filled the room. Haven was the only one present. She had begun her workout with a series of stretching exercises. At present she was hanging upside down from an apparatus that allowed her whole body to dangle freely and fall into perfect natural alignment. Her eyes were closed, and she didn't hear Ian's approach across the padded floor mats.

Ian knelt down so that their eyes, when Haven opened hers, would be at the same level. "Haven," he whispered, and her pale aqua lids flew open.

"There's something very peculiar going on here," he advised. "Men have been disappearing at an average of two per year, and the superintendent isn't even remotely concerned. At best, men have been killed in accidents that have been covered up. At worst, they've been murdered and their bodies tossed down the incinerator chute. My job is to solve the mystery and arrest whoever is responsible. I hope to do it quickly, and then I promise not to disappoint you."

Since Haven had left him standing in the hallway she had had plenty of time to replay their initial conversation. In fact, that was all she had done, and she was badly embarrassed by how quickly she had blurted out her adolescent crush on him. That did not mean that she could accept the cool nonchalance of his reaction, however.

Fans often approached her with the presumption that she would regard them as friends. In her first year with the Flames she had learned how to tactfully turn away lovestruck fans so as not to hurt their feelings, but she had never stooped to lying about her identity to discourage them. Coming upon Ian without warning as she had, she had had no opportunity to shield her emotions, and they had betrayed her. Alert to that danger now, she would not repeat her earlier mistake.

Haven curled up in one easy motion, grabbed the top bar of the bat unit with one hand, released the belts holding her ankles with the other, and dropped down into a confident stance. She put her hands on her hips and watched Ian stretch to his full height. That he was no more than six feet three or four amazed her. She truly had believed him to be taller.

"I'm sure your work is fascinating, Mr. Wyatt—"

"Hyatt," Ian corrected. Her face was flushed, and with her hair at last knotted atop her head, he noticed the pair of crystal studs in her ears. Reflecting the bright light in the gym, they sent sparkling rainbows across her cheeks. His glance traveled down her sleek red suit, and he could not help but wonder whether she had one of the full body tattoos that were so popular. He was inclined to believed that she did, and did not want to have to speculate too long on what it might be. She wasn't the type for flowers, but he knew whatever motif she had chosen, if indeed she had one, it would be as bold as her steady gaze.

Haven noted the direction of Ian's glance and reached out to cuff his chin, forcing his gaze up to meet hers. "Stop drooling," she scolded. "I haven't the slightest interest in your assignment. To make things even more clear between us, by lying about who you are you've already disappointed me too badly to make up for it. The sign on the door makes it clear this gym is off limits to all but Flames' personnel. Leave now, or I'll call security to evict you."

Despite her harsh words, Ian couldn't resist the impulse to touch her again and reached out to run his fingertip along her cheek in a gentle caress. She quickly batted away his hand. "Who's hurt you so badly that you can't trust me?" he asked.

For an instant Haven debated shouting for security, but she was too angry to let them have all the fun of handling Ian. "You expect me to believe that you're not Ian St. Ives," she challenged, "and then criticize me for not trusting you? It's clear which one of us isn't trusting the other, Ian, and I'm not the one who's at fault. Now get out of here."

Ian knew she had an excellent point, but he dared not confide in her more than he already had. He always worked solo, and this job would be no exception. "Haven, please," he cajoled, still admitting nothing. He raised his hands in a plea for mercy as he began to back away. "Just give me a few days."

Haven covered her ears. "Lies now or lies later—what's the difference?" She turned her back on him and walked over to the barre running along the back wall. She hooked her right heel over it and continued her warm-up drill.

Ian watched her for a long moment. Like most tall women, she had long, slender legs and a captivating, lithe beauty. He had to force himself to turn away, and for the first time in his life he felt torn between what he had been sent to do and his desire for a woman. Haven Wray wasn't just any woman, of course, but that knowledge didn't make the ache in his chest any less painful. He walked out and, with a newfound determination, promised himself that he would solve 317's ridiculous mystery before she played her first game.

Chapter Three

Annoyed by the unwelcome disruption of routine John Hyatt's visit posed, Egon Rascon squeezed the arms of his chair with a merciless grip. Hyatt had impressed him as being a thorough—if unimaginative—individual who would undoubtedly pursue his investigation with coldly relentless precision. A man of action himself, Egon would do all he could to appear helpful. The tour of the mine was merely his first gesture, but he would make it so brutal that the investigator would be unlikely to venture below a second time.

Later he would provide Hyatt with complete access to the mine's records, and he would schedule interviews with whomever the investigator wished to meet. He would suffocate Hyatt in a veritable avalanche of facts, without ever revealing any of 317's fascinating secrets. Pleased with the strategy he had chosen, Egon relaxed slightly, laced his fingers, and extended his arms in a lazy stretch.

He had been looking forward to another quiet dinner with Haven Wray, and now he would have to invite John Hyatt to join them. He doubted Haven liked the intellectual type, but still, they would have to be polite and include the investigator in their conversation. The rest of the Rocketball players would be arriving soon, along with all their coaches and trainers, and it would be difficult, if not impossible, for him to spend any time with Haven. He was convinced that she liked him, and he intended to extract every last drop of whatever mild affection she might feel for him.

He laughed to himself as he imagined Haven twisting her long, lovely body around John Hyatt. The investigator would be sure to blush and stammer as he demanded to know her intentions. Egon would never waste such a splendid opportunity, however. He sighed softly and imagined himself entertaining the delightfully agile Ms. Haven Wray with every implement a man had ever used to make an unwilling woman his slave. And what a splendid slave she would be!

His thoughts straying in a totally inappropriate direction, he had to force himself to straighten up and attend to business. He scanned the last shift's production reports. By the time he heard his electronic secretary greet John Hyatt a second time, he was satisfied that the mine was operating at its usual peak efficiency. Confident that he deserved the credit, he left his office eager to begin an extended tour.

Ian had changed into a pair of worn gray pants he wore for workouts, training shoes, and a baggy tan shirt whose generous folds served to disguise his well-conditioned physique. "I'll need to observe the entire operation of the mine," he commented. "Not that I expect to traverse the whole length and breadth of it, but I would like to see the real work of it firsthand."

Egon gestured toward the hall. "Good plan. Let's get started." He led Ian out into the corridor and turned left toward a double set of steel doors. They were painted beige to match the walls but provided a thick, fireproof barrier between the mine and the rest of the complex. As soon as the men had passed through them, they were assailed by a burst of cold air and surrounded by the deep, vibrating hum of the massive cooling system.

Egon had to shout to be heard. "Quite naturally, the deeper we go, the warmer it gets. By constantly pumping cold air into the tunnels we're able to maintain the temperature of the mine between ninety and one-hundred degrees."

After walking quickly through the chill network of pipes, valves, and gauges they entered a huge domed chamber. Three stories high, this was the main entrance to the mine. The triangular gridwork overhead sheltered the miners and supported the machinery that ran the massive buckets used both as elevators for the men and to hoist the astronium ore from below. Even expecting the noise, Ian was forced backward by the harsh clanging intensity of it.

Egon allowed Ian a moment to observe the crew funneling a bucketful of ore into railcars that would be sent to the docking bay for loading on the waiting transport ships. Then he led him over to a bank of lockers, opened the first, and tossed him a pair of white coveralls. "Here, slip those on; then we'll pick up a helmet and boots for you."

"Thanks." Ian donned the loose-fitting garment in an easy stretch. Still appearing to be fascinated by the men loading the railcars, he leaned back against the lockers and observed Egon from the corner of his eye. As the man swapped his tunic and pants for a set of coveralls, Ian took note of an unusual tattoo on the smooth inner flesh of his left arm. It was placed just far enough above the wrist to be covered normally by his sleeve, even when he reached for something, but in a single quick glimpse Ian had recognized the tightly interwoven design as a Celtic knot.

Tattooing was an enormously popular form of decoration, but the choice of an ancient design, coupled with a location that was so easily concealed, struck Ian as doubly odd. Believing the tattoo was most probably the mark of a secret society rather than some purely personal motif, he did not comment on it, though he fully intended to research it later. He pulled on the heavy boots Egon gave him, and then the hood that provided not only protective headgear but insulation from the racket, and a communication system as well. A light strip above the clear faceplate provided a constant source of illumination. The last item of apparel was a pair of thick gloves.

Now fully clad in a miner's anonymous garb, Ian followed Egon through the narrow gate leading onto the platform surrounding the main shaft. As they passed through, sensors read the code on their suits and flashed the identification numbers in blue on an overhead screen.

"This is how we track the crews," Egon explained. "The shift currently working below is shown in blue. I've already assigned that guest suit to you; should we be delayed for any reason, your number will appear among the men listed as overdue. Any time you go below, make certain that you not only notify me, but wear that same suit so that your location can be tracked.

"When we come up we'll just reverse our direction through the gate. I'm sure I don't need to warn you not to try anything foolish like removing your suit before you walk through it, either. I don't want my emergency crews wasting their time searching for you if you're eating dinner in the mess hall."

"Yes, I understand." Ian scanned the neat rows of blue numbers. "I assume there must be a record showing the missing men passed through here as they left the mine after their last shift?"

"Yes, I can access them in my office."

Ian folded his arms over his chest. "Good, but

all you can prove is that someone wore their suits out, right? The missing men could still be in the mine."

Egon began to swear, then caught himself. "As I suggested earlier, please complete your tour before you attempt to draw any more conclusions."

Ian rocked back on his heels. "Yes, that would undoubtedly be wise. Shall we continue?"

Egon gestured broadly. "There's an elevator in the auxiliary shaft that runs parallel to the main shaft. I like to keep it in reserve for emergency use, but if you'd find riding in the bucket frightening, I could make an exception for you."

Ian was grateful the concealing folds of his hood relieved him of the tiresome necessity for affecting a terrified expression, but he still took the precaution of adding a slight tremor to his voice. "No, not at all," he gasped. "I insist we follow the mine's usual procedures."

"Good." Egon couldn't stifle a devilish chuckle as he waved Ian on up the ramp curving around one side the bucket. After making certain the bottom of the bucket was securely closed he swung himself over the side. Crusted with a thick layer of astronium dust, the heavy container reverberated with a deep bell-like tone as his feet struck the bottom. A puff of sparkling gray dust swirled around him as he raised his hand to urge Ian to join him.

Ian hung on tightly to the rail above the ramp and leaned way out to look down into the peculiar conveyance. "What keeps the bottom of the bucket from opening while we're using it as an elevator?" he called down to Egon.

"The mine's equipment is fully computerized," Egon said. "The only time the bucket will open is when it's pulled away from the shaft to empty ore into railcars." He jumped up and down to demonstrate the strength of the hinged bottom. "See? We've never had a single miner fall out while he was en route to work. When you get in just hook your arm over the inside rail and you'll be completely safe."

Hoping to appear skeptical, Ian counted to ten before climbing down into the bucket. Then he grabbed the inner rail with both hands. "How long does it take to reach the bottom?" he asked.

Rather than reply, Egon signaled the operator to begin lowering them into the shaft. The bucket rocked wildly for a moment, and then plummeted with a speed that sucked the breath right out of Ian's lungs. Dizzy, he clung to the railing. Even knowing Egon was trying to frighten him, he was infuriated by the childish prank.

As they continued to fall, the tunnels that branched off from the main shaft sped by as brief bursts of light, followed by another stretch of darkness so deep, Ian began to fear they had dropped into hell. His stomach lurched upward and his chest ached with the effort to breathe, but the force of their fall flung him back against the side of the bucket and there was no way he could reach Egon to drive his fist clear through the grin he was certain lit his face.

Positive he could survive the wild ride if Egon could, Ian gritted his teeth and held on, but by the time the bucket's perilous speed finally began to slow, he could barely stand. Refusing to let Egon know how angry he was not to have at least been warned what to expect, he let out a wild whoop. "What a rush!" he exclaimed. "Is it as much fun riding up?"

Egon stared at Ian, but with the faceplate in his hood fogged slightly all he could make out was the bright gleam of his amber eyes. He had meant to give Ian such a terrible fright it would keep him out of the mine; having failed, he could only shrug. "Sorry, the ascent is much slower."

"What a shame." There was a metal ladder welded inside the bucket, and Ian summoned the strength to climb it. They were now two miles below the surface, and the mine's sweltering inner heat closed around him, choking him again, though the filters in his hood allowed him to suck in the cool air that was constantly circulated through the mine. It was an odd sensation, and one he hoped he did not have the opportunity to learn to tolerate.

Egon was enjoying what he could observe of Ian's discomfort immensely. "Can you see why this work pays so well?"

Ian nodded. "Yes, indeed."

Egon grasped his arm and guided him onto a temporary platform to observe the work of the crew directly below them. "The rock is loosened with carefully targeted laser blasts; then robotic equipment performs all the heavy digging. Men drive it, of course, as well as the scrapers that remove the loose ore and dump it into another of the buckets like the one we rode down."

Content to observe the men work for several minutes, Ian was soon overcome with the sheer monotony of their task. Their white suits dusted with gray, the crew moved with the precision of a living machine. First they swept the exposed face of the rock with short laser blasts. Then the powerful rigs fitted with huge claws moved forward to gouge out the shattered stone, followed by the scrapers that cleared it away. As the sequence was repeated, the miners carved their way through the asteroid's heart by fiercely won inches.

While he had to admire their skill and determination, Ian could not envision himself as part of the crew. He was never affected by claustrophobia, but he was seldom called upon to work several miles underground either. Being surrounded by rock, it was all too easy to imagine being sealed in a tomb, and he had just turned to Egon to suggest they move on when a sharp jolt shook the whole shaft. The powerful lanterns strung around them swayed and dimmed, for a moment leaving only the light strip on each man's hood to brighten the darkness of the shaft, but then the lanterns came back on full strength.

Egon looked over the platform to make certain the twelve-man crew had sustained no injuries before he spoke. "That's an example of the seismicity I mentioned. We experience a great many minor tremors. Most are like that one and cause no damage other than to our nerves. Cave-ins, and killer rock bursts, are a rarity here."

Seizing the opportunity the quake provided to enhance his image as a timid soul, Ian edged toward the bucket rather than remain near the bottom of the shaft. "I'd like to see the work in one of the tunnels now, please."

Egon chuckled to himself. He could not plan tremors, but he was elated one had occurred while they had been there to feel its full force. "The ones closest to the surface have been worked the longest, but they are still being extended and are producing quality ore."

Ian climbed down into the bucket first, and again slipped his arm through the rail. He braced his feet, but their ascent, unlike their rapid drop, was slow and smooth. Egon stopped at the second level, and here they caught a ride in one of the small rail cars that carried the ore from the ends of the tunnel to the main shaft for transfer to buckets for the trip to the surface.

The railcars gathered speed as they bumped along the track providing an exhilarating if uncomfortable ride, but Ian offered no complaints as they reached the end of the tunnel where another crew, identical to the one they had observed in the main shaft, was hard at work. It was several degrees cooler here, but the racket made by the machines echoed off the rock with the same grinding whine. The protective headgear minimized the noise, but for a man accustomed to the blissful silence of glaciers, it was nearly deafening.

Ian took note of the beams used to reinforce the tunnel, the ventilation ducts, and the overhead lanterns, satisfying himself that the mine was structurally sound and superbly maintained. That fact would mean little to the fifteen missing men, however. He waited for Egon to suggest it was time to move on, and they returned to the main shaft and rode the bucket up to the surface. As soon as they had passed through the gate at the entrance, Ian yanked off his hood and started a new line of questioning.

"What's the average stay here at 317?"

Egon opened his locker and tossed his hood on the top shelf. "The average is three tours, or eighteen months, but there are men who barely make it to six months, and some who stay for several years." He paused before removing his coveralls. "If you're hoping to find friends of the missing miners, it's doubtful there will be any except for the last few."

"And you've already questioned them?" Ian asked.

Egon pulled open the closure running down the front of his suit and shrugged it off. "I most certainly did. They were as puzzled by the disappearances as we are. Regardless of what you told me, I still think the men left on shuttles."

Ian pretended to mull over Egon's opinion while he waited for another glance at his tattoo. Inked in iridescent blues and greens, the design's tightly interwoven swirls recalled the colorful illumination on medieval manuscripts. He still believed it held a significance other than a purely decorative one, but preferred to add it to his private investigation rather than inquire as to its source.

He followed Egon's example and shook the gray dust off his suit before replacing it in the locker with the hood, boots, and gloves. "If the men disappeared while they were off duty, what's become of their white suits?"

Egon smoothed the hem of his tunic over his hips and reached down to pick up the rust-colored boots that matched his uniform. "They were cleaned and returned to supply. Why? What could you possibly learn from their work clothes?"

Ian pursed his lips thoughtfully. "Perhaps nothing. Then again, they might have been filled with clues. Now we'll never know. Could we find the suit belonging to the most recent victim?"

A slow smile slid across Egon's lips as he reached over to touch the coveralls hanging in Ian's locker. "You were wearing it. The general feeling was that it ought not go to a new man, as it might prove to be unlucky. Miners tend to be a superstitious sort, and I chose to respect their beliefs rather than call them silly."

"I'm sure that was wise." Ian cast a lingering glance over the coveralls in question before closing the locker. "Are all the men assigned to twelve-man crews?"

"Yes. We have a variety of equipment, but each crew has twelve members. They work together as teams. Men don't wander the tunnels by themselves, Hyatt. Even if they did, the main entrance is the only way out, and they all exit through the gate, where their numbers are recorded at the ends of their shifts."

Ian turned back toward the center of the cavernous room. The main shaft was large enough to accommodate five of the gigantic buckets. The emergency elevator Egon had mentioned held a wire cage that could hold easily fifty men. At the start of each shift men went down into the mine and sent up buckets of astronium ore. It was a simple, if hazardous routine, and for a man to disappear from his crew eleven of his co-workers would have to be in on it.

Ian had learned from experience that secrets had a way of revealing themselves. One man often found it impossible to keep his own dark secret hidden. With two men, one was sure to betray the other. But eleven men could never keep a dangerous secret—unless, of course, they had sworn a blood oath, and might even wear the sign in a compelling tattoo.

Suddenly Ian found this case infinitely more intriguing. "I'd like to follow the ore to the docking bays," he announced. "Transport ship pilots are not nearly as reliable as those commanding shuttles, and it's just possible the missing men made their way off 317 aboard them."

Egon reached out to slap Ian on the back. "That's brilliant, Hyatt. I hope you're right."

Ian smiled with what he knew would pass for modest pleasure, but he doubted the missing men had left 317, and certainly not alive if they had.

* * *

Haven spent her day training and reviewing recorded games of the Flames' three opponents in the finals. They had already played each team during the regular season, and she knew the strengths and weaknesses of each. But, as her coaches stressed, there was always something more to be learned. Each team had key players, and each of them had her own mannerisms and idiosyncrasies, which had to be studied in order to counter their best moves effectively.

Haven was well aware that her rivals were undoubtedly studying her technique just as intently to strengthen their chances of winning. She played for the sheer thrill of the game, however, and had never been threatened by competition. In fact, there were several women she was actually looking forward to facing, and beating again.

As she showered and changed for dinner, she didn't know whether or not to hope Ian St. Ives would join them in the executive dining room. Egon Rascon was a gracious host, and his staff personable, but she really did not feel up to another evening of mining stories. Not that they weren't exciting, because they certainly were, but she found her mind wandering so frequently, it was difficult to make appropriate comments.

She leaned over to brush out her hair with forceful strokes and was overwhelmed with a nearly forgotten memory of a man easing the brush from her hand. It had been a long while since a man had brushed her hair. Too long, and she missed being pampered. As she straightened up, her hair dipped across her forehead in a silken veil, but she quickly swept it aside and secured it at her nape with a gold clasp.

Blake had loved to brush her hair, or at least he had said he did. Now she didn't know if that had been merely another of his seductive lies. Aren would be arriving tomorrow or the next day, and for the duration of the finals she would be unable to avoid him. He was a superb team doctor, but she would never allow him to delve into her all-too-painful past.

He had misunderstood the cold facts in her chart, twisted everything, but what did it matter now? She had made a series of disastrous choices, beginning with marrying Blake Ellis when she was only nineteen. She had paid dearly for that mistake, but there was no point in explaining why to Aren, or anyone else.

Thoroughly depressed by the sad direction of her thoughts, Haven considered dining alone in her room but, fearing she had been without company too long, she decided she would be better off with Egon. If Ian appeared, she would maintain the same polite distance she showed the other men on 317. His purpose in assuming a false identity did not concern her. The evening carefully organized in her mind to fill the time, if not lift the darkness of her mood, she stepped through her door. But her plans dissolved in a warm amber blur when she found Ian waiting in the hall.

Ian was again dressed in a gray tunic and pants and, despite having spent a strenuous day, appeared relaxed as he moved forward. "I thought since we were both dining with the superintendent we ought to go together."

Haven regarded Ian with a decidedly skeptical glance. "I can't imagine why. Were you afraid you might get lost on the way to the executive dining room?"

Haven's bright red gown was artfully draped to complement her spectacular figure, but rather than pay her compliments Ian ran his finger down her bare arm before taking her hand. He felt the most delightful tingle and, seeing her shiver slightly, knew she had experienced the same unexpected thrill. They would be very, very good together; he had to fight to shove that delicious thought to the back of his mind.

"No. I have an excellent sense of direction, but it would have been extremely rude of me not to provide you with an escort, Ms. Wray; and I do have another reason."

His grasp was warm, and Haven left her hand in his a moment longer than she had meant to before drawing away. "You needn't worry," she whispered. "I'll not give you away."

Ian didn't try to recapture her hand, but remained closer than necessary as they walked to the end of the hall. In no hurry to summon a tram, he turned to face her. "Thank you, but that wasn't it."

Haven had never met a man with such a compelling gaze. It wasn't simply the delicious amber shade of his eyes either, or the thick fringe of dark lashes that framed them. Perhaps it was the firm, masculine definition of his brow that added depth to his expression; the sum of his features was subtle perfection. Unable to dismiss him with a toss of her head, as she would have liked, she swallowed hard to find her voice.

"If you wanted tickets to the finals matches, I'm afraid I don't have any."

She had sounded as though it pained her to disappoint him, and Ian couldn't help but laugh. "No, it's not tickets either. Because you've been here a few days, I wondered if you've noticed anyone with an unusual tattoo on the inside of his left arm." Rather than use his own arm for the demonstration, Ian touched her wrist and slid his fingers past the pulse point. He traced the design on her skin.

"It's a tightly laced pattern that resembles Celtic scrollwork. Have you seen anything like that?"

Amazed by the absurdity of his question, Haven backed away to break the contact between them. Ian was incredibly smooth; she had to give him that. His voice was deep, and the intimacy of his tone lent each of his words a provocative edge. His glance was as seductive as his touch, but despite the magnetism of his appeal she heard the ready insult in his question.

She took a deep breath to steady herself and then replied in a rush. "There's obviously an enormous difference between the way male fans behave when they meet me and the way women must greet you, but let me assure you: Had any of the men here begun peeling off his clothes when we were introduced, I'd have gladly used them to strangle him."

Haven slammed her palm against the call button for the tram, but Ian moved to block her escape. "He'd deserve it too," he agreed with a low chuckle. "Forgive me. I seem continually to say the wrong thing to you. I merely wondered if you'd seen someone with such a tattoo. I didn't assume it had to have been under . . . well, less than formal circumstances."

Even if he had not been implying that she must have seen some, if not all, of the men stationed there nude, it had certainly sounded that way, and Haven believed her angry reaction was fully justified. A hot threat of tears stung her eyes, and she reconsidered dining alone in her room before she realized Ian did not always create the problems between them. She was just so close to the edge of reason, the slightest nudge to her composure enraged her. But surely that was better than weeping uncontrollably, as she so often feared she might do.

She didn't dare look up at him. "I came here early because I wanted to get away from everything. The end of the season is always difficult. Everyone is under a great deal of stress, and I had hoped having some time alone would help me restore the balance to my life. I've kept to myself since I arrived. I've not seen any tattoos that I recall. Is the one you described important to your investigation?"

Ian felt the rumble of the approaching tram and used it as an excuse to take her hand again.

He knew exactly how difficult the stress of constant competition could be, and how many fine athletes' lives were ground into tiny bits by it. He did not want to see that happen to her, but clearly that was a very real possibility. For now, all he could do was answer her question. "It might be, and then again, it might not. If you should happen to notice such a design, tell me. Don't comment on it to whoever's wearing it."

The tram slid soundlessly into their station. Haven entered, chose the closest seat, and slid over to leave room for Ian. She doubted she could eat a bite, but suddenly dinner seemed likely to be far more exciting than she had anticipated. "I'm used to answering questions rather than asking them. You needn't worry about me."

Ian smiled, but he was already more worried about her than he had any right to be.

Chapter Four

As Haven entered the executive dining room, Egon Rascon rushed forward to welcome her, but his smile faltered when he saw Ian a step behind her. He had hoped to share a few minutes' conversation with the stunning athlete before the investigator arrived, but he recovered quickly and included Ian in his greeting.

"As I promised earlier, Mr. Hyatt, we're blessed with a talented chef who prepares some of the most delicious meals any of us has ever tasted. I can provide entertaining company as well. I see you've already met Ms. Wray, but come; let me introduce you to some of my staff. Because we operate the mine in three shifts, we're never all together at once, but you're sure to meet everyone eventually."

"Yes. I intend to," Ian assured him.

Rather than listen to the introductions, Haven excused herself, skirted the group at the bar, and moved on toward the far end of the room, where thickly padded chairs and ottomans covered in a burnt sienna fabric had been arranged to encourage conversation. A viewing screen was recessed into the wall, and soft music was coming from hidden speakers. The inviting area provided many off-duty amusements for the mine's executives, but Egon was pained by how quickly Haven had chosen it over his company. Disappointed that the evening wasn't going as he'd planned, he sent her a regretful glance.

Feeling forgotten, Ian cleared his throat noisily, prompting Egon to finally escort him to the bar, where four men were clustered around the room's only other woman. The group parted to include them. While Ian had never been recognized before that day, he felt an uncharacteristic tremor of apprehension after his experience with Haven. He held his breath until it was plain in the curious expressions that greeted him that no one had any idea who he was before Egon stated his name and purpose for visiting 317.

Egon first introduced Chella Bergh, the physician in charge of the hospital unit. She was petite, with dark brown hair clipped short as a boy's and big brown eyes sparkling with a lively intelligence. She swept Ian with an appreciative glance and broke into a delighted smile.

"I do hope you'll be able to discover what's happened to our missing men before there's another disappearance. Have there been similar incidents at any other mining colony?"

"Not that I know," Ian replied. Before he could inquire whether she held a theory, Egon introduced Douglas Garabedian, a tall, broad-shouldered man, as the associate superintendent. Doug's features were as craggy as the chiseled tunnels of the mine, and his eyes were the pale gray of astronium dust. He responded with a distracted nod and hurried away to join Haven.

"Don't be offended," Chella whispered to Ian. "It's difficult for anyone to compete with Haven Wray."

"I wouldn't even want to if Doug was the prize," Ian confided. Taking hold of his upper arm, Chella muffled her giggles against his sleeve, and Ian had to force himself to remain where he stood rather than lurch backward to put more distance between them. She was apparently the type who enjoyed petting men, but he had never cared to receive such affectionate gestures from strangers. A perceptive woman, when she noted the humor of his words wasn't reflected in his cool golden glance, she was embarrassed and stepped back on her own.

"Ruben Flores," a slender, dark-haired man announced before Egon spoke his name. A handsome fellow, with a gesture as relaxed as Chella's cuddling, he looped his arm through hers and drew her close. "I supervise the robotic equipment," he said with a sly grin, "and we've not lost a single unit."

The others in the group laughed at Ruben's

joke, but Ian did not see anything amusing in his comment. "Robots are programmed to be obedient, though, aren't they," he chided, "and not given to straying off on their own."

"Yes. That's certainly true," Ruben agreed. "Or, at least, not yet, they haven't."

"And they won't," Egon insisted. "I'd like you to meet Daniel Corbett, another of our fine engineers, and Glenn Mott, one of the geologists who monitors our seismic activity."

Daniel Corbett, a fair, blue-eyed young man, smiled broadly and offered a few words of welcome, but Glenn Mott was no more friendly than Douglas Garabedian had been. A redhead with pale, almost translucent skin, Mott placed his empty glass on the bar and snapped his fingers impatiently to hurry the bartender. "You look as though you could use a drink, Hyatt," he said. "If colonial wines don't suit you, ask for something stronger."

Ian hesitated for a moment, and then made a request. "I will admit to a fondness for Martian ale. Do you have some?"

"Certainly, sir," the bartender replied. "Would you prefer it warm or chilled?"

"Warm." Ian watched him fill a tall glass with the thick amber brew. Regardless of his assignment, he allowed himself an occasional ale. He could nurse one all evening and, while potent, it had no effect on a man his size when sipped over several hours. He took a single swallow, then held his glass in a relaxed grasp while his companions joined Glenn Mott in having refills of wine.

Before Ian could lead them into a discussion of the mine's mystery, he felt a warm, tingling sensation creep up the back of his neck and knew he was being watched. Certain Doug wasn't neglecting Haven to study him, he was pleased to think she must find him attractive. He waited a long moment and then scanned the room, as though he were merely admiring the sophisticated decor. When his eyes locked with Haven's she quickly glanced away. Amused by that show of guilt, Ian couldn't help but smile. He took another sip of ale and continued to study the furnishings.

The executive dining room was decorated in a pale salmon shade brightened with white accents. A clear acrylic-table set with white linens was placed at one end. The attractive grouping of chairs and ottomans where Haven and Doug sat occupied the other. With the mine executives and Chella clad in rust-colored uniforms and Ian wearing gray, Haven's flattering dress provided the room's only splash of brilliant color.

Ian attempted to steer the conversation toward the missing men, but all he received for his efforts were polite shrugs. Egon soon urged everyone to take their places at the table, and when Haven had slipped into the seat at his right he gestured for Ian to take the chair at his left. Daniel sat next to Ian; then Ruben and Chella took their places at the end. Douglas sat down beside

Haven, and Glenn dropped into the last chair on that side of the table.

Ian waited until Egon was distracted for a moment, then winked at Haven. Startled, she completely lost the thread of Doug's conversation, which had not interested her to begin with. She shook her head to warn Ian to stop. Misunderstanding her gesture, Doug rephrased his remark.

"I was certain you would feel the Rocketball season is too long, while all of us would like to have the games run continuously. Your games are so exciting, I could watch the Flames play every day and never grow bored."

"It's marvelous to have such loyal fans," Haven replied, but she was speaking directly to Ian rather than Doug. Ian responded with a barely perceptible nod, and again she wished that she had not been so open in her admiration. Not that he was any disappointment in the flesh; but she would definitely keep that thought to herself.

They were served their salads then, and Haven pretended to concentrate on the chopped greens. The colorful assortment was freshly harvested from the mine's hydroponic gardens, flavored with a delicately spiced dressing, and sprinkled with sesame seeds. All the food she had been served there was as good as Egon boasted, but even after working out all day she had little appetite.

All too aware of Ian, she was surprised by how subdued he had become. His manner had changed the instant they had entered the dining room; the confidence he had shown in their earlier conversations was muted now. He appeared to be paying close attention to the opinions expressed at the table, but he offered none of his own. She assumed he was being paid to listen and observe, but she wished he would just be himself.

The main course was a saffron-tinted rice dish laced with steamed vegetables and tender morsels of meat. Lost in her own thoughts, Haven did not realize the conversation was still centered on Rocketball until Egon began to praise her skill. She was embarrassed to think that, while Ian deserved even more enthusiastic accolades, he had not even been recognized. She hastened to change the subject.

"I merely play a game for a living," she reminded Egon. "I can't work miracles. Now, could we talk about something else, please?"

Thinking her request absurd, Egon responded with a deep chuckle. "You're the highest-paid athlete of all time but too modest to accept our praise graciously. I find that incredibly endearing, Haven. You deserve our attention. Don't you realize that?"

Haven sighed wearily, rolled her napkin into a tight ball, and jammed it under the edge of her plate. "The other players will be here soon. I hope you'll entertain them all with the same enthusiasm you've shown me." Having had more than enough insipid adulation for one evening, she shoved back her chair. "Now I must ask you to

73

excuse me. Rather than wait for dessert, what I truly need is rest."

Fearing he had offended her, Egon began to rise, but Haven was already out of her chair. She rested her hand lightly on his shoulder. "You needn't walk me to the door. I'll see you all tomorrow." She gave a slight wave and included the others at the table with a smile that lingered on Ian, then hurriedly left the room.

"I thought she liked talking about Rocketball," Doug Garabedian exclaimed.

Ian opened his mouth to comment, then thought better of it. He knew exactly how it felt to be treated as a celebrity rather than a person. As for the remark about Haven's income, Egon had been tactless, and she had every right to be insulted. He ate the rest of his dinner in silence while his companions continued to discuss the upcoming tournament. He understood how thrilling the event would be for them, but he was tired of the subject. After a taste of the exquisitely light fruit sorbet served for dessert, he again brought up the disappearances.

"I'll make appointments to speak with you all privately," he began, "but please be thinking about the missing men. If you knew any of them well, they might have made a chance remark about being bored here, or some vague reference to home that didn't strike you as anything out of the ordinary at the time but could be a valuable clue."

Still unhappy that Haven had retired early, Douglas Garabedian puffed out his cheeks with an exasperated sigh. "None complained to me, nor would they if they had planned to jump their contracts."

A low murmur of agreement passed around the table, but Chella smiled helpfully. "I don't recall any special problems among the missing men, but I'll check their medical records. A bout of depression would have been noted, and could account for strange behavior."

"Is vanishing merely strange?" Ruben teased.

"Well, no, I suppose it's more mystifying than anything else," Chella admitted, "but I do want to help in whatever way I can."

Glenn Mott leaned back in his chair. "My job doesn't require me to have much contact with the miners. I can quote statistics on our seismic activity for hours, but that's not going to do you any good. The miners themselves should be able to tell you more than any of us ever could. Aren't you going to question them?"

They were seated at opposite corners of the table, but Glenn wasn't looking at Ian as he spoke. As a matter of fact, the geologist had avoided eye contact with Ian when they met. Perhaps Glenn always displayed a coldly distracted attitude, but his averted glance might also mean he was hiding something. While Ian would make no accusations without evidence, he never discounted his initial impressions either.

From what Ian had observed that day Egon Rascon did not like to have his authority questioned and regarded the investigation as a troublesome nuisance. Rather than being of any help, Douglas Garabedian seemed far more concerned with impressing Haven. Glenn Mott was just plain obnoxious, and Ruben Flores was a comedian who had kept Chella giggling throughout the meal. As for Chella, her flirtatious manner made it clear she enjoyed being one of the few females at the mine; but then, what woman wouldn't? he asked himself.

That left Daniel Corbett, who was at least friendly, even if he didn't have any valuable information to offer. Someone suggested watching a film or playing a game of cards, but Ian was in no mood to socialize with the people he was investigating. "Thank you; another night perhaps. I've got a lot of work planned for tomorrow, and I'll need to turn in early."

Chella made a soft mewing sound, as though she was sincerely disappointed, and Ruben Flores's amused expression slipped slightly, betraying his disgust. Apparently he considered the diminutive doctor his property, but Ian was no threat to their romance. He bid them all good night and returned to the guest quarters. He did have some preparation to do before he began questioning everyone tomorrow, but it wasn't urgent. Not in the least bit tired, he rapped lightly at Haven's door.

Unwilling to be disturbed, Haven didn't leave the recliner until the knocking became an insistent summons. Forced to roll off the comfortable seat, she swore the whole way to the door. She hit the button on the security panel with her fist, and Ian's face, marred by an impatient frown, appeared on the small viewing screen. She uttered a particularly foul oath, debated a long moment before her curiosity overruled her need for solitude, and then pressed the button to open the door.

Prepared for bed, Haven was clad in a bright blue robe with the Flames' logo embroidered on the breast pocket. Her feet and legs were bare, and Ian doubted she was wearing anything beneath the robe. All he would have to do was reach out and give the belt a quick tug to appreciate all of her superb body. He was sorely tempted, but they had just met, and he didn't dare try such a playful trick on her.

He had gone to her room rather than his own on an impulse, but her questioning glance demanded a reason for disturbing her, and he quickly provided one he was positive she would accept. "It must be very difficult receiving constant attention for what you can do on a Rocketball court, rather than for the person you are, but I hope you won't want to avoid me as you do the others."

Astonished by the ridiculousness of his remark, Haven shook her head sadly. "I'm sorry, but you have me completely confused. Weren't you the one who wanted to avoid me?"

Ian rested his hand against the doorjamb. He couldn't deny her accusation, so he laughed instead. The sound echoed down the long empty hallway in rich, rolling waves. "Yes, that was me, but you made it clear you wouldn't let me get away with it." He glanced past her, hoping she would invite him in, and glimpsed the shadows flickering over the walls. The Dreamer's haunting images were unmistakable, and he was appalled to find her watching them. He straightened up quickly, all trace of humor gone.

"You're the last person I'd ever guess would tune in the Dreamer. Hasn't anyone warned you against it?"

Aren Manzari had warned her so many times she had lost count. Exasperated to have Ian do the same, Haven rolled her eyes. "I realize this little apartment may not be much, but for the time being it's my home, and I'll do whatever I damn well please here. As far as I'm concerned, the Dreamer is a harmless diversion that helps me get to sleep, which is what I intend to do. Good night."

She reached for the button to close the door, but Ian grabbed her wrist before she made contact. Taking a quick step forward, he pushed her back into her room. "You're in far worse shape than I thought if you have to rely on the Dreamer to relax." Haven tried to twist out of his grasp, but Ian spun her around and yanked her back against his chest. He used his free hand to press the button to close the door, then crossed his arms over her chest to put an end to her struggles.

"Calm down," he whispered in her ear. "We're two of a kind, and I just want to talk with you for a minute. Now tell the room's computer to shut off the Dreamer."

Haven could have broken free, but not without

resorting to vicious tactics that would have left
Ian severely injured. Unwilling to hurt him, she
laid her hands over his and thought fate had a
peculiar way of making her adolescent dreams
come true. She had often longed to be in Ian St.
Ives's arms, but not like this.

"I came here early to escape a man who
thought he knew what was best for me. I don't
need another. Do it yourself."

"You know it won't respond to my voice, and
the one in my quarters won't obey you."

Ian had not slackened his hold, and while Haven could feel only the hard planes of his body
through her thick robe, the heat of his hands was
enough to send a sizzling thrill clear through her.
She felt it each time they touched, and the blissful sensation promised so much more than her
fantasies ever had. That was an experience she
would have to postpone until after the games,
however.

No fool, she would not give in without first getting something she wanted in return. "You denied that you were Ian St. Ives but haven't argued
when I've treated you as though you were," she
began. "I want the truth. Just who are you and
what are you really doing here?"

Ian gave her a fierce squeeze and rubbed his
cheek against her hair. Still in a braid, it held a
delicious hint of a deeply distracting perfume.
That was the last thing he needed, but he couldn't
bring himself to let her go. "For now I'm John
Hyatt, and you must know from the conversation
at dinner that what I told you about searching

for missing miners is true. When I complete this assignment I'll go home and be myself, but nothing that happens between us between now and then will be pretense."

Unimpressed, Haven scolded, "You can do better than that."

Ian hesitated. He had already told her about the Celtic tattoo, which was undoubtedly a mistake. The Dreamer sent a shadowy chain of dancing children circling the room, and he gritted his teeth as he thought of how easily Haven could lose herself in illusion when her need for a real life was so plain. He made a fervent promise. "I can give you so much more than the Dreamer."

Haven's response was husky with the desire she wouldn't indulge. "You won't even tell me your name."

Her challenge presented Ian with a clear choice. He could walk out, pursue his assignment with his usual relentless vigor, and hope Haven would deign to speak to him when he was through, or he could break one of Control's cardinal rules and confide in her. He had felt torn when he had left her in the gym, but now he could actually feel his heart begin to rip. He could not shut her out, but he could not make her his accomplice either. Somehow he had to find a way to thread his way between the two impossible options.

"I want your promise that this will be your last question," he demanded.

Why Ian St. Ives would masquerade as an insurance investigator was certainly puzzling, but

Haven was willing to settle for his name alone now. After all, they could always make additional bargains later. "Agreed," she murmured, as though it was a concession. Ian had softened the firmness of his hold until she was snuggled in an affectionate embrace, but she wasn't even tempted to escape him.

"I'm trusting you with my life, Haven. I am Ian St. Ives, all right, but that's a secret you must keep."

Haven turned slightly to look up at him, and Ian nuzzled her throat with teasing kisses that enchanted her more deeply than his touch. She had to swallow hard to find her voice, and even then, it wavered. "Why would anyone send an Artic Warrior to an astronium mine? You're completely out of your element here."

Ian's chuckle was muffled against her braid. "It's been eleven years, Haven. I've learned a few new tricks. Now turn off the Dreamer."

What he wanted was clear, but Haven refused to be rushed. "Cancel the Dreamer," she called, and the swirling shadows dissolved into a golden light that lit her quarters with the warmth of late afternoon sunshine. She slipped out of Ian's arms and turned to face him.

"I appreciate your concern," she said. "Yes, it is difficult to accept constant praise from people who never stop to consider that I might be tired, or sad, or desperately lonely. It's as though I was an actress with a touring company. No matter where I go, I'm presented with the same questions, and expected to give the same answers;

and preferably provocative ones, at that. Most men are intimidated by me, though, whereas women must have adored you."

Ian shook his head. "Not me. The Artic Warrior image was what they adored." He reached out for her again, but she backed away. "What's wrong? Are you really disappointed that I'm not taller?"

"No, I'm not disappointed at all." Haven tightened her belt, unconsciously sending a message. "I make it a practice not to become involved with men while I'm playing. Rocketball can be a deadly sport, and I don't intend to become one of the casualties."

"I don't want that to happen either," Ian exclaimed, "but if you have to resort to using the Dreamer to get to sleep, you'd be much better off letting me relax you."

His sly smile made it plain how he wished to go about it, but Haven wouldn't change her mind. "I wouldn't use any man like that; least of all you."

Ian took a step forward, but when Haven moved back to maintain the distance between them, he remained where he stood. "I wouldn't feel used, Haven. I plan to enjoy it as much as you."

Haven had to look away. "You asked for a few days to complete your assignment," she reminded him. "Why have you changed your mind?"

Ian clasped his hands behind his back and looked down at the toes of his boots. "It's standard operating procedure. I never mix work and play. It's not simply unwise; just as it is in your case, it's dangerous. With you, however, I believe the greater danger would lie in not breaking that rule."

Haven frowned slightly. "You're willing to make an exception for me?"

"Does that strike you as ridiculous? I think we'd be a far worse distraction to each other if we didn't become, as you described, 'involved.' I'm trying to save us both, Haven. Help me."

Haven longed to agree but held back. She would never forgive herself for letting Blake tell her what was best for her, and no matter how good Ian's intentions might be, she trusted her own instincts rather than his. "No. I don't want to rush into anything, and I don't want either of us to risk his life for what might well be a fleeting passion. This is the best choice for us both, Ian. Please go."

Ian wasn't used to being turned down and, coupled with the fact that Haven had refused to make the exception for him that he had made for her, it stung. He stared at the pulse throbbing at the base of her throat. She sounded cool, but he had definitely moved her. It was a small consolation.

"Haven Wray," he breathed out softly. "I watched some of your games on my way here. You are the best."

"Thank you, but so were you."

"Oh, yes, I was."

He was gone before Haven realized how final his good-bye had sounded. "Choices." She sighed unhappily. Life was filled with impossible choices, but knowing she had made the right one didn't ease the ache in her heart. She slid onto the recliner and again asked for the Dreamer's channel. The lights dimmed and a sapphire haze crept up the walls, then took on the slow-rolling motion of the sea.

Haven loved the sea dreams. She took a deep breath as a sparkling light danced on the tips of the waves and fish as bright as tropical blooms swam in the depths. Foam kissed the shore, and a hushed melody lapped against her ears. Certain such a beautiful scene could not possibly be harmful, Haven drank it in. After a few blissful moments her eyes closed and, her pain washed away by the Dreamer's magic, she fell into a deep sleep where her own dreams were filled with precious images of Ian St. Ives.

Egon assembled the Circle at midnight in the antechamber of the maze. A select group of executives and miners, they guarded one of the galaxy's most fabulous secrets with a jealousy bordering fanaticism. That night the mood was subdued, but Egon sensed a deep restlessness he knew he would have to contain or risk losing his place as their leader.

Lanterns carried by the members at the rear sent an eerie light bouncing over the rocky arch above them, but the Circle itself was cloaked in deep shadow. Only three of the original members remained; the others had been invited to join them, a precious few each year. Originally a group of daring miners, the Circle had invited Egon to join them, hoping he would use the power of his position to guard the Circle's secret. He had not disappointed them, and in time other executives had been recruited.

The majority of the Circle were still miners, however, and always would be. A tough, surly lot, they pressed Egon to begin as deep voices echoed off the angular walls of the domed tunnel. "What have you learned of the outsider?" they called.

Egon raised his hands to still the rumbling. "Hyatt can be controlled," he assured them. "He'll ask tedious questions, comb the records, compare dates, and probably make a few wild accusations. But in the end he'll leave 317 convinced the missing men shipped out on transport ships. After all, when no other explanation can be found he will have to propose that conclusion or risk appearing an incompetent fool."

"We've been careless," a man toward the front complained. "It can't continue."

Egon agreed. "An accident will be a simple matter to fabricate. If we lose another of our number, we'll stage one to cover his death."

"We can't afford to risk losing anyone with Hyatt here. We must close the maze until he leaves," another member proposed.

That demand was met with shocked gasps followed by sharp protests, but Egon saw the wisdom in the decision and urged agreement. "Think for a moment," he cautioned. "No one wants a permanent closure, but a temporary halt to our explorations will protect us all." He waited for a moment, but the scattered dissent was quickly quelled.

"It is agreed then. From this night, until Hyatt departs, the maze is closed. Give me your hands on it." He stepped forward and extended his right palm upward. Following his lead, the others stacked their hands above his until the last member placed his at the top. "May the fires of the Maze burn us all if we break this oath," Egon intoned and, raising their voices in a single shout, the Circle backed away and returned to the only lives they would allow John Hyatt to observe.

Chapter Five

Ian was up early the next morning, and he went to the mess hall to have breakfast with the miners working the first shift. He took a tray of fresh fruit and a container of juice to a table that was already half full. He did not ask if he could join the group; he just sat down and introduced himself.

"I'm here to discover what's happened to the missing men. I'll be happy to listen to whatever theory anyone might have."

Strangers were a rarity on 317, and the man seated opposite Ian squinted slightly, as though he were observing a real curiosity, then let out a hoarse, rasping chuckle. "Every last one got sucked into the void. That's my guess."

Ian picked up an orange and rolled it between his palms before he began to peel it. "You think they just strolled out the airlock? Wouldn't an alarm have sounded?"

"Maybe, maybe not," the man muttered before stuffing half a muffin in his mouth.

Ian had not expected the miners to have much in the way of table manners, but he had to look away as muffin crumbs sprayed across the table. "Are you talking suicide, or murder?" he asked as soon as the man had swallowed.

"Can't say. I didn't know 'em."

"How about you?" Ian called to the next man. "What do you think?"

That miner turned in a tight coil as he rose from his seat. "I think it's none of my business." He carried his tray over to the next table and sat down with his back to Ian to finish his meal.

Ian didn't really care whether he learned anything of value that morning. His goal was simply to make his presence known so that anyone who had something to say would know he was there. Most of the men were having protein cakes lathered with whipped syrup, and he had to speak loudly enough to be heard over the clanking chorus of forks scraping against the metal trays.

"There's a reward for information," he announced. "Alado doesn't want another miner lost."

A bearded man seated at midtable leaned forward to look past his friends. "There's not a one of us who isn't already lost, and as for a reward, how about a night with Haven Wray?"

That remark was met with loud whoops and several graphic descriptions of the imaginative perversions such a wonderful night might entail. There were posters for the tournament prominently displayed around the room, and the one for the Flames was a glorious image of Haven leaping into the air to make a shot. He didn't blame the miners for wanting her when he couldn't deny how badly he wanted her himself, but listening to their crude jokes was sheer torture. He forced a smile, as though he was as amused as his companions, but he would much rather have demanded that the men offer Haven the respect she deserved.

When Ian couldn't take any more of the lurid talk he picked up his tray. "Pass the word that I'll pay for information," he said in parting. He got to his feet and moved across the aisle. At least no one there asked for a night with Haven when he offered a reward, but before he could learn anything helpful a buzzer sounded, and the room cleared as the men exited hurriedly to suit up and begin their shift.

Ian remained in the mess hall to finish his breakfast. He ate very slowly, and before long the spacious room began to fill again with the men coming off duty. They had showered and changed clothes, but fatigue slowed their motions. Rather than breakfast, these men picked up dinner trays and shuffled down the narrow aisles between tables to their favorite places. When a man walked up to Ian's table and stared at him angrily, Ian knew he wanted his seat. Unfortunately, he did not feel like moving.

"If I'm in your usual place, choose another,"

Ian ordered firmly. "I came to find the missing miners, not to win friends."

The miner would have demanded he move had he not noticed the fierce gleam in Ian's eyes. They were a warm amber when he was in a pleasant mood, but as he looked up now, they smoldered with the heat of molten gold. The miner stepped back slightly to better judge Ian's size; then, sensing a temper he ought not test in a man with Ian's reach, he shrugged as though he did not really care where he sat and moved two tables away.

A young man with spiked blond hair gave a low whistle. "I thought you might get off with no more than a bloody nose if Sam was in a good mood. I've never seen him walk away from a fight. Whoever you are, you're one lucky bastard."

As Ian saw it, he had been careless. He was supposed to be a timid insurance investigator; he should have apologized hurriedly and changed seats rather than confront Sam. He smiled as though he was sincerely embarrassed. "You're right. I've always been lucky. Name's John Hyatt. Got any thoughts about the missing men?"

"T. L. Rainey," the young man replied. "Stands for Thomas Lee, but everyone here calls me either Too Little or Too Late." He paused to wind a long string of melted cheese around a bite of squash. "I don't plan to be here more than six months, but from what I hear the guys who disappeared had been here several tours. They should have known better."

"Better than what?" Ian prompted.

"Better than to get mixed up in whatever they did," T. L. explained. Apparently bored with the subject, he turned to the man beside him and began discussing the Rocketball tournament.

Ian glanced around the room. Like T. L., most of the miners were in their twenties, but there were a few, like Sam, in their thirties and, scattered about, even some who looked to be in their forties. He waited for a lull in the conversation at the table and again announced Alado's offer of a reward.

"We're all truly touched by Alado's concern," a man at the end called out, and the whole table erupted in laughter.

Ian waited until the last chuckle had died away. "Fifteen men can't disappear without anyone knowing what happened to them," he commented. "I'm betting someone here does. If you don't know for sure, I'd still like to hear your best guess. My name's John Hyatt. Leave a message for me with central communications and I'll find you."

A couple of miners looked away too quickly, and Ian was certain they knew more than they cared to reveal in public. "Alado's a generous firm," he coaxed. "Don't pass up the reward if you know enough to earn it." He grabbed his tray and empty beverage container and carried them over to the chute where he had seen the miners toss their dirty dishes. It would lead directly to a service robot that would scour, wash, sterilize, dry, and stack them for use at the next meal.

Ian took the tram to the library, found an

empty cubicle, and removed a miniature computer link from his hip pocket. He flipped it open, accessed the computer onboard his ship, and recorded his impressions of his initial conversations with the miners. His review of the mine's personnel records had already indicated that the missing men had served more than a single tour on 317, but he thought it significant that a newcomer like T. L. Rainey knew their histories so well. That had to mean that there was talk circulating about the missing men, and he was encouraged by the fact that it was accurate rather than mere speculation.

He leaned back in his chair to plan his next move. Control had already given him whatever pertinent records existed, but he would have to spend the better part of the day studying the files in Egon's office. Because that would essentially be a performance rather than true investigation, he was in no hurry to begin. Instead, he asked his ship's computer to scan for the use of a Celtic knot as the symbol for any group past or present.

While he waited, he drew in a deep breath and sought the peace of meditation. While his body relaxed easily, his mind betrayed him, filled with taunting images of Haven Wray. He had never experienced such a strong response to any woman, and he wasn't certain he liked it. The physical aspects certainly felt good, but he sensed that becoming involved with her would require a whole lot more of him than he might care to give. The simple fact that she intruded on his thoughts so frequently warned him that he might not have a choice, and that annoyed him too.

He had already sensed that the attraction between them was stronger than mere chemistry. He had never believed in the concept of soul mates. Until Haven Wray. She certainly shared his passion for sport, but that was scarcely enough to form a lasting bond. Perhaps they would discover a multitude of similarities, but that still wouldn't cancel out the most important difference.

She was the most popular athlete alive and drew swarms of fans and abundant media coverage everywhere she went, while he worked undercover. Though that was his present occupation, he would not be able to continue as an intelligence operative long if he began appearing at Haven's side. With that kind of exposure, soon his face would become as familiar as hers. His past glory would overtake him the instant he was recognized, and he didn't want that. Then he recalled the sadness of Haven's expression when she had admitted to a desperate loneliness, and he ached for her.

There was simply no way lives as divergent as theirs could be woven into a single strand. Yet the more impossible their chances of ever being a couple, the more he came to want it.

An insistent beep from the computer link reminded him that he was supposed to be working. He looked down at the small screen in his hand and saw there was no record of a Celtic knot in any of Alado's files. Next he requested information on any group with a Celtic logo; again, Alado had nothing.

There were listings of secret societies involving miners, but none had been in existence since the twentieth century. Ian made no claim to being clairvoyant, but he trusted his instincts and felt certain he had more than a serial killer on his hands. A secret society might have dangerous rituals, or even sacrifice an occasional miner. Every crime left a trail; but in this case, unless someone talked, it might take him months to find it. He didn't have the luxury of time. He had been told to wrap up the case before the tournament began.

Growing restless, Ian sent the signal his ship would relay to Control confirming his status, then left the library to report to Egon's office. He was suspicious of the man, as well as of his peculiar tattoo, and would be on his guard.

A brief detour would have taken him by the gym. Though he really wanted to look in and say hello to Haven, he remained focused on his assignment and avoided her, drawing on reserves of will power he had not been called upon to use since he had left the Artic Warrior competitions.

Haven spent the morning working out in the gym and the afternoon practicing her serve on the Rocketball court. Her timing was off and she felt slightly queasy, unable to remember if she had eaten lunch. Taking a break, she sat down in a corner, wrapped her arms around her legs, and rested her cheek on her knees.

The empty arena held an eerie silence, but next week the tiered seats would be packed with fans shrieking the names of their favorite players. The wooden floor of the court would vibrate with the thunderous noise. "Ha-ven, Ha-ven, Ha-ven," some would chant, using her name as an incantation.

It had been exhilarating once, but she was all out of magic. She was so terribly tired, she didn't see how she would make it through the tournament, let alone lead the Flames to another title. With any luck, the stars of the opposing teams would be equally exhausted and she wouldn't have to play hard until the final round.

Elida Rivard would love that, Haven thought. Elida lived for the chance to substitute for her. Elida was only twenty-two, and so eager to play, she never seemed to tire. Haven had been just like her once, but no more. She closed her eyes and exhaled on a melancholy sigh. She wasn't going to make it through another season if she didn't find a way to regain the fire that had made her the pride of the Flames.

There were people, like Elida, who believed she had it all; but wealth and fame were scant consolation when she awoke alone each morning. The guest quarters to which the teams were assigned varied so little from post to post, most of the time she couldn't even remember where she was.

"Lost," she murmured to herself, "as lost as the miners Ian is never going to find." She used her arm to brush away the stray tendrils that had escaped her braid and struggled to her feet. There was still time left to practice, but as she hurled the ball against the end wall, it echoed with a thud as hollow as her life. Feeling utterly defeated, she continued to practice like the champion she was, but her broken heart just wasn't in it.

The eight other members of the Flames and their trainers and coaches arrived on 317 that same afternoon. As soon as Aren Manzari located the room to which he had been assigned, he tossed his gear on the bed and went looking for Haven. When she wasn't in her room he rode the tram to the gym. Finding it empty, he took another ride to the arena. As he approached the huge double doors, Haven came through them. She was wiping her face on a towel and he was badly disappointed that she didn't find a smile for him when she glanced up and saw him.

"I was hoping you would look rested," he called, for it was immediately apparent from the slowness of her gait that she had gotten little benefit from the time she had been on her own. He waited for her to reach him, then took her racquet and bag of balls. "I never should have let you come on ahead alone."

"It wasn't your choice, Aren," Haven reminded him. Now that he was here, and again smothering her with unwanted attention, it seemed as though they had never been apart. She hurried to distract him. "How is everyone?"

More interested in her, Aren searched her ex-

pression as he described her teammates. He
didn't want to scold her again, but as the captain,
she ought not to have deserted the team. She
ought not to have deserted him either, but he
kept that private sorrow to himself as well.

"Rita Blanco sprained her right ankle again in
training, but she should be fit by the second
game, if not the first. Everyone else is healthy,
and the team's optimistic about another win."

"That's good." Haven draped her damp towel
around her neck. "Have you already checked in?"

"Yes. My room's just across the hall from
yours."

Haven was sure he would be pleased, but she
certainly wasn't. She had not missed him one bit,
but she could tell by the intensity of his glance
that he had missed her. She also knew he
wouldn't wait long before he began the relentless
barrage of solicitous advice she didn't want to
hear.

They had reached the tram stop and she
pressed the button for him. "Take the tram," she
suggested. "I'm going to jog back to our quarters.
See you at dinner."

Aren made a grab for Haven's arm, but she
spun away, waved, and sprinted around the corner. He swung her racquet toward the wall but
checked the motion at the last instant. He feared
Haven was disintegrating before his eyes, and
she wasn't going to let him do a damn thing to
help her. It was his job to certify the Flames' fitness to play, but he doubted threatening to put
Haven on the injured list would force her to ac-

cept counseling. That she was so independent was her strength, but it was also her greatest weakness.

He climbed on board the tram, holding Haven's equipment cradled in his arms. She was not simply the finest athlete of her time, but an extraordinary woman in all respects. He would just have to find a way to help her—and soon.

When Aren reached the team's quarters he caught a glimpse of Lyne Lee, captain of the Satin Spikes, and could barely stifle a groan. Blake Ellis would be with them, and from what Aren knew of Haven's ex-husband, he would take a malicious delight in baiting Haven in hopes of upsetting her badly enough to throw off her game. It wouldn't take much to do that with Haven as distracted as she was. Determined not to let Blake near her, Aren showered and dressed for dinner in plenty of time to warn Haven that the Satin Spikes had arrived.

Ian paced his room to burn the restless energy he had had no time to work off in the gym. He was far too active a man to enjoy poring over files all day long, and he decided to schedule interviews for the next day rather than repeat the ordeal. He still had not seen Haven, but he had passed several of her teammates when he left the tram in the guest quarters. Tall and lithe, they had moved aside with an agile grace, but none had drawn more than a polite nod from him.

Their arrival meant he had lost whatever slight opportunity he might have had to enjoy Haven's undivided attention, but he wasn't prepared to stand in the background either. Intending to again escort her to dinner, he went to her room several minutes early, but tonight he wasn't content to wait outside. She answered his knock promptly, but sent an anxious glance up and down the hall. She was wearing another attractive red dress, but she was barefooted and her hair was still loose.

"Were you expecting someone?" Ian asked.

"Dreading is a better word, so I'm not disappointed it's you. Come on in. I'm almost ready."

That was scarcely an enthusiastic welcome, but Ian followed her through the door and quickly closed it. He had taken little notice of her room last night, but now he saw it was identical to his: small, and decorated in a sandy beige with what could well be described as institutional charm. Tonight the air was sweetly scented with incense burning in a small clay jar. Placed on the ledge that served as a shelf or desk, the lid was pierced to allow the fragrant smoke to escape. While it was a bit strong for Ian's tastes, he had to admit it conjured up a wealth of erotic possibilities. Haven had been so definite about avoiding any involvement with men during the games; he was very curious as to what she might be up to.

Haven stepped into the bathroom to finish combing her hair. She neglected to close the door, and Ian chose to regard what might have been simple carelessness as an invitation to observe. He crossed his arms over his chest and leaned against the doorjamb. "Do you always wear red?" he asked.

"Always." Haven twisted her hair atop her head and secured it with a gold clip. Meeting his eyes in the mirror, she picked up her comb and carefully withdrew a few seemingly errant wisps at her nape to create a charming, innocent style. "First because the Flames' management encouraged it, and now because it gives my spirits a boost. Now all I need are my boots."

She turned away from the mirror, but Ian refused to move aside to allow her to pass. "Why are you burning incense?" he asked. "There wasn't a trace of it when I was here last night, but now I'm nearly choking on jasmine."

There was a smugly superior arch to his brow, and though his manner was nothing like Aren's, the effect of his impertinent question was precisely the same. She could not abide having each of her actions analyzed so intently. "I fail to see why my habits are any concern of yours. Now get out of my way so I can find my boots or we'll be late for dinner."

"Are you certain that wasn't what you had in mind?" Her dress had a high neck and long sleeves, but it caressed her slender figure as beautifully as the one she'd worn last night. He couldn't help regarding her with an openly admiring glance. "You were obviously expecting someone, and the room is scented for seduction. Why did you invite me in? Were you hoping to make another man jealous?"

Ian was smiling now, as though he might actually enjoy watching a rival draw a completely erroneous conclusion. Disgusted with him, Haven rested her hands on her hips. "We've probably had similar training in self-defense. I could snap your neck with a single blow, but you'd probably break my arm as I tried. I wouldn't be able to play in the tournament then. The money wagered would undoubtedly be less than Alado anticipates, and you'd be blamed.

"To save us both such unnecessary misery, jettison your romantic fantasies and get out of my way so I can get my boots."

Amused rather than insulted by the sharpness of her tone, Ian stepped aside. As Haven passed him, there was an insistent knock at the door. "Right on cue," he teased. "Go ahead and answer. I'll just stand here and look innocent."

His smile had widened to an insufferable smirk, and Haven was sorely tempted to wipe it away with a well-placed slap. "Why do I get the impression that you've had a lot of practice in that skill?" she asked.

"Because I have," Ian assured her confidently. "Now answer the door."

Haven hoped it was one of her teammates but relied on the viewing screen in the security panel to make certain. Discovering Aren waiting in the corridor, she swore under her breath while Ian broke into deep chuckles. She shot him an angry glance, then used the speaker rather than open the door.

"I'm not quite dressed, Aren. Can it wait until dinner?"

Not wanting to broadcast the bad news, Aren lowered his voice. "I just wanted you to know that the Satin Spikes are here, so you wouldn't walk into dinner unprepared."

Haven sucked in a breath. She had not really been hungry in the first place, and now she lost all interest in food. She glanced down at her bare toes while she mulled over her options. She wanted to stay in her room but didn't dare risk being accused of cowardice. She would have to force herself to dine with the others, but she did not have to like it.

"Thanks, Aren," she finally replied. "I'll see you at dinner." Preoccupied when she turned, she was startled to find Ian only a step away. He didn't look in the least bit amused now. Clearly his moods shifted as rapidly as hers, and she found that unexpected kinship strangely comforting.

"That was Dr. Manzari, our team physician," Haven explained. "I'm not fond of the Satin Spikes' personnel, so I appreciate his warning."

Relieved that she had dismissed the doctor so quickly, Ian forgot him too. "Do you really take the rivalry between your teams that seriously?"

Haven slipped by him to get to the closet. She grabbed a bright red boot and leaned back against the wall to maintain her balance as she tugged it on. "Let's just say I respect some opponents more than others."

Ian watched her yank on the second boot with far more force than was necessary and knew there was more to this story than she was telling.

He watched her smooth her dress over her hips and then followed her to the door. "I'll be happy to run interference for you," he offered.

Tempted, Haven made the mistake of looking up at him, and the tenderness reflected in his amber gaze made her heart lurch. She longed to slip her arms around his waist and hold on forever. In the next breath, however, she was ashamed to be so weak and found the courage to refuse.

"You've got your own work, Mr. Hyatt. You take care of it, and I'll handle mine."

She hit a button and, as the door slid open, they came face to face with Aren, who had been anxiously pacing back and forth. The conscientious physician took one look at Ian and could think of only one reason why he would be in Haven's room. Devastated to discover how she had really been spending her time on 317, he turned his back on her and strode off alone.

"Aren!" Haven called in a hushed plea, but he kept right on going.

The silent confrontation had been over almost before it had begun, but Ian felt a sickening sensation swell in his gut. "Don't tell me I was right. Were you really using me to make the doctor jealous?"

Haven clenched her fists and swallowed the shriek of frustration that threatened to burst through her lips. Aren was the dearest of men, and while she abhorred being the object of constant scrutiny, she would never have hurt his feelings deliberately. "No, absolutely not," she swore. "It was the farthest thing from my mind.

Aren can't separate his professional obligation from his personal interest in me, but I'd never stage such a ridiculous encounter just to hurt him. This is going to be a perfect evening; I can see that right now."

Haven started off down the hall with such a furious stride that Ian had to run a step to catch up with her. "Look, I've obviously stumbled into the middle of an embarrassing situation. I prefer women who are satisfied with one lover at a time, so I'd like you to be straight with me."

Haven came to a halt so quickly, Ian now had to retrace a step to face her. She raised her fist and shook it at him, but her voice was controlled in a low, dangerous hiss so as not to alert the other occupants of the corridor to their argument. "I should rip off your head for that insult, but because you once meant a great deal to me I'll let you off with a warning: I do not regard men as toys and I never play with their emotions. I don't need even one man in my life, let alone two. So if you're afraid of being used, it's your own paranoia. Now for the remainder of our time here, I suggest you stay as far away from me as you can get!"

Haven again took off down the corridor at a pace just short of a run, but Ian lengthened his stride to keep up with her. Her cheeks were filled with a vivid blush and her luscious mouth was set in such a hostile line that he did not doubt the sincerity of her vow for an instant. What he did doubt, however, was his own resolve. He wouldn't argue with her now, but one day soon he was going to turn the flame of her temper to white-hot desire and make her beg him to come as close to her as her own heartbeat.

They had to wait for a tram, and Haven did her best to ignore Ian until it came. The problem was, her whole body was all too aware of him. She had never been so hungry for a man, but there was no other word for the desperate craving even the sight of him caused. He had been completely wrong about the incense; she had lit it in a futile attempt to create a few moments of tranquillity rather than a mood of seduction, but all hope of finding peace had eluded her once he had entered her room. *And she had invited him in!* she agonized.

A tram arrived, and as she and Ian stepped on, she heard Elida Rivard call for them to hold it. She saw Ian hesitate, then slid her hand over his to touch the panel to keep the tram at their stop. Another mistake she vowed not to repeat, for the heat of his skin scorched her palm. She quickly drew her hand away.

Elida and two more of her teammates joined them then, and Haven attempted to smile as though she had missed them, while Ian moved to the rear, as though he were no more than a passenger who had just happened by at the same time. She could still feel his presence, however, and when Elida eyed him appreciatively, Haven sent her a challenging glance that had nothing whatsoever to do with their rivalry on the Rocketball court.

Chapter Six

Creative use of movable partitions allowed the mine maintenance staff to enlarge the executive dining room to accommodate the addition of the Flames and Satin Spikes. Each team traveled with nine players, plus coaches, trainers, a physician, and a manager, for a total of fifteen. That many guests required five tables, and to minimize what Egon assumed would be a natural animosity, he had designated the seating at four of the tables to separate the players by team but had mixed the support personnel at the fifth.

He had asked his executives to serve as host or hostess at each table but, wanting to keep a close eye on John Hyatt, he had put him at his own table. He assumed the investigator would be discreet enough not to discuss his case with the players, but he wanted to be able to interrupt and silence him if he did. He had observed Hyatt studying the mine's personnel records with a commendable diligence, but Egon had long ago erased the only evidence that would have connected the missing men. Confident Hyatt would soon tire of his fruitless search, he looked forward to an immensely entertaining evening.

As Haven entered the dining room, she saw only that it was larger and cared not at all how much planning Egon had put into making the evening a success. Her sole interest lay in the guests. Most of the Flames were already there, but only a few of the Satin Spikes. Blake Ellis wasn't among them. Relaxing momentarily, Haven sought out Aren, who was carrying a drink away from the bar. His back was toward her, but she caught up and cut in front of him rather than call out his name.

Aren's hands were shaking, and he took a quick sip of wine to avoid an embarrassing spill. The pause also served to curb his impulse to call Haven the foul name he thought she deserved but feared he would soon regret. "I don't want to hear your excuses," he said in a malicious hiss.

Haven took his free arm to make it appear they were merely having a friendly chat, but she cautiously kept her back to the rest of the guests. There was music playing—a shimmering chorus of flutes and chimes—and bright laughter came from people standing near the bar, but she was still wary of being overheard. "You recently accused me of being unable to move past a casual friendship with anyone. Now you've seen a man

107

in my room and you're acting like an outraged lover. John Hyatt is an insurance investigator, of all things, and there's nothing—not even friendship—between us. Even if there were, you still would have no right to behave as though you've been betrayed."

Aren was hurting so badly, he found it difficult even to look at Haven, much less to accept what she had to say. "There is something between us," he argued, "even if it is dreadfully one-sided, and I saw the look on that man's face. He was more at home in your apartment than you were. Don't tell me he hadn't been there before, or that you hadn't welcomed him."

Because at least part of Aren's bitter speculation was true, Haven couldn't dispute the rest. Thoroughly disgusted with him, as well as herself, she released his arm and walked away. Ian was lounging against the bar, observing her rather than talking with the others clustered nearby. Wanting to avoid him, she started across the room, intending to speak with Rita Blanco, who was seated in one of the deeply padded chairs with her right foot propped on an ottoman.

"Haven?" Blake Ellis intercepted her before she reached Rita. "We need to talk."

Haven had to force herself to turn toward her ex-husband. He was now the head coach of the Satin Spikes and was dressed in their silvery gray. At six feet, four inches, and 210 pounds, he was as perfect a physical specimen as the women on his team. His dark brown hair had a healthy sheen, his hazel eyes were clear, and his smile, as always, was too wide to be sincere. She had once thought him handsome but now knew just how little character there was behind his attractive facade.

"I can't imagine why," Haven replied, "and even if we did, this is neither the time nor the place."

Haven would have continued on toward Rita, but Blake reached out to catch her hand and draw her back to his side. "Wait," he begged softly. "This might be the only chance we'll have until after the tournament, and I don't want to miss it."

"It's always what you want, isn't it?"

Blake winced. "Just give me a chance, Haven. I've a lot to say."

Haven shook her head. She knew precisely how persuasive Blake could be, but the pain he had caused her had imparted a strong immunity to his charm. She pulled her hand from his grasp and wiped her palm on her dress to remove all trace of his touch. Her stare was cold. "The Flames are favored to win the tournament again this year, and nothing you could possibly say will upset me so badly that I won't be able to play my best game. We both know that's all you're trying to do, Blake. It's a pathetic trick and it won't work."

"You've got me all wrong," Blake protested. He leaned close to whisper, "This is personal, Haven. It's not about the games."

"Liar."

Even from across the room Ian could read that insult on Haven's lips. Thinking she might need his help to escape a man who was obviously being obnoxious, he set his glass of Martian ale on the bar and joined them. "The way I see it," he interjected, "the contest between the Flames and the Spikes doesn't begin for several days. Why don't you stay on your side of the room?"

Refusing that bit of unwanted advice, Blake turned fierce. "Stay out of this," he ordered harshly. He regarded Ian with a challenging stare, but when Ian didn't even blink Blake was forced to look away first. Far from beaten, he chose to ignore the intruder and concentrate on Haven. "If not here, then give me a time and place and I'll be there."

"What a charming invitation," Ian murmured. "Let's make it a threesome."

For a brief instant Haven feared Blake was going to throw a punch, which she felt certain Ian would dodge. She shuddered at the thought of the hellacious brawl that would surely ensue, but at the last moment Blake's posture relaxed.

"He's pretty enough, but I doubt one of Alado's men can keep up with you," Blake leaned close to whisper. "Meet me at the arena at ten."

The warmth of his breath caressed Haven's cheek as he turned away, bringing a bittersweet memory of what they had once shared. She waited until he had reached the bar to scold Ian. "I didn't need your help, if that's what you thought you were giving." She watched his expression fill with doubt and knew she hadn't sounded convincing. Ian could convey an amazing array of emotions with such slight effort, she wondered if it had been part of his training. Suddenly realizing the danger he was in, she dropped the sarcasm.

"If Blake wasn't so damn self-absorbed, he might have recognized you. I don't think you ought to mingle with the teams."

While Ian was thrilled by the new note of concern in her voice, he remained cool. "There's so little interaction between Artic Warriors and Rocketball stars that there's a minimal risk anyone here will know me. Unless, of course, you and Blake are so well acquainted that you admitted to once having had a passion for me."

A questioning light filled his amber gaze, and Haven did not disappoint him. "Blake's my ex-husband, but I've no idea what he recalls of our conversations."

Ian had known she was divorced, but he would have been a lot more hostile to Blake had he known who he was. "Stay with me this evening," he offered, "and I'll keep him at bay."

"You needn't bother," Haven assured him. "He's just trying to distract me so the Spikes will win the tournament, and I've already told him it won't work."

"Are you going to meet him later?"

"You heard?" Haven was appalled. "No. He said more than enough to me while we were married." Ian inclined his head slightly, encouraging her to confide more, but just being in the same room with Blake was making her too sick to her stomach to want to. "I'm not the subject of your investigation, Mr. Hyatt. How is it going, by the way? Have you located any of the missing miners as yet?"

"Not a one," Ian admitted, "but I will soon." He slid his hand down her arm to take her hand. "Let's find out where we're to be seated for dinner so we can switch places with others if we're not together."

Blake had demanded a great deal from Haven. Aren merely spewed advice and complained when she refused to follow it. Now here was Ian St. Ives, the man of her dreams in the flesh, assuming more than he had any right to expect when she had only known him two days. "I'd rather sit with the Satin Spikes," Haven replied. Thinking she had made her point, she broke away and finally went to talk with Rita.

Ian smiled as though their exchange had been pleasant, but he was disappointed he was making no more progress with Haven than he was in finding the missing miners. He returned to the bar to retrieve his ale, then continued to appear as though he was enjoying the evening as he moved around the edge of the expanded dining room and studied the players from both teams. The Flames were clad in a stylish assortment of dresses and boots in the same bright hues featured in their uniforms, while the Satin Spikes wore matching short silver dresses trimmed in hot pink with pink boots. It was impossible to tell which was the better team from a glance at the players, but none of the other women present moved with Haven's fluid grace.

In addition to having superb coordination, Haven also had a remarkable talent for conflict with men, Ian mused silently. The room was full of beautiful young women with supple bodies and enticing smiles, but Haven was the only one who interested him. He was in good company, it seemed. Her team's physician was still eyeing her with a sullen frown, and whenever Ian paused to search the room for Blake he found him also watching Haven intently. Blake's expression was difficult to describe, but Ian judged it as more remorseful than angry. Perhaps he sincerely regretted their divorce and wanted Haven back.

Ian took a sip of ale and contemplated that possibility. After all, Haven had married Blake once, and from what little he knew of her she would not have made the commitment had she not loved him. A woman with her passionate temperament would surely love deeply, and expect her marriage to last a lifetime. He was very curious as to what had gone wrong. He would keep his distance for now, but at ten he was going to take a stroll by the arena to see just who was there. Content with his own company since he could not have Haven's, he was annoyed when one of the Flames approached him.

"Hello. I'm Elida Rivard, and I couldn't help but notice how lonesome you look. You're not here for the games, are you?"

Elida had golden skin, luminous brown eyes, and curly black hair that spilled over her shoulders in a long, wild mane. She was an attractive woman, but she stood so close to him that her arm brushed against his. Ian had to back away. He gave her his name and a brief reference to an insurance problem to justify his being on 317. "I hope to be able to see the Flames play before I leave," he added.

"Do you have tickets?" Elida ran the tip of her tongue across her lower lip and again moved closer. When Ian shook his head she flashed him a predatory smile. "There are always a few reserved for friends of the players, so I can get you some."

"Do you always make friends so quickly, Ms. Rivard?"

Elida responded with a throaty laugh. "Only with men as appealing as you, Mr. Hyatt."

That was an invitation Ian probably would have accepted had he not met Haven Wray, but he wasn't interested and didn't encourage her. "What do you think of the Satin Spikes' chances?" he asked.

Not realizing he had just signaled her that he would rather discuss the games than her offer of friendship, Elida boasted proudly, "They'll be eliminated in the first round, and the Flames will win the championship again."

Ian kept Elida talking about the tournament and, inspired by his interest, she provided lengthy derogatory descriptions of the other teams until dinner was served. He was relieved that she wasn't seated at his table, but then, Haven wasn't either, which was disappointing. He could see Haven, though, and he wasn't surprised when she again excused herself before dessert was served. She was the most elusive woman he had ever met, but he had always relished a challenge.

Blake Ellis reached the arena early and sat down in the stands for what he feared would be a futile wait. He had rehearsed what he wanted to say for months, but now he went over it again just to make certain he hadn't forgotten any of the tender phrases he hoped would soften Haven's heart. When ten o'clock came and went without any sign of his former wife, he was beyond anger. Leaving the arena, he shoved open the double doors with outstretched arms but came to an abrupt halt when he saw the blond man who had interfered in his earlier attempt to speak with Haven. Ian was leaning against the wall, wearing an amused smirk that made Blake wild.

"You kept her away," he shouted accusingly, and before Ian could respond he rushed toward him.

It had been a while since Ian had had to defend himself, but he had not lost his edge. Rather than adopting a defensive pose, he waited where he stood. Then, at the last instant, he stepped aside, and Blake went barreling right into the wall. "Careful," Ian cautioned as he moved to the center of the corridor. "You'll hurt yourself."

Shaken, Blake peeled himself off the wall and called Ian a filthy name. They were nearly equal in size, but Blake lacked Ian's speed and skill. He faked a move to the left, then came at Ian from

115

the right. Not fooled, Ian spun away, then slammed the heel of his hand across the back of Blake's neck in a vicious chop. Blake's knees buckled, and with a sad cry of surprise he went limp and fell forward. His right brow smacked against the floor, and had he not already been unconscious, he would have knocked himself out then.

Ian waited for Blake to rise, but when he hadn't stirred after several minutes Ian gave him a nudge in the ribs with his toe. "Looks like you're the pretty one who can't keep up." He laughed, then left Blake where he lay. When he reached the tram a young man with spiked blond hair was seated in the back row and gave him a nod of recognition.

"Pretend you don't know me," T.L. Rainey whispered.

Ian swung into a seat two rows ahead of him. They were the only two in the tram car but, hoping T.L. had some much needed information, Ian went along with his desire for discretion. He rubbed his right hand to work out the soreness from striking Blake and waited.

At the first stop T.L. left his seat and walked by Ian without pausing. "Don't get too curious," he warned softly, "or the mine will swallow you too."

Ian let him go, but he was encouraged by the young man's words. T.L. had only been there for a few months, and if he knew something, then other men did too. Recalling his tour of the subterranean tunnels with a shiver of revulsion, Ian could easily imagine the mine as a ravenous beast eagerly devouring miners. "But where does it spit out the bones?" he asked himself. He hadn't a clue.

On the way to his room Ian stopped by Haven's. He doubted she would invite him in, but he did have some interesting news. When she used the speaker on the security panel he couldn't keep the chuckle out of his voice. "Your ex-husband got more than he bargained for at the arena. You might want to have a medical team check on him."

He went on to his room without waiting for her reply, but even if he hadn't seen her reaction, he could imagine a combination of surprise and satisfaction. He stretched out on his bed and propped his head on his hands. Haven had made his stay on 317 far more entertaining than he had imagined possible, but that did not mean he would neglect his assignment.

He had never failed to complete a job and he had no intention of breaking that enviable record now. He frequently had been sent to rescue other agents who had gotten themselves entangled in difficult situations, but this case wasn't so much difficult as it was baffling. Fifteen men were missing and no one here cared. That just couldn't be true. Someone had to have lost a good friend. That someone was going to have to start talking and soon, though, or he was going to run out of ways to make Egon think he was working while he waited for the valuable tip that had to come.

Until then, he sighed, there was always Haven

Wray, and she provided more than enough excitement to enliven the dullest assignment in the galaxy. Now all he had to do was convince her that he was exciting, too.

The remaining teams competing in the tournament, the Zephyrs and the Pagans, were due to arrive the following day, but the Flames and the Satin Spikes chose not to wait for them to begin practicing in the arena. Times were determined by the coaches, with the Flames having the morning and the Spikes the afternoon. Even with Rita Blanco sitting out the practice, the Flames had eight healthy players to form two squads and play each other.

Haven was the captain of one squad, and Elida Rivard captained the other. During the regular season they were seldom on the court at the same time, and then always on the same side, so practice games were the only times they were pitted against each other. Haven's squad won the first two matches, but Elida's came back to win the third by a single point. It wasn't until they took a break before the fourth game that Haven noticed Ian was seated in the stands.

She didn't know how long he had been there, but he made her uneasy. She could block out the distraction of an arena full of shrieking fans, but ignoring him was far more difficult. Believing Blake had deserved whatever he had gotten, she had not called the medical unit to request assistance for him, as Ian had suggested, and then had felt guilty because she hadn't. After an uncomfortable hour spent debating what she ought to have done, she had finally gone to the arena herself but found it deserted.

Perhaps Ian had only been teasing her. She certainly hoped so. Many women would be flattered to have two handsome men fighting over them, but Haven was not one of them.

Tory Norton, the head coach, shouted for the next game to begin, and Haven walked out on the court. She was careful not to glance Ian's way before serving the first ball.

Ian sat forward and watched all the action on the court, rather than simply concentrating on Haven. Her squad played together well, working as a cohesive unit to score or block their opponents' shots, while Elida's careened about the court and missed as many shots as they made. Elida was a strong player, but she fought her own side for shots just as hard as she fought Haven's. Haven's squad won again, and so easily that Ian was convinced she had merely let Elida's win the third game to enliven the competition.

It was clever of her, but not something Ian would encourage. Getting caught up in the play, he moved down behind Aren, Tory Norton, and Christine Barry. The women had once led the team as players and now served as coaches. Ian listened to their comments as the fifth game began, then had to make one of his own.

"Excuse me," he whispered. "I realize you're attempting to build two winning squads, but if you play your two strongest players together, you can run up the score so quickly, none of the other teams will be able to catch you. It's been a long season. You owe it to your players to win the tournament in the fewest games possible. Elida's too wild. Rein her in, and then she and Haven will be an unbeatable combination."

Astonished by Ian's advice, Tory and Christine turned and simply stared, but Aren had plenty to say. "The Flames have the best record in their league, and they'll win the tournament without any help from you."

"I've reviewed tapes of your games," Ian argued. "You've won so many because Haven's the best player Rocketball has ever seen. She's carrying the rest of the team on her back, and you're going to burn her out if you don't make some constructive changes. That wouldn't just be tragic; it would be criminal."

"I thought your field was insurance," Aren countered, "not competitive sports."

Ian rose rather than contradict the physician. He spoke instead to the coaches. "Give my ideas some thought for Haven's sake. She deserves a lot more support than she's getting on the court, and it shows."

Haven had not seen the exchange, and the next time she glanced toward the stands Ian was gone. Relieved, she relaxed, then collided with Elida as she went for the next shot and nearly went sprawling. Saved by her natural agility, she missed being injured but had come too close not to be angry.

"That was deliberate," she shouted.

"It was not," Elida exclaimed innocently. She looked up at the coaches. "I'm just playing to win.

Isn't that what I'm supposed to do?"

Not eager to mediate the dispute, Christine Barry checked the time and decided that they ought to leave the arena before the Spikes arrived. "That's enough for today. Cool down, shower, and we'll talk strategy after lunch."

"Are you going to let her get away with that?" Haven called to the coaches.

Tory Norton came forward and rested her hands against the mesh screen separating the spectators from the playing area. "Save your anger for the tournament. Now let's go. Clear the court."

Haven saw Elida turn away to hide her smirk, but she wasn't about to allow the willful girl to play so roughly. She removed her helmet and walked up to her. "You try that again and I'll see you're the first player traded in the off season. Don't think I don't have that power, because I do."

Elida's eyes widened. "It was an accident, Haven. Don't make more of it than it was."

"You'll have no second chance," Haven warned. She walked off the court, but as she entered the locker room she found Blake Ellis waiting for her. His right eye was ringed by one of the most colorful black eyes she had ever seen, but she did not care to admit she knew exactly how he had gotten it.

"Looks like you had a rough night," she said instead.

Blake was in no mood to admit anything either. "I slipped and fell. Where were you last night? Why didn't you come to meet me?"

Haven rested her racquet on her shoulder. "I had better things to do, just as I do now." She heard the door open and turned to find Aren had followed close behind her. "The rest of the Flames will be here any second," she told Blake. "Let's spare them a regrettable scene."

Blake looked far from pleased. "Tell your boyfriend I'm going to make him sorry he ever tried to come between us."

"You're the one who came between us," Haven reminded him.

Blake shook his head, as though her opinion was absurd, then brushed past Aren and went out on the court.

"Was he bothering you?" Aren asked.

"Forget it, Aren. It doesn't concern you."

Haven left for the showers before Aren could insist her well-being was indeed his concern. He was as annoyed with Elida as she was, which he would tell her later, but he wouldn't reveal the fact that John Hyatt apparently believed he had the right to offer the coaches advice. There was only one place he could have gotten that assumption, and it was from Haven herself.

She might deny it, but Aren was positive John Hyatt had been in her room for a purpose, and it wasn't to discuss insurance. He frowned slightly as he recalled Hyatt's confident assessment of the Flames. There was something familiar about the man, although he was positive they had never met before yesterday. He struggled with the sense of recognition but couldn't push past the vague feeling to anything concrete. Perhaps Hyatt merely reminded him of someone, but he could not remember whom.

The Flames flooded through the locker room on their way to the showers, and he needed to check the schedules of their massages with the trainers. It was difficult to concentrate on business when he was so worried about Haven, but given her recent history with men he was confident John Hyatt wouldn't be a problem for long. Then he realized that this was the first time she would not even admit she was interested in a man. That had to mean there was something different about Hyatt, and he began to fret all over again.

Ian spent the remainder of the day interviewing every last person on the mine staff who might possibly know anything at all about the missing miners, and learned absolutely nothing other than the fact that Chella Bergh was still interested in him. When he reached his room and found the message light flashing on the communications panel he hardly dared hope it might be a lead, and it wasn't.

The voice on the recorded message was Haven's, however, which wasn't at all disappointing. She sounded breathless, as though she had urgent need of him, and he left right away to see why. He tapped lightly on her door, and she opened it immediately and quickly pulled him inside.

She was again wearing the blue robe, but she

did not look as though she had been relaxing. "I scarcely know where to begin," she exclaimed. "I wasn't certain you were serious about calling the medical unit last night, but Blake has a truly beautiful black eye, which has to be your fault, although he wouldn't admit it."

"He fell," Ian swore convincingly.

Haven was no more amused by his lie than she had been by Blake's. "Sure he did, right after you hit him. That's really beside the point. I want you to leave him alone. I won't have you two fighting over me. It has to stop immediately. Do you understand me?"

"Yes." Ian straightened his shoulders proudly. "But I believe that's between Blake and me."

"Not when I'm in the middle, it isn't."

An erotic image of her sandwiched between them filled Ian's mind and he couldn't suppress a sly smile. He was wise enough not to describe it to her, though. "Men have always fought over women. It's in our genes," he insisted, "but if you want Blake back, I'll get out of the way. There is a certain percentage of people who remarry the spouses they've divorced, but often they just divorce them again for the very same reason they left them the first time. I'd hate to see you make the same mistake twice."

Haven combed her fingers through her hair. She'd washed it after practice and left it falling free. "Regardless of what Blake may wish, he and I will never, ever, be a couple again. That's what makes any argument between the two of you so damn stupid. I'm the one making the choices here, and he's not even in the running."

Enormously relieved, Ian tried not to gloat. "I knew you were a smart girl the first time I saw you."

"Please, we both know that wasn't your first thought. Now that Blake's out of the way, I have something else to say."

Ian placed his hands behind his back and rocked back on his heels. "I can hardly wait to hear it."

Exasperated with him, Haven picked up the glass of juice she had been drinking before he arrived and took a long drink. She did not offer him any as she replaced the glass on the shelf beside the incense burner. She pulled her belt tight, and then continued. "You were at the Flames' practice this morning."

"I'm flattered you noticed."

"Aren't you ever serious?"

Ian took a moment to consider her question. "The fact is, I'm probably the most serious individual you'll ever meet, but I can't seem to resist teasing you. I'll try to do better if it annoys you."

Haven sincerely doubted he could. "Please do. I can't imagine why you'd attend a practice, but don't do it again. It's difficult enough to concentrate without your being there to distract me."

Ian knew she would really be enraged if he revealed that he had spoken with the Flames' coaches, so he simply nodded. "If that's what you want, I'll stay away, but don't ask me to skip the games. I really want to see you play in the tournament, and you'll not be able to pick me out in the crowd."

Knowing that she would still feel his presence, Haven had to look away. "Come to the games, if you must," she agreed softly. She had another topic to discuss but needed to show him something first. She took a step toward the communications panel and inserted a small disk. "I didn't realize I'd brought this with me, but you ought to see it."

Her mood had changed so swiftly from defensive to melancholy that Ian knew something must be very wrong. He moved up behind her and slid his arms around her waist, but he held her in a gentle embrace rather than a confining hold. He held his breath, waiting for her to break free, but she relaxed against him.

He was about to slip his hand inside her robe to caress her breast, but it seemed she was able to read his mind and placed her hands over his. "Don't," she begged. "Just hold me for a minute."

Ian muffled an anguished moan against her throat. "It's not nearly enough."

Haven took a deep breath, but it didn't help. "I know, but anything more will be too much, and I won't be able to stop you."

She sounded as troubled by that prospect as he. "Do you even want to stop me?" he asked.

Haven closed her eyes but saw his face clearly in her mind. She knew his features as well as her own and could have sculpted the angle of his cheek and jaw. The sweetness of his mouth lingered in her memory. She could feel the tension in his muscles through her robe. If only she could feel his bare skin against hers for just a moment, but neither of them would be able to stop there. And if they became lovers, how could she play in the tournament when a single distracting thought could cost her her life? She was going to have to be the strong one, for both their sakes, if they were ever to have a future.

"No," she confessed, "but I would have to, and then you'd be even more angry than you will be when you see this." She asked the room's computer to show the disk. The lights dimmed instantly, and snow-covered landscape flashed across the viewing screen. "I've had this for years. I didn't even realize it was still in my things. I suppose it's lucky for you that I'm never in one place long enough to unpack."

There was still a faint trace of jasmine in the air, but it didn't distract Ian from her, or the images on the screen. It was coverage of the final seconds of an Artic Warrior competition. He had always dressed in gold to match the medals he had won, but had never bothered to attend the awards ceremonies. He had not needed applause; winning had been all that had mattered to him.

This was an early contest, one he had entered in his teens. As he shied away from the finish line, some ambitious reporter only a year or two older than he had followed him with a camera. He had raised the smoked visor on his helmet and laughed rather than reply to questions, but he was easily recognizable. His image lingered on the screen to be enhanced, and enlarged, as his prospects for sweeping the Artic Warrior competitions were discussed by some unseen expert. He had been predicted to win every contest he entered, and he had.

It was the only interview Ian had ever given, if it could be called that, and he had forgotten it. "Who else has seen this?" he asked as he released her.

Haven felt him drop not only his arms but his affectionate manner, and there was a sharpness to his voice that alarmed her. "No one that I can recall, but it's enough that it exists, because that means others may have seen it. Aren might recognize you. So could Blake, or any of the press who'll soon arrive. You never should have come here during the games."

Ian wanted the disk, and badly, but he knew Haven would never let it go. He could not even say how he knew, just as he had known in the moment he had first seen her face that no woman would ever mean more to him. "Do you believe in omens?" he asked.

Haven nodded. "Yes, I do, and surely this is one."

"Yes. It's definitely inspired me to get back to work." Ian walked to her door. "But it could also be one for you. You win the tournament, and I'll find those poor lost souls. Then we'll celebrate together."

Haven let him go, then replayed the disk. She had fallen in love with the cocky kid on the screen, but he was now an entirely different man, and while he might still be recognizable, the innocently adoring girl she had once been was gone.

Chapter Seven

Aren was standing at the end of the hall, conferring with one of the trainers, when Ian left Haven's room. Despite her denials to him, this was additional proof that she was indeed seeing John Hyatt. Aren was heartsick at the thought. He managed to complete his conversation without revealing his distress, but as soon as he entered his room, he sank down on the bed and put his head in his hands.

It did not matter that Haven had never really been his. His torment was as deep as any caused by a failed love affair.

Even before Haven had mentioned it, Aren had been aware that the other women on the team were attracted to him. He saw their admiring glances and enticing smiles but dismissed them without regret. He wanted Haven with a yearning no other woman would ever satisfy. Hot tears of frustration and shame filled his eyes and he fought to blink them away. Having observed how reluctant Haven had been to form serious relationships with the men she dated, he had never been jealous. Instead he had been patient, confident that eventually she would turn to him and accept the love he was so eager to give.

Now John Hyatt went in and out of her room as though it was his own, and Aren was badly worried. He simply did not know what to make of the man. He had seen Hyatt confront Blake Ellis to protect Haven from her ex-husband, but not ten minutes later he had observed him chatting with Elida Rivard. Wasn't Haven woman enough for him? Aren wondered. Was he out to seduce the entire team?

His thoughts dark, Aren had to force himself to dress for dinner. Not feeling up to making amusing conversation, he arrived at the dining room just minutes before the meal was to be served and was disappointed to find Haven absent. He had no problem with her dining in her room when she was tired, but John Hyatt was nowhere to be seen either, and he could not abide the thought that they were together. Believing he had a legitimate complaint about his rival, he approached Egon Rascon.

"How did your practice go today?" Egon inquired, greatly enjoying his role as host of the tournament.

"Very well, thank you, but as many games are won off the court as on."

Egon had planned to bet on the Flames. Now, seeing an opportunity to gain a valuable piece of inside information, he nodded thoughtfully. "Are you referring to injuries?" he asked.

Aren shook his head. "Not really, although it is my job to keep the Flames fit. I'm more concerned about motivation. Sometimes a player is burdened by personal problems and unable to give her best."

Really intrigued now, Egon moved closer. "I've been divorced three times, so you needn't tell me about personal problems. But how do you handle such a crisis?"

Aren feigned the confidence he didn't actually feel. "I do whatever I can to resolve or remove the problem. That's really why I wanted to speak with you." He scanned the room, making a last search for Haven and John Hyatt, but they still hadn't appeared and he was now positive that they wouldn't.

"I wonder if you could tell me something about John Hyatt," Aren said. "Haven Wray seems to be taken with him, and she ought not to become involved with anyone who might be a detriment to her career."

Egon was astonished by Aren's remark. "I don't know what to say," he blurted out. He turned to look for the pair, but even in the crowded room he quickly ascertained their absence. He had been badly disappointed when Haven had not warmed to his attempts to impress her, but that she would prefer someone as dull and soft-spoken as John Hyatt was insulting.

"Don't misunderstand me," Aren cautioned. "They're adults and don't need our supervision, but if you could vouch for Hyatt's character, it would put my mind at ease."

From the general impression Egon had received of John Hyatt, he would never have guessed that any of the glamorous women on the Rocketball teams would even notice him. That the colorless investigator had somehow accomplished a seemingly impossible feat was completely beyond his comprehension. "I barely know the man," Egon explained, and added a vague reference to insurance. "He arrived two days ago, and I imagine he'll soon complete his investigation and leave. He's such an unassuming individual that, quite frankly, I'm amazed Ms. Wray would be interested in him."

"Unassuming?" Aren repeated incredulously. "No, he's scarcely that. In fact, I'd describe him as confident to the point of arrogance. He reminds me of someone. I just can't recall who, but it will come to me eventually."

Egon was growing more nervous by the minute. He had dismissed John Hyatt as an innocuous clerk whose absorption in extraneous detail would never endanger the Maze, but if the investigator had a more commanding side to his personality—one that could captivate a beauty like Haven Wray—then there was a great deal more to the man than he had been led to believe. That discovery called for a complete re-evaluation of the situation, and he knew the Circle would not be pleased to learn his original recommendations had been incorrect. The possibility of incurring their anger terrified him.

"We don't seem to be discussing the same man," Egon prompted, grasping at the faint hope that Dr. Manzari had confused John Hyatt with another man at the mine. "The John Hyatt I know is tall, blond, and dresses in the gray uniform of Alado's administrative staff."

"Yes. That's him."

Egon took a gulp of his wine and nearly choked, but recovered quickly. "What makes you believe you might know him?" he asked.

Aren looked away and frowned slightly as he struggled to find precisely the right words to make himself understood without giving away the real reason for his concern. "As physician for the Flames, I meet a great many professional athletes, and Hyatt has an athlete's build and confidence. Of course, I've no experience with Alado's Insurance Division. Perhaps all the men are trained to his level and walk with a swagger."

"I rather doubt it," Egon said, although he had never noticed anything even remotely appoaching a swagger in Hyatt's walk. That Hyatt might appear meek with him and bold with Haven and Aren didn't make sense. People didn't change their basic personalities to suit the occasion. He doubted Hyatt could be suffering from a multiple personality disorder, but the physician's perceptions differed so widely from his own that it had to mean Hyatt could convincingly portray two completely different individuals.

Could he have been trained to play a multitude

of roles? Egon agonized silently.

"Hyatt pilots his own ship, and pilots often have a cocky attitude," Egon added to cover his mounting dismay. "Is that what you've seen from him?"

Aren smiled at the apt comparison. "Precisely. Thank you. There's too much of the adventurer about Hyatt for me to believe he'll be content to follow Haven from game to game, and I don't want to see her heart broken."

Egon shrugged. "Well, I'm sorry I couldn't be more helpful, but as I said, I've only just met the man. I could check his employment history for you, but Alado's standards are exceptionally high, and if he didn't possess a fine character, he'd not be with the corporation."

Aren had hoped to learn some scandalous bit of gossip that would influence Haven to avoid John Hyatt, but it was obvious Egon Rascon didn't know him well enough to provide any. It wasn't the type of material personnel files contained either, so there was no point in asking Egon to review them. Discouraged, he brought their conversation to a close. "I'm sure you're right," he offered agreeably. "Please don't share my concerns with him. It would embarrass Haven terribly if he reported that I didn't believe she could make wise choices for herself."

Egon assured Aren that he wouldn't, but he had a difficult time swallowing his dinner over the sticky lump of panic clogging his throat. Aren Manzari had impressed him as a thoughtful, conscientious physician; if he saw John Hyatt so differently, it was undoubtedly because Hyatt behaved differently with him. In the conversations Egon had had with Hyatt, the investigator had been extremely professional. Had he only appeared to be obsessed with detail because that was what Egon would expect from someone who spent his days studying facts and figures? It seemed an excellent possibility.

And what about Haven Wray? That Egon had failed to win more than an occasional distracted smile from her was galling. She could not possibly be fascinated by a meticulous insurance investigator who would probably make love with a sex manual open on the bed for handy reference. That had to mean she saw the same exciting man Aren had met, rather than the introvert he knew.

Certain something was terribly wrong and unwilling to risk jeopardizing the Maze any further, he sent the first of the signals that would summon the Circle as the guests left the dining room. He dreaded discussing the situation with them, but they would have to decide how to stop John Hyatt before the danger he posed overwhelmed them all.

As was their custom, the Circle assembled at midnight in the antechamber of the Maze. In the past, the mood had been one of eager anticipation as lots were drawn for turns to explore the ancient labyrinth but, as in their last meeting, tension rather than exhilaration filled the air tonight. The lanterns illuminated narrowed eyes and mouths strained taut. Whispered accusations moved through the group.

Egon had been chosen as leader in recognition of his ability to protect the Maze, rather than for his eloquence, but he had had time to compose not only himself but a statement that minimized the damage John Hyatt might possibly do. "Our secrets are safe," he assured the Circle. "Hyatt is far more clever than we first realized, but now that we know he is not what he seems, we have regained control of the situation. Think a moment, then give me your best ideas on how to handle him."

"We'll have to rid ourselves of him permanently," one member urged.

"He's offered a reward," another remarked, "so he'll be easy to lure into the mine."

Relieved that he had not been blamed for not acting sooner, Egon nodded as the Circle continued to offer suggestions. Some were elegant in their simplicity and others brutal, but at last they came to an agreement. Egon extended his hand, and the others joined him in swearing the oath. They dispersed, confident as always that the Maze would provide the answer to this and all their future problems.

Haven slept poorly and had a difficult time maintaining the energy required during practice the next morning. The Zephyrs and the Pagans were due to arrive that afternoon, and with arena time limited during the final days of practice, she wanted to give her best effort. The problem wasn't entirely one of stamina, however, but also one of focus.

The mental discipline that had been second nature to her was suddenly lacking, and more than once she caught herself turning to search the stands for Ian when she ought to have been following the play. Alarmed, she had jerked her head back toward the ball, and fought all the harder to play well. Rocketball had always been her joy and salvation, but the thrill eluded her today. When she walked off the court at the end of the session she felt drained, and she didn't even try to hide her downcast mood from the coaches.

Tory Norton came forward to meet her. She had been mulling over Ian's advice ever since he had given it but could see from the way Haven was dragging her racquet that she wasn't up to discussing changes in the player roster. "You were way off your game today. Have the trainers help you out if it's physical. If it's something else, come talk with me later."

"Thanks, Coach." Haven breezed on by her without admitting a thing and again was the first to reach the locker room. She was relieved not to find Blake waiting for her again and went straight into the showers, peeling off her practice uniform as she went. Turning on the spray, she leaned back against the wall, closed her eyes, and let the water spill over her shoulders and rush between her breasts in a heated cascade. She kept telling herself that the tournament wouldn't last more than a week, and she could get through it one game at a time.

When she at last left the shower the soft cushioning of the trainer's table was so inviting, she fell asleep before anyone arrived to give her a massage. When she awoke everyone else had gone, and Aren was seated in a chair by the door, apparently standing guard. She tucked her towel around her breasts as she sat up. "You needn't have waited for me."

"Someone had to," Aren scolded. "Hyatt must really be something. Did he keep you up all night?"

Haven reached for her robe, slipped her arms into the sleeves, and tied the belt without bothering to drop her towel. She leaned back against the table and folded her arms across her chest. "You apparently have a very short memory in addition to your overactive imagination. I was alone last night."

"You were alone?" Aren scoffed. "I suppose John Hyatt will say the same thing if I ask him."

"He might. I've no idea how he spent the evening. Would you please call a trainer? I'd rather have a massage than argue."

Aren left his chair and came forward. "They've already gone to lunch, but I'll be happy to take care of you."

Haven shook her head. "That's not a good idea, Aren. Besides, didn't you tell me that you'd rather one of the trainers saw to my needs?"

Aren recalled that conversation vividly. He had thought touching her was agony then; now he knew not touching her was even worse. "Yes, but since none is available, neither of us has a choice."

Haven pushed away from the table. "Thank you, but I still have a choice, and I'll skip the massage today."

As she started past him, Aren reached out to loop his arm through hers to stop her. "The finals begin in two days. You can't let the team down just to spite me. Get back up on the table and I promise to concentrate on smoothing the tension from your muscles rather than annoying you."

It wasn't Haven's muscles that were troubling her, but an uneasiness so deep it brushed her soul. She hesitated a long moment; then, valuing her friendship with Aren too highly to end it, she nodded. "All right, but save your advice, please."

Aren waited until Haven had sloughed off her robe, then took it from her and hooked it on one of the pegs lining the wall. He waited until she had returned to the table before responding. "I promise not to offer any advice, but I can't help but wonder how much you know about John Hyatt. Egon Rascon told me he's just been posted here temporarily, and he'll soon move on."

"So will I. Now hush." Haven rested her cheek on her crossed arms as Aren wrapped his hands around her instep and began to press with his thumbs. Because she had already encouraged him to focus his attentions on her teammates, she also refrained from providing advice, but she did so wish he would find a woman who could return his love.

She closed her eyes and wondered how Ian St. Ives's hands would feel moving up her calf. She felt a twinge of shame, daydreaming about Ian while Aren was doing his best to help her relax, but it didn't block his image from her mind. Ian had been with her too long. She had been little more than an ambitious child when she had first seen him win an Arctic Warrior competition.

So many years had passed since then, and yet Ian excited her just as strongly today. It wasn't only the impossibility of their situation that made her crave his touch either. It was something more, something far stronger, deeper; a knowing that did not even have a name. She exhaled softly and conceded how pointless it had been to send Ian away when she would never be able to exile him from her mind.

She spent the afternoon in a team meeting, but it was a constant struggle to give the coaches the required level of attention. She debated whether to go to dinner, and finally ordered a meal sent to her quarters rather than join the others in the executive dining room. By the time she finished eating she realized her mistake, for without companionship the evening grew dreadfully long. Of course, there was only one companion she cared to have, and she had been so adamant about refusing his company that she knew he would never come looking for her.

She lit some jasmine incense and tried to meditate, but her mind stubbornly refused to seek a blissful calm and she was tormented by doubt. She knew avoiding Ian was the right choice, the only sane choice considering their situation, but she felt as though her skin were itching on the inside and knew she had made a horrible mistake. The last time she had failed to follow her heart there had been catastrophic consequences, and she could not bear the thought of causing herself that same agonizing pain.

Surely when the wisest course of action made her so miserable, her emotions were warning her of a dreadful mistake. At last accepting that truth, she knew exactly what she had to do. She gave Ian time to dine with the others, then dressed in one of the red outfits he had admired. She gathered her courage and prayed it would not desert her as she walked the short distance to his room.

Rather than endure more of Egon Rascon's company, Ian had eaten in the mess hall with the miners coming off duty. He had yet to receive the vital clue he needed and he grew more frustrated by the minute, in no mood to welcome callers. Summoned by a soft knock, he activated the security screen, intending to rid himself quickly of whomever stood in the hall. But when he found Haven waiting outside he lost all interest in being alone.

As the door slid open, Haven noted Ian's bare chest an instant before his smile. She had expected him to have a handsome build, which he did, but the jagged scar that sliced across his rib cage surprised her. She reached out to touch it, then caught herself and dropped her hand.

"You were right," she confessed as she slipped past him into his room. "Being with you could not possibly be more distracting than being apart." His uniform jacket lay tossed over the back of the recliner, and for the moment she was content to run her fingertips over the soft folds. She heard the door close and waited for Ian to speak, but the wait grew uncomfortably long.

Until then, she had not stopped to consider the fact that Ian might have changed his mind about her. After all, she had repeatedly sent him away, and if he had lost interest in her, she would have no one to blame but herself. Suddenly she felt very foolish. "I'm sorry. If this isn't a good time, then—"

Ian came forward but stopped at a respectful distance. He watched a pretty blush creep up Haven's cheeks and was sorry she doubted how very welcome he wanted her to feel. She glanced down, but he knew she had seen his scar and had to be curious about it. Like so many things about himself, it was better left unexplained. He could at least acknowledge it, however.

"I'm accident-prone," he teased, "and just haven't gotten around to having the last scar erased. Does it bother you?"

Ian was making Haven exquisitely nervous, and she didn't know where their conversation was leading. "No," she answered softly, but his aloof manner certainly did. "These rooms are awfully small, aren't they? They all look so much alike that there have been times when I've had to

143

post a sign by the door to remind myself of where I am."

Ian nodded. "I've done that too, but I have a home to return to. What about you?"

Haven had never felt so awkward. She had expected Ian to be as eager to be with her as she was to be with him. No conversation was even necessary in her view. Of course, he was entitled to his feelings too, but she was very sorry they weren't in sync with hers. She leaned against the back of the recliner and wished she had been smart enough to devise a way to leave his apartment with her dignity intact. As it was, she felt stranded, unable to move forward or make a graceful retreat.

"I was born in the original Mars colony, but I haven't been back in years. I suppose I should schedule a visit soon, perhaps after the tournament."

Her red dress sculpted her curves superbly, and Ian traced the luscious swell of her breasts with a hungry glance. "I've wondered since that first day if you have a tattoo."

His voice had dropped in pitch, at last giving Haven the hope she wasn't simply making a fool of herself. She licked her lips. "You'll have to wait and see."

Ian doubted he could wait much longer, but he wanted to prolong the night, so he remained where he stood. "Take off your dress," he urged.

Haven was already too warm, and it wasn't due to any malfunction in the carefully controlled temperature in his apartment. It was an inner heat that made her breath come in short gasps. From another man she would have refused the command, but it had left Ian's lips as a plea. She didn't want to undress herself, though, and turned her back toward him. Her hair was knotted atop her head, out of his way.

"You'll have to help me," she responded in a sultry whisper.

Ian finally closed the distance between them, fighting the need to rub against her as he slit her dress open from her nape to well below her waist. The beautifully contructed garment was too snug to fall on its own, so he peeled it down over her hips, where it was loose enough for her to step out of it. She tossed it over his tunic and turned to face him.

Her lingerie was as bright a red as her dress, and the lacy pattern clung even more tightly. He watched as she kicked off her boots. Had her creamy skin not been so beautiful in itself, he would have been disappointed that she had no tattoo. "Take your hair down, or do you need my help with that too?"

Enjoying the effect she was obviously having on him, Haven stepped into his arms. "Yes. You'll have to do it."

Ian found two long pins, and when he removed them her hair spilled down over her shoulders in gentle waves. He brought a ringlet to his lips and kissed it lightly. It was the color of spun gold and softly scented with her perfume. He could not wait another second to kiss her, and when he dipped his head she reached up to meet him with an eagerness that inflamed his need. He slid his arms around her waist to pull her close and lost himself so completely in her delicious taste, he could not bear to break away until he was dizzy from lack of air.

"I was afraid you'd changed your mind," Haven murmured against his shoulder.

Ian gave her a nearly bone-crushing squeeze. "Does that feel like indifference?" he asked.

Haven slid her hand down between them, but he didn't need any coaxing; he was already hard. "No, and neither does this."

Ian smothered a laugh against her hair. "Most women regard me as cold," he confessed, "but you'll have a far different story to tell."

Alarmed that he would even imagine such a possibility, Haven drew away slightly. "Have women slept with you simply because they wanted to be able to brag about being with an Artic Warrior?" The answer crept into his expression, and she had to ask the most obvious question. "Is that all you think I'm doing?"

Ian felt her posture stiffen and chose his words carefully. "No. I think you have the same problem with men and are doing this just for yourself."

Haven swallowed hard, uncertain whether to scream or cry. She rested her forehead against his chest. They barely knew each other, and yet the smoothness of his skin felt achingly familiar beneath her fingertips. The sound of his voice had echoed in her dreams. With him, she had never felt the awkwardness strangers feel upon meeting; but then, she had known him, or believed that she had, for years.

She had mistakenly believed she had made only one tragic mistake in her life, but surrounded by Ian's warm embrace, she knew she should never have waited for a chance meeting to bring them together. She should have searched the whole universe for him the instant she had had the means to do so. "I don't take lovers," she whispered, "and not because I don't trust men's motives. It's because I never feel anything for anyone. It would have been like sleepwalking, and I'd not have remembered a thing."

Ian didn't care whether she had had a hundred lovers, or only Blake Ellis, but he didn't want her to change her mind about being with him now. He ran his hands down her back and pressed her hips against his. She felt so incredibly good to him that he wondered if nature hadn't molded their bodies to form the perfect pair.

He slipped his fingers under the narrow shoulder straps on her lacy teddy and pushed them aside. Obligingly, she pulled her arms through so he could finish undressing her. He wanted to taste all of her, but as he rolled down the bodice of her lingerie to free her breasts, the sight that greeted him was so captivating in itself, he could do nothing more than stare.

"You asked if I had a tattoo," Haven responded with a husky laugh. "Well, now you know."

Ian watched in awestruck silence as Haven stepped out of the red teddy with a slow, sensuous dip. She laid it on her dress, then turned slowly, so he could appreciate the whole wildly erotic design. A circle of bright flame danced around her hips. The yellows, oranges, and reds were inked into her pale skin with such exquisite detail, she appeared to be in grave danger of being consumed by the fire. The flames coiled around her waist and then burst over her breasts, licking the pale pink nipples with blazing tongues.

"My God," Ian moaned. He turned her again, then traced the path of the flames with his fingertips. "I thought you were perfect before I saw your tattoo. Now, I think it's a shame that you ever have to wear clothes."

"Fire and ice," Haven mused, praying they would not destroy each other.

While Ian knew he could be aptly described as the ice half of the pair, he felt anything but cold now. He pulled Haven back into his arms and kissed her with a fervor that left them both trembling with desire. Her mouth was as hot as his, and it drew him back again and again until the lush fullness of her breasts against his chest grew too enticing to ignore. He bent to lick the hard buds at their center, sucking first one and then the other into his mouth. Haven slid her hands through his hair, keeping his face pressed close to her heart, and her own luscious scent was as seductive as her exotic perfume. Desperate to sample still more of her, Ian dropped to his knees.

Rocked back on her heels, Haven leaned against the recliner to maintain her balance. She was far too entranced by Ian's passionate loving to insist they move to his bed. She closed her eyes and gloried in the delicious sensations as his tongue darted into her navel and then continued lower in an adoring trail. She rolled her hips, luring him to take still more, and he understood her unspoken invitation.

He teased her at first, flicking his tongue over her most sensitive flesh until it swelled to brush his lips. He probed more deeply then, drinking his fill of her essence and all the while luring her toward a climax that shuddered through her so deeply, it rocked him as well. Unwilling to take her on the floor, he rose to his feet, swung her up into his arms, and carried her to the bed. He kicked off his pants and stretched out over her. Her eyes were still glazed with pleasure and, fearing she would be exquisitely sensitive, he eased into her slowly, stretching her, filling her until he was buried so deeply within her pulsing heat that he could never have pulled away.

A silvery hank of hair fell across Ian's eyes as he began to move with forceful thrusts, and Haven reached up to push it away. She wanted to look into his eyes, to see the amber turn to a burnished gold as he chased the rapture he had just given her. She was intent upon watching his pleasure, but his lunging strokes were so wildly exciting that he rekindled the fiery bliss deep within her. She arched up beneath him, defiantly capturing his ecstasy as she was again flooded with her own. She felt him stiffen as it burst forth and muffled his joyful cry with a kiss that was filled with the same haunting hunger as her first.

When Ian at last lay in a pleasure-drenched stupor in her arms, Haven wrapped him in a fierce embrace and savored his glorious heat along the entire length of her body. The moment was as perfect as she had once dreamed it would be, but she couldn't force her mind past it to imagine a shared future for them, and that brought a terror unlike any she had ever known.

Chapter Eight

Ian had never lingered in bed with any of his other partners, but the restlessness that usually drove him from his lovers' arms was absent that night. In fact, he could not recall ever feeling so blissfully content. Not wanting to spoil the mood, he didn't withdraw. Haven was running her hands over his back in a light, rhythmic caress, so he knew she wasn't burdened by his weight. He sighed softly against the curve of her throat and wished he had asked the room's computer to dim the lights earlier, because now he lacked the energy to speak.

Haven was also savoring the moment, but with a desperate sadness. Her life was one of constant motion, and it seemed so was Ian's. Their itineraries would coincide no more frequently than the planets were aligned. She longed for a thousand such glorious nights but feared it was far more likely they would have only this one. Because it would not be nearly enough, she decided fantasies were better left unrealized if there was no future beyond their fulfillment.

Haven lay beneath him perfectly relaxed, and yet Ian sensed her sorrow and raised himself up on his elbows. Her wistful smile tugged at his heart. He wanted to shout, he was so happy, and she looked ready to cry. He brushed her lips lightly, then kissed her with a slow, sensuous abandon that took her breath away.

"You must be sufficiently relaxed to sleep," he whispered, "but I don't want you to leave. Spend the night here with me." Ian could see she was tempted, but the slight furrow of her brow warned him he would have to do more to convince her to stay. He nuzzled the smooth curve of her cheek, nibbled her earlobe, and kissed her softly, gently, tenderly beseeching her to remain in his bed.

What Haven craved were the passionate promises Ian seemed reluctant to give. She slid her fingers through his hair and turned his sweet kiss into a fevered demand for another fierce coupling. Not caring if she shocked him, she wrapped her legs around his hips to keep him trapped within her. As she ground her pelvis against his, she felt him again growing hard and exulted as though she had won an important victory when, in truth, Ian had surrendered readily.

He cradled her in his arms and his next kiss seared her lips with an equally fervent desire. He chose only light, fluttering strokes that brushed her core with a teasing intensity until he felt her whole body tremble with imminent release. He drove into her then, swiftly, deeply, and yet retaining control until she was past caring how badly he needed his own blinding climax. Only then did he allow it to flood through him. Basking in the brilliance of their shared joy, he fell into a dreamless sleep still locked in her embrace.

It was past midnight when the door to Ian's room slid open and four members of the Circle, their identities concealed beneath their white miners' coveralls and headgear, entered. One closed the door and remained there to block their quarry's escape, while the other three approached the bed. That Ian wasn't alone didn't faze them, but before they could inject the drug that would keep the slumbering pair from awaking for hours, Ian sensed a menacing presence and rolled off the bed.

He would have gone for the closest man but felt the heat of a laser pistol's targeting beam on his chest, and knowing he would be of no use to Haven dead, raised his hands. He couldn't make out the miners' features through the smoked face masks in their hoods, but he felt certain they were among those he had spoken with in the mess hall. He had not realized he had gotten close enough to 317's secrets to alarm the culprits responsible for the disappearances, but clearly he had.

He glanced over his shoulder and found Haven

sitting up, clutching the spread to her breasts. She looked angry rather than frightened, and that was most inspiring. He turned back to face the miners. "I've been offering a reward for information. You'd be wise to trade what you know for immunity."

The communication system in the miners' headgear had not been designed for use with someone not similarly clothed, so the response was muffled. Ian understood the profanity clearly, however. "You're making a very grave error," he cautioned. "If anything should happen to me, Alado will be relentless in finding those responsible. Tell me what you know, and you'll be protected from prosecution. You have my word on it."

The man carrying the laser pistol gestured for Ian to step away from the bed, but he refused. "Leave Haven out of this," he demanded. "She has absolutely no idea what's happening here." He watched one of the other men pull an injection canister from the pocket of his white coveralls and was relieved to see it was a drug that would leave him unconscious, rather than dead. Still, he continued to argue.

"If any harm comes to me, Alado will send in security forces. The mine will be closed, and you'll all be out of work. Don't take that risk. Let's cut a deal for immunity. I'll fly you out of here tonight, and you'll have Alado's protection for as long as it's required to bring those responsible for the disappearances to justice."

Haven listened as Ian spoke in a calm, reasonable tone. She had to admire his courage. The thick soles on the miners' boots combined with their hoods gave them all an imposing height, but it was the laser pistol that frightened her most. A single blast could sever a limb or explode a heart, and she didn't want Ian to risk either grisly peril. Afraid anything she said would only make matters worse, she kept quiet, but she didn't see any way out of this for either of them. Then Ian looked over his shoulder and winked. Clearly he had nerve enough for them both, but she was badly frightened.

"Look," Ian cajoled, "you can't possibly get away with this. Side with Alado, and I'll have you out of here within the hour."

The pistol-wielding miner motioned more emphatically for Ian to move away from the bed. "Alado will never touch us," he boasted loudly enough to be understood clearly this time. "You and Ms. Wray are going to elope tonight. That you'll not be seen again will sadden everyone, but eventually your elopement will become a wonderfully romantic legend."

"But that's absurd," Haven cried. "No one will ever believe it!"

Ian hoped it was not merely an elopement with him that struck her as absurd, but there was no time to request a clarification of her meaning before the three miners pushed forward and the injection canister was slammed into his arm. A terrible weakness overcame him, but he could still hear Haven's screams as he slid to the floor.

* * *

Ian had no idea how much time passed before he regained consciousness. His whole body felt as though he were buried beneath an immense weight, but as his thoughts gradually cleared, the uncomfortable sensation diminished. He and Haven were lying on a bed of delicate blue moss, and when he raised his head to look around he found they were encircled by high stone walls. Disoriented, he tried to sit up, but Haven's hand closed around his neck to keep him down.

"Be careful," she whispered. "They may still be watching us."

Ian heard only an eerie silence, unbroken by any sound other than their own quiet breathing. "No, we're alone," he assured her. He sat up and raked his hair out of his eyes. He was relieved to find the miners had dressed him in his uniform pants. It was a sign of compassion, albeit a small one. From what he could see, his tunic fit Haven like a baggy dress, but he wasn't about to criticize her choice of attire. He just hoped all the miners had done was dress her.

"Where do you think we are?" Haven asked anxiously. She raised herself up on her arms and then waited a moment, as though fearful of drawing laser fire.

The warmth gave away their location, but Ian tried not to frighten her. "We're in the mine, and from the temperature I'd say we aren't more than a few levels beneath the surface."

Haven searched the high walls surrounding

them with a disbelieving gaze. "Is this how the mine looks?"

"No, but this is how it feels." Ian stood and gave Haven a hand up. When she stood his tunic reached to mid-thigh, but the sleeves drooped over her hands. He rolled them up for her. "There's no natural source of oxygen on 317, which means we're breathing air pumped into the mine. That's proof we're close to the tunnels and, therefore, an escape route."

Ian was still behaving with a reassuring calm, but Haven was trembling all over. "This is all my fault," she agonized. "I should have accepted your need for time to clear up the problems at the mine. If only I'd stayed out of your way, this wouldn't have happened."

The anguish that brightened her eyes was so painful to observe that Ian drew her into his arms and hugged her tightly. "Nonsense. You never made any demands on me. If fact, it was quite the opposite; I'm the one who placed you in danger by inviting you into my bed."

"But if I hadn't come to your room—"

Ian placed a kiss on her forehead. "Hush. What's done is done. Now help me figure out where we are so I can get us out of here."

Haven stepped away but held on to his hand tightly. "This looks like some ancient burial chamber," she offered in a hushed voice. She turned slowly as she counted. "There are eight sides, and four doors. Where do you suppose they lead?"

Ian gave her hand a fond squeeze, then released it and walked over to the closest wall. The moss that grew over the floor cushioned his step, but he could feel the stone underneath and wished the miners had given him his boots. He ran his hand over the wall. The stone was the same dull gray as that in the mine, but it had been cut in perfectly proportioned cubes and set in place without mortar. He looked up at the craggy dome overhead.

"This appears to be a natural cavern, but there's nothing natural about these walls. They're the product of an extraordinary mason. This chamber is well-lit, but rather than lamps strung along the walls as in the mine, here the lighting appears to come from a source recessed in the top." He stood back to gauge the height and judged it at twelve feet.

Haven didn't understand why he was so fascinated by their stone enclosure, when all she wanted was to get out. "I'm sure this chamber would fascinate an archaeologist, but I'm not all that eager to hang around. Let's pick a door and leave."

Haven's hair was loose and mussed from sleep, and she looked so pathetically eager to go, Ian didn't have the heart to point out that leaving couldn't possibly be all that easy a feat. "The miners brought us down here," he explained as he walked toward her, "so there's obviously a way in and out. Just as soon as we find it, I'll race you right out of here, but let's be careful not to overlook anything. The clue to the exit might be no more than a seam in the stones that's a milli-

meter wider than the rest. It could be a subtle
change in the lighting, or a worn place in the
path. We've no food or water, so we can't afford
to run around and exhaust ourselves."

Haven knew he was right, but she could not
help feeling resentful. "I'm beginning to understand why women might describe you as cold,"
she replied. "We're trapped in some ghastly dun-
geon and you're not even slightly perturbed."

Taking their situation into account, Ian wasn't
insulted by her criticism. "Alado keeps me well
rewarded for remaining cool. Try to consider it
an asset." As he looked down at Haven, he
thought it a terrible shame that they had been
forced from his room. They should have awakened in each other's arms and made love again
before they parted for the day.

"I'm used to working alone," he explained,
"and this is an assignment, after all. I'm sorry you
got thrown into the middle of it, but don't doubt
for an instant that I will be able to get us out."

While she desperately wanted to believe him,
there was good evidence that he did not always
escape harm. Haven laid her hand on his ribs and
rubbed her thumb over the jagged scar. "I know
you'll try, but this looks as though someone
meant to stab you in the heart and you weren't
quite fast enough to block the blow."

She barely knew him, so Ian understood why
the gruesome scar fueled her doubts. His voice
was deliberately low and soothing. "You're right,
but I walked away and the man with the knife
didn't. You can trust me to take care of you. I'll

see that we both get out of here without any additional scars."

Haven had little choice but to trust him, and forced a smile as she took his hand. "The miners don't expect us to get out, do they?"

Now that she had voiced that fear, Ian felt safe in agreeing. "Probably not, but that was a serious error, because we are going to find our way to the surface, and we'll know that whoever announced that ridiculous story about an elopement put us here." Ian debated briefly, then decided they were in so much trouble, she had every right to know the truth.

"I'm not with the insurance division, but with Alado's intelligence branch. I've been checking in with Control, my superior, at regular intervals. When my signals stop he'll know something's wrong and send help immediately. I wasn't making idle threats when I said the mine would be closed. Whenever one of his operatives is in trouble, Control responds immediately."

"And whom does he usually send?"

Ian chuckled in spite of himself. "Most of the time, he sends me."

That she was trapped below ground with the very man Control would have sent to rescue them struck Haven as wildly funny too. "Then we're damn lucky you're already here, aren't we?"

That was the Haven Wray Ian knew. "I like your spirit."

"Save the compliments until we're out of here. Which door should we try? All four appear identical."

Ian had already taken note of that fact. The moss was flattened where they had been lying, and he used that as a clue. "They would probably have carried you, but I bet they just dragged me in here. Come, let's see if they left a trail."

Haven returned to the spot where they had awakened. The outline of her body was faint, but Ian outweighed her by nearly a hundred pounds, and the indentation he had made was still clear. She knelt and studied the growth pattern of the moss. The tiny leaves were petal-soft. "Have you ever seen this blue moss anywhere else?" she asked.

"No, but botany isn't one of my specialties." Pleased that she was following his lead, he waited for her to point out the trail the miners had inadvertently left.

Haven found it in the next instant. "Look," she exclaimed. "Someone tried to cover their tracks by sweeping the moss with their hands. It's that fan-shaped pattern that's visible, rather than footprints."

Ian reached for her hand. "Come on; let's see if they've left a trail the whole way."

Haven hardly dared hope that the miners had, but as soon as they had passed through the door, they were on a stone walkway rather than moss, and she swore angrily. "That would have been too easy, wouldn't it?"

"I'm afraid so." They were standing in a long hallway, and Ian glanced back over his shoulder into the octagonal chamber.

"Do you want to try another door?" Haven asked.

"No. We've proof they left this way. Let's try it."

The walls here were also fashioned of superbly crafted masonry. Ian knew his boots would have echoed with a low, hollow ring down the length of the corridor, but barefooted, their steps were silent. When they reached the end the hall branched to the right and left, but rather than being wide enough to allow them to walk hand in hand, it was so narrow they would have to move in single file in either direction.

Haven waited for Ian to make the decision, then followed him down the right corridor. The path was illuminated by the unseen overhead lights, but she felt uneasy, fearing the walls might close in on them at any moment. "I'm beginning to suffer from claustrophobia," she announced fearfully. "Can you see anything ahead?"

All that loomed in front of Ian was a passage similar to the forbidding one they had just traversed. "Not yet," he replied in as comforting a tone as he could manage. When they came to another split he again took the right-hand fork, but it went on and on like the others, and when it split again he stopped and turned back to Haven.

"This appears to be some sort of maze," he remarked with forced calm. "It's deliberately confusing, but if the miners have mastered the secret to finding their way in and out, so can we."

Haven wanted to believe him, but she was rapidly losing what little optimism she had had. She was used to running up and down the Rocketball court and longed for that uninhibited freedom. Here the corridors were so narrow, she couldn't stretch out her arms. "We're caught in that Celtic knot you asked me about, aren't we?"

"Only temporarily," Ian assured her, and he meant it with all his heart. He flashed her an encouraging grin, then continued on down the corridor. He wasn't used to having anyone trail behind him, and while Haven wasn't following too close, her presence in itself was distracting. He certainly couldn't complain aloud, but he wished he could have left her in the central chamber and returned for her when he had found the way out.

The path turned abruptly, and he cried out in anger and surprise as they stepped through a doorway and found themselves right back where they had begun. "Don't panic," he warned as he turned to face Haven, but tears were already welling in her eyes.

"I guess we'll have to try it again and bear to the left this time," Haven suggested bravely.

Ian was used to calling the shots, but he nodded. "In time the fanlike pattern won't be visible in the moss. We should have torn up a patch to mark the first door we used. Let's do it now."

Haven waited while Ian studied the airy blue carpet, and breathed a sigh of relief when he found the trail. It led to the door to the right of the one where she stood. "Do you suppose the missing miners all got lost down here?"

Ian wished she hadn't asked that. He pulled up

a couple of handfuls of moss and tossed them aside. "It's a possibility, but not a certainty as yet."

"What kind of proof do you need, a neat pile of bodies?"

She was tugging on the hem of his tunic, and in the oversized garment she looked very child-like and innocent. He recalled last night too vividly to believe that was her true self, however. "I should have said something about last night," he mused aloud.

Haven came toward him. "I was too frightened to remember much. Did you recognize the voice of the only miner who spoke? From where I was on the bed it wasn't clear enough to identify."

Ian rested his hands on her shoulders. "I was thinking of earlier."

Haven reached up to grasp his wrists. He hadn't made any pretty promises at the time, and she didn't want any tardy reassurances that she was special. "Skip it," she said flippantly. "Let's stay in the present. Do you want me to lead this time? Not that your bare back isn't handsome, but I'd like a chance at a different view."

She had shut him out so quickly, Ian didn't know what to say. He thought they made an incredible pair, and he couldn't believe she wouldn't at least acknowledge it. "Now wait a minute . . ." he argued.

Haven pushed his hands off her shoulders. "Fine, you lead, but let's get going. You might want to take a couple of days off, but I've got a championship tournament to play."

She started to go around him, but Ian moved to block her way. "Just listen to me," he ordered. "Last night meant a lot to me. I thought it did to you too. I'm not at all pleased by the way it ended, but that doesn't cancel out how good it was."

Haven shook her head. "Please, let's wait until we're safely out of here before we begin to reminisce."

Ian had always believed the pleasure he gave women was sufficient thanks for their company. For the first time ever he wanted to give more, and Haven didn't seem in the least bit impressed. Obviously he had expected too much of her.

"Believe me, I want to get out of here just as badly as you do," he assured her darkly. He was tempted to tell her precisely what he thought of her for lightly dismissing what they had shared, but he didn't want to waste the time. "I'll lead the way," he stated firmly, and headed back through the doorway they had chosen first, grateful she couldn't see the anger in his eyes.

There was room to walk side by side here, but Haven made no effort to catch up to him. She stayed several paces behind and tried to focus on a spot midway between his shoulder blades to distract herself from the high walls on either side. As they swung left and the corridor narrowed, it was more difficult for her to force down her panic, but she clenched her fists tightly and refused to shriek for fear the sound would echo around them endlessly.

"How's it look?" she called.

"Bleak," Ian shot over his shoulder, no longer making any effort to spare her feelings.

Haven lowered her glance to his waist. He had a marvelous physique, with wide shoulders and narrow hips, but the perfect triangle of his proportions didn't soothe her mounting terror. In her whole life she had never been lost. She had never even been separated from her companions and experienced a momentary panic. Perhaps she had spent too much time in gyms and on Rocketball courts to put herself at any risk, but she had never felt so helpless, and it grated her nerves raw.

Ian had been counting the turns and, just as he had feared, the last left brought them right back to the central chamber, only this time they were at the door to the left of the one they had used. He walked out over the moss and looked up at the craggy dome above. "Don't be discouraged," he told Haven. "Every dead end brings us that much closer to the exit."

Haven stepped out on the moss, bent over, and put her hands on her knees. She drew in great gulps of air. "It better. I can't take much more of this."

Ian watched her for a moment and realized her distress was real. "My God, you really are claustrophobic, aren't you?"

Haven looked up at him through a curtain of tangled curls. "Don't tell me you enjoy walking along such narrow corridors."

Ian came to her and knelt down by her side. "No, of course not, but if I let the discomfort stop me from searching for a way out, we'd be stuck here, and that worries me far more."

"This isn't about worry, Ian. It's plain old terror." Haven straighened up and brushed her hair out of her eyes. "Look at you," she complained, "half naked and you're still gorgeous, while I must look like something not even a space pirate would touch."

Ian rose and took hold of her upper arms. "I don't know," he teased. "From what I've seen, space pirates aren't all that particular."

Haven laughed in spite of herself, and slipped her arms around his waist. "What are we going to do if we can't get out, Ian? People can't survive very long without food and water, and I know those miners aren't coming back."

Ian rested his forehead against hers. He had been angry with her just a moment ago, but she felt so good in his arms, it was difficult to remember why. "I've gotten out of worse situations," he assured her. "Don't forget that Control will send help. It has to be morning by now, which means my first signal is overdue. When the second is missed he'll be on his way."

Haven licked her lips. "We're supposed to be eloping. That has to mean the miners have programmed your ship for some destination, even if it's deep space. Maybe they just put it in orbit above 317 and rigged it to explode. Will Control believe we were blown to bits with it?"

Amazed, Ian rolled his eyes toward the dome, but if the route out were marked on it, he couldn't find it. "What a colorful imagination you have. I'll introduce you to Control at my first opportunity. He's an amazing man. He's small, and his features are pinched in a perpetual frown, but he has a rare grasp of human nature. He knows that his agents' ships don't just explode. Even more importantly, he'll never believe you and I eloped."

Haven took a step backwards and crossed her arms. "Why is that so impossible to believe? I'm not considered undesirable." She blew a curl out of her eyes. "Or at least I didn't used to be."

Even disheveled, Ian thought her extremely desirable, but that really wasn't the issue. "Let me rephrase that. He knows I like living alone. An Arctic Warrior is trained to survive in a silent world, and women have a way of creating a great deal of noise."

Cut to the quick by that insult, Haven refused to let it show. She raised her chin to a stubborn angle. "I bet you use that line all the time, don't you? And women must tie themselves in knots trying to prove you wrong. Well, you needn't worry that I'll ever make domesticating you one of my priorities. Now let me lead this time. Maybe I'll bring us some much-needed luck."

Haven started toward the next door on the right, and Ian was so glad to see she had pulled herself together, he didn't fight for the privilege of leading the way. "Take each right turn," he shouted after her.

Haven ran her hands along the walls, unconsciously pushing them away as she headed down another long, dim corridor. This one seemed to go farther before it reached a fork and here, unlike their two previous attempts, they were greeted by stairways. The one on the right led up and the one to the left went down. Haven paused.

"Do you still want to go to the right?" she asked. "It's so dark, I can't see the top, but it's more light on the left."

Ian peered around her to confirm her observations. "I'd choose the lighter path, but this is a maze, and it must have been specifically designed to confound us. Let's go up the stairs."

"All right," Haven agreed shakily. She started up, but after several steps the stairway narrowed, the steps became more shallow and, rather than lead to a second floor they ended at a blank wall. "Damn. It's another trick." She turned to face Ian and caught him before he had time to erase the dismay from his expression.

"This isn't some playful labyrinth constructed by miners, is it?" she asked. "We're moving through a sinister city built by someone else entirely." She ran her hand along the smooth stone walls. Everywhere the stones were joined with the same mortarless perfection they had seen in the central chamber. "Who owned the mine before Alado?"

"An independent concern. They began their operation seven years ago, and sold it to Alado three years later." Ian saw in the seriousness of Haven's expression that there was no point in attempting to hide the truth from her. "I think you're right. Miners know how to blast and burrow through rock. They've absolutely no training

169

in stone construction, and what we're seeing here is the work of experts. There's no way to give it a date, but from what I read in 317's records, the asteroid was uninhabited until seven years ago."

Haven was standing on the step above Ian's, placing their eyes at the same level. "It seems probable, then, that this maze was built prior to the arrival of anyone from any of the Earth corporations. Are you thinking what I'm thinking?"

Ian could read it in her eyes. "Yes, this could be the first evidence of a civilization other than those coming from Earth."

Haven looked over his shoulder, her apprehension plain. "Do you suppose the builders are still here?" she whispered. "Could they be watching us, waiting for us to stumble into their trap?"

Ian put his hands on her waist, scooped her off the step, and set her down beside him. "Absolutely not," he insisted confidently. "We'd feel their presence if they were, and a great many more than fifteen miners would have disappeared had the builders regarded humans as a delicacy. Come on; let's take the more brightly lit path."

Haven left her hand in his as he led the way down the stairs, but she wasn't at all certain they weren't being watched by some curious creatures who were having a great deal of fun at their expense. She had had a pet rat once who had loved to run inside a wheel. She had not thought of Mom Rat for years, but suddenly she was very sorry she had ever kept her pet caged.

Chapter Nine

As they moved down the stairs toward the light, Haven's steps quickened and her hopes soared, but when they reached the bottom they found themselves in a small circular room with no exit other than the one by which they had entered. Her claustrophobia now intense, she bolted back up the stairs and down the long corridor that led to the central chamber. She was trapped there as well, but at least she had the space to move around and breathe.

Ian remained behind for a moment to make certain they were not overlooking anything. He ran his fingertips along the seams in the stones and pressed against the edges, searching for a release that might turn one of the walls and open up another passageway. When he rejoined Haven in the central chamber he hid his discouragement as best he could, but he couldn't pretend not to see the fear in her eyes.

He eased his hand over her back. "Let's sit down a minute and rest. I stayed behind to look for an opening to a secret tunnel. I didn't find one in that little room, but that doesn't mean we haven't passed another." He tugged on her hand to pull her down beside him on the moss. "I want to go back through the first tunnels we explored and concentrate on the walls, rather than where they lead. I can't end up anywhere but right back here. Can you wait here for me without growing too anxious?"

Haven was still struggling to catch her breath. She tucked his tunic between her legs for modesty's sake and hugged her knees. "Probably not, but I'll seize any excuse to avoid walking through those awful hallways again. I'm sorry to be a burden. Space travel doesn't bother me, but then, the Flames have their own ship and the accommodations are spacious. I've never experienced anything even remotely like this."

"Neither have I," Ian assured her.

His smile was relaxed, and so charming Haven was ashamed she couldn't be of more help. Searching the corridors more thoroughly was an excellent idea, but she didn't want him to leave her just yet. "I know you're from Earth, but there were never any details of your life in anything I ever read about your Artic Warrior competitions. Where were you born? What were your parents like? Did you come from a large family, or—"

"Hey, give me a minute to answer your first

question before you ask a dozen more." Ian glanced away as he considered just how much to tell. Control knew more of his background than anyone else, but that was only because he had the capability to conduct a thorough investigation. With anyone else, Ian brushed aside all inquiries into his past. Now, trapped here with Haven, refusing to confide in her would have been unkind, as well as totally unnecessary.

"I was born in Iceland, not far from where I have my present home. It's remote, but not so far from Reykjavík that I can't have a taste of civilization whenever the need arises."

Haven feared that wasn't often but didn't interrupt him to ask. "Iceland," she murmured instead, and nodded to encourage him to continue.

Ian ran his fingers through the moss. It was a beautiful sky blue, and so delicate that he almost felt guilty crushing it with his weight. "My parents were childhood sweethearts. They were so deeply in love that when my mother died shortly after my birth my father never really recovered from the loss. It left him a tormented and bitter man. He never spoke of her, but he didn't part with any of her belongings, and she was always an unseen presence in our home. He'd been an Artic Warrior, and from the moment I was old enough for my first pair of skis, he devoted himself singlemindedly to training me to excel. Fortunately, I had the talent to succeed and didn't disappoint him."

Afraid a bitter man could not possibly have been a loving father, Haven reached out to give his arm a sympathetic squeeze. "Where did you go to school?"

"Ah, yes, school," Ian hedged. "My father tutored me until I could read and write well enough to join a computer link-up, and then I had the same education children in distant colonies receive. There isn't much I can't do, so apparently it was effective."

Haven could easily imagine his home, set in a vast, snowy landscape. He would have been a handsome boy, but she could scarcely comprehend a child thriving in such a sterile environment and wondered how he had survived. "What about friends? Did your father train other young men?"

"No, I was his only pupil." Ian saw a hint of pity soften her gaze and rejected it forcefully. "It was the perfect upbringing for an Artic Warrior, and I don't regret a second of it. I could ski and shoot better than anyone. That's why my records still stand."

"As well they should," Haven agreed. "Is that why you retired? Was there no longer any thrill left in the contests?"

Ian gave her question a moment's thought, and then responded with another ready grin. "In my last couple of years I had so little real competition, I was just piling up scores for the record books. When it got to be a chore I quit. Now do you see why I never did interviews? I'd rather make a dozen deep-space voyages than talk about myself. Being closemouthed is an asset in my present job, though, so I'm well suited to intelligence work."

He looked very proud of himself, so she stifled the impulse to remind him that at present he wasn't doing all that well. "You must admit it's an unusual choice of occupation for an Artic champion."

"Not at all," Ian argued. "I work well alone because that's all I've ever done. I'm self-reliant, and have an abundance of survival skills. Because I didn't have the advantage of having playmates, I cultivated a vivid imagination to keep myself entertained. You're the only person who's ever recognized me; but then again, I had intended merely to modify my manner rather than use a disguise for this job. When it comes to assuming false identities I'm considered a master. Recently I posed as an itinerant monk and performed a marriage ceremony in a pirate's den, but that's too long a story to begin now."

Ian started to rise, but Haven caught his hand to keep him beside her. "Wait. I would love to hear about some of your more exciting assignments, but when you're not actively shielding your identity, who are you really?"

Startled, for a brief instant Ian felt the chill winds of home swirl around them. He quickly shook off the sensation. *Who was he?* Haven had asked. He had denied his identity when they had met so he supposed she was justified in asking. Perhaps she feared all he had ever shown her was a pose, and for the life of him he couldn't swear that he hadn't.

He leaned over and kissed her soundly. "You know me better than anyone," he assured her, and re-entered the maze before she could stop him a second time. Her question plagued him as he searched, however, and while he could supply a lengthy list of useful skills or admirable achievements, they struck him as irrelevant. Haven had been seeking insight into his character, not gathering information for a job résumé.

He pressed the corners of the next stone and felt the exact same stubborn resistance he had encountered with all the others. If there actually were a secret passageway, at the rate he was progressing he would be a very old man before he found it. He stopped to rest and wiped his forehead on his arm. The way his luck was running, if he did find a hidden tunnel, it would probably have such slippery sides that he would just careen straight into the asteroid's molten core. Sickened by that gruesome thought, he gave up his fruitless search and returned to the main chamber.

Haven hadn't moved. She sent him an expectant look, but he shook his head. Not wanting to leave her behind again, he grabbed her hands and pulled her to her feet. "Do you feel up to giving the last door a try?"

Haven shuddered slightly but drew herself up to her full height. "No, but I'm going to do it anyway. You're the captain of this expedition. Lead the way."

Ian responded with a cocky salute and approached the last door with the very real fear that it would be like the first three and provide only sharply angled corridors that would lead right back to the center. Then he stepped over the threshold and found such a narrow hallway, he had to turn sideways to move down it. "I think you'd better wait outside," he called over his shoulder. "This is too cramped for someone with claustrophobia."

Praying she could contain her fear, Haven followed him anyway, but she closed her eyes and tried to pretend she was moving down the center of a Rocketball court, where lack of space was never a problem. "No, I'll make it," she promised, and kept up with him with nervous side shuffles. "Do you see anything yet?"

Ian saw a change in the light ahead, but after their last disappointment he chose not to report it for fear of offering false hope. Remaining quiet, he pressed on, and gradually the corridor widened sufficiently for him to face forward. Grateful, he let out a whoop, and Haven bumped into his back. "Come on," he urged. "We can make better progress from here on."

Haven opened one eye, observed the change in the passageway, and hurried after him. When they came upon an opening in the wall she peered around Ian's shoulder to see what lay beyond. He moved over to give her a better view, but rather than the portal to freedom, they were looking down into a pit so deep, the bottom was lost in shadow. Haven sagged back against the opposite wall.

"This corridor may be different from the others, but it's no better. Do you suppose we've been down here long enough for help to be on its way?"

Uncertain, Ian rubbed his chin, then felt his cheeks. He hadn't shaved in a day, but his skin was still smooth. Like many blonds, he didn't have a heavy beard, but his whiskers grew as rapidly as any other man's. Or at least they always had. He stared at Haven as the horrible possibility that they might have died and gone to hell washed through him, but he absolutely refused to accept it. He might not have been the most righteous individual ever born, but he hadn't done anything to merit being tossed into this wretched maze for eternity either.

"What's wrong?" Haven asked, frightened by the darkness of his glance.

"Nothing; just my imagination playing a cruel trick on me." He wrapped his arm around her shoulders and pulled her close. "You're damn good company, Haven. I'm sure glad I'm not alone."

Haven did not even want to think of being alone in such a distressing place. "Thank you. You're a great source of comfort to me too; now let's keep going. I'm starting to get hungry, and I'd like to rejoin my team in time for dinner."

Ian feared she was being overly optimistic but didn't dash her hopes. Twenty feet past the pit, the corridor made a sharp turn to the left, then one to the right, then another jog to the left. Ian was so intent upon studying the path, searching for deep scrape marks that would signal the presence of a secret door, that he missed seeing the high window until Haven began to pound on his back.

"Look," she exclaimed. "We've not come upon a window before. Can you reach it?"

Ian raised his arms, but even after he jumped it was a good foot above his reach. He swept Haven with an appraising glance. "If you stand on my shoulders, you should be able to reach it easily." He laced his fingers together to provide a convenient step. "Come on; let's give it a try."

Haven's first thought was that a woman without underwear ought not to stand on a man's shoulders, but she quickly made an exception in this case. She took hold of Ian's shoulders and, grateful to be agile, put her right foot in his hands. As he raised the makeshift platform, she caught a handful of his hair to gain the leverage to place her left foot on his shoulder. Blinded by her tunic, Ian swayed slightly, and she had to grab for the wall to keep her balance as she brought up her right foot.

"Hold still!" she cried.

Ian thought he had been remarkably stoic in not shrieking in pain when she had used his hair as a handhold. "I'm trying to. Just be glad you're not the one on the bottom."

Haven had never particularly cared for gymnastics. She couldn't recall ever being part of a human pyramid, but despite a shaky start she was standing on Ian's shoulders. He had such a fierce grip on her legs, she was confident she would not fall, but bruises were a certainty. She grabbed for the windowsill and leaned in. The opening was several feet deep, but it was backed by another blank wall.

She cried out in frustration. "Get me down. There's nothing up here but more stone."

As badly disappointed as she, Ian swore under his breath. "How do acrobats accomplish a dismount?"

Lacking an acrobat's training, Haven grew cross with him. "Do you honestly expect me to leap into the air, turn a couple of back flips on the way down, and land on my feet?"

Ian could understand her annoyance, but he had been serious. "No," he replied with forced calm. "I was just asking if you cared to give me a few pointers." Because she hadn't, he did not provide her with another chance to lodge a complaint. Instead, he shoved her forward, stepped back, and caught her as she dropped into his arms.

Haven's expression was a priceless depiction of sheer terror, but Ian was really quite proud of himself. "For quarters this crowded I'd say that wasn't half bad. Do you want to try it again?"

The wind knocked out of her by the force of his catch, Haven sputtered angrily. "Why do you take such a perverse pleasure in torturing me?"

Ian set her on her feet with exaggerated care. "That was teasing, not torture. Besides, I'm sure I apologized for it a couple of days ago."

Haven tugged on her hem but didn't feel a bit more secure. "Yes, you did, but obviously you weren't sincere."

Ian started to laugh, and his rolling chuckle echoed all around them in a deep chorus. "I'm sorry, but could we please have this argument later? I want to get out of here."

Exasperated, Haven stared at him for a long moment, then couldn't suppress her own laughter. "How did we ever get ourselves into such an awful mess, Ian?"

"From what I've seen, we both have a talent for finding trouble." He longed to renew his promise that he would see them safely out of the maze, but he had made such little progress thus far, he doubted he would sound convincing. Added to that, he now feared not nearly enough time had elapsed for Control to begin to worry. Maybe they had been unconscious only an hour or two, rather than most of the night. He was usually fairly accurate with his estimates of time, but his beard—or lack of it—was ample proof that he wasn't able to judge it well now.

"How long do you suppose we've been down here?" he asked casually.

Haven brushed the hair out of her eyes as she tried to make a good guess but found she had no real sense of time and frowned. "I'm sorry. I don't really know, but it's definitely long enough for me to get hungry. Aren't you hungry too?"

A painful ache had indeed begun to fill Ian's stomach, but he repressed it. He had had assignments where he had gone several days without food or sleep, but he hoped this was not going to be another of them. "Yes. Just try to think about something other than food. Once you distract yourself, the hunger pangs will disappear."

"I don't dare become distracted, or I'll miss a window that will finally lead somewhere. You can't see everything, Ian, so I can't afford to just tag along behind you daydreaming."

"That's an excellent point." Ian tousled her mussed curls, then headed off down the corridor. This time he watched the walls as well as the path, but there were no more windows, fake or otherwise, up ahead. The corridor continued to gradually widen, and at last they came to a huge stone column. An arched doorway in the base revealed an interior staircase. Without a railing, the graceful spiral curled up around the inside of the column and eventually disappeared in what could be either another dead end or salvation.

Enjoying the open space, Haven flapped her arms as she walked around the column. "What are the odds that the stairs actually lead somewhere this time?"

Ian bent down to peer up into the column. "I don't want to gamble on our prospects, but if it does, my shoulders may be too wide to allow me to get very far. You'd better go first this time."

Like the rest of the maze, the staircase was illuminated from an unseen source, but Haven still had eerie visions of danger. She rubbed her arms and tried to work up the courage to begin this latest challenge. "At least this corridor continues, rather than leading directly back to where we began. That has to be a good sign."

"Yes. I believe it is." Ian was anxious to move on, but he did not want to prod Haven. He waited, but was nearly at the end of his patience before she finally dipped under the arch and began to climb the stairs. He followed, but stayed several steps behind, not wanting to increase her discomfort by getting too close.

"How are you doing?" he whispered.

"I'm trying not to think about it," was Haven's muffled reply.

Cut into the interior wall of the column, the stairs' tread was nearly triangular in shape, forcing Haven to place her foot near the inner edge. She crept along, bravely hugging the wall, and kept her eyes focused on the next step, rather than the open center of the column. A single slip would cause a terrible fall, and she couldn't bear to look down into the open core to see how far they had come. She just kept moving up the winding path, her heart in her throat, and clung to the desperate hope that they had finally found the way out.

The stairs were a challenge for Ian as well, for he had to lean back against the wall to have enough space to move. Stepping sideways, he hoped the climb was worth the effort, but all too soon he heard Haven choke back an anguished sob and knew she had found another dead end. "Come back down to me," he encouraged.

The stairs ended in a wide platform that mocked Haven's soft cries with whispered echoes. Trapped inside a small dome, she cursed not only the builders of this maniacal torture chamber but herself as well, for being so stupid as to have hoped they had finally discovered the escape route. She heard Ian's call but didn't acknowledge it. She couldn't do more than sit and sob.

As soon as he realized that Haven wasn't coming down on her own, Ian pushed on up the stairs. The incline grew increasingly steep as it neared the top, and he was experiencing a hint of claustrophobia himself before he reached Haven. He looked past her and saw they were surrounded by more gray stone. There were no initials playfully incised in the walls, but if he had had a knife, he would have left theirs.

He patted Haven's knee lightly. "Let's get out of here. The corridor continues, so we needn't stop here."

Haven peeked at him through her fingers. Her eyes were bright with tears and her voice was husky. "What did the miner say about our elopement becoming a legend? Hasn't it occurred to you that there isn't any way out of here, that this maze just goes on and on like a giant wheel spinning in place?"

A wonderfully romantic legend had been the exact phrase, but Ian didn't repeat it for her. "The miners underestimated both me and Control," he insisted. "Neither of us quits before an assignment is over. I wouldn't work for the man if he didn't back up his agents with the necessary force."

"How can he provide backup if he can't find us?"

"There isn't anything the intelligence branch can't find; now stop crying." He brushed the last of her tears from her cheeks with his fingertips; then, certain he had been too stern, he softened his tone. "I don't like it in here any better than you do, Haven. Let's go back down to the corridor and find another route to explore."

In a daze of despair Haven looked around, noticed how the walls curved toward the domed ceiling like giant claws, and would have bolted past him had there been room. "Fine, let's go. Hurry."

" 'Hurry,' " he muttered as he attempted to negotiate the first turn. Going up, the curve to the ceiling hadn't hindered their progress; now he was forced into an awkward backward slant as he started down the stairwell. He could feel Haven coming along behind him and was grateful he did not have to turn back and go after her. When they burst out of the column in a rush he pulled her into his arms and hugged her tightly. She didn't squirm to break free, but she didn't relax against him either, and he quickly released her.

"There's got to be another fork up head. You call it: left or right?"

He had chosen the right each time they had encountered a split and that had gotten them nowhere. "The left," she announced clearly, "and let's hope there's a cafeteria that way."

Ian's gaze narrowed slightly. "Let's also hope that you're not beginning to hallucinate."

"How could you tell down here?" Embarrassed that she had given way to tears, Haven straightened her shoulders proudly and waved him on.

Just as Ian turned, a sharp jolt rocked the corridor, slamming him back against the column. He reached for Haven and pulled her close, shielding her head with his arms, but the tremor wasn't repeated. "Seismic activity is common in the mine. Don't let it bother you," he said as he released her.

"What you mean is earthquakes, isn't it?" Haven sent a frantic glance over the stone walls surrounding them, but there were no cracks that she could see. That was scarcely reassuring. "Maybe that wasn't a natural quake. Could it have been the result of blasting? We might be closer to the mine than we think."

Ian recalled the detailed maps in Egon Rascon's office and gestured as he spoke. "The mine has a central shaft that branches off into side tunnels at each level. From what I saw the day I went down into the mine, most of the laser cannon work is going on at the deeper levels. It's really hot down there too, so I'm still convinced we're near the surface."

"So that was probably a natural quake then? With our luck, we'll be crushed under one of these blasted walls before we even come close to discovering the way out."

Ian placed his hands on her shoulders and squeezed hard. "Stop it. What do you do when the Flames fall behind in a crucial game?"

Haven's gaze took on a sheen of insolence. "We're one of the best Rocketball teams ever assembled, so that seldom happens."

"Congratulations. Now tell me what you do on

the rare occasions when it does." Ian was continually surprised by how natural it felt to touch Haven. It didn't matter if the gesture was an expansive hug or merely a quick tap. They all brought such enormous pleasure, he left his hands resting where they were.

"We have to play harder," she conceded reluctantly.

"Exactly. I said the miners underestimated me, but I should also have factored in your abilities. We may not be playing Rocketball down here, but we'll need the same determination and courage you always display on the court. They couldn't possibly have realized what a great team we'd make, or they would never have made the mistake of keeping us together."

Haven felt certain he was only offering praise to make her feel better, but she couldn't fault him; it worked. "Thanks, Coach." She managed a smile, if only a faint one, and he again led the way down the corridor. Unlike other junctions, here they could go either left, right, or straight ahead. Ian went to the left. There was another quick left, and then a zigzagging path that had them thoroughly confused before bringing them back out into the main corridor.

"What was that?" Haven complained. "Another joke?"

"Undoubtedly. Let's stay on this main channel for a while."

Haven reached for his arm. "No, wait. We ought to try the right-hand path too." Ian nodded, and went back to find it. It was curved with steps leading down and then back up before it also rejoined the main corridor. "Sorry. That was just another worthless detour," she conceded darkly.

At first Ian had expected Haven to get in his way, but having to keep her spirits up as well as his own was sufficiently distracting to keep him moving, and he was positive that was the best thing to do. "No, I disagree. Each digression serves to make us more acutely aware of our surroundings. We're going to beat them, Haven. Keep your eyes open, and we'll be out of here in no time."

Growing serious, Haven tried to sound as confident as he. "It's all right, Ian. I'm not going to break down in tears again. I just let my hopes get too high and I won't make that mistake twice. I don't want to go back to the octagon with the moss, but I sure hope we find a good place to rest up ahead."

Ian knew she had a fine athlete's stamina, but stress was wearing them both down. "If we don't find one, we'll make do with whatever we do find. Let me know when you're tired and we'll stop for a while."

Haven nodded, but she didn't really want to stop until she felt as though they had actually accomplished something. She ran her hands along the walls as they moved forward. The roughness of the stone was familiar now, but she hated every inch of it. She looked up and thought the walls were getting higher. Perhaps the path declined at such a gradual angle that it wasn't noticeable in any other way, but she doubted it was a good sign.

The corridor suddenly branched not simply in two directions but in four, and Ian halted abruptly. "Let's begin with the far left passage and work our way across if it doesn't lead anywhere."

"We've yet to find a strategy that works," Haven replied, "so that's as good as any." She still felt confined, but the path was wide enough for her to swing her arms without scraping them against the stone, and that helped her to breathe more easily. They hadn't gone far when the path split into three more trails. They proved to be interconnected and, cursing the whole way, they went back to the first split and tried the second passage.

It was the most intricate of any they had found yet, with six channels cut into each side, but each led right back out to the center path, and they felt as though they had just traced the steps of some ridiculously repetitive dance. The third branch held gradual curves that lured them deep, then curved back on itself. As they walked back out, Haven couldn't hide her frustration.

"There has got to be some logical sequence to this place," she exclaimed. "Even if we've seen only a small part of a gigantic maze, there has to be a key."

She stood with her hands on her hips, wearing the same defiant expression Ian had seen too often directed at him. He preferred anger to tears and readily agreed. "You're right, but whether it's

189

short, straight corridors, those with sharp angles, or those with wide, looping curves, we're just going to have to traverse them all until we finally come to the exit. Trial and error is too slow, I know, but the only way to speed up the search is to split up and travel separately. I'm not willing to do that as yet. Are you?"

Haven sagged back against the wall and closed her eyes. It was bad enough being trapped in such a horrible place; she could not bear the thought of going on alone. When she looked up at Ian she was surprised to find real concern etched deeply in his expression. She pushed away from the wall.

"We're both loners, Ian, but staying together makes far more sense to me than betting everything on the hope one of us will make it out alive. I say we stay together."

Ian was grateful she saw the situation as he did, but he was worried about her. "Let's sit down here for a while and rest. The last passage in this chain has to lead somewhere, and we'll be better able to explore it after a short nap."

Haven peered down the passage and saw only the same uninviting stone hallway as all the others they had encountered. It seemed foolish to rush into another disappointment; she sat down beside Ian and rested her head against his shoulder. "If only the miners hadn't had the laser pistol. The two of us could have taken them."

Ian covered a wide yawn. "I've never fought with a nude woman by my side, but I think you're right. That sight alone would have been so distracting, I could probably have gotten in half a dozen savage punches before they realized they had been hit."

Ian was teasing her again, but Haven was too tired to care. She was still hungry too, but she wouldn't mention it again. For the time being all she wanted was a brief rest, and then she was going to have to find the courage to press on, but she lacked Ian's steadfast belief that they would eventually find a way out. He had asked her to show the same courage she gave to Rocketball, but she hadn't had the heart to confess that it was all gone.

She sighed sadly and fell asleep, thinking that becoming a romantic legend wasn't all that bad a way to be remembered.

Chapter Ten

Egon Rascon leaned forward and studied the corner screen on his desk with an intense gaze. After the last disappearance the Circle had installed sensors in the cavern roof. It had been a divisive issue, and had he not already known Alado was sending in an investigator he would not have voted for it. Now he was grateful to have a means to track John Hyatt and Haven Wray. The sensors registered the pair's location with pulsing dots on a grid, but no one had wanted to subject themselves to any more invasive scrutiny when they ran the maze.

Egon would have liked to have been able to see the pair's expressions and overhear their conversations, but he tried to be content with knowing they had found their way out of the octagon. They were still traveling blind, however, and exploring each branch they encountered with a thoroughness that meant they would be unlikely to ever solve the mystery of the magical maze. Not even all of those in the Circle had made that leap of faith.

Quickly growing bored with observing his hapless prey from such a rudimentary perspective, Egon requested a sweep of the mine's lower levels. Instantly the grid was cleared from the screen and replaced with sharp images of men and equipment gouging out astronium ore. He sat back to observe the progress of the current shift and felt confident that he had handled the threat to the maze both imaginatively and well. Unfortunately, when he met later with the Circle some still felt uneasy. Not taking it as a personal insult, he let the discussion continue until it grew heated. Then he broke in to reassert control.

"I don't believe that Hyatt and his reluctant bride will ever escape the maze, but blocking their exit in the unlikely event that they do would be such a small challenge for us. In the interest of harmony let's agree to be cautious." He waited until a low murmur of consent had rolled through the group; then he nodded to the most vocal advocates of that course of action.

"Lay the explosive charges. Then if we need an avalanche to block their exit, we can set it off without delay."

The Circle moved back to form a ring, extended their hands to repeat their oath, and then hurried away without a twinge of guilt clouding a single conscience.

* * *

Ian closed his eyes, but he couldn't sleep. He had had many an assignment where another operative's life had depended on quick action on his part, but he had never been responsible for the welfare of an innocent bystander, and that's all Haven should have been. That she had been sucked into a trap meant only for him was entirely his fault, and he was determined to succeed in getting them both out. Positive affirmations weren't going to be nearly enough to accomplish it, however.

He kept coming back to the question of time. Did the maze only appear to make time stand still, or did it actually accomplish what had always been considered an impossible feat? It seemed ridiculous to believe a set of confusing passageways constructed of stone could have any effect on anything, other than to dampen their spirits, but it was such an intriguing possibility, he couldn't entirely banish it from his mind.

If they had stepped into a time warp—and one apparently built by alien beings at that—they would emerge no older than when they had entered. Their metabolisms continued to need fuel to burn to maintain their bodily functions, hence the need for food, but the aging process would stop. At thirty-six, he had lost none of his youthful vigor, but he doubted he would be able to say the same thing ten years from now. It would not be a bad thing to remain thirty-six forever, but he did not want to spend eternity lost below ground. He would not doom a vibrant woman like Haven Wray to such a terrible fate, either.

The circle, a line without beginning or end, was an ancient symbol of eternity. Perhaps the Celtic knot provided another layer of meaning, but the circular element of the swirling design wasn't lost. Somehow 317 housed not merely a fabulous time-stopping maze, but a secret society that guarded it so jealously they thought nothing of sealing Haven and him in what could very well be their tomb. Without food and water they would grow thirsty and thin, but no older, and that fact would surely keep them alive long enough for Control to set them free.

Never one to passively sit and wait for rescue, Ian grew anxious to move on. When Haven stirred slightly he shook her shoulder to wake her. "I can't rest any longer. Let's go."

Haven straightened up, then stretched her arms over her head in an effort to shake off what had not been a particularly refreshing nap. Ian had already gotten to his feet, but she remained seated. "Wait a minute," she asked through a lazy yawn. "Who had the Celtic tattoo?"

On the off chance that she survived and he didn't, Ian did not want her to trust the wrong man. "It was Egon Rascon. He's a geologist as well as an administrator, so it makes sense that he would have been privy to all of 317's secrets."

Haven took Ian's hand when he offered it but couldn't hide her distress. "Aren asked Egon about you. He was trying to prevent what he saw as an unfortunate attachment on my part, but Egon apparently had no derogatory information

195

to provide, so he didn't get anywhere."

Ian responded with a curse so vile it would have made 317's miners blush. "I'm sorry. This isn't your fault, but I didn't want Egon to discover we were even acquainted, much less close enough to inspire Aren to pry into my past. I had created a specific image for Egon's benefit, and you wouldn't have been attracted to that officious soul."

Haven recalled how quiet Ian had been the night they had sat at Egon's table for dinner. It had upset her that he had not gotten the recognition he deserved but, of course, that had been his goal. She sighed unhappily. "Aren couldn't possibly have known that."

Ian noted how quickly she had defended the physician and shook his head. "Don't get me wrong: I'm not blaming my current problems on Aren. I made some classic mistakes all by myself." Inwardly he was still seething; rather than anything he had said to the miners, it now seemed likely that it had been Aren's questions that had caused Egon to become suspicious. How could he have been so damn careless? he agonized.

Haven preferred to focus her gaze on the clear definition of Ian's abdominals rather than his face. That he was such an attractive man didn't distract her from the issue at hand, however. "Namely seeing me—is that what you mean?"

Ian reached for her hand and pulled her along behind him. "You can't be that insecure, Haven." He knew that wasn't the reassurance she had probably hoped to hear, but if she doubted him after what they had been through together, he knew words would never satisfy her, no matter how poetic he might make them.

Before Haven could yank her hand free they entered a segment of the maze honeycombed with so many passageways that they could scarcely count them all, let alone choose where to begin. Ian went barreling straight ahead, and they soon discovered the corridors intersected at sharp angles, divided and then rejoined, only to divide again into a dozen new splinters. They ducked under low arches, craned their necks to look up into high vaulted ceilings, and got so thoroughly confused that when they burst upon a serenely elegant courtyard neither could believe what they had found.

The stones paving the courtyard had been laid in a pattern of concentric circles that framed a fountain from which bubbled a clear, sweetly perfumed liquid. The design of the fountain itself was a graceful stone tower pierced with gentle curves that caught, cupped, and caressed the fluid as it tumbled on its way into a pool large enough to allow swimming. An artistic masterpiece, it beckoned invitingly to the weary travelers.

Haven rushed toward it, but Ian caught her around the waist to hold her back. "Wait!" he cried. "It may be poisonous."

Haven could not believe anything of such heavenly perfection could possibly be harmful.

"It couldn't be!" She beat on his hands, but he refused to release her.

"Calm down," Ian ordered firmly. "Think of where we are. This is a maze, and nothing is as it seems. The fountain may very well contain something we'll find not only delicious but nourishing as well, but it could just as easily be an acid that will dissolve your hand clear to the wrist when you try to scoop up a mouthful."

Nauseated by that ghastly image, Haven sagged back against his chest. "Wouldn't it stink and fizz if it was some evil acid?"

"It might, and it might not. We don't know who built the maze, so we've no idea what their sense of humor might be." He bent down to nuzzle her cheek. "Let me try it first. If it's safe, you can drink all you want and I won't stop you. I'll even wait while you go swimming."

The liquid moved through the fountain, creating as delicate a melody as a wind chime, and Haven couldn't believe it would harm them. "My intuition is seldom wrong," she said, "and all I sense here is a blissful calm. I don't usually face such dangerous situations as you do, though. What do you feel?"

With her in his arms, if was difficult to sense anything other than her enticing beauty, but Ian tried. He closed his eyes and listened to the fountain for a moment. It had a happy sound, like the chirping of brightly colored birds. He released her but waved her back as he approached the fountain.

"I don't detect any sinister presence, if that's

what you mean, but that may have been the builder's intention. I'll risk a portion of my little finger to test how it affects the skin."

Haven took only a tiny step forward. "No, wait. You ought not to have to do that."

She looked terrified, and he was flattered for a brief instant until he realized that she might very well be more frightened for herself than him. "Well, I'd be happy to test the liquid another way if you can suggest one."

Haven thought a second and then came forward. Her bare feet were sore from walking on the rough stones, but she attempted to smooth out her stride rather than limp. "I could dip a bit of my hem into the fountain. If it eats the fabric, we won't have to sacrifice your finger to know we ought to go on."

"True; but it might have no effect on cloth and still eat holes in us." Ian could actually see her pushing her mind for another solution and hated to torture her needlessly. "All right. Come close and we'll see what it does to my tunic. Let's keep it well away from your legs."

Haven held her breath as Ian grabbed a hunk of the hem, pulled her against the edge of the circular fountain, and dipped it in. He waited only a brief instant and then, after flinging the excess droplets toward the center of the pool, bent down to examine the fabric. "It looks fine to me," Haven said.

"So far," Ian cautioned. He squeezed the damp fabric between his thumb and forefinger and experienced no ill effects. "Don't start cheering yet. Let me try my hand."

Haven caught his arm. "This is worth the risk, isn't it? After all, we do need something to drink, and this is all that we've found."

Ian could not find any reason to give her hope that their situation wasn't as dire as it seemed. Rescuers might already be on the way, but that did not mean they wouldn't be trapped in the maze several more days. "Yes," he assured her. "It's well worth the risk." He saw another question in her eyes but didn't pursue it before dipping the little finger on his right hand into the pool. If he had been with another agent, he would have screamed in mock pain just to scare him, but he wasn't even tempted to play such a nasty trick on Haven.

He shook his hand, but other than being wet, the perfumed liquid had no effect whatsoever on him. "I'm fine, but I'm going to wait a few minutes before I take a sip. Sometimes caustic materials don't burn on impact, but after a few minutes they do."

"What do we do if that happens?" Haven looked around the courtyard. "If we had some of that moss, we could use it to wipe off your hand. Maybe we can use this tunic again." She was still holding the damp portion away from her leg. "I can get along without a dress better than you can without a finger."

"Don't panic. Alado's medical unit can make me a whole new hand if I need one."

Haven couldn't bear the thought of him being

so horribly injured and turned away. "I'm afraid I'm going to be sick."

"Fine. Just don't vomit in the pool. It might be all we'll find to drink."

Haven really did feel sick, but she had not eaten in so long, she would have had nothing to vomit. Dropping her hem, she crossed her arms over her stomach to hide how badly her hands were shaking. "Is this the type of thing you do all the time? Do you just go from one harrowing adventure to the next?"

Ian nodded. "That's one way to describe it, but as I said before, I'm well compensated for the risks I take."

"Yes, so am I," Haven mused, "but I always thought I'd live long enough to enjoy it." She ran her toe along one of the paving stones. Perhaps five inches square, they resembled medieval cobblestones. "Whoever built this awful place must have been close to our size. The proportions of everything fit us well."

"Yes. They do." There was not even the slightest tingling in Ian's finger, and it was as fine a time to take a drink as he was likely to have, with Haven distracted momentarily. He bent over the pool and scooped up a long swallow.

"Ian!" Haven shrieked. She locked her hands around his left arm and held on with a fierce grasp. "Why didn't you warn me you were going to do that? Are you all right?"

Ian licked his lips as he straightened up. He waited a long moment but experienced no burning sensation in his mouth or throat. In fact, the liquid had been cool, and had slid down his throat as easily as water. "I'm fine," he promised. "It tastes like the children's punch at a wedding. It's much too sweet for me, but you might like it. I want you to wait a while though. Let's give it time for any adverse effect it might have to show."

Badly shaken by his reckless daring, Haven clung to his arm. "I don't like this, Ian, not at all."

"I've had better days too," he agreed with a low chuckle. "Now it's your turn to answer my questions. Let's sit down here and talk while we wait." Ian saw a shadow cross her gaze but couldn't decide if she was provoked at having to wait or merely reticent to confide in him. He opted for the latter.

"Let's agree that nothing we disclose here will go any farther," he urged. "I won't share your secrets with reporters. Can I trust you to guard mine?"

Haven nodded as she lowered herself to the stones, but she had no intention of unburdening herself, and nothing Ian had told her would make sensational news. She fidgeted with the hem of his tunic so she would not be seated on the damp edge, but the subject, not the oversized garment, was what was making her nervous. "I was blessed with an extraordinarily loving set of parents," she began as soon as he was seated across from her.

"My earliest memories of home are extremely happy ones. My parents were nutritionists by profession, but also avid amateur athletes who recognized my talent. I was very good at running, jumping, and climbing, but it was all play to me then. I began competing in races when I entered school, and won quite a few."

"Aren't you being too modest?" Ian coaxed. "I'll bet you won every race you entered."

Haven paused to brush her hair out of her eyes, but his comment had made her smile. "As a matter of fact, I did. That's how I was noticed by Kate Jandy. At the time she was the best coach in the galaxy, and when she explained to my parents just how remarkable she believed me to be, they allowed me to go and live with her at her training camp. I was seven years old."

This part of her life held no sadness, and Haven met Ian's gaze easily. "Kate had about a dozen promising young athletes training at her facility. We attended small classes to keep up with school, but sports were always our main focus. As you can see, I learned everything I was supposed to. I joined the Flames when I was seventeen, and ten years later—well, you know more than enough about my present situation."

"Those were the same facts I could have read in the tournament program," Ian chided. "Tell me something more. How did you happen to marry Blake Ellis?" He chose not to ask *why,* because he knew her well enough to know it must have been for love.

Haven glanced toward the fountain. "How do you feel now? Dizzy, nauseated? Do you have any strange symptoms?"

"Not a one," Ian swore. "But I still want you to

wait a little longer. Don't try to distract me again. Tell me about Blake. You must have made a striking couple."

They had been that, all right, but Haven did not want to force her mind back over those brief golden days. "I was married at nineteen and divorced a year later. It's an experience I've done my best to forget, so you'll have to forgive me if I can't provide any details. I've worked too hard to suppress them to want to dredge them up now just to keep you entertained."

Not satisfied with that flippant refusal, Ian pressed her to continue. "Just give me your impressions of marriage, then. Even if you weren't successful, do you still believe in the institution?" He caught a glimpse of the same dark shadow that had marred her gaze moments earlier. It gave her a touching vulnerability, but he did not want to leave such an important matter unresolved.

"I'm scared to death you're going to go into convulsions and die right here in front of me and you want to know my thoughts on marriage?"

While Ian was flattered, he was positive she could be more forthcoming. "That's right. There are some people who believe there are only two topics worth discussing: love and death. If these are my last minutes of existence, then we ought to be talking about something worthwhile." Ian had only been teasing, but when huge tears welled up in Haven's eyes he knew his joke had been in very poor taste. He moved close and pulled her into his arms.

"I'm sorry, Haven. I'm not used to having anyone care whether I'm around in ten minutes or
not. I didn't mean to frighten you so badly."

Haven leaned into his embrace but bit her lip
rather than weep openly. She had never had such
strong feelings for another man, not even Blake.
She rubbed her cheek against Ian's bare shoulder
and wished they were anywhere but here in this
strange underground world where nothing made
any sense. As abruptly as her composure had
crumbled, she pulled away, wiping her eyes on
the back of her hand.

"I'm sorry." She rested her hands lightly on his
shoulders to push herself to her feet, then took a
step toward the fountain. "I don't care if this stuff
is too sweet. If it was going to eat a hole through
your stomach, it would have done so by now."

Ian rose with an agile stretch and followed
her to the edge of the pool. "Every choice we
make in life has an element of risk," he stated
calmly. "You waited as I asked you to, and I
appreciate that. If we later discover this was a
tragic error—"

Haven shook her head. "You needn't warn me
again. I've been making all my own choices for
as long as I care to remember. If I suffer even the
smallest consequence from taking a drink, I
won't blame you."

Ian could not recall ever meeting another
woman with such swiftly changing moods, but
that was undeniably part of Haven's charm. She
was like quicksilver—impossible to hold—and

yet that very quality made her infrequent surrender almost unbearably sweet. He sat down on the edge of the pool. "I've not doubted you for an instant," he swore convincingly. "Go ahead. Take a sip."

Haven didn't torture herself with dread about the fountain's purpose. Instead, she just leaned over and scooped up a drink as smoothly as Ian had. She closed her eyes as she swallowed, waiting for some ghastly reaction to overtake her, but there was none. She straightened up. "I think it tastes more like some insipid perfume than punch, but it's wet, and that's all we truly require."

She had shut away her sorrow with a maddening ease, and Ian wondered if winning her trust wouldn't be every bit as difficult as escaping this cursed maze. Intrigued by her description, he scooped up another handful of the fragrant beverage. "I've never heard a taste likened to a scent, but you're right. If perfume had a taste, this would definitely be it." He got up and walked around the pool, but the source of the strange liquid was hidden beneath the tower.

"I've seen fountains on Earth placed at a level below the rivers that fill them so that they run on the force of the current alone. It's an ancient design, and that seems to be what's happening here. I don't see any moving parts, and there's no sound to give away the presence of a mechanical means by which to keep the fluid bubbling through the fountain."

As with his appreciation for the excellence of the masonry, Haven thought his appraisal of the power source for the fountain was totally irrelevant. "That would undoubtedly fascinate an engineer, but what you and I need is a map to the exit."

Ian saw the wisdom in her comment. "True. Let's use the fountain as a reference point. If we return to it frequently to ease our thirst, we'll soon be able to recognize details of the maze we're missing now."

"That makes sense."

As far as Ian was concerned, everything he said made a great deal of sense, but he could understand why she might be unwilling to concede that now. "I offered you a chance to go swimming. Do you want to give the pool a try?"

Haven's hands were sticky and she knew a swim would only make her feel uncomfortable all over rather than refreshed. "No thanks. If you're ready to move on, so am I."

Eight doors opened onto the courtyard, and Ian used the design of the fountain to identify the one by which they had entered. He gestured toward it. "We know that way doesn't lead anywhere. Let's take the door directly across from it." He extended his hand and, after a slight hesitation, Haven took it and joined him in another lengthy and unproductive search.

They returned to the fountain and went out again. The next door led to a dizzying array of steep stairways that met beneath another dome, then plunged down into a heated gorge that was well below the level where they had started. They went back up the way they had come, tired and discouraged that they had so little to show for their efforts.

"We've at least found a fountain," Ian stressed as they returned to the courtyard. "It may be a very small island of comfort, but it will do for tonight."

"Is it night already?" Haven asked. She had not even worn her crystal earrings to his room, let alone a watch. All of Alado's installations followed Earth's patterns of sunlight and darkness. Here at the mine, the lighting in the hallways dimmed to signal the approach of evening, and she missed that valuable cue.

The courtyard was open to the cavern above, and lit with the same intensity as the octagonal chamber. "How do you suppose the lighting works, Ian? It's even throughout the maze, and yet we've not come across a single place where we could see its source. I could manage a brief nap, but how are we going to sleep when it's so bright in here?"

Ian sat down by the fountain to use the low wall surrounding the pool as a backrest. "The lighting probably comes from a chemical source that once activated burns indefinitely." He watched her pace restlessly and was sorry she wasn't ready to go to sleep too. "If you're going to walk around, we might as well finish our conversation on marriage. Give me your honest opinion. Don't feel you have to censor your remarks to protect my feelings."

Haven recognized his teasing tone now but was no more interested in the subject than she had been the last time he had brought it up. "My parents had a blissfully happy marriage," she finally confided, "but they were older than I was when they wed and knew a great deal more about life."

"What didn't you know?"

Haven peered into a doorway that they had not explored as yet and, finding still another long, gray hall, crossed the courtyard and sat down beside him. She leaned back against the pool but didn't feel nearly as comfortable as Ian appeared to be. She rested her hands in her lap and gave his question the consideration it deserved.

"Kate Jandy trained me to be a superbly conditioned athlete, but there's more to life than winning at sports, or at least I hope there is."

She sent him a questioning glance, and Ian nodded to urge her to continue. "Such as?"

They were straying dangerously close to the argument that had torn apart Haven's marriage and, quite naturally, she quickly shied away. "Being able to relate well with others. Knowing what's truly important in life."

"My father would have sworn winning was all that mattered," Ian replied.

From what little Ian had revealed of his father's personality, Haven believed it was a very good thing she was stranded with him rather than that morose and bitter man. "He isn't here, though, and you are. What do you value most?" It was the question she should have asked Blake before they married, not afterward when it was too late to rectify her mistake.

Ian took her hand and brought it to his lips. He placed a light kiss on her palm and then rested her hand, still laced with his, on his thigh. "Being a man of honor," he finally replied. "If a man lacks good character, no amount of other attributes will make up for that failing."

That wasn't exactly what Haven had hoped to hear, but it was a comforting answer all the same. "I'd not thought of it that way, but I agree. A woman ought to have a good character too. The problem is, a man—or a woman—can appear to have an admirable character when things are going well, but if they start going wrong it shows as clearly as a missed shot on a Rocketball court."

"We've all had our disappointments," Ian mused thoughtfully, but he believed she was referring to her ex-husband, and he was talking about the men he had met in his profession. "Is that why you divorced Blake?"

The old anger filled Haven's throat, and she had a difficult time choking it down. "That was seven years ago, Ian. Leave it alone."

"No one forgets their first love."

"Not unless they sincerely want to," Haven countered. "What about you? Was there some dazzling beauty who broke your heart?"

A slow smile crossed Ian's lips and threatened to spread into a wicked grin. "Not yet," he confessed slyly.

Haven saw past that arrogant boast to the promise reflected in his amber gaze. He had never let another woman come close enough to break his heart; but then, he had probably never been forced to trek through an endless maze with another woman either. She already knew she could love Ian, and not merely as she had as a child. The question was whether she ought to. Would it be wise? Or was she being incredibly stupid to believe she even had a choice where he was concerned.

Unable to pursue that line of thinking without inviting the same suffocating dread entering the maze brought, she looked away. "Control may not believe that you and I eloped, but Aren surely did. It must have broken his heart to think I'd leave without telling him or the team good-bye."

Annoyed by another mention of the meddling physician, Ian almost missed the real value of her comment. "No, wait," he cautioned. "He must know you too well to believe you'd abandon your career for a man you'd only known a few days. We're back to character again, Haven. A woman of good character wouldn't have thrown her team into a panic by eloping on the eve of the championship tournament. There may be more people searching for us than we believed."

Clearly he was excited by the thought, but Haven couldn't agree. "Aren warned me repeatedly that I was pushing myself too hard. He probably believes I simply snapped. Elida Rivard must be ecstatic that I'm gone. Now she'll have her chance to prove she can carry the team."

Ian responded with a very uncomplimentary prediction as to how Elida would do. "I watched you practice, remember? You're the consummate team player, but she's out for herself, and this is one championship the Flames will never win if they have to depend on her."

"You want to place a little bet on that?"

"Right now all I've got is a pair of pants, and I sure don't want to lose them."

"I'd not take your pants. Let's make it something else—like a fabulous vacation at one of Alado's best resorts when we're out of here." She offered her hand, and Ian took it.

"Now I feel bad for betting against your team."

"It looks as though I won't be there to play, so I don't feel insulted. Besides, I still think we'll win."

Her eyes sparkled with a charming glow, and Ian leaned over to kiss her to seal their bet. He longed to make love to her again, but the last time they had fallen asleep in each other's arms, they had landed in so much trouble he did not want to take the risk. He released her hand and patted his thigh. "Stretch out and use my leg for a pillow. Then maybe you won't have such an uncomfortable night you won't be able to explore tomorrow."

Haven felt the very same sweet longing for more than a brief kiss but followed his suggestion. His leg did make a passable pillow, and the soft gurglings of the fountain were soothing, but she did not feel any more safe than she had when they had awakened that morning on the beautiful blue moss. "Tomorrow has to be better," she mumbled softly.

Ian stroked her hair lightly. "Hush; go to sleep," he cajoled, but he had no reason to even hope she would be right.

Chapter Eleven

Sleep was a long time coming, and then Ian's dreams were haunted by vaporous images floating through the twisting corridors of the maze. The ethereal creatures beckoned with graceful gestures, then withdrew as soon as he gave chase. He ran harder, his arms pumping, his feet flying in a desperate attempt to catch one and force it to speak. But when he at last trapped a pale apparition at a dead end it mocked him by dissolving into a fragrant mist.

Close on that disappointment, a rumbling tremor surged through the courtyard, sending the contents of the pool sloshing over the low wall in a cresting wave. Drenched as well as shaken, Ian and Haven came awake in a furious tangle. Sticky and wet, they rose unsteadily.

"Another minor quake." Haven shook her head

sadly. Ian had gotten the worst of it, but his tunic had been dampened and her hair soaked. "As if we didn't have enough to contend with down here." Sore from lying on the unyielding stones, she twisted and turned to work out the resulting stiffness. "I had the most awful dream. We were chasing these lovely beings who were no more solid than smoke, and—"

"You saw them too?" Ian interjected. He used his fingers to comb wet hair away from his face but knew he must look like some sloppy mechanic who styled his hair with grease and wasn't at all satisfied with the result. What the maze needed was not an oversized punch bowl but fresh-water showers where they could rinse off the sticky spill.

"Shared dreams are damn odd," he added.

"This whole place is odd," Haven grumbled. "Do you suppose it's haunted? Could the ghosts of the missing miners have appeared to us in dreams?"

Ian searched the courtyard for a better place to rest while he considered her question. He didn't so much mind getting wet, but the stickiness of the sweetly scented pool was annoying. He never bothered to wear men's cologne and didn't appreciate smelling like some whore's boudoir either.

"Did they look like miners' ghosts to you?" he called over his shoulder.

Now that Haven was fully awake she couldn't recall them clearly. "They were like some of the Dreamer's softer images," she remarked absently, "and yet their silhouettes were distinct against the stone. I've not had any experience with ghosts. Have you?"

Ian shot her a deeply skeptical glance. "There are no such things as ghosts."

Haven rubbed her upper arms briskly. "We could debate that issue endlessly, but I've always enjoyed ghost stories far too much to believe none of them actually happened. I suppose having fanciful figures appear in a dream isn't the same as being pursued by menacing demons while awake, but the fact that we had similar dreams makes me wonder. If not the miners, could the builders of the maze be trying to reach us?"

Ian chose a wall across from the fountain, where he would not be sprayed should there be another tremor, sat down, and stretched out his legs. "Damn near anything is possible," he conceded, "but I sincerely doubt the builders left behind holograms we could access only in our dreams."

Intrigued by that possibility, Haven crossed the courtyard and knelt in front of him. "Perhaps that's the only time we're sufficiently relaxed to be receptive to them. The problem was, I couldn't get close enough to understand their gestures. Could you?"

Ian shook his head, then pointed to the pool. "Besides being in the maze, the liquid in that glorious fountain is the other thing we shared. I don't feel drunk, but our twin dreams could be no more than a hallucination caused by that per-fumey liquid."

Thinking he might very well be right, Haven turned back toward the pretty fountain. It was as beautifully crafted as the rest of the maze, and she couldn't bear not to know who had built it. "We didn't drink very much, but I'm not thirsty for more."

"Neither am I; but at least it doesn't affect us while we're awake." Ian frowned slightly. "I doubt I'll be able to get back to sleep. Are you still tired?"

Deeply puzzled by their dreams, Haven wasn't eager to repeat them. "No. But I've no sense of having been asleep for an extended period. Of course, there have been occasions when I've lain down for a nap and awakened thinking hours had passed when it's only been a few minutes. Not being able to track the time accurately is un-settling. Do you want to go on?"

"If you're ready."

Haven pushed herself to her feet, and this time she gave Ian a hand up. Their palms were equally sticky, and they wiped them on their clothes. "Despite your theories on what makes the foun-tain function, that sugary liquid can't possibly be a natural substance. Someone must have filled the pool, just like a punch bowl. The courtyard is large enough to host a dance for a large group. Maybe the builders had parties here."

"Do you suppose they could all find their way here on time?"

"Oh yes. That must have been part of the fun."

Haven followed Ian through a new doorway, where they were again forced to turn sideways to traverse the corridor. Hoping to fool her senses, she closed her eyes, but that blocked only a small part of her dread. She placed her hands on the wall opposite her and felt her way with light pats until, with a hoarse cry, Ian made a lunging grab for her right arm and shoved her back the way they had come.

"My God, what's wrong?" Ian was blocking the corridor so completely, Haven couldn't see past him to whatever hazard he had found, but she knew he would not have manhandled her so roughly had he not had just cause.

Ian took a moment to catch his breath, but when he replied his words were still punctuated with deep gasps. "The hall continues here, but the path just drops away. Lucky for me you were right here to grab on to, or I might still be falling. There's a break of perhaps ten feet here before the path reappears. We could probably clear it with a running start, but with the passageway so narrow that's not an option. You'll have to lead the way back out."

Haven swallowed hard. Just moments earlier they had been analyzing dreams, and now Ian had nearly plunged to his death. What if he had actually fallen? Where would she find the strength to go on?

"Just give me a minute," she begged, but she felt as though the corridor had narrowed to trap her where she stood. She couldn't step to her right and shove Ian off a precipice, but she

217

couldn't seem to make her left leg move either. Wedged tightly in the passageway, she was so near hysteria she couldn't break away.

Ian did not like being trapped in the uncomfortably cramped hallway any more than Haven did, nor the thought of how easily the path might crumble from beneath their feet if they had another sharp tremor. "Haven," he urged firmly, "a cork might enjoy being stuck in the neck of a bottle of fine wine, but I'm not enjoying being forced to stand here one bit. Your feet will move if you give them the command. Do it."

Haven heard Ian's order, but for a terrible instant she felt as though she were being swallowed whole. She held her breath, waiting for needle-sharp teeth to pierce her flesh and crush her bones, but, mercifully, none did. Ian spoke to her again, his tone even more forcefully persuasive. She gripped his hand tightly. Because focusing on a Rocketball court had helped her in a similar situation earlier, she concentrated her energies on creating that same illusion. The court was wide and long, with plenty of room for the wildest play any team might dare to slip past the referees.

In a heroic attempt to conquer her fears she forced herself to remember the plays in the last game of the finals. Concentrating with all her might, she could actually feel her racquet connect with the ball and the whiplike recoil shoot up her arm. She heard her own labored breathing and the rhythmic thud of running feet as she and her teammates sprinted across the highly polished wood. She recreated the scene in such exquisite detail that while she didn't move with the speed Ian would have preferred, she finally managed to lead the way back out into the courtyard. Once there, however, she sank to her knees and put her head in her hands.

Haven wasn't crying, but she was so clearly distressed that Ian couldn't bring himself to scold her. He knelt beside her and hugged her shoulders tightly. "I didn't mean to be harsh with you, but that wasn't a place I wanted to stay."

Haven nodded. She was shaking all over and didn't know if she could stand without his help. She brushed her hair out of her eyes and looked up at him. "You'd better explore the next tunnel on your own. I can't take going back into the maze."

Ian did not want to take her back in if there was a risk she would become hysterical. But he couldn't leave her alone out here either. "I won't leave you," he assured her softly. "Either we keep searching together or we wait here."

"I hate this place," Haven swore darkly.

"I'll not come back here to vacation either, but first we have to get out." Ian had no phobias of any kind, and Control would promptly exclude him from intelligence work should he ever develop one, but he could see with his own eyes how terribly frightened Haven was. Her fears might have been of her own creation, but they were as real as his terror at nearly falling off the path had been.

He treated her gently. "You pulled yourself together to lead us out. How did you do it?"

Haven was embarrassed to explain that it had been with visual imagery but finally did. "You see," she pointed out, "all I've ever done well is play Rocketball. Even trapped down here, that's all I can do."

Self-pity was the last thing Ian would have expected from Haven Wray but, considerate of her feelings, he concealed his dismay. "You're a woman of extraordinary talents, Haven, and whatever you use to help us succeed will be most welcome." The wretched sadness didn't leave her eyes, though, and he knew he hadn't reached her.

He brushed her lips with a light kiss. "You're so much more than simply a superb athlete."

His voice held a seductive resonance that Haven couldn't mistake, but she did not want to lose herself in him when it would only postpone rather than resolve their real problem. "Please look for a corridor wide enough for us to move freely, and then I'll come with you."

Ian doubted she could actually die of fright, but he did not want to test the theory. "There's no rush. Let's wait a while."

"I want to play in the tournament," Haven reminded him. "That's an excellent reason to hurry."

Ian straightened up. He did not want to encourage her in what could so easily prove to be a futile hope, but she had set the tournament as a goal, and he did not want to belittle her determination. "I was looking forward to watching you play. Let's see you get there. Just give me a minute and I'll find a good tunnel for us."

Haven watched him walk away, his posture proud despite their ordeal, and she was thoroughly ashamed of herself for not having more courage. She knew her problems hadn't begun with this cursed maze, however. Her life had been disintegrating around her long before she had come to 317, but the decline had certainly accelerated once she had arrived. No, she argued silently; she had met Ian here, and he had been a joy.

Ian entered the next corridor and found it comfortably wide. As soon as he was out of sight, he leaned back against the wall to assess their rapidly deteriorating situation. Trapped belowground, most women would have posed problems related to their strength and endurance, but Haven was so well conditioned that the physical rigors they faced hadn't fazed her. Her problems were of the emotional variety, and Ian felt completely unqualified to help her in that area.

He had tried to draw her out, but she had glossed over her childhood and dismissed her marriage as too painful a subject to discuss. That left only Rocketball; while it was certainly an exciting sport, discussing it with her would not tell him anything more than he already knew. As he turned that dilemma over in his mind, he gained a sudden insight into just how much Haven had inadvertently revealed. Rather than being critical of herself by claiming her success was limited to Rocketball, she had been wishing for a great deal more. Inspired to pursue that line of inquiry, he went back out into the courtyard and sat down beside her.

"I found a corridor that looks good," he began, "but then I had an idea. You asked me who I was when I wasn't posing as someone else. That's not an easy question to answer, but how would you respond if I asked you who you are when you're not forced to wear the champion's crown as the star of the Flames?"

Once alone, Haven had tucked herself into a tight ball. She hugged her knees and began to rock back and forth slowly as she replied. "I've never had the opportunity to be anything else."

Ian reached out to caress her cheek. "Then you'll have to seize one," he urged.

Haven closed her eyes for a moment, but when she looked deep inside herself, rather than hope for the future, she found only a desolate emptiness that made her whole body ache with the loneliness she had fought for too long. She was far too proud to make such a pitiful admission to Ian, however, and she met his sympathetic gaze with a sullen frown. "We have to get out of here before I can consider making a career change. I'm sorry to be such a coward. I didn't mean to add to your worries." She pushed herself to her feet, then waited for Ian to stand.

Ian recalled how angry Blake Ellis had been the night Haven had failed to meet him outside the arena. He had had no sympathy for the man that night, but if Blake had had as little success breaking down the high wall Haven had built around her heart, then he owed him an apology. "You're no coward," Ian denied quickly, "and certainly not a burden. Now that you know how to beat the claustrophobia, you'll be able to conquer it again should the need arise."

Not at all cheered by that horrible possibility, Haven reluctantly followed Ian back into the maze. The corridor he had chosen curved and looped with the grace of a wide satin ribbon, then began to climb in a lazy swirl that took them winding around the outside of a thick column. With every step Haven dreaded reaching another dead end, but when the passageway at last widened they found themselves in a rotunda framed with stately arches leading to half a dozen more tunnels.

It was paved with the same circular pattern as the floor surrounding the fountain, but it was the curious cabinet occupying the center of the spacious chamber that captured their attention. Carved from a single block of stone, it was taller than Ian and half again as wide. The corners were decorated with fluted columns and molding incised with interlocking circles adorned wide bands at the top and base. Adding to the strange chest's commanding sense of mystery, its contents were hidden by a pair of highly polished doors.

Ian walked around it, then traced the design cut into the base with his fingertips. He placed his palms against the back. The stone was warm, as it was throughout the maze. "What do you make of this?" he asked.

Haven was as astonished as he. "This is the first piece of furniture we've found. If that's what it is." She peered into the crack between the doors, but the interior was too dark for her to see anything. "I don't suppose there's even the remote possibility that this contains charts that will help us find our way out of here."

Ian came around to the front and ran his hands over the satin-smooth doors before searching for a release. "I want you to go stand in the corridor that leads to the fountain. In the event of an explosion you'll not be hit with flying debris."

Haven shuddered and made a horrible face; if that were the case, part of the debris would be bits and pieces of him. "Do you really think this might be an elegant booby trap?"

"It never hurts to be cautious, Haven. Now go."

Haven didn't move. "And miss being splattered with your blood? I'll stay."

Ian thought her devotion, if that was what it was, was misguided. "If this contains a bomb, blood will be the least of your problems. The whole cabinet will fly apart in a hail of jagged shards, and the dome above us will probably collapse from the force of the blast. If you're not killed outright, you might be trapped under the rubble and suffer horribly for days before help arrives. I won't allow you to chance that. Now do as I say."

Haven doubted many people argued with Ian when he used that tone, but she wasn't intimidated. "I thought we were in this together."

"We are, but that doesn't mean that you have

to take dangerous risks just because I do. You've nothing to prove here, Haven."

Haven wasn't trying to prove anything. She just didn't want to be left alone in the maze should the catastrophe Ian imagined come to pass. She widened her stance and crossed her arms over her chest. "Open it," she directed firmly.

Ian eyed her with a darkly determined gaze. She was tall but slender, and he doubted she weighed more than 130 pounds. He could pick her up easily and carry her out into a corridor, but not without a fight. He could be brutal when he had to get his way by force, but that was the last option he wanted to use on her. "Do it for me if you won't do it for yourself," he said as calmly as he could.

Haven wouldn't back down. "There would be no joy in living if you were dead. Go on; open it. Maybe the blasted thing doesn't open in the first place, and this argument has been as useless as our explorations."

That Haven wasn't frightened by the prospect of imminent death surprised Ian. An intelligence operative confronted his own mortality early in his career and either made peace with whatever fate might have in store or left the unit for less hazardous work. Haven's background was completely different from his, however. "The prospect of death doesn't trouble you?"

Believing he might try and trick her somehow, Haven remained wary. "I couldn't play Rocketball if living past my prime was a priority. It isn't.

I've had a good life, and if it ends here, I'll not feel cheated."

"I would," Ian replied. The thought of losing her brought a swell of emotion that caught him completely off guard. He wanted to say something profoundly moving, something she would always treasure should they survive, but he could not even think over the wild beating of his heart, let alone compose a touching vow.

To hide his distress, he turned toward the doors and prayed the magnificent cabinet contained nothing more than several centuries' worth of dust. He took a deep breath, then placed his hands on the doors and leaned against them with sufficient force to trip the latch should there be one. He heard a slight scraping sound and shot Haven one last pleading glance. Again refusing to leave him, she shook her head, and as he drew away, he reached for her hand, meaning to pull her down on the floor and shield her body with his own should his worst fears materialize.

For a nearly unbearable instant the silence of the maze was unbroken, and then with a slow, dull rasp, the doors swung open to reveal a bank of eight deep drawers, each with a semicircular dip at the top to facilitate its removal. Ian finally exhaled, then embraced Haven with an ecstatic whoop. "We're safe for another few minutes at least," he breathed against her ear.

He was all sticky, but his warmth felt so good to Haven, she didn't mind. She returned his hug, then broke away and directed his attention to the drawers. "Shall we open them in sequence or at random?"

That she had bolted from his arms was a disappointment. But, after all, he could scarcely order her to leave him one minute and complain in the next when she refused to stay. Then again, he wondered why her behavior was equally contradictory.

"Let's begin at the top." Ian gave the first drawer a yank, and it slid easily from its compartment. Made of the same stone as the cabinet, it was heavy, and he held it low enough for Haven to examine its contents along with him. He counted twelve irregular spheres with a corklike covering. "Are these nuts or seeds?" he asked.

"I think nuts are seeds," Haven murmured, "but I don't recognize these." She removed one of the hard, spotted objects and rolled it between her palms. "It feels like the shell of a nut, but it's awfully hard, and we've no way to crack it."

"We could put it on the floor and crush it with this drawer," Ian suggested.

"We'd probably break the drawer before that happened, and we ought not to risk that. As an archaeological find, if for no other reason, let's keep the cabinet intact."

"I suppose that's a good plan, but I was hoping to find something to eat." Ian returned the drawer to its slot and removed the one beside it. This time he placed it on the stone floor and knelt down. "Well, look at these." He reached in and scooped up a handful of what looked and felt like shelled nuts, even if he wasn't certain exactly what kind.

"Wait," Haven urged. "You insisted upon taking the first drink from the fountain, so now it's my turn."

He had lost their last argument but, again asserting control, Ian grabbed Haven's wrist as she reached into the box. "No. I'm being paid for this dangerous escapade and you're not."

Exasperated with him for being so dense, Haven's temper flared. "This isn't about money; it's about survival. How will you enjoy your pay if Alado has to forward it to your heirs?"

She had a good point, but Ian wouldn't concede it. "I don't have any heirs," he explained, "so you needn't sacrifice yourself to save me."

The nuts were a little larger in size than an almond, but they were deep red rather than tan. As with the fountain, Haven had no premonition of impending doom, and she doubted they would harm her. "Look at it this way," she coaxed. "If these poison me, you'll still have an excellent chance to get out of here on your own. If something happened to you, I'd just have to sit with your body and wait for rescue, because I'll not put myself through the ordeal of traveling through that ghastly maze alone."

Ian could actually see the logic to her argument, but it didn't sway him. "I'm here by choice, Haven, and that means I take the risks."

Haven sent a pointed glance to the fierce grip he had maintained on her wrist. "You're hurting me." She twisted her arm, and when Ian released her she plucked a nut from the box. Before he could stop her she popped it into her mouth. A triumphant grin lit her face for only an instant, however, before the nut's highly spiced coating set the inside of her mouth on fire. She spat it out, but coughed and gagged so violently that Ian assumed she had been poisoned.

He picked her up in his arms and, careening at a wild run through the winding passageway they had just traversed, he carried her all the way back down to the fountain. With her still clutched in his arms, he knelt beside the pool and, in a frantic bid to save her life, he scooped up several handfuls of the perfumed liquid and forced them into her mouth. Haven sputtered and choked but finally caught her breath and swallowed deeply. She scooped up the next drink by herself and then, worn out, slumped against Ian's shoulder.

"I've never cared for spicy foods," she finally explained, wiping away her tears on the back of her hand. "I swear ten thousand chilis aren't that hot. That was just awful."

Ian was so greatly relieved that she hadn't died in his arms, he could almost forgive her for giving him such a terrible scare. Almost. "It was just too spicy?" he asked incredulously. "My God, I thought you'd swallowed a lethal dose of some exotic alien poison and were dead for sure."

Although still trembling, Ian's sarcasm pushed Haven to her feet. "You sound as though you're disappointed that I'm not." Feeling slightly dizzy, she sat down on the wall surrounding the pool and hugged her arms. "Let's wait a few minutes. There's still a chance I might expire."

Thinking this was no time to be flippant, Ian straightened up, sorely tempted to shake her. He shoved his hands into his pockets to control the impulse. "That isn't in the least bit funny. I don't want you dead. What I do want is for you to follow my orders when I give them. We're both lucky the cabinet wasn't rigged with explosives, but I won't tolerate another confrontation from you. Now if you feel up to walking, let's go back to the cabinet and see if we can't find at least one thing in it that we can eat."

Haven could see right through him. Rather than admit she had been right in assuming the cabinet posed no threat to their safety, he was upset because she had defied him. Twice. As she saw it, his pride was the problem, not her defiance. She did not waste her breath pointing it out.

"I'm afraid my mouth is in shreds."

Ian took her hands and pulled her to her feet. "Let that be a lesson to you then. From now on, I'm the official taster for this expedition, and that's final." Haven had withdrawn again, and that worried Ian more than any lingering discomfort she might be experiencing. He pulled her close. "I don't want to crush your spirit. I just want us to be able to work well together without either of us getting hurt."

That was a noble goal, but Haven was used to leading, not following. She wiggled out of his embrace. She doubted they would ever encounter a worse situation, but she was positive the fact that they could not get along well was a very bad omen. "I don't recommend the red nuts," she finally said, "but maybe you'll find something to your liking."

Exasperated that she hadn't thanked him for bringing her to the pool, Ian watched her walk away. That proved to be a tactical error, because she had the most beautiful pair of legs he had ever seen. She knew the way back up to the cabinet, so he didn't shout for her to let him go first; when the view from behind was so good, he did not really mind following.

Chapter Twelve

As Haven followed the corridor up to the cabinet, she bit her lip to force back the tears threatening to overwhelm her. She ached to escape these endless passageways with the same longing for release that had robbed Rocketball of its lifelong thrill. She wanted to get out of the trap her life had become and had foolishly believed that if she could just hang on until the Flames won the tournament, somehow she might be able to find herself in the off season. Now she doubted she would even be able to play in the tournament, and what little hope she had clung to for the future was rapidly slipping away.

After her ghastly experience with the highly spiced nut she was more than willing to allow Ian to sample the curious rations they found, and she slowed her step as she approached the cabinet.

She had wanted to accept her share of whatever danger they might encounter, but she had done such a poor job of it, she hung back as Ian withdrew the next drawer. He placed it on the floor to examine the contents. She no longer expected anything good, so she didn't kneel down beside him.

This drawer held dried fruit. Ian ruffled the leathery circles to separate them, then held up one. It was translucent, with a wavy, irregular edge. "This looks as though it might have come from a nobby apple. Let's hope it's delicious." When Haven didn't speak, Ian finally noted her downcast expression and straightened up.

"What's wrong?" he asked.

"What isn't?" Haven studied the slice of dried fruit in his hand rather than meet his gaze. Ian tipped her chin to force her to look up.

"I'm just as depressed as you are," he said.

"That's impossible. You're in the middle of another tough assignment. That's all this is to you, but things haven't been going well for me for so long, I can't even remember being happy."

Ian had noted the sadness in her eyes soon after they had met, but he had hoped knowing him had made a difference. "I would have sworn that you were as happy as I was a couple of nights ago."

Rather than a sarcastic boast, Ian's tone was so wistful that Haven couldn't help but smile. But the expression fluttered across her lips and was gone in an instant. "Yes, I was; and look how badly we were punished for it."

Fearing she would pull away if he embraced her, Ian could only offer words for comfort. "I should have taken better care of you; then you wouldn't have been drawn into this with me. But that's the only thing I regret about that night. I hope these are edible, because a good meal will brighten our spirits."

Past caring about hunger, Haven responded with a distracted nod. She watched as Ian tore off a bite of the dried fruit; by the pleasant warmth of his features she knew it must taste passably good. "I can already tell that it's better than the nuts."

Ian nodded. Slightly sticky, the fruit was a chore to chew, but he rolled it off his teeth with his tongue, swallowed, and took another bite. The second sample brought no ill effects either, but he still asked Haven to wait a few minutes before she tried it. "I'm not used to being responsible for anyone but myself, so I'm probably being more cautious than necessary. Please be patient with me."

At the fountain Ian had angrily asserted his authority; Haven was surprised that he had now grown contrite. Believing she must look even more pathetic than she supposed, she was embarrassed rather than relieved. Her hair was a sticky mess; she attempted to smooth it down but swiftly gave up the effort as hopeless. "I've never much cared for dried fruit, so I don't mind the wait."

Ian swallowed the last bite of that piece. "It's awfully sweet. Whoever built this place definitely

had a sweet tooth." Not wanting to keep Haven
waiting any longer, Ian bent down to get a slice
for her. "Perhaps you can identify this."

Treating his question as though it deserved the
utmost concentration, Haven took a bite of the
shriveled circlet and chewed slowly. She compared the flavor with fruit she had sampled in the
past. While it resembled a dried apple in texture,
it was unique. "No. It's fruit, but nothing I've
tasted before. Let's check the other drawers.
Maybe we'll find something better."

Glad he had succeeded in distracting her sufficiently to encourage hunger, Ian replaced that
drawer and removed the next. "These look like
cookies," he exclaimed. "Didn't these people eat
anything but snacks?"

"Maybe they weren't people," Haven reminded
him, "and had entirely different needs."

Ian set down the drawer, selected a thin wafer,
and popped it into his mouth. It melted before
he could chew. "Too light for anything other than
some stilted society affair." He replaced the
drawer without giving Haven a sample. "Let's
keep going," he urged, moving down to the next
row and finding a drawer with strips that resembled beef jerky.

He snapped one in two and brought it to his
nose. "It doesn't smell highly spiced, but jerky
often is." He broke off a bite and began chewing.
After a moment he nodded slightly. "Sweet again,
but with a hint of something like cinnamon." He
offered Haven the other portion.

Haven waited even without his asking. Jerky

wasn't one of her favorite foods either, but when she tried the stringy tidbit it at least tasted good, even if it took too much effort to chew. The next drawer had a similiar substance formed into squares that were so tough, Ian could not even bite off a hunk to try. "Let's save that one until we're desperate—or more desperate, I should say," she suggested.

Disappointed that the cabinet held such insubstantial rations, Ian readily agreed. The bottom drawer on the left contained what looked like huge raisins. They were even more gooey than the leathery circles with which he had begun, and he quickly tossed several to Haven. "I think we're lucky our hosts aren't here to notice our lack of enthusiasm for their food. Then again, it's doubtful anyone who thrived on a diet that was this exhausting to consume would be all that great a menace."

Haven tried one of the raisins. She rolled it around her mouth, found it had little in the way of flavor, and then gave a hesitant chomp. "These are more tart than raisins, but the fruit must be a grape or wild berry. I don't know what I was expecting, but certainly something better than this."

Ian pulled out the last drawer, but all it contained were sugary crumbs. "Looks like someone beat us to the really good stuff. Well, that leaves us with nuts we can't crack, others too spicy to eat, cookies lighter than air, and an assortment of dried fruit it may well take us the whole day to chew. Let's sit down and rest while we eat what we can."

Haven reached into the drawer with the rippled circles and took three. "I liked these the best. Should we ration the supplies? If this is all we find, we'll have to make them last until your troops arrive."

"Or we get out," Ian reminded her. "I'm not really very hungry. Are you?"

Haven took several of the crisp cookies for dessert and sat down in front of the cabinet. "No; and as sweet as this stuff is, I won't be able to eat much."

"Fine. Then we won't ration anything yet." Wanting to leave the circlets for Haven, Ian chose the jerky strips and sat down beside her. He would have offered conversation to distract her from their meager meal, but she wore a preoccupied frown. Thinking she might have already had more of his company than she wanted, he kept his thoughts to himself. She had asked to hear about some of his adventures, but as he began sifting through his most recent assignments, he feared his exploits would sound more brutal than entertaining to Haven. In fact, even his brief stint as a monk had had dark repercussions.

When Haven finished the fruit she took a bite of the cookie. "Hazelnuts," she murmured. "These taste as though they could have been made with finely chopped hazelnuts. Perhaps not exactly like hazelnuts," she qualified, "but close." She rolled the crunchy bits around in her mouth.

"These are the best thing in the cabinet." She quickly ate the ones she was holding and stood to get a few more. "Would you like some too?"

Ian had dismissed the crisp wafers as too light to be considered real food but, inordinately pleased by Haven's smile, he nodded. "Please."

Haven made a quick count of the remaining wafers. "There are close to fifty. That will last us a while." She handed Ian five and gave herself another three. She sat down again and grew more relaxed as she ate another wafer. "It's pitiful how little it takes to give a person hope, isn't it?"

Ian ate a wafer whole. Again it melted before he had a chance to savor the flavor, but he did notice just a hint of hazelnut this time. "That's an asset, Haven, not a flaw in human nature."

"Well, yes, I suppose." Haven savored another wafer and felt a delicious warmth fill her stomach and roll slowly through her limbs. She wasn't tired, though; in fact, her senses were becoming exquisitely acute. She glanced toward Ian and found him framed by an iridescent rainbow that pulsed with his every breath. He smiled at her, his amber eyes glowing with desire, and she quickly finished the last two wafers. She brushed off his tunic with a distracted swipe and leaned toward him.

"You are a very handsome man," she whispered seductively.

Ian was beginning to feel rather warm himself, but he thought it was merely the heat in Haven's glance that was affecting him so strongly. He slipped another paper-thin cookie into his mouth. "Thank you." His eyes widened as Haven began to tug on the waistband of his pants. He reached out for her, and she crawled up over him. The wafers were in his way, and he shoved the last of them into his mouth. "Come here," he sighed against her lips, and as she moved astride him their kiss was flavored with a nutty sweetness.

That first kiss blurred into a dozen more; then Haven arched her back and, with a languid purr, pulled Ian's tunic off over her head and flung it aside. She rocked against him, brushing the tips of her flame-kissed breasts across his chest. She ran her hands down his sides and along his scar, then raised up on her knees to give him the opportunity to discard his pants, which he promptly did.

She settled back down on his bare lap, gently tucking his hardened shaft into her slippery cleft. Seeking more, he bucked beneath her, but she teased him and slid up and down to heighten her own pleasure rather than allowing him to penetrate her. She grabbed handfuls of his thick blond hair and smothered his moans with deep kisses until, awash in glorious sensation, she was completely satisfied.

Then she spread a taunting trail of passionate kisses down Ian's chest and over the flatness of his belly. He wound his fingers in her hair to direct her mouth lower, but she already knew what he wanted and how to bring him the most exquisite of pleasures. Her senses bombarded with the dazzling colors spinning wildly in her mind, she lost herself in him. His rapture was now hers, and when he pushed her down onto the paving stones to seek his release deep within her, she coiled around him, coaxing him past reason to the ultimate bliss.

As Haven looked up, the dome above them spun from a scarlet core to a bright orange that blurred into radiant yellow. The colors mirrored the graceful flames of her tattoo, came together in a frantic swirl, then burst like fireworks in a sparkling rain that fell all around them. Ian's face was bathed in that spectacular light, and when Haven called his name her voice reverberated around them in shimmering waves of laughter.

Still hard, Ian rolled over with Haven cradled in his arms and brought her up astride him. He rubbed her nipples between his fingers and thumbs, tugging on her breasts in time to the rhythmic motion of her hips. Dipping down over him in a graceful swoop, she used her hair as a silken whip across his chest, then threw her arms wide and leaned back until he grabbed her waist to pull her down into his arms.

She locked her arms around his neck and flexed the muscles that kept him lodged deep within her. Ian rolled over again, now seeking to dominate her with grinding thrusts that served only to sharpen their blinding need for each other. He kissed Haven deeply, longing to absorb her very soul as another stunning climax stole through them with a shattering grace. They needed no more time than it took to catch their

breath before their hunger for still another release again drew them together.

This time Ian slid down over Haven, tracing
the pattern of her tattoo with his lips and tongue.
He turned her in his arms, savoring each dip and
lick until he had at last explored every delectable
inch of her. Her taste was sublime; still he had
not had enough. He rubbed his cheek against the
tender flesh of her inner thigh and, craving more
of her intimate kisses, crawled up over her. Her
mouth was hot, eager, and Ian begged for more,
and more, taking her with him on an erotic quest
that ended only when they were exhausted by the
ecstasy they had shared and fell asleep in a languid tangle neither sought to escape.

Haven came awake with a start, then realized
the weight pressing her down into the unyielding
stones was Ian. He was lying sprawled across
her, his head nestled against her left shoulder,
his legs woven through hers. He was sleeping so
soundly, she doubted he would wake for hours.
Thinking it was very nice to wake in his arms,
even if it was on the hardest of floors, she raised
her fingertips to his nape and combed his hair
gently.

She licked her lips and could still taste the
nutty flavor of the crisp wafers. They had been
as delicious as Ian's kisses, but as she pushed her
memories past their skimpy meal, a heated blush
rose to her cheeks. She recalled the vivid colors
that had turned the drab gray stone maze into a
paradise of sparkling hues, and the musical

sound of her own laughter. Even more clearly she remembered making love to Ian with a wild, wanton, insatiable need. That his desire had matched hers had doubled their joy, and after the first dizzying rush of memory she felt no lingering sense of shame.

The first night they had spent together had been a celebration of unspoken love, but the second time they had been possessed by a fiery passion that even now left her feeling not merely blissfully content but completely drained. She wanted to hug Ian tightly, to never let him go, but she felt so terribly weak that she could barely hold him in a relaxed embrace. They had had very little to eat, and only a strange sweet liquid to drink, but she knew her fatigue was caused by something far more dangerous than lack of food or drink.

Perhaps the delicious cookies were not only a potent aphrodisiac but also a deadly treat. She was not certain how it felt to die but imagined the weakness that kept her trapped beneath Ian had to be close to the gradual dimming of energy at the end of life. The dome no longer throbbed with magical colors, but Haven felt the same wonder-tinged joy she had previously found in Ian's arms. A tear rolled down her cheek, but she wasn't saddened by the possibility that she might die where she lay. It was where she belonged, but she wished they could have shared so much more than these few fevered days.

Haven had fallen asleep again before Ian awoke, and when he did he feared he must have crushed her and quickly moved aside. He laced his fingers in hers and brought her hand to his lips. Her eyes came open and she smiled, but he could only moan.

"I feel as though I've been asleep for at least a century."

"Maybe we have," Haven replied.

Ian's memories were as sharp as Haven's, and while he knew he had every right to be tired, he felt as though he had had an extended sleep without gaining any of the usual benefits of rest. He brought his free hand up to check his beard and found his cheeks were still smooth. That they were trapped in time as well as the maze chilled him.

"I'm so sorry," he murmured. "I didn't think to make an allowance for the difference in size between us. I should never have let you eat those cookies when I hadn't tested them thoroughly."

"Maybe it wasn't the cookies," Haven mused languidly. "Maybe it was the giant raisins that worked the magic, or maybe a combination of everything in the cabinet."

Ian knew he ought to get up and pull on his pants, but lying on the floor naked was all he could manage for the moment. He covered a wide yawn with his hand and then gave Haven's hand a fond squeeze. "We may have to wait right here for Control to find us, but I'll help you dress if you'll just give me a few minutes."

Haven was too comfortable with her body, too relaxed with him to be ashamed of being nude. "Take your time. If we can't manage our clothes, or your clothes since we're both wearing them, will Control be shocked to find us like this?"

Ian inched closer to snuggle with her. "He's the type who expects to have his orders carried out with diligence and precision, but he's not above congratulating an agent for getting a job done by unconventional means."

"We haven't found the miners," Haven reminded him, "so he's unlikely to be pleased to find us lying here as limp as soggy bread. In fact, I'm afraid you're going to receive a rather severe reprimand. Blame everything on me if you like."

While it required an enormous effort, Ian slipped his arm under Haven's neck to cradle her head on his shoulder. "You're the last person I'd ever blame for anything. Let's just rest a while longer; then we'll surely feel strong enough to move on."

"And if we don't?"

"Hush," Ian begged. "The worst that can happen is that one of my friends will find us in each other's arms. I won't be embarrassed about it, and I hope you won't either."

Haven looped her arm over Ian's waist. "I think I'm past the point of embarrassment." She truly was afraid they were dying, but because Ian had not grasped that fact himself, she did not want to give voice to her fears and force him to share them. Silent tears filled her eyes.

Ian felt Haven's tears splash on his bare chest and hugged her as best he could. "Please don't cry, Haven. I'll get us out of here and we'll be fine. Trust me."

Haven did trust his intentions, but when they were too weak to move she did not understand how he was going to manage to make his brave promises a reality. Believing it was enough that he made them, she fell asleep still crying softly in his arms.

Ian drew in a deep breath and exhaled a silent string of bitter curses. It was clear to him that they had been drugged, and while the erotic aspects of the cabinet's contents had been spectacular, this prolonged period of exhaustion afterwards was a bitter price to pay. At least their minds hadn't been dulled to the same level of languorous stupor that filled their bodies, and he was cheered by that. Still, he was anxious to get up and push on with their efforts to escape.

He rested as Haven slept, and with each deep breath felt himself growing stronger. He experienced several jarring flashbacks that nearly blinded him with bright bursts of color, but they tapered off as his strength returned. More worried about Haven than he had admitted to her, he waited for her to wake on her own, and prayed that when she did she would have regained her strength as well.

Haven's sleep was unmarred by dreams, and when she awakened for the third time she felt well enough to stand with Ian's help. He slipped his tunic over her head, and then quickly yanked on his pants. She seemed none too steady on her feet, so he wrapped his arm around her waist to help her walk.

"Let's go down to the fountain and have a

drink. Then, as soon as you feel up to it, we'll explore the corridors that meet here."

"I'll be all right," Haven argued, but she didn't wiggle out of Ian's comforting hold. Instead, she rested her arm around his waist as they started down the corridor to the fountain. The winding path was familiar now, but she felt slightly dizzy, and when they reached the portion where the corridor should have begun to loop back on itself, she was surprised to find a set of stairs.

"Wait a minute," she urged. "There aren't any stairs on the hallway to the fountain."

"I know," Ian replied. He was as startled as she to discover they had taken the wrong corridor. "I was certain I chose the right path, but obviously I didn't. I'm sorry; we'll have to go back. Shall I carry you?"

"No, I can make it," Haven assured him, but her steps remained shaky. When they returned to the chamber with the cabinet she uttered a small cry of alarm. "Oh, no, look. This is exactly where we entered this chamber before. You didn't make a mistake. We were in the corridor that should have led to the fountain, but it's changed."

Ian searched her fear-stricken expression with a troubled gaze. Had he been alone he would have afforded himself the luxury of a few moments of well-deserved panic, but he wouldn't give in to it in front of Haven. "I know this looks like the angle at which we approached the cabinet, but obviously it isn't. Now I want you to sit down here and wait while I check a couple of the other corridors."

Haven grabbed hold of his arms. "No! Don't you see? We didn't blunder into the wrong corridor. The maze has changed!"

"How could it change?" Ian asked. "It's made of stone. We must have made a careless error. That's the only explanation that makes any sense."

"Nothing makes sense here!"

While Ian had not known Haven long, he was positive she was not given to becoming hysterical without good reason. Still, he couldn't accept her theory without proof. "Please. Sit down and rest. I'll check the corridor again and come right back."

"No. If the corridors can shift form and direction, then we don't dare separate for even a minute or we might never be able to find each other again."

Ian straightened up to his full height. If he was not the best of Control's agents, then he was a close second, but nothing in his extensive training or wide experience had prepared him to escape a trap that changed form. That had to mean someone or something controlled the maze and, therefore, their fate. He rejected the idea even as on a deeper level he accepted it as the truth.

Haven watched Ian closely, but there wasn't a trace of fear in his expression. Instead, he appeared to be even more fiercely determined to get them out of the maze safely. If it were possible to read the quality of a man's character in his face, Haven was positive she saw only strength and goodness in Ian's. There was an umistakable wildness as well, but knowing a defiant spirit was what they needed most to survive, she welcomed it as the best of traits.

"You know I'm right," she coaxed. "We've already decided the construction of the maze is beyond the miners' capabilities. Miners couldn't have rearranged the stone walls while we slept either. For all we know, we're no more than pawns in some alien child's game. Well, they've made a stupid mistake, because I play every game to win."

That Haven would respond to this new challenge so bravely was all the inspiration Ian required. He kissed her soundly and took her hand. "We'll stay together. Now because we know we were on the right path, let's go back and see where the stairs lead. If the corridor no longer leads directly to the fountain, it might still take us somewhere worth going."

Haven glanced back toward the cabinet. "We might not be able to find our way back here, so we'd better take some of the dried fruit with us. I'm willing to bet it was the cookies that provoked the passion, and I'd like to leave those behind."

Ian responded with a smile. "You're what provoked my passions, Haven. The cookies may have increased my stamina, but I still want you just as badly."

Haven did not know if this was the worst or the best of times to fall in love, but love him she did. She raised her hand to his cheek and he placed a kiss on her palm. "I've waited a long time to meet you, Ian St. Ives, but you were well worth the wait."

"So were you," Ian answered easily. He winked at her and, forgetting the need for rations, they went back into the corridor they knew had led to the fountain. The new set of stairs took them on a steep descent that ended not abruptly at a blank wall but simply broke off in midair. Ian leaned out to look over the end, but deep shadows hid whatever lay below.

"There could be a five-foot or a fifty-foot drop, and there's no reason to explore this route any farther with that kind of risk."

Haven agreed, and they retraced their steps to the chamber with the magnificent cabinet. "Let's use the inedible squares for markers so we'll know which corridors we've explored," she suggested.

"That's fine with me." Ian grabbed one but, remembering their earlier decision to take along some of the rations, he stuffed his pockets with jerky strips and big raisins. "I'm sorry there aren't any pockets in my tunic. But this ought to last us a while."

They chose the corridor to the left of the one they had just explored, and placed a square beneath the arched entrance to mark their route. The passageway proved to be long and dark, with sharply angled turns and steep inclines that eventually wound back down and spilled out into the chamber where they had begun. They stood in the doorway to the left of where they had entered and, after Ian had sworn a particularly inventive oath, he went to get another square to mark the corridor as explored.

"Do you suppose this is going to be like the first chamber, and all the doors will lead right back here?" Haven asked.

"Don't forget there was a way out," Ian cautioned. "We'll just keep going until we find a clear passageway here as well."

Haven took his hand as they ducked beneath the next arch. This passageway led to another honeycombed stretch where the corridors intersected at right angles so often, they swiftly became confused, but when they finally stumbled out onto another courtyard, it was one where the paving stones had been cut to the size of tiny mosaic tiles and set in the swirling curls of ocean waves. A single glance at the floor made Haven dizzy.

"Please, I've got to sit down for a minute." She sank down without waiting for permission from Ian and put her head in her hands. She hoped with all her heart that they were making progress toward freedom but feared all they were really doing was staying in the same place while the maze spun around them.

"This is a good place to rest," Ian said. He sat down beside Haven and offered her a couple of the peculiar raisins. "Let's eat just one of these, then wait a few minutes to see how we feel."

Haven popped one into her mouth. She ran her tongue over the badly wrinkled fruit and wished it had more taste. "This just isn't the stuff of wonderfully romantic legends," she mused softly, "but then, maybe all the beautiful love stories are lies."

Ian could not recall ever being put in a position to defend love, but he knew it was real. "I told you I'd played a monk recently, and performed a wedding in a pirate's den. The groom was another of Control's agents, and I'd been sent in to check his progress when his loyalties were questioned. He was angry with me for interfering with his mission but absolutely infuriated that I had posed as a priest when he wanted a real wedding. Control wasn't about to allow one of his agents to marry a pirate's daughter and ended the operation with a successful raid."

Ian paused there, but Haven's curiosity was far from satisfied. "Well, what happened?" she prompted. "If that's supposed to be a story about the triumph of love, it needs a better ending."

Ian nodded slightly. "The official story is that the woman escaped from detention but died soon after."

"So that wasn't a beautiful love story after all?" Wondering why he had told her such a dreary tale, Haven began to chew the second raison without waiting to see if the first caused any problems.

"No, I said that was the *official* story. The truth is another matter entirely. I'll be happy to tell you, but only if you'll trust me with the truth of what happened between you and Blake Ellis."

Appalled that he would want to strike such a

251

despicable bargain, Haven started to rise, but Ian reached out to pull her back down beside him. "Don't you think I've earned that much?" he asked. "It's plain the pain is still eating away at you. Regardless of what happened, I won't think any less of you."

Haven shook her head sadly. "You don't understand," she replied sadly. "I'm the one I can't forgive, not Blake."

Ian had expected some dark tale of betrayal, or even abuse, and he didn't understand how Haven could possibly blame herself for the breakup of her marriage. "We all make mistakes, Haven. But you're right: Sometimes we're a lot harder on ourselves than we are on others. I've uncovered more than my share of shameful secrets in my work, and I can promise you now that nothing you could have done will shock me. It's obviously upsetting you, though. Let's put a stop to it. Secrets lose their power once they're told."

Haven could see the sweetness of Ian's expression clearly through her tears. Aren had begged her to get therapy, but she had seen no point in sharing her mistake with some kindly person who was paid to nod and smile sympathetically. That wouldn't have restored her loss. But now, as she gazed into Ian's beautiful amber eyes, she realized that the secret formed an impenetrable barrier between them. She would risk whatever they might have if she told him, but not telling him might cost her far more. He had promised his opinion of her would not change, but if she saw even a glimmer of disgust in his gaze, she wouldn't care if she did not survive the maze.

Chapter Thirteen

Haven was quiet for a long moment as she tried to find the best place to begin the story that up until then only Blake and her parents had known. She had kept it locked in her heart for too many years to access it easily, and she frowned with the effort to make herself understood. She couldn't look at Ian and instead focused her attention on the swirling design of the mosaic floor.

"I'd been with the Flames a year when Blake was hired as lead trainer. You've seen him; he was just as handsome then as he is now, and I was thrilled by how often he singled me out for special attention. Growing up at Kate Jandy's, I'd had boyfriends, but that's all they had been—boys— and Blake was a very attractive man. Rocketball kept us together constantly, and when he asked to see me one night, I honestly believed he wanted to talk about our next game. I was wearing gym clothes when he came to my room, and he was dressed to take me to dinner.

"It was probably the single most embarrassing event of my life. Blake saw it too. Rather than laugh or tease me, he acted as though the misunderstanding was entirely his fault, apologized, and gave me time to dress properly. Off duty he proved to be even more charming than he had been as a trainer. After our first date he began giving me presents, little things like a piece of music or a colorful poster for my room. He was never extravagant, but his gifts were thoughtful and served as constant proof of how much I meant to him.

"We kept dating, and when after several months he asked me to marry him I didn't need even a minute to consider my decision. I loved him with all my heart, and as soon as the Flames had won the championship, he went home with me to Mars. We were married there. My parents adored Blake, and they believed, as I did, that we'd have the best of lives together.

"That was such a long time ago," Haven remarked pensively. "I don't know how I could have been so naïve."

"You were only nineteen," Ian reminded her, "and no one raised as an athlete is sophisticated outside his particular sport."

Ian was striving to make her confession less painful, and while Haven loved him for it, it was an impossible task. "I should have known," she argued. "The signs were all there, as big as the posters announcing our games. I was too much in love to see the truth, but Blake was focused entirely in the present and avoided all mention of the future. We always had a game to play, or a strategy to devise, and whenever I expressed a desire to make plans for our life together he would promptly distract me."

Haven laughed at herself, but there was no happiness in the sound. "I was very easy to distract then, and for a while the pleasure we shared was enough. Our life as a couple consisted of following the Flames' schedule. We were constantly training, and playing, or moving on to the next round of games. After our brief honeymoon there never seemed to be an opportunity for us to go away together. Because we would have several weeks leisure in the off-season, I convinced myself that we would have plenty of time to map out our future then." Haven sighed sadly.

"Unfortunately, that time never came. The Flames led in the finals, and just before the championship tournament began I found out that I was pregnant. I was absolutely thrilled because to me it meant that we would be a real family, as my parents and I had been. Perhaps I had romanticized the years I'd spent at home with them, but having a real home rather than a succession of sterile rooms in visitors' quarters meant a great deal to me. That's what I had expected of marriage, you see: not merely love, but all that love creates. It was a jolt to discover that Blake had an entirely different view."

Ian now had to agree that Haven had been incredibly naïve to assume a lead trainer would marry one of his team's most promising players in the hope of having a home and family. He knew how her story would end without having to hear another word but, believing she desperately needed to confide in someone, he waited for her to continue on her own.

"The Flames had lost a key player the previous year, and while we had a good chance of winning the championship, it was by no means certain. To me the choice was clear, however: I was pregnant, and I wasn't going to subject myself to the hazards of the game. Rather than accept the wisdom of my decision, Blake acted as though I'd not merely betrayed him but the whole team by making what he described as a purely selfish choice. The entire time I'd known him, he'd never even raised his voice to me, but he was beyond anger then.

"I felt betrayed as well, because for the first time it was abundantly clear that my dreams for our marriage weren't the same as his. Aren Manzari wasn't the team physician then, but Blake asked the woman who was to assure me that I could play without any risk to either my health or the baby's." Haven paused to wipe away her tears.

"To say Blake put pressure on me to play doesn't begin to describe what he did. He was relentless in his insistence, constantly ridiculing my fears for the baby's safety. I knew he was wrong. You know how rough the games can be, and while I wasn't frightened for myself, I didn't want to take any risk with my baby."

Ian's voice was hushed. "But you did?"

Overwhelmed with guilt, Haven nodded. "Even though I knew I shouldn't. Even though I knew Blake was wrong, I gave in and played to please him. The Flames won the championship, and I was still in the locker room when I began to hemorrhage. I was lucky to survive, but the baby didn't. I was devastated, but Blake shrugged it off as though it meant nothing to lose a child. All he could talk about was supervising my training in the off season so that I would be at my peak when the games resumed.

"I lay there in my hospital bed and listened to him discuss my physical condition as though I were a piece of expensive equipment. I finally realized that was all I was to him. He had linked his career to mine with the expectation that I would be the greatest player of all time, and that he would be at my side, directing my every move. He spoke of that goal as though it were a holy quest, but by then he was the last person I wanted in my life.

"I gave him twenty-four hours to file for divorce. He was stunned by my demand, but when he realized I was serious he was gentleman enough to divorce me quietly. He took a job with the Satin Spikes, and whenever we're at the same arena we do our best to avoid each other. Or at least we always have until he approached me here. Seeing him made me terribly sad because I once truly loved him, but I should never have let him influence me to do something I knew was wrong. I lost everything because of that mistake—not merely my respect for him but my respect for myself as well. It was a bitter lesson."

Haven looked smaller somehow, very frightened and alone. Ian moved behind her and pulled her across his lap. Her skin was still slightly sticky, her beautiful hair matted and tangled, but he didn't mind at all. He needed to hold her as much as she needed to be held.

He wouldn't offer another comforting cliché about mistakes, or attempt to distract her with love the way Blake once had. He longed to ease her guilt over her tragic error but didn't know how. He hugged her tightly and wished he were an expert at love rather than the many other skills he had, which were useless when it came to mending a broken heart.

Haven rested her head on Ian's shoulder and closed her eyes. "I don't suppose anyone asks the right questions when they fall in love, but you can't sacrifice yourself, or go against your own instincts to please another person. It's a futile effort really, because it's impossible to love someone else if you come to despise yourself in the process."

Ian leaned down to rub his cheek against hers. "That's why you're alone, isn't it? You've avoided men rather than take the risk of having another love affair end badly."

Haven quickly corrected him. "I lost a great deal more than a casual lover."

"Yes, I understand. You lost your beautiful

dream of what your life was meant to be. That was a terrible tragedy, Haven, but it's even more tragic that you blame yourself when Blake is the one who was at fault. He simply took advantage of your youth and innocence to boost his own career." Disgusted, Ian drew in a deep breath and released it slowly. "I should have killed him when I had the chance."

Shocked by the vehemence of Ian's tone, Haven leaned back to look up at him. The seriousness of his expression left her with no doubt as to his sincerity. The threat glowed in his narrowed gaze. His amber eyes had always fascinated her, but until this moment she had not understood that he was fully capable of carrying out dangerous deeds.

"You've killed people, haven't you?" she whispered anxiously.

Too late Ian realized he should have kept his thoughts about Blake to himself. He forced a smile and brushed Haven's lips with a fleeting kiss. "Let's just say that upon occasion I've had the opportunity to rid the galaxy of some of its worst influences. I don't kill for sport."

"How does Control refer to you?" Haven asked. "As an assassin, or an executioner?"

"Neither." Ian had wanted to make her feel better and was disappointed that he had only succeeded in frightening her. She deserved so much more. At the moment, though, he had damn little to offer her. "Do you feel well enough to go on?" he asked.

Haven pushed herself up out of Ian's arms and

smoothed his tunic down over her hips. The fabric was wrinkle-free for the lifetime of the garment, but she felt far from fresh. "Yes, let's keep looking as long as we can. The path of the maze is uncomfortably lifelike, isn't it, with nothing but twists and turns. Still, staying here wouldn't achieve anything."

Stiff again after sitting on stone, Ian had to work to conceal his body's lingering awkwardness but managed to rise in a lazy stretch rather than an ungainly hobble. "I don't know," he replied. "I think each time we've stopped we've learned something valuable about each other."

Haven feared she had revealed too much. "Yes, but was it anything we wanted to know?"

Ian rested his hands lightly on Haven's shoulders. "Part of getting to know someone is accepting the weaknesses as well as the strengths in her personality. We can't simply focus on the admirable qualities and ignore anything that doesn't please us, or we'll have a very narrow view of each other. You may have thought I was a magnificent Artic Warrior, but if what I do now erodes that memory, you'll cheat us both of something worthwhile."

That Ian was more concerned about what she thought of him than he was about the mess she had allowed Blake Ellis to make of her life cheered Haven immeasurably. She still ached with regret, but it was bearable as long as Ian did not compound it with scorn. "I'm sorry," she offered hurriedly. "I shouldn't have sounded so critical, but please, don't confront Blake again. I shut him out of my life seven years ago, and I don't want you letting him back in."

"Is that what you think I'm doing?"

"Not intentionally, perhaps, but I don't want to give him the power of a single thought. If you're baiting him—well, he'll be impossible to avoid."

"I understand."

He took her hand and surveyed the four arched doorways leading from the chamber. "I neglected to bring along any of the squares. Shall we leave a raisin in front of the door we choose?"

"No, you'd better save them. Besides, if this place is moving whenever we look the other way, it won't matter which doors we mark."

"Excellent point." Ian gestured broadly. "Pick a door."

Convinced it did not matter which way they went, Haven led him toward the one opposite where they stood. As they entered the passageway, she shivered slightly. "Is there a draft in here?" she asked.

Ian drew to a halt, then went back a few steps. The variation in temperature from the chamber was slight, and even without a shirt he would have missed it had Haven not commented, but now that she had, he was elated. "It's more of a whisper than a draft, but yes, it is cooler in here, which means we must be close enough to one of the tunnels to feel the cool air seeping in. I told you we'd have to be careful not to miss a valuable clue, and this may be exactly what we've been searching for."

Ian dropped Haven's hand and felt along the

seams between the stones lining the hallway, but he failed to find the leak. Not discouraged, he led the way as they continued their search. The corridor extended a long way before it intersected with another. They paused at the crossing, closed their eyes, and waited until they again felt a breath of cool air caress their cheeks.

"The left?" Ian asked.

Haven agreed. They had not walked far before the corridor began to curve upward in a tight spiral. When they reached the end they found a small circular room with a central column that extended all the way to the domed ceiling. Frustrated to come upon another dead end, Haven was about to let out an anguished shriek when she noticed that there was a stone missing where the wall began to curve up into the dome. She grabbed Ian's arm to point it out, but he was already studying the gap.

"Do you suppose that's another of those blasted blank windows?" she asked.

"It could be," Ian agreed, "but then again, it could be a way to get out and travel over the top of the maze." He scanned the small room, searching for a means to climb to the opening, but there wasn't a hand or foothold in sight. He leaned against the wall and attempted to brace his feet against the column, but the distance was too great for him to get the proper leverage to scoot his way up the wall.

"Ordinarily," he assured Haven, "I can outclimb a spider, but this room appears to have been designed specifically to defeat such an attempt."

Haven swept Ian with a quick glance and then looked up. "Let me try balancing on your shoulders again. The gap's higher than the window, but I think I can reach it."

As Ian judged it, she was going to come up several inches short, but he did not want to discourage her by declaring the effort impossible. "It might work," he offered. "Do you feel strong enough to try?"

"Yes, if you promise not to drop me this time."

Ian laughed at the memory. "I didn't drop you; you landed in my arms."

"You know what I mean." Haven walked around the column, certain there had to be a way to use it if they could just think how. It had too great a girth to climb like a pole, and it was too far from the wall to use as a brace, but still, she felt it had to be useful somehow. "Is this just a tease, or are we missing something here?"

"I don't know what."

Certain Ian knew far more than she did, Haven gave up on the column and motioned for him to clasp his hands. She put her foot into the impromptu step and, rather than his hair, used the column and wall for support as she pulled herself up to his shoulders. He wavered slightly but held his position as she reached toward the opening.

"Come this way a bit," she coaxed.

Ian inched toward the wall. "Is this better?"

Haven trusted him to hold her, but as she stretched up, her fingertips barely brushed the ledge. "I can feel the cool air," she cried.

"Great. Can you reach it?"

Haven debated for a moment. "I can if I jump," she observed cautiously. "Let go of my ankles."

Ian wasn't even tempted to release her. "That's too dangerous. Come on back down."

Haven felt along the stone for a crack she might grasp that had not been visible from the floor, but there was none. She reached out for the column but couldn't get a hold on it either. "Do you think you could jump?"

"With you standing on my shoulders?"

"Yes. Can you do it?"

Ian did not even want to try. "Haven," he coaxed as calmly as he could, "come back down."

Haven was too close to a real discovery to give up now. "Coward. Let's go on the count of three. All I need is a little lift. Give it to me."

Stymied for a moment, Ian swiftly came up with a better idea. "Rather than try to jump, I'll give you a push. I should be able to lift you the last couple of inches."

Haven did not doubt that Ian usually possessed sufficient strength for the trick, but with only dried fruit for energy it seemed unlikely now. Of course, what did they have to lose? she asked herself. She closed her eyes briefly and when she opened them she had the same clear focus she maintained during a game.

"All right, let's try it," she called out. "One, two, three!"

Haven lunged for the opening as Ian straightened out his arms to raise her upward. Her fingernails scraped the sill, but for a terrifying instant she feared she wasn't going to make it. She yanked a foot free of his grasp and kicked out toward the column. When her toes hit hard she pushed with her last bit of strength. Rather than a solid cube, the stone below the opening was only six inches deep, and when she caught hold she was able to hang on and pull herself up into the gap.

Haven's head and shoulders disappeared into the opening. "Well," Ian yelled, "is it another blank wall?"

Mesmerized by the sight that greeted her, Haven stared out over the top of the maze. Each winding curve, dome, and arch was visible, along with miles of interlocking tunnels. It was a magnificent feat of engineering, completely surrounded by a ring of fire that shot plumes of flame against the cavern roof. There was none of the snap and crackle that she associated with fire, nor was there any heat, but the fire raged with an intensity that rivaled the sun's in beauty.

"Haven!" Ian shouted, growing annoyed. "What can you see?"

Haven craned her neck to look as far to the right and left as she could, but everywhere her view was blocked by the encircling blaze. She dangled there in the high window, desperately searching for the words to describe what she had found, and at the same time fighting not to lose all hope of escape. Finally she called over her shoulder, "Are you ready to catch me?"

Provoked that she had failed to describe the view, several sarcastic replies came to mind, but

Ian forced himself to remain cool. "That's what I'm here for." He watched her scoot back out of the window and lower herself down the wall until she was dangling from the ledge. "You're doing a fine imitation of a spider yourself," he encouraged. "Let go. I'll catch you."

Exhausted by the ordeal, Haven dropped into Ian's arms and didn't even care that his tunic was bunched up around her waist. She clung to him even after he put her down. "There is no way out of the maze," she blurted out. "Even if we were able to find a place where we could both get out to walk over the top, the way's blocked by a wall of flame. The whole cavern's on fire. There's no way to escape."

Ian did not doubt the sincerity of Haven's fervent account, but he stubbornly refused to accept it. He gripped her arms tightly and spoke in a low, controlled tone. "If there were no way out, then we couldn't have gotten in. Let's keep on looking for another break in the walls. There has to be a place where I can get through too."

"Not if the maze is capable of shifting there doesn't." Haven fought back her tears. "Maybe there's an entrance the miners use, but if it seals itself shut while they're inside, they're lost. Could that be what's happened to the missing men? Is that what's happening to us? Were we brought in through a doorway that no longer exists?"

"That's a plausible explanation, I suppose, but not one I intend to accept. We've been searching for a corridor that would lead us out, but let's shift our focus to finding another opening where we can crawl out over the top of the maze."

"But what about the fire?"

"Let's deal with that problem when we come to it," Ian said. "For the present our goal is simply to find a place where the walls are open to the cavern roof as they were in the first chamber. Then we'll find a way to climb out."

Ian made it sound so easy, but Haven's arms were scraped and sore from her effort to scale the wall, and her knees were skinned as well. As if that discomfort wasn't bad enough, she felt the small room closing in around them and shuddered. "Let's get out of here." She brushed by Ian and when they came to the intersection where they had paused earlier, she went straight rather than turn back to the chamber with the mosaic floor.

Ian feared Haven was again nearing hysteria, but giving her the opportunity to run off her excess energy, he kept up with her rather than call her back. They were sprinting along the corridors now, dodging right and then left as they entered another section crisscrossed with interlocking passageways. Ian scanned the walls, seeking any break, no matter how small, but none appeared before Haven sank down in an archway to rest. He slid down beside her, and reached into his pocket for some raisins.

Haven accepted the one Ian offered, but rather than eat it quickly she rolled it around her mouth and sucked on it for a long while. Thoroughly depressed, she didn't feel up to talking, but when she turned to Ian she wondered aloud why he still looked so good. "I've lost track of how long we've been down here, but don't you have to shave occasionally?"

Ian rubbed his hand across his cheek and chin and still felt no trace of stubble. "My beard grows as fast as any other man's—or at least it did until we ended up in here. Even with no way to keep track of day or night, I feel certain we've been down here a couple of days at least. Perhaps time moves more slowly in the maze, and we haven't been inside long at all."

Haven leaned back against the wall and closed her eyes. They had encountered so many dead-ends that the corridors they had explored were all a blur to her now, but she did remember the fountain, and the cabinet with its strange supplies. She was positive they had slept several hours, if not all night, after they had finally sated their desperate hunger for each other. It was disorienting not to be able to judge the time accurately.

"How can time move more slowly down here?" she asked. "It passed at the usual rate in the mining colony."

"Yes, it did. But as we've learned, nothing makes any sense here. Except for you and me, of course. We make a lot of sense." Ian laced his fingers in Haven's and squeezed tightly. "I just wish we weren't so damn sticky."

Haven laughed in spite of her best attempt not to. "That's not really the major issue here, is it?"

"No, but it's annoying." Ian's hair felt as stiff as a helmet, but he did not voice that complaint when Haven's resembled badly tangled vines. "We've got to stop feeling sorry for ourselves," he warned. He rose and gave Haven a hand up. "Let's find another courtyard where we can spend the night . . . if it is night."

Haven nodded, but her step was slower now as she trailed him. The path soon broke off at sharp angles, splintering into a dozen narrow lanes, but she balked at having to turn sideways to squeeze through another passageway. "Wait," she begged. "Let's go back and take another turn."

Haven's fright was etched so clearly in her expression that Ian couldn't mistake her mood, but he believed retreating now would be a mistake. "Wait here," he said. "I'll check what's up ahead first. One of these corridors might prove promising."

"Don't go far," Haven cried.

In an effort to bolster her courage, Ian kissed her soundly, but her lips trembled beneath his and he knew he had failed. He added a warm hug. "I'll just take a few steps down each passage, and if it remains too narrow for you to be comfortable, I'll come right back. If it turns into something promising, I'll come back to get you."

Haven had a good reason to reject his plan as unwise. "I know we've not actually seen the maze shift, but the fountain did disappear, and that's enough for me. I don't want you to be swallowed up while I'm left standing here alone."

"Swallowed up?" T. L. Rainey had used those exact words, and Ian was beginning to wonder if the young man had not known a great deal more than it had first appeared. "I'm sure the maze would promptly spit me out. Now stop being so melodramatic and start counting. I'll be back before you can reach five."

Not wanting to be a burden, Haven ceased to argue and began to count very slowly. As promised, Ian reappeared before she reached four. He ducked into the second tunnel and was out again by three. By the time he entered the third she had relaxed somewhat, but she continued to count the seconds he was out of sight. When she got to six she called his name, but there was no respose.

"Ian!" she shouted, but again there was no answer. This opening was as narrow as the others, but Haven inched toward it. "Ian!" she screamed, but it was her own voice that echoed all around her. What if the path had made a sharp drop and he had failed to see it in time to avert a fall? Her own fears dissolved in concern for him, and she rushed into the passageway where he had disappeared.

"Please," she prayed softly, "don't let anything happen to Ian." She crept along, stretching out her foot to make certain the path was still there before she took the next step. The corridor was blessedly short, and when it opened out into an octagonal chamber she found Ian bending down, studying the seam between two stones in the far wall.

"Thank goodness you're all right," she cried. "I was terrified you'd fallen."

Ian straightened up slowly, but he was more puzzled than pleased by her comment. "Why didn't you wait for me?" he asked. "I would have returned as quickly as I did from the other two tunnels."

Haven put her hands on her hips. "Well, you may have intended to, but you didn't. When you didn't answer my calls I was too worried to stay behind."

"Why didn't you count to keep yourself occupied?"

"I did! Oh, look, let's not argue. Let's just stay together. Did you find something?"

"I'm not sure yet." Ian motioned for her to follow him to the wall. "Can you feel the cool air seeping in here?"

Haven knelt beside him and instantly felt a draft brush her cheek. "Is this stone loose enough to push out of our way?"

Ian gave it a shove, and while he wasn't certain, he thought the stone had given way slightly. "Help me," he said. He waited for Haven to move into position next to him and then they both exerted pressure on the stone. They heard a dry, scraping noise and, encouraged, shoved again. When they paused to gauge the position of the stone it had moved perhaps half an inch.

Ian looked up at the low ceiling. "This might take a while, but if we can push this stone out into the open space between the walls, we can climb up on it and pull ourselves up to the top of the maze."

Haven was also studying the stones overhead. "If the rest of the stones in the wall remain in place, that just might work, but if they don't, and the ceiling caves in on us, there won't be much left for Control to find."

Ian had already thought of that. "It's your call," he offered. "Help will come eventually, but this might very well be our only chance to get out on our own."

Haven remembered the high wall of fire. Ian had not seen it, but if he had he might become as discouraged as she. Or he might find a way to defeat it as he had all the other obstacles that they had encountered thus far. She tried to smile. "I've no other plans for the evening. Let's do it."

That was the Haven Wray Ian loved and, after kissing her again, he leaned against the stone. This was either going to be the escape of the century or utter disaster, and he hoped for both their sakes they weren't about to be buried alive.

Chapter Fourteen

When Ian nodded Haven joined him and pushed against the loose stone with all her might. All she felt was a faint tremble. Discouraged, she sat back. "I need to rest a minute," she begged. She closed her eyes to shut out the smallness of the chamber, but its tomblike dimensions remained oppressively vivid in her mind's eye, and it was a chore to simply breathe in and out without gasping.

Ian cast a nervous glance toward the dome. Without mortar to filter down on them in a fine mist, it was impossible to tell if they had jarred the stones overhead and put themselves at risk. From what he had seen throughout the maze, the stones were wedged into place so tightly that the loss of one on the bottom row would not endanger the chamber. Then again, if the maze could shift, then the stones had to be less securely placed than they appeared.

"I'm sorry," he said. "This is too much for you, isn't it? Why don't you wait outside? I'll call you as soon as I break through."

Ashamed not to be of more help, Haven straightened up. "No, absolutely not," she insisted. "I'm staying with you."

The wild gleam in her eyes warned Ian not to order her to go, and after a moment's reflection he knew he could not have sent her away had he tried. He slipped his arm around her shoulders to draw her close and kissed her very gently, then with an almost painful need. Rather than return his ardor as he had expected, she drew away with a shy, averted glance.

"There have been so many times when I've wished that I knew what to say to you," Ian murmured. "The words just don't come to me easily, but—" He watched Haven's gaze grow more troubled rather than hopeful and knew he had again failed to reach her. He had never given any of the women with whom he had had brief romantic liaisons the promises he longed to make to Haven. Now, without ever having had any practice, he did not know how to speak what was truly in his heart.

"I will get us out of here," he assured her again. "Don't lose heart."

"I haven't lost my faith in you," Haven replied. "You needn't worry that I will. I just wish I were stronger. All my training has been to increase my endurance and speed, but it doesn't take nearly as much strength to hurl a Rocketball against the wall as we need to move this blasted stone."

"I can do it on my own," Ian teased. "I just didn't want you to get bored."

"There's little danger of that." Haven leaned toward the stone and Ian moved back into place beside her. She focused her attention on his hands, and this time when they began to shove the stone scraped against those surrounding it and moved forward almost two inches. Astonished, Haven let out a small cry of triumph.

Ian winked at her. "Let's not stop to celebrate just yet." He gave Haven a minute to catch her breath, but when their next push proved to be even more successful, Ian was the one to let out the wild whoop. They still had more than a foot to go, but he was confident they could do it now.

"I sure hope on the last push this stone doesn't just topple into an abyss, or I'm going to be real angry."

"I hadn't even thought of that," Haven moaned. "If it does, we'll have to dismantle the whole damn wall to build a set of steps to get out." She looked up and cursed softly. "Without getting crushed beneath the dome when it collapses. Ready?"

They made another combined effort, and with a coarse grating the stone slid back several more inches. Now deeply recessed in the wall, it was more difficult to reach, and Ian took over. He sat back, braced his hands against the floor, placed his feet against the stone, and used the powerful muscles in his legs to dislodge it further. "We're almost there," he exclaimed, but it took several more forceful thrusts to shove the stone all the way through to the other side.

Haven bent down to observe. "It didn't fall!" she exclaimed. "It's resting on a ledge, or an interior corridor wide enough for us to use." She got out of Ian's way and, elated by their success, he gave the stone a final shove to push it back far enough for them to scramble through the opening.

"I'm going first," Ian announced in a voice that brooked no argument. "Give me a minute to make plenty of room for you to follow. Then as soon as I get my bearings I'll call for you."

They had been trying to escape the maze for so long, Haven could not believe the moment had actually arrived, but they would still have to face the fire. She nodded, but as soon as Ian disappeared through the opening they had created she began to shake. She trusted him not to abandon her, but she did not trust the maze not to separate them. She knelt by the hole and could see the flames' flickering light reflected on the stone they had removed but, unable to see Ian, she panicked.

She hated being so weak and choked back her tears. "Hurry up," she urged. She could understand the need to reconnoiter, but leaving her behind for so long was simply cruel. She got down on the floor intending to follow Ian to the other side, but the opening suddenly seemed very small. She had watched Ian crawl through. His shoulders were wider than hers; if he had made it easily she knew she should be able to also, but logical arguments didn't ease her fears.

Not only did the opening appear too small, the tunnel looked far longer than the length of one stone. How was she ever going to crawl through it when every inch would be the most agonizing of tortures? She rocked back on her heels and locked her arms around her knees. Why was everything so terribly difficult for them? She knew, of course. She had let herself care for Ian, and they had both been severely punished as a result.

She did not want to believe love always led to the painful anguish she felt now, but that was all she knew. Lost in sad memories, she didn't hear Ian call her name until he repeated it for the third time. She leaned forward and peered through the opening in the wall. "Yes?"

Ian laughed in spite of himself. "What are you waiting for? Come on."

Haven swallowed hard. Hoping her aversion to the small chamber might give her an incentive to move, she glanced over her shoulder, but the sickening dread that churned through her stomach kept her rooted in place. Even knowing how stupid it was to be afraid, she couldn't make herself crawl through to Ian.

"I can't do it," she cried. "I'll get stuck."

Ian doubted he had heard her correctly. "Haven, you can't possibly get wedged in there. Close your eyes if you have to, but get yourself over here."

Haven remained poised at the opening, her

heart thumping in her ears. The ominous rhythm compounded her fright, and while she could hear Ian coaxing her to come to him, she just couldn't do it. Certain he must regard her fear to enter the tunnel childish, if not a great deal worse, she hated herself for disappointing him.

Ian was well aware that Haven suffered from claustrophobia, but that she should be unable to crawl through the wall completely amazed him. He soon realized a string of comforting words was having absolutely no effect and scooted back into the chamber. Haven flinched slightly as he crawled out beside her, and he was sorry she was afraid of him as well as the small tunnel.

He took her hand and brought it to his lips. "Let's try another approach," he offered without a hint of scolding. "I want you to turn around and wiggle through the tunnel backwards. Just watch me until you make it to the other side. You'll move out into a wide corridor where there's no danger of any kind."

"I'm so sorry," Haven mumbled. "What must you think of me?"

"I think you're the bravest woman I've ever known," Ian assured her truthfully. He gave her a quick hug and then coached her with gentle praise to move her into place. "I'll come right behind you, so you won't be alone out there for more than a couple of seconds."

Haven had hated each of their brief separations, but the challenge of crawling through the small, dark opening in the wall absolutely mortified her. She focused her attention on the hope lighting Ian's eyes, but just getting her feet and legs into the hole made her shake with dread. His tunic bunched up around her waist, and she had to yank it back down before she could crawl. The stone flooring was warm but rough, and with her knees already skinned, it hurt to travel on her stomach.

"You're doing fine," Ian assured her. He remembered the earthquakes that had rocked them before and prayed one wouldn't rumble through now, while Haven was so vulnerable. "Your feet are already on the other side. Can you feel the cool air against your skin?"

Haven nodded and gave another tentative push. She had to draw her arms into the hole now and scraped her left elbow against the stone. She bit her lip rather than cry out, but it hurt. Ian was smiling confidently. He believed in her, or at least he was projecting a convincing sense of trust, but her wretched insecurity didn't lift. She closed her eyes as she ducked her head and, seeking a memory to provide focus, concentrated on the passion they had shared, but the images had faded into a dreamy haze. Angered that something precious had been lost, she crept through the wall without again falling victim to her claustrophobia.

The instant she pushed free, she opened her eyes and scrambled to her feet. She had to lean back against the outside of the chamber to maintain her balance, but by the time Ian joined her she could manage a smile. She was still badly embarrassed, but he smothered her apologies with tender kisses.

"It was a small problem, Haven. Let's not dwell on it." He pointed to the wall facing them. Perhaps six feet in height, it posed little in the way of a barrier to the determined pair.

"We're in the space between corridors. I moved the loose stone so that it makes a convenient step. I'll climb to the top of the corridor and pull you up beside me. From there we should have as good a view of the maze as you had from that narrow window."

"We were looking for a place to spend the night," Haven reminded him. "I hope there's room up there to stretch out."

Too excited to rest, Ian stepped up on the stone. From there he grabbed hold of the edge of the corridor, swung a leg up, and pulled himself up on top. He didn't pause to look around before leaning down to give Haven a hand. She was tired but made the climb with only a minimal amount of help from him. Arm in arm, they stood to look out over the maze.

The domes were brightly lit by the flames' reflected light and caught their notice first, but gradually they widened their focus to sweep the twisting, turning passageways that had confounded them with an abundance of dead ends. There were sharp angles and wide, lazy coils, but even from this view of the baffling structure there was no clear path that led to the way out. Haven sighed softly and waited for Ian to comment on the flames.

Haven had warned him that they were completely surrounded by fire, but Ian had hoped she had missed sighting a bridge or stone staircase that would allow them to break through the flames unharmed. He could not see anything promising, however, and tightened his hold on her. "The fires must be fed by natural gas seeping up into the cavern. Let's see if we can't find a place where we can climb high enough to leap over them."

Haven admired Ian's enthusiasm, but she was too tired to search for anything other than a place to rest. "We're going to have to stop," she said. "We haven't eaten much, and I feel as though I've been awake for days."

Ian knew better than to push Haven again, and he sat down right where he stood. "This is as good a place to rest as any." He slipped his hand into his pocket and withdrew a couple of strips of jerky. "Would you like to try this instead of the raisins?"

Haven knelt beside him, and while she did not want either item he offered, she did not blame him for the scarcity of their rations. She took the jerky and broke off a tiny bite. "Do you think we can sleep up here without rolling off?"

"I certainly hope so. Do you frequently fall out of bed?"

"No, never."

"Then you'll sense the edge here as well." Ian chewed the jerky and watched as a sudden bright burst of fire shot toward the roof of the cavern. "You'd think whoever built the maze would have

281

been satisfied without a blazing moat."

"Apparently not. The only fires I've ever seen were built in fireplaces for romantic atmosphere. That obviously wasn't the purpose here."

"No, indeed. This fire's meant to contain anyone clever enough to escape the maze, but we'll find a way to beat it as well. Just being outside where we can see the whole cavern has given me new hope."

"You've always sounded so confident, I didn't realize you'd harbored any doubts."

Ian shrugged. "I didn't, but it's good finally to have made some progress toward getting out of here. Do you want to try and sleep? You can use my leg again for a pillow."

Haven finished the last bite of her jerky, then snuggled down beside him. She had never considered herself weak, but she couldn't keep up with Ian. Her feet hurt from walking on the stones, and she was scraped from her climb. "It is better to be out here," she agreed through a wide yawn. "At least we can breathe more easily, and there's no danger of being crushed in a cave-in."

Ian rubbed her back in a slow circle. She had been slender, but now he could feel her backbone through his tunic. He grew worried that dried fruit wasn't going to be nearly enough to keep her alive. "Go to sleep," he coaxed gently, and while she replied with a distracted murmur, in another minute she was sleeping soundly. For a long while Ian was content to study the flames, but he soon discovered they had no pattern. He eased

Haven's cheek from his thigh and rose slowly.

He waited until he was certain she would remain asleep and then started off toward the flames. He turned back frequently to keep Haven in sight but leapt across the space between corridors to shift direction whenever he could find a shortcut. The maze spread out around him with a taunting complexity, and while he had thought they had broken out close to the ring of fire, he soon discovered the blaze was too far away for him to risk traveling the distance alone.

Disappointed, he started back toward Haven, but he had just begun to retrace his path when she disappeared from view. He was positive he had not strayed in the wrong direction, but suddenly there was a dome obscuring his view. Unwilling to allow Haven to wake alone when he knew how badly she would be frightened, he hurried on, swinging first to the left and then to the right, but even after lengthening his stride he couldn't seem to travel past the dome.

The fear that the maze might be shifting even as he ran across the top propelled him along at an even faster pace until he was confronted with a gap that was much too wide to leap even at a run. He stopped and rested his hands on his knees while he caught his breath, but he now knew leaving Haven had been the worst mistake he could have made.

He could wait for her to wake; he knew she would immediately start yelling for him and he could locate her by sound if not sight, but that wouldn't spare her the initial fright of being alone. Quickly rejecting the idea, he retraced his steps and attempted to circle the dome from the other side. He ran across the zigzagging corridors, leaping the breaks to follow the most direct route, but he got no closer to the dome than he had in his previous attempt.

He approached it next at a walk. Each of his steps was taken with deliberate care to bring him past the dome in a few minutes' time, but again his efforts came to naught. It did not matter if he ran or walked; he could not reach the dome. Now positive that Haven lay sleeping just beyond the enigmatic structure, he knelt down to plan his next move. He could thank his father for the early training that enabled him to keep a cool head regardless of how dire the situation. That asset had served him well on arctic quests, and he drew upon it now.

He had continually offered Haven reassurances that he would see them safely out of the maze, and he had every intention of keeping that promise. He would have nothing to celebrate, however, if Haven were so traumatized by the ordeal that she bid him good-bye the instant they escaped. He had sincerely believed he might find something important if he searched on his own, but he had not considered how actively the maze would work to thwart him. Perhaps it could actually feel him running along its back, the stones laughing as they continually blocked his path.

When Control had first described this mission Ian had known it was not one he wanted to undertake. Haven Wray had been the only intriguing element, but she should never have been subjected to this danger. Now he wondered how he was going to explain her involvement to Control.

Control forbade agents of either sex to indulge in romantic entanglements while actively engaged in missions. Ian had never argued the wisdom of the policy because he believed Control was absolutely right, but somehow Haven had been impossible to resist. She was an extraordinary woman, and he could not have avoided her even if Control had been sharing his room on 317.

What Control understood was success. He provided his agents with sufficient freedom to accomplish their assignments without any tedious procedural constraints. In fact, he was often willing to overlook just how his agents' objectives were met. In this case, however, Ian was without a clue, except for an unusual tattoo that might have nothing to do with the case, and he was going to be hard pressed to convince Control that he had handled his assignment with his usual skill.

Then again, he really didn't give a damn what Control thought. Right now his only concern was finding Haven.

Ian glanced up from his musings with a gasp. To his utter amazement the maze stretched out before him in a familiar honeycomb pattern and, not twenty feet away, Haven lay sleeping as soundly as when he had left her. He turned, searching for the dome that had confounded his every move, but it had disappeared as silently as it had arisen. Not wanting to push his luck, he hurried toward Haven and reached her in half a dozen flying steps.

He stretched out beside her and slipped his arm under her neck to cushion her head on his shoulder. She murmured his name and cuddled close. He wanted her very badly, but let her sleep for now. When he closed his eyes he still saw the flames that surrounded them and found it impossible to rest. He relaxed his body, but his mind continued to churn.

He felt a rolling tremor surge beneath them, but Haven lay undisturbed in his arms. He envied her. Except for the cookies that had left them in a drug-induced sleep, he had slept only fitfully since arriving in the maze. He had pushed himself to complete other assignments but never without the expectation of soon having a chance to rest. Here nothing was certain, and the longer he went without sleep, the more likely it was that he would be exhausted just when he needed to be at his best.

He slid his hand over Haven's bare hip, but the smoothness of her skin wasn't in the least bit soothing. Instead, touching her had merely increased his need for more. She was warm and soft and alluring as she slumbered in his embrace, but he ached for another taste of the joy they had already shared. He fought to distract himself, but Haven's tug on his emotions had become too strong to be denied.

He shifted his position gradually so as not to jar her awake, but when he could no longer delay kissing her, he traced the outline of her slightly parted lips with the tip of his tongue to entice her from her dreams. She sighed and nestled against him but didn't open her eyes, so he tried again, this time nibbling her lower lip playfully. "Haven," he whispered, desire deepening his voice.

Charmed by Ian's gentle teasing, Haven opened her eyes and arched her back to rub against him, but when he spread her legs with his knee she knew he was past the point of leisurely affection. She raised her arms to encircle his neck and lured his mouth to hers for a kiss she deepened as he entered her with a single, diving thrust. She felt him shudder as he surged even deeper, and wrapped her legs around his thighs to hold him tight.

Even without the magical cookies, his passion inflamed hers, and she writhed beneath him to intensify her own pleasure as well as his. He raised up slightly, and as he looked down at her, the dancing flames that lit the cavern were reflected in his amber eyes. For an instant he seemed to burn just as brightly, but she saw a god rather than a demon, and ran her fingernails up his ribs in a stirring caress that brought him back down into her arms.

In control of his body, if not his desires, Ian knew precisely when to stroke and when to hold still to savor Haven's inner heat. Pacing himself to carry her higher and higher, he prolonged his own release until she had found hers in a shimmering climax that gripped him with deep, joyous tremors. He bore down a final time to ride the waves of her rapture as he chased his own; then, as before, he couldn't bear to let her go.

Perfectly relaxed, Haven wished Ian had given her time to discard his tunic so that she could feel his bare chest against her breasts. She could remember wishing for that in what now seemed like another lifetime. She felt his eyelashes brush her shoulder and knew he wasn't asleep.

"When I had your photographs taped up in my locker, I used to dream of being with you like this. Certainly not here, but exactly like this. When you hold me this close I can't tell where my body ends and yours begins. There are people who live their whole lives without ever experiencing a moment this perfect. I feel so lucky to have shared it with you."

While her words were complimentary, the wistfulness of her tone frightened Ian. He withdrew so that he could again cradle her in his arms. "It doesn't have to end," he promised.

Haven had no such hope, but for now this was enough. "We ought to go on," she mused aloud.

Unwilling to describe just how difficult he had found that to be, Ian sat up and pulled his pants back into place. "I didn't mean to interrupt your nap."

Haven leaned on her elbow. "You can't honestly have expected me to have slept through that."

A grin spread over Ian's lips. "I hope not, but I should have been able to wait until you woke up on your own. I honestly meant to, but—"

Haven reached out to catch his hand. "You

needn't apologize for wanting me, Ian. I want you too badly to ever refuse." She gave his fingers a quick squeeze, then rose and stretched her arms above her head. "Do you really think we can get across the flames?"

"I know we can," Ian assured her, completely without justification. He stood and took her hand. "It may take us a while to find the right place, but we will get across. Can you still feel a breeze? It might lead us to the mine."

Haven looked down over the side of the ledge where they had stopped to rest. A pale beam of light shone through the hole they had made in the wall and illuminated the trench below. "The space between corridors must act as a duct. Let's just follow along beside it toward the flames."

"Good plan," Ian replied, but he had scant hope they would ever reach them. He had sincerely believed the maze would be less confusing once they had broken through to the outside, but thus far that had not proven to be the case. They moved into single file, with him leading the way, and before long he was astonished to find they were actually making progress toward the encircling blaze.

They had to double back when the corridor they had been following ended abruptly, but they found another route that, while curved, took them a long way before they had to jump onto another. Ian kept expecting the maze to grow beneath their feet, stretching the distance they had to cross until it extended into eternity, but after another change of route they reached the edge.

Haven came up beside him, and he held her hand tightly as they looked down into the gorge that held the fire.

The golden flames danced with scarlet plumes and shot silver sparks high into the air. Translucent, the blaze mocked them with a deceptive delicacy, while the depths of the gorge glowed with the intensity of molten lava. The raging fire created its own warm wind that brushed their skin in a silent warning to keep their distance.

"Why is it so quiet?" Haven asked. "If it's burning natural gas, shouldn't there be a hiss or roar as it reaches the surface and ignites?"

Ian shrugged. "I've given up trying to predict what ought to happen here. The cavern wall curves up too sharply to provide us with room to walk along the other side should we cross the flames here. Let's find a better place to jump."

"Aren't we too close to judge?"

Ian stared down at her. "What do you suggest?"

The darkness of his gaze discouraged comment, and Haven chose not to elaborate. "Let's see what we find," she said instead, and she followed Ian as he turned to trace the edge of the maze. He moved out ahead of her, walking with a long, rapid stride, and she had to jog to keep up. She could understand why he was anxious to get over the flames, but each time she glanced toward them she grew less certain it was possible.

They had traveled a long way before Ian finally found a place where the cavern walls receded into darkness behind the fire. He stopped and rested his hands on his hips as he studied the breadth of the gorge they would have to leap. Then he looked back over his shoulder to gauge the length of the corridor where they stood. There was room enough to get a running start, and he hoped that was all they would need.

"I'd go first, but once I'm safely on the other side I won't be able to come back and get you if you find you can't follow me on your own. I won't leave you here, Haven, so we'll have to jump together."

Haven bent down and studied the golden flames. "How wide is the gorge?" she asked.

When they had been in the maze, tricks of perspective had often made the corridors appear longer than they were, and outside Ian had found things were not what they seemed either. Because such an admission would serve no useful purpose, he kept it to himself and knelt beside her. "It might be ten feet, but the ground falls away on the other side, so even if it's farther, it won't be impossible to leap. I've seen you run, and I know you can make it."

"But nothing's certain down here, is it?"

"Just you and me. Let's do it." Ian rose and pulled Haven to her feet. "You'll need a couple of days rest before playing in the finals, so we've no time to waste admiring the fire." He didn't give her a chance to argue before he led the way down the top of the corridor to provide plenty of room for a running start.

Haven swallowed hard. "We make quite a team, don't we?"

Ian had never been a team player, but with Haven none of his old rules applied. "We sure do. Do you want to make a practice run?"

Haven shook her head. "No, let's just go full-out one time. Count to three."

Ian brought her hand to his lips. He was confident he was strong enough to pull her across if she balked at the last second, but he didn't want to have to resort to yanking her across when it would probably dislocate her shoulder and keep her out of the finals. *As if that was his only worry*, he thought to himself. "That beautiful tattoo of yours is going to bring us good luck."

Haven was positive Ian made his own luck, but she smiled bravely and turned toward the flames. She felt none of the paralyzing fear that had kept her from crawling out of the small chamber and easily drew in a deep breath. Ian's voice was calm as he began to count, and when he started to run she raced him toward the edge of the maze. They went barreling off the end with a flying leap and passed through the flames without feeling more than a whisper of heat.

Rather than having to pull Haven across, Ian had had to press to keep up with her. When they hit the ground he reached out to catch her before she tumbled over onto the rocks and kept them both from falling. They had landed on solid rock, and he felt the force of the impact all the way to his hips, but they were out of the maze, and that triumph was glorious. He lifted Haven off her feet and spun her around.

"I told you we'd make it. We should be able to

pick up a trail leading to the mine and be out of here in no time."

Also jolted by the landing, Haven clung to Ian for support, but his optimism was infectious and she was soon dancing in his embrace. "Let's search for another draft. It's sure to lead to the mine."

They were standing on a broad ledge that led away from the maze, and Ian hoped they had already found the way out. "Let's try this path first. Stay behind me."

The trail was lined with crushed rock and, barefoot, Haven had to pick her way gingerly along it, but she knew Ian had to be suffering the same discomfort as she and kept quiet. She had to stop every few steps to brush away the bits of rock that had become embedded in the soles of her feet, but she did not let him get too far ahead of her. The temperature was growing cooler. Elated to think they were close to escape, she tiptoed over the gravel and hoped they did not have much farther to go.

As they moved away from the fire, the shadows covering the path deepened. Uncertain what lay ahead, Ian was forced to remain close to the face of the cavern. He felt a vibration and braced himself for an earthquake. But rather than another small tremor, he heard a roaring blast, and the steeply angled path slipped right out from under him. He yelled Haven's name, made a grab for her, and caught hold as he was slammed into a crevice in the cavern wall.

An avalanche poured by them in a thunderous

rush. Jagged shards of stone slashed Ian's back, but he protected Haven with his body until the air grew so thick with astronium dust, he could no longer breathe. He felt Haven grab for him as his knees buckled, and with his last conscious thought was grateful he had saved her life even if it had cost him his own.

Chapter Fifteen

Choking on the suffocating dust, Haven struggled to drag Ian farther into the protective depths of the crevice. It was so narrow that she had great difficulty hanging on to him, but she didn't suffer even a twinge of claustrophobia. She coughed and wheezed and grew faint from lack of air, but maintained a frantic grip on Ian.

With no interior souce of light, the cleft in the cavern wall was as dark as their hopes for survival, but seeking the safety it offered, Haven dragged Ian as far away from the opening as she could before sinking to her knees. She eased his head into her lap and felt through his hair for a lump, or a gash in his scalp. With no way to treat any injury, her hands trembled badly as she searched, but she was greatly relieved not to find the stickiness of blood.

She placed her hand over his heart and was comforted by the steady beat. She prayed that all he needed was fresh air to breathe. By the time the avalanche had slowed to a mere trickle of pebbles, the mouth of the crevice was nearly blocked by rubble. Desperate for a source of air, Haven gently moved Ian's head aside and crawled forward to begin enlarging the opening.

She tossed out the smaller pieces of rock over the top of the debris and rolled aside those too heavy to lift. The harder she worked, the more dust she dislodged, and she had to stop frequently to let it settle. As soon as she cleared a path large enough to permit them to venture out, she went back to Ian and tried to lift him.

"Can you hear me?" she cried. "We've got to move out into the cavern." When Ian didn't respond she shook him. "Breathe for me, breathe." She didn't want to slap him but was close to resorting to it when he moaned softly. "That's it. Wake up, Ian. I need you."

Ian's whole body protested when he tried to sit up. He fell back but reached out for Haven, lacing her fingers tightly in his. Only a thin beam of light shone into the crevice from outside, but he could see she was safe and tried to smile. Even that hurt. He wiggled his toes, and was relieved to find he wasn't paralyzed, then realized if he were, he would not have to deal with such agonizing pain.

Haven squeezed his hand. "You saved my life by shoving me back in here. If only I had moved a little faster, you wouldn't have been hurt. Do you think you can get up and walk?"

"Just give me a minute to work up to it."

"Oh, Ian, what are we going to do? We were so close to reaching the mine, and now—"

Ian recalled the avalanche with painful clarity. He had felt something—a vibration, a slight tremor—then what he swore was no mere act of nature. "Did you hear an explosive charge before the rockslide hit us?"

Haven did not even want to consider what that implied, but nodded. "Yes. There was something unusual. I want to call it an echo, but that might have been because we were so close to the cavern wall that it reverberated all around us. My initial thought was that we must be near the mine, but as I looked up, I saw a whole wall of rock coming toward us. Had you not reacted so quickly, we would have been buried alive."

Ian felt as though that was precisely what had happened to him. He rolled onto his right side and propped himself on his elbow. If his ribs weren't broken, they were undoubtedly cracked, and it made drawing each breath an exercise in pain. With no extra cloth to bind his chest he would just have to bear it.

"I'm starting to become annoyed," he confided. "It was one thing to drop us into the maze but quite another to start an avalanche. We must have been close to escape; whoever is behind this can't allow that to happen."

Haven found it difficult to believe anyone could be so malicious. "Then we would have been better off waiting for Control to find us.

Would you have been as anxious to escape the maze if I hadn't been here?"

Her hair and skin coated with gray dust, Haven looked even more bedraggled than she had before this latest catastrophe had befallen them, but Ian was confident he had made the best choices for them both. "Yes," he assured her. "I wouldn't have changed a thing. Besides, those wild cookies wouldn't have been nearly as much fun had I been alone."

Haven leaned close to caress his cheek. "Thank you, but what are we going to do now? Could we have set off the avalanche simply by moving toward the mine? Or are we being watched?"

Ian needed a moment to consider her question, then offered his best guess. "Egon has screens mounted on his desk to allow him to monitor the operation of the mine without ever having to leave his office. That means they have equipment to perform relatively sophisticated tracking. I haven't seen any sensors, which means that if they do exist, they must be mounted in the cavern roof, rather than in the maze. If that's the case, the avalanche might have knocked out the ones in this sector."

"Which brings us right back to my original question: What are we going to do?"

"The safest thing might be to stay right where we are, but if anyone comes to make certain we're buried under the avalanche we'd make too easy a target. Help me up, and we'll choose another place to hide."

Haven rose but didn't reach for him. "Wait a

minute. If we stay here, they might come and find us, but if we move, they might track us wherever we go. Is that the choice?"

Ian knew those weren't attractive alternatives and did not try to fool her. "Precisely, but it's never wise to confront an enemy on his own turf. That puts us at a disadvantage regardless of where we are down here, but we can at least be a challenge to locate."

Haven had hoped the avalanche would be the last peril they would have to face. Now she silently berated herself for being so stupidly optimistic. "How would they track us? With body heat?"

"Yes, or movement."

"Then if we stay near the flames, which have both warmth and motion, would we be invisible?"

"I like the way you think," Ian replied. "It's worth a try." Hoping the fires were not too far away, he eased himself up onto his hands and knees. His ribs complained with a renewed burst of pain, but he clamped his teeth together tightly to stifle a cry. His back hurt too, but he was too anxious to move on to allow a few superificial injuries to stop him.

He looked up at Haven. "At least it's too dark in here for you to see how ridiculous I look. Give me a hand and I'm sure I can stand."

"There isn't anything in the least bit ridiculous about you, Ian." Haven took his arm and drew him to his feet. He swayed slightly, and she quickly slid her arm around his waist. "There.

I've got you. If you can't make your way over the rubble easily, I'll clear a wider path."

"I'll make it," Ian swore, but when he had to bend down to crawl out over the loose rock the pain in his back became even more severe. He swallowed hard and hoped he wasn't hurt even worse than he supposed. Internal bleeding would be the most dangerous possibility, but he was stubbornly determined not to pass out again, leaving Haven to fend for herself.

As soon as they left the crevice, there was enough light for Haven to see the long slashes on Ian's back. Tears came to her eyes, but she didn't want to make him feel worse by crying in front of him and blinked them away. She kept her hold on his waist and they picked their way over the rock that spilled across the trail in a broad fan. Slipping and sliding over the treacherous mound, it took them a long while to reach the level ground encircling the ring of fire.

"Let's keep going for as long as we can," Ian suggested, but he was hurting so badly, he could barely remain on his feet.

Haven searched the way in either direction, hoping for some sort of shelter, but found only the rough curve of the cavern wall. Ian was leaning against her, and with his back so torn, she had to take care to keep her arm low around his waist. "Maybe we ought to stay right here," she said. "At least here there is a generous supply of rocks to throw and we'll be able to defend ourselves."

"That all depends on how many laser pistols they have."

"I don't even want to think about lasers." Haven nodded toward the right, and they stumbled on down the path. She kept glancing toward the maze. Even from the outside it was as forbidding as an ancient fortress, and she longed for a change of scene. She looked back over her shoulder to judge how far they had come and decided it wasn't nearly far enough.

"I wonder what day it is?"

Ian responded with a hoarse chuckle. "Exactly what I was thinking."

"You were not," Haven scolded. "I was just wondering if Control has had time to arrive. It would be far easier to survive the next few hours if we knew we were close to being rescued."

"I'm sure we are," Ian stressed, but he kept watching the trail. "Look: The wall curves inward up ahead. It's just a small pocket, but it offers the only protection we've seen."

Haven helped him reach it, then stood back to give him ample room to lower himself to the ground. He had lost his characteristic grace, and she knew each awkward lurch must cost him a fresh burst of pain. Once he was settled in place, he looked up at her and smiled. It was such a small gesture, but an exceedingly brave one. She knelt by his side.

"I can remember from the stories my mother read to me as a child that even a rabbit is smart enough to have a rear exit to his hole. The miners must have another exit here. They might even

301

have half a dozen. If I stay close to the flames, do you think it would be safe for me to search for another way out?"

Ian made his decision quickly. "I want you to listen to me carefully. Sometimes despite the best of intentions an operation goes awry. I won't take you down with me, Haven. I want you to stay far enough away from me that should the miners come back, they won't catch you as well. I'll tell them you died in the avalanche, and the way I look, they're sure to believe me."

The coldly determined glint in Ian's eyes made his plea convincing, but Haven was outraged. She pushed herself to her feet. "You bastard. It looks as though we're a team only when it suits you. Otherwise I'm on my own. Well, I have a different version of loyalty, and I won't desert you. Is that all you expect from me, or any woman?"

Ian didn't understand how she could have twisted his words to come up with such a bizarre conclusion. "No! But I didn't save your life to watch you throw it away in some misguided attempt to protect me."

Haven's glance turned as cold as his. "That's my choice to make, not yours. Now I'm going for a walk. Maybe you'll come to your senses and apologize to me when I get back." Her anger dissolving the soreness in her feet, Haven crossed to the flames with a long, quick stride. She walked as close to the lip of the gorge as she dared, and didn't slow down until she had moved out of Ian's line of sight.

She didn't care how many times Ian begged, ordered, or demanded she leave him—she wouldn't go. She turned toward the flames and studied their leaping dance. She was close enough to reach out and touch them, and in a burst of self-destructive violence, she thrust her hand into the fire. She had meant to jerk it back out, but the flames licked her skin with the gentle warmth of a whispered kiss rather than searing heat.

That the blaze behaved strangely wasn't all that odd, considering where she was, but Haven was still puzzled. She leaned out over the gorge and looked down into the molten core, where the lava bubbled and popped and then trickled over its hardened crust in scarlet rivulets. It was a splendid fire, a thrilling combination of beauty and danger, but as she swung her hand through it a second time, she still felt only a minimal amount of heat. That such a raging blaze would merely tease her senses was deeply perplexing until she remembered how swiftly the corridor to the fountain had changed shape.

Inspired by an idea she couldn't wait to share, Haven hurried back to Ian. He was leaning against the cavern wall propped on his left shoulder, looking even more miserably unhappy than when she had left him. She knelt beside him and raised her hand in a plea for silence. "We know the maze can transform and reconfigure itself, but how does it do it? Can you think of any plausible explanation?"

Ian started to take a deep breath, caught himself, and froze on the edge of pain. He had not expected her to come back so soon but was relieved she was no longer infuriated with him. "It could be controlled by mechanical means. The gears and rails could be hidden underneath, and the walls switched along tracks."

"Sort of like the sets for an elaborate play?"

"Yes. A revolving stage is controlled from below, and scenery can be moved into place by a variety of means." Because she would undoubtedly accuse him of abandoning her, he did not describe the difficulty he had had approaching the flames while she slept. He could not forget the terrible frustration, though. "I see where you're going with this. If we knew how the maze worked, we'd be able to find the way out."

"Exactly. But what if the maze isn't run by mechanical means? What if, like the Dreamer's images, it's an illusion?"

Ian could barely move, but he shook his head sadly. "That avalanche was no illusion. It damn near killed me."

"No, it wasn't, but it occurred in the cavern wall, not in the maze. I just put my hand in the flames, and they're barely warm. I wondered why there wasn't the roar a fire makes, and now I think it's because it's no more real than the Dreamer's beautiful fantasies."

"You just stuck your hand in the fire?" Ian exclaimed in horror. "Why? What were you trying to do? Get back at me?"

Haven reacted immediately to the inherent arrogance of his question. "As difficult as it may be for you to accept, it had nothing to do with you. I was just watching the flames. They possess a near-hypnotic beauty, but despite the appearance of an inferno they generate precious little heat. If the maze is an illusion, perhaps created by brilliant alien minds, it stands to reason that it can be defeated by thought as well."

Ian had read of experiments involving psychotronic machines, but the studies were more often hoaxes than true scientific investigations. There were people who could move objects with their minds alone, but damn few of them, and no one had been able to harness their unusual ability as a reliable power source. "Brilliant alien minds?" he repeated numbly.

"Perhaps that's giving them too much credit," Haven explained. "Maybe the creatures who built the maze were of merely average intelligence, but they knew how to construct a maze that would endure, and could be adapted to defeat any challenge. Do you feel well enough to try concentrating with me?"

"No, but I'll give it a try." Ian reached for her hands. "Touching might boost whatever power we have."

Haven doubted he was taking her seriously, but she'd not be stopped by whatever misgivings he might hold. She moved closer so he would not have to stretch and gripped his hands tightly. "Let's focus on the flames. They haven't the solidity of stone and ought to be easier to affect."

"The flames," Ian repeated. He closed his eyes and let his mind fill with bright, dancing flashes of color. They dipped and leapt around the ring, confined to the gorge, and yet free to soar into the air. It was a pleasant vision, but he soon realized he had no real idea what it was they were trying to accomplish. He opened his eyes and found Haven still deep in thought. Despite her disheveled appearance he found her enchanting. He looked past her toward the flames and couldn't see any difference in them.

"Haven," he whispered, then waited until she opened her eyes. "I think we need to be more specific. Just concentrating on the flames doesn't affect them. We need to send a command."

"Of course. I should have known that."

"Don't apologize. Your field is Rocketball," he reminded her. "What do you want to try? Shall we fan the flames with our thoughts, or try to extinguish them?"

"Be serious, Ian."

"I am. The fire's already there, so let's stoke it. If we can make it brush the cavern roof, we'll have proof our thoughts can influence it." Ian slid his hands across Haven's palms and grasped her wrists. "There, that's better."

As she gripped his wrists as well, Haven drew in a deep breath, closed her eyes, and pictured a roaring blaze. It shot sparks high into the air, and the colors deepened from yellow-orange to a vibrant red. The flames rolled, tumbled, and screamed with blistering tongues of fire. It was such a beautiful image, she couldn't draw away her attention to check the fire behind her. She could only stare at the glorious inner vision until a figure began making his way toward her through the flames.

He walked through them with a relaxed stride, and when he came close enough to be recognized, Ian's expression bore no trace of fear. He reached out to her, beckoning her to join him on what she now recognized was a funeral pyre. Horrified, she opened her eyes and found Ian staring at her with a curious gaze. She quickly looked over her shoulder, but the ring of fire was unchanged.

"I'm sorry. I was trying to concentrate on the fire, but I saw you, and—" Haven fell silent as she noticed that Ian was now sitting up straight, the anguish gone from his expression. "Do you feel better?" she asked.

Ian was almost afraid to admit that he did. He took a breath, gently inflating his lungs so as not to renew the agony in his chest, but when he felt no pain he sucked in more air. Still not experiencing any discomfort, he shifted position slightly, and relaxed visibly. "Yes, surprisingly, I do. Tell me what you saw," he encouraged her.

Haven did, but she couldn't suppress a shudder. "It frightened me."

"I saw the same thing," Ian replied. "But you needn't worry; the pyre didn't belong to me. I can breathe more easily now, so let's keep going."

The pride had returned to Ian's posture, and while Haven had hoped they could influence the maze with their thoughts, she had not even considered attempting to heal his wounds. "Wait a minute. How did that happen? Was it merely a coincidence?"

"I don't know, Haven. I've never tried to link my thoughts with another person's. As long as we get beneficial results, let's not stop to analyze the process. Close your eyes if you like. I'll watch the ring. Concentrate again on increasing the intensity of the fire."

"Do they still have funeral pyres anywhere," Haven asked apprehensively, "or did we see an ancient rite?"

Ian shrugged, and smiled when his back didn't hurt. In fact, it itched slightly, as though the cuts were almost healed. He squeezed her wrists. "I imagine it was simply a random illusion conjured up by thinking of fire. Don't dwell on it and let it depress you. Let's focus on the here and now."

While Haven thought his advice wise, she couldn't forget the fright the pyre had given her. No matter what he believed, she took it as an omen of death. Shaken, she closed her eyes and, rather than the fire, she concentrated on the warmth of Ian's hands. Slowly his image took shape in her mind. He was wearing a dark blue uniform she didn't immediately recognize, and when he held out his arms she was the woman who stepped into his embrace. The scene seemed real, and yet it was surrounded by a dreamy aura.

She was wearing a dress Haven had never owned but had seen in history tapes. It was elegant, but the lace and ruffles were dreadfully out of style. The couple began to dance, and others joined them in what was clearly a wedding celebration. She watched the joyful scene with a longing that brought tears to her eyes. She was dreadfully embarrassed when Ian began to laugh.

"This isn't working," she complained. "I'm getting ridiculous images rather than anything useful."

"Would it be ridiculous to marry me?" Ian asked. "We could have used some newer clothes, but it looked as though we belonged together."

Haven licked her lips nervously. "The maze is playing more tricks on us. These images are different from the ghosts who appeared to us in our dreams at the fountain, but this is still just a shared hallucination, and it's not getting us anywhere."

"I disagree. It's making me stronger, and no mere hallucination could do that. Besides, what if we're watching memories, rather than fantasy?"

"Memories? Of what? Past lives?"

"I realize that's not something we've experienced elsewhere, but there seem to be limitless possibilities here. Let's see what we find this time. Ready?"

Haven was about to remind Ian that she was still mad at him, but he obviously felt too well to send her away now and she didn't want to continue the argument. Uncertain what her focus ought to be, she sat back and waited for whatever vision might appear. For a long moment nothing came to her; then she heard a woman singing a lullaby in a hushed soprano and saw herself rocking an infant. Again her clothes were lovely but quaint, and when Ian leaned over the back of the chair she saw he was wearing still another uniform. He was looking down at her and the babe with such a tender expression that this time she couldn't suppress her tears.

Haven yanked her hands from Ian's and wiped her eyes as she got to her feet. "I'm sorry, but this isn't helping us escape." She turned her back on him and walked out to the fiery ring. She couldn't bear to think that she and Ian had been together in the past when the happy scenes mocked the present so cruelly. It was all a trick. She was certain of it, and she despised the builders of the maze for taunting her with a glimpse of a life she would never have.

Ian couldn't understand why Haven wasn't as entertained by the intriguing visions as he. Putting his miraculous recovery to the test, he rose without strain and walked up behind her. "The first time I saw your photograph I knew you'd be different from any other woman I'd ever known. Now I know why. We've been together before, Haven, and we must still carry the happiest of our memories deep inside us. I don't know if we'll be able to explore those memories when we leave the maze, but I'm more than willing to plumb them now."

Haven envied Ian his appreciation of the touching images, but she had had enough. "I'm sorry, but I'm not."

Ian slipped his arms around her waist to pull her back against his chest and again thought they fit together perfectly. "Does it make you sad to think we've known each other in previous lives?"

Haven placed her hands over his. She wasn't sad about the past, only desperately sorry to think how quicky they would part in this life. She turned to look up at him. "That you're feeling well enough to walk around on your own is wonderful. If the maze did that, then I'm very grateful, but it really doesn't matter if we knew each other in a hundred past lives when our present lives are at risk. Now I think the visions are merely a distraction, and I don't want to waste another minute on them. Let's attack the maze instead."

That was quite a challenge, but Ian accepted it. Keeping hold of her hand, he moved closer to the flames. He didn't feel much in the way of heat either and plunged his whole arm into the ring of fire. It caressed his skin with the same comforting warmth as a hot shower, and when he withdrew it the hair on his forearm wasn't even singed.

"You're right," he agreed. "The flames are a clever illusion."

"Then the visions of our pasts might be an even more clever defense. If we're distracted, we can't dismantle the maze."

Ian did not share Haven's belief that they held such enormous power. "I've had more experience putting my fist through a wall than thinking it away, but if you want to work in that direction, I will."

"Thank you." Haven gripped his arms tightly and tried to smile. "Let's clear our minds of all thought except the flames."

Ian nodded. "The maze is magic," he swore, "but so are we." He held her tightly and willed the flames to expand and grow. This time when there was no immediate reaction he did not give up, but simply painted an even more brilliant picture in his mind. In response, the ring of fire flicked out toward the roof of the cavern, and in the next second sent up a huge burst of flame that showered them both with glittering sparks.

Haven opened her eyes and gasped in awe as the fire took on the wild raging spirit she had seen in her mind. "It's working!"

"Yes, and you deserve the credit for suggesting we try. Now what shall we do, try to crack the maze or play with the fire?"

Haven's expression mirrored her resolve. "Let's go after the maze. We want it to show us the way out."

"Set us free," Ian intoned in a firm command.

"Yes! Set us free." Haven chanted the words in her mind, calling to the spirits haunting the maze. She felt Ian calling to them too, and kept her head bowed in concentration. She knew there was a way out, and she couldn't wait another minute to find it. *Set us free! Set us free! Set us free!*

Ian watched the maze through the flames. He repeated the plea for freedom in time with the pulse throbbing in Haven's wrist. Lovely images of her strayed into his mind, but he refused to allow them to distract him, forcing them away. There was only the maze, and he willed it to give them a sign.

The gray stone mocked him with silent strength, but he refused to be beaten. He felt Haven's doubts and knew she was wavering, but he crushed her in his arms and urged her to repeat the chant aloud. Her voice was muffled against his chest, but he heard the words clearly in his mind and felt their combined power soar. He dipped into the reserves of energy the images of their past lives had restored and sent the maze a final demanding command to set them free.

As if on cue, the flames responded with graceful, looping coils that spun above their heads and then slid down into the gorge to form a golden ribbon of light. One moment it enclosed the maze with a bright blur and in the next it leapt out of the confining moat. Snaking through the maze in a living swirl, it stretched across the labyrinth with an inviting brilliance.

Ian sent Haven a questioning glance and saw her response in her ecstatic smile. She wasn't afraid and neither was he. Their hands locked in a deathless grasp, they stepped up on the golden path and with flying strides raced toward the end of the shimmering trail.

Chapter Sixteen

As they ran, Ian and Haven looked ahead rather than down at the glorious beam of light. The golden path curved over the top of the maze, then made a gradual descent to the other side. Glowing with a dazzling brilliance, it spanned the now empty gorge, then curled around the inside of the cavern before spilling down into a ravine that ran deep into the heart of the asteroid. Finally, the magic fire pooled around a set of stone steps leading up to a wide door.

Once Ian and Haven had reached the doorway the flames lapped at their ankles, then shrank to a narrow dancing line and withdrew, leaving the pair to confront the next challenge on their own. Still holding Ian's hand, Haven turned back to catch a last glimpse of the ribbon of light, but it had already vanished without a trace. There was a stone walkway beneath their feet, but she was positive they would never have found it on their own.

Awestruck, she could only shake her head. "I don't think I'll ever be able to describe what just happened."

"Describing it won't be my problem," Ian complained. "It will be being believed." There was a large ring in the door, and Ian released Haven's hand to grab it. "If this leads to the mine, then we're finally free. But if it's the gate to another maze, we'll have to go back and begin again."

"Oh no, it couldn't be." Haven wrapped her hands tightly around the ring and yanked with Ian. At first the massive stone door held firm, but after a tense few minutes it succumbed to their combined efforts to wrench it open. The hinges protested with a metallic whine, but the door slowly swung wide. Haven slipped around Ian to see what lay beyond. "More steps?" she asked fearfully.

Disappointment filled her eyes with tears, but Ian wasn't ready to concede defeat. "Don't cry. I didn't really expect the doorway to open out on a tunnel. This passage must intersect with the mine somewhere, though, or the miners would never have discovered the existence of the maze. I still have some of the dried fruit. Do you want to stop and eat before we go on?"

Haven's expression darkened. "I'm in no mood for a picnic. I just want to get out of here."

"So do I. Let me go first," Ian urged, but he

reached for Haven's hand to bring her along with him.

As Ian turned away, Haven was astonished to see that the slashes in his back had healed, leaving only pale pink trails. She reached up to trace one with her fingertip. "Ian, the avalanche left a half dozen deep cuts on your back, but they're gone. I know they were there, but the scars are so faint that I'd not have noticed them had I not seen the slashes earlier."

Ian had already felt the change in the diminished pain, and he ran his thumb down the scar on his ribs. "I don't need any more scars as souvenirs of this place and I won't miss them. Now let's just get out of here. We can discuss the healing phenomenon later."

Haven was trembling, and he would have offered more encouragement, but the doubt clouding her emerald gaze stopped him. Believing action would mean more to her than promises that might quickly prove empty, he started up the stairs. They were steep, and climbing them was so tiring after all they had been through that he soon had to pause for a rest.

"Are you all right?" he asked.

Haven didn't even try to hide her distress. "I'm so afraid this is a trick. If it leads to another dead end, I don't know what I'll do."

Ian cupped her face tenderly in his hands. "If our thoughts can influence the maze, we don't dare expect anything other than a route to the mine. Concentrate on playing in the finals, and we'll be out of here before you know it."

When he lowered his mouth to hers Haven responded with a hesitant kiss, then slid her arms around his waist and hugged him tightly. She would always be grateful for his courage and, wishing she could show more spirit, she released him with a quick shove. "I'm fine," she exclaimed with an embarrassed smile. "Let's keep going."

Ian could see that she was anything but fine, but he winked at her and continued on up the stairs. "It's getting cooler," he noted.

Haven also felt the drop in the temperature, prompting a renewed burst of fear that they were being manipulated. But she quickly suppressed the negative emotion with silent curses. *This is the way out!* she shouted in her mind. "I've never been in a mine. What's this one like?"

Ready for another break, Ian stopped again. "There are huge tunnels with tracks laid for railcars to carry the astronium ore. Unlike the cavern, which is a natural structure, the tunnels are braced to protect the miners from cave-ins. Lights are strung along the walls, along with sensors to record seismic activity and, oh damn, scanners that we'll have to hope Egon isn't monitoring when we walk by."

Like the maze, the stairway was lit from above, and as Haven looked past Ian, it seemed to extend for miles. "Maybe these stairs lead to the surface of the asteroid rather than the mine. What will we do then?"

Haven never ceased to amaze Ian. "You do love to worry, don't you?"

"No, not usually. But I've never been trapped

below ground before either. Maybe we should have something to eat."

"Good idea." Ian motioned for her to sit on the step below his, then sat down behind her and straddled her shoulders to provide her with a backrest. He reached into his pocket and came up with a handful of dirt left by the avalanche, plus the last two strips of jerky. He brushed them off and gave her one. "Without doubt, this has been one of my strangest adventures. Will you help me write my report?"

"I doubt I could add anything."

"You'll have different recollections, and including your thoughts will give a more detailed account of what we've seen."

"How many ways are there to describe a blank wall?"

Ian had never met another woman with such a well-developed dark side. But he doubted Haven had had a pessimistic outlook on life before her brief marriage to Blake Ellis, which was another reason to make the bastard pay for hurting her so badly. He bent down to kiss her cheek.

"There was a tranquillity about you in my visions," he revealed softly. "I hope to help you recapture it when we're safely out of here."

Unable to think past the moment, Haven stopped chewing in midbite. She had also noticed the remarkable serenity of her features in the visions and, unlike Ian, had recognized it as the glowing reflection of love. And love was the one thing he had never offered. "I still think the visions were distracting illusions and nothing more."

Ian was amused by the defiant tilt of her chin. "Perhaps, but they must have come from somewhere, and I still believe the fact that we were together and blissfully happy is significant. Even if it was only a shared dream, it must have been what was in our hearts."

Such sweetly sentimental comments made Haven horribly uncomfortable. "I've found dreams seldom become reality."

Ian finished the last bite of his jerky. "Have I been a disappointment?"

Haven rested her cheek against his knee, and Ian leaned down to nuzzle her nape. "No. Not at all."

That admission was slurred by what Ian feared were more tears. Not having meant to upset her, he rubbed her arms, then stood. "Come on. Let's keep going. I have a feeling we're nearly there."

Haven felt badly torn. She wanted out of the maze, but deliverance would bring them that much closer to saying good-bye. Because they couldn't survive where they sat, she struggled to her feet and turned to face him. "Let's go then."

For a moment Ian was filled with such an intense longing to be with her that he was tempted to remain right where they were, but Haven was looking past him at the stairs and he knew she wouldn't share her thoughts no matter how eloquently he phrased his request. He had thought he was the one who had difficulty confiding his emotions, but it was suddenly painfully obvious that she was no more skilled at that delicate art than he. In many respects they were too much alike, but he hoped they would discover a way to turn their similarities into an asset, rather than allow them to become a liability.

He turned and continued up the long flight of stairs, but the muscles in his calves were aching painfully before they finally reached a landing. Here they were greeted by another door, identical to the one below. "Hell must be like this," he mused under his breath. He leaned back against the stone portal and waited for Haven to reach the landing. She was moving so slowly, he knew she couldn't take much more.

"Sit down and rest," he encouraged. "I'll open the door."

Haven lacked the energy to argue and sank down on the top step. She knew Ian would carry her if all they found was another flight of stairs, but she couldn't bear the thought of being an even greater burden to him. "Wait a minute," she begged. "Don't open it yet."

Ian raised his brows. He had expected her to be as eager as he to discover what lay ahead, but seeing the slump to her shoulders he knew she was anticipating another horrible disappointment. Though he had begun to believe they were almost free, relentless optimism on his part would do little to relieve her anxiety. He recalled another matter that he could set right, however. He sat down beside her and wrapped his arm around her shoulders.

"I'm sorry about asking you to leave me. I

should have known you were too fine a woman to abandon an injured man. Can you forgive me?"

Haven could remember being furious with him at the time, but now all she felt was numb. "There's nothing to forgive."

"Is that a no?"

Haven rested her head on his shoulder. "No. It's a refusal to consider your request."

Ian was about to insist that she must, but when he looked down at her she was fast asleep. Eager to move on, he was annoyed but, remembering how he had awakened her the last time she had had a chance to sleep, he felt too guilty to disturb her now. He was almost painfully alert, however, and prayed the mine lay on the other side of the door at his back.

"It damn well better be," he vowed in a hushed whisper. He rested his cheek against the top of Haven's head and tried to relax, but none of the methods he had used in the past were effective now. Growing apprehensive, he looked over his shoulder to scan the stones surrounding the door and was relieved not to find any sensors. They were safe for the moment, but Ian was by no means complacent.

His thoughts drifted to imaginative ways to punish the miners who had abandoned them in the maze, and the time passed quickly until Haven stirred in his arms. He gave her a quick hug and urged her to her feet. "Nice nap?" he asked.

"What? Yes, I suppose. I didn't have any strange dreams." She hadn't meant to fall asleep and now she hurriedly moved beside him to grasp the metal ring. Still yawning sleepily, she began to tug on the door. Like the first, it resisted their initial attempts to draw it open, but after Ian swore several particularly colorful oaths it also groaned on its hinges and swung wide.

A rush of cold air hit them, and Ian drew Haven through the doorway into a narrow corridor that veered sharply to the right. "I can see a ray of light ahead," he whispered, but as they drew near, they were faced with navigating a narrow gap without knowing what lay beyond it.

Ian gave Haven a quick kiss. "Can you squeeze through here?" he asked.

Haven cringed but didn't believe she had any choice. "I can make it if you can," she promised.

"Good." Ian inched ahead, but he kept hold of Haven's hand and gave her a gentle tug to encourage her to follow. Perhaps ten feet long, and little more than a foot wide, the passageway appeared to be a natural fissure in the rock. "Just another few steps," Ian called out. "We're almost there."

Haven shut her eyes and pursued Ian so closely, she bumped into him every time he brought his feet together. "Sorry," she offered, but she wanted to get out of the narrow hallway so badly that she was moving faster than he. When he at last drew her out into a brightly lit tunnel she was blinded for a moment, then could scarcely believe her eyes.

"Is this one of the mine tunnels?" She turned back toward the rocky wall, but the passageway they had traveled was so cleverly concealed behind an outcropping of rock that a thousand miners might have passed by without ever noticing a crevice. And even if they had, they would never have guessed its wondrous significance.

Overwhelmed with relief, Ian pulled her into his arms. "Yes, this is the mine." He gave her an enthusiastic hug, and then stepped back. "Because we don't know which miners we can trust, if any, we're going to have to get out of here without being seen. We're still covered with so much dust, we just might blend into the walls, but let's take care to avoid the scanners if we can."

He searched overhead for monitoring equipment and didn't find any nearby. He knelt beside the tracks and placed his hand on the closest rail. It was cold, and without any hint of vibration. "There may be no one working in this tunnel today. We must be near the surface, perhaps at the second or third level."

"Look!" Haven beat on his shoulder. "There's a sign pointing to the level three exit."

Ian straightened up and followed her wild gesture. The illuminated sign was some distance away but clearly legible. He had not paid any attention to the level markers when he had toured the mine with Egon but was elated to find that the mine had them. He could easily imagine the men getting disoriented if there were an explosion or fire, and that safety precaution would be a great help to him now.

He extended his hand. "Let's see if we can't get home in time for supper."

"I'll settle for a crust of bread." Haven followed his example and hurried along, pressed close to the far wall. When he spotted a scanner up ahead they moved to the opposite side of the tunnel to pass beneath it. Using the same crisscross strategy, they moved all the way down the tunnel to the central shaft without being observed. But they could hear a deep rattle and hum coming from the other arm of level three, where miners were excavating, and grew still more cautious.

There were several scanners mounted here, but Ian took care not to stray across their range, reaching up to tilt their glowing eyes toward the top of the tunnel and away from them. Then he pulled Haven into the shadows behind the elevator cage. There were emergency ladders on either side of the shaft, but he did not want to risk using one.

"The miners send huge buckets of ore up to the surface. If we wait here, we can catch one on its way up. When it arrives at the top the ore is funneled into railcars and sent out to the docking bay for loading on transport ships. It's a noisy, dirty process, and we ought to be able to slip onto a railcar and ride out to the docking bay without getting caught. We can find flight uniforms or mechanics coveralls there, and then move around without being recognized."

Haven's eyes took on a skeptical glint. "Wait a minute. I want to make certain I understand your plan. We're going to hop on a bucket of ore, and when it reaches the top somehow get into a railcar without being crushed beneath several tons of ore when the bucket drops its load?"

Ian nodded. "Trust me. I do this sort of thing all the time."

"And you have the scars to prove it," Haven reminded him.

"Only one," Ian argued. "This isn't going to be nearly as risky as it sounds. There's a handrail encircling the inside of the bucket, so we can hold on when it empties. Then we'll drop down onto the railcar before the empty bucket is swung aside. Our stay in the maze has given us a dusty coat of camouflage; we'll blend in against the gray ore. Then we'll just ride out to the docking bay."

"Where we'll again have to avoid being buried under several tons of rock?"

Ian really didn't see that possibility as being much of a hazard. "We'll be on top of the ore, Haven, not in the railcar itself. I imagine the cars must sit for a minute or two before they are unloaded onto the transports, and that will be plenty of time for us to get out and move clear."

Completely dismayed, Haven gasped. "You imagine?"

"I observed the operation the first day I came here," Ian replied. "I didn't time how long it took to load the ore onto the transports, but it wasn't instanteous by any means. I'm sure this won't be nearly as frightening as it sounds, but if you'd rather wait here until I can find help and come back for you, you're welcome to stay."

Haven leaned from behind the elevator cage to search for a better place to hide and couldn't find one; the platform surrounding the central shaft was clear and brightly lit. She supposed she could go back down the tunnel and hide on the steps leading down into the maze, but that wasn't at all appealing now that they had finally gotten free.

"I suppose if we survived the maze, catching a ride on a bucket of ore won't be much of a challenge. Then again—"

Ian rested his hands on Haven's shoulders. "I'm afraid climbing up one of the ladders would bring us out in plain sight, but if you'd feel safer, we can use one."

"My legs are still shaky from climbing all those stairs. I'd never make it."

"Then you'll ride up in the next bucket with me?"

Haven couldn't believe they had come this far only to die beneath a load of ore. "You've done a fine job leading this expedition so far. I won't mutiny."

Ian couldn't help but laugh. Haven was a bright and beautiful woman who looked as though she had been sucked through a trash disposal chute, and still she had faith in him. Before he could thank her the cables in the shaft came alive with a deep, wrenching groan. He grabbed her hand.

"There's a bucket now. Let's catch it."

Haven followed him out to the edge of the shaft and peered down. She had not expected it to be so deep, but staring into the mine's dark core made her so dizzy, she had to step back. "I'm sorry. I'm not usually afflicted with vertigo."

"That's a relief. Close your eyes and I'll tell you when to jump." He leaned out to watch the bucket rise to the surface, but it was coming from a long way down and moving slowly. "We've a while yet." As he watched it rise, he realized that they would have to be careful not to get tangled in the cables. This was precisely the type of wild stunt he frequently encountered, but never with an untrained partner.

"If this doesn't look as easy as I thought, we'll let this one pass and catch the next," he assured Haven.

Haven's heart was pounding with fright, but she swallowed her complaints. She just waited, shaking all over, as he provided intermittent reports on the bucket's approach. When he began to count down from ten she repeated the numbers in a hoarse whisper, praying she would find the nerve to go through with what was only the first part of his dangerous plan.

Ian waited until the bucket was a scant two feet below their level. "Jump!" he cried, and Haven dropped down with him onto the ore. They both pitched forward on their hands and knees but managed to scramble over to the handrail and catch hold. Haven's face was white beneath a fine coating of astronium dust, and she returned Ian's elated grin with a trembling smile.

"I don't believe I'm cut out for your line of work!" she shouted above the whine of the cables.

Ian laughed, then motioned for her to keep her

head down. The bucket wasn't filled to the top, so they could crouch below the rim, but he didn't want to take any chances with their being seen when they reached the top. What he hadn't anticipated was the jarring lurch that shook the bucket when it swung out and away from the shaft. The ore slid to one side, then careened back over them, and Haven lost her hold on the handrail just as the hinged bottom of the bucket dropped open.

Ian made a grab for her arm and caught her, and the thunderous crash of the ore into the railcar drowned out her scream, but they were both so badly shaken that they wouldn't have made it out of the bucket had the operator not chosen that particular moment to go on a break, leaving it hanging in place above the railcar. Ian was breathing hard as he dropped Haven down onto the ore. He quickly joined her atop the railcar; then, lying flat, he looked around to make certain they hadn't been seen.

There were only two men standing nearby. They were talking together, but they had their backs to them and posed no threat. After a few minutes one moved away to access the controls for the railcar, and slowly it began to roll. Ian slipped his arm around Haven's waist and pulled her against his side as they left the entrance to the mine and entered the tunnel leading to the docking bay. He whispered in her ear, "Hang on. We're almost there."

Haven felt as though she were lying on a bed of nails. The sharp edges of the ore poked and jabbed through the fabric of Ian's tunic and all down her bare legs. She knew Ian must be hurting too, but she was near tears by the time the railcar rolled out into the docking bay. "I can't take much more of this," she whispered.

"You won't have to," Ian answered. The instant the railcar reached the end of the track, he raised his head up slightly. Half a dozen men were adjusting the position of the chute used to fill the transport ships' holds, and he did not want to wait for the railcar to begin to tilt. He nodded for Haven to follow him, picked his way as quietly as he could over the ore, and swung down over the side of the railcar.

Terrified that she still ran the risk of being buried under a ton of ore, Haven lurched along after him. There was a ladder welded onto the side of the car, and she used it to reach Ian's arms. He took her hand and, sprinting away with her in tow, dipped under the nose of the transport ship to reach the other side. Another ship lay moored just beyond, and as soon as he was certain the way was clear, he led her to it.

Ian paused at the bottom of the ramp. "If anyone stops us, let me do all the talking," he warned.

"Gladly. I've no idea what to say. We must look like refugees from some ghastly frontier rebellion."

"That's rather good; I'll use it if I have to." Ian winked at her. They went on up the ramp and entered the crew's quarters. Just as he had expected, no one was on board. They entered the

329

first officer's compartment and helped themselves to a couple of khaki flight suits. Ian tossed one to Haven and yanked on the other. He tried on the man's boots, and while they were not as comfortable as his own, they fit well enough to wear.

"I'll check the bridge for helmets and find you a pair of boots. Wait here."

"What if the first officer shows up?" Haven cried.

"Entertain him with stories of the rebellion until I get back." Ian brushed her dusty cheek with a kiss and hurried away.

Haven crossed to the mirror, and then was sorry she had. Caked with dust, her tangled hair resembled some wild animal's, and her face was streaked with tears. She was amazed that Ian had wanted to kiss her, then remembered that he had looked no more civilized himself. She wanted to believe they were safe, but she wouldn't truly feel secure until the tournament was over and they had left 317. She paced the small cabin with an anxious stride until Ian reappeared.

He was carrying a pair of boots and two black helmets. "Ordinarily I'd suggest we wash up, but it would only increase our chances of being recognized. Let's just risk looking ridiculous a while longer." He pulled on his helmet and waited for Haven to don hers. She sat down on the bunk to try on the boots and nodded approvingly when they fit comfortably.

Ian had grabbed the first pair he had found but allowed her to think he had a discerning eye.

"There's a communications panel by the exit. Let's see if we can raise Aren."

Aren struck Haven as an odd choice until she realized that Flames personnel were the only ones on 317 they could trust. "What are we going to tell him?"

Ian wasn't sure how she meant that. "I'm going to insist that he not tell a soul that I've spoken with him, and ask him to meet us at his quarters. We don't even know what day it is, Haven. Other agents might already be here, and if they are, I'll find a way to contact them."

As Ian started out of the cabin, Haven touched his sleeve. "No, wait. Let me talk to Aren. He was too jealous of you to be helpful, but he'll do whatever I ask."

She had spoken matter-of-factly, but Ian felt uneasy at her words. "Fine. I should have remembered that he's as loyal as a pet. Swear him to secrecy and give him no more than five minutes to reach his quarters if he isn't there already."

Haven didn't understand what had brought the edge of hostility to Ian's voice but assumed he was worried that the miners might discover they had survived the avalanche. "You needn't worry; I'll be brief." She followed him down the ramp and, mistaken for transport ship officers, they attracted no notice from the men working in the docking bay. She had to hurry to keep up with Ian as they strode toward the communications panel.

She pressed the button on the panel and asked

to have Aren Manzari paged. As they waited, Ian kept his back to the bay, but he didn't offer any encouraging smiles, prompting her to comment on the obvious darkness of his thoughts. "I'd hate to have you for an enemy," Haven whispered.

Surprised by that unexpected comment, Ian frowned slightly. "You never will, but you're right—I make the very worst of enemies for the type of people who deserve to be caught."

The wait grew uncomfortably long before Aren answered his page, but when he did Haven was ready for him. "Listen closely," she ordered in a hushed whisper, "and don't speak my name aloud. Don't tell anyone you've heard from me. Just go to your room in the guest quarters and wait for me there." She broke the connection before Aren had a chance to reply and looked up at Ian.

"I think it's time to tell Aren who you really are."

A slow smile brightened Ian's dirt-smudged face. "I intend to, but let me be the one to do it."

Haven nodded, and followed him to the tram stop. She climbed aboard and, playing the part of a weary transport ship officer, slid into the seat in front of Ian for the ride to the guest quarters. She slumped down and folded her arms across her chest to hide the name embroidered over her breast pocket should any passengers glance her way. Sick of this wretched game, she couldn't wait for it to be over.

Ian reached up to slap Haven on the shoulder. He was proud of her and he had forgotten to say so. There was a lot more he intended to say, but not until he had arrested every last miner who had ever had anything to do with the maze. Until then, he was finally going to give this assignment the single-minded concentration it had deserved all along.

Chapter Seventeen

Aren Manzari was in the locker room when he heard the page. Since Haven's elopement, the Flames' staff had been besieged with requests for interviews. Assuming it was another reporter eager to gather his impressions of the man the star of their team had married, he was slow to respond. The few times he had been cornered by reporters, he had been hard pressed not to angrily blurt out how he felt.

Annoyed by the repeated page, he had answered intending to promptly disconnect. Then he had heard Haven's voice, and his heart had ceased to beat. He had made a quick excuse to Tory Norton and waited for the Flames' head coach to acknowledge it with a slight nod before he left the team meeting. He had sprinted the whole way to the tram. He left his seat as it neared the guest quarters, and exited at a run as soon as the car slowed.

His only thought was that Haven must have come to her senses and left John Hyatt. Why else would she have sworn him to secrecy? Elated, he dashed around the corner of his corridor and saw what at first glance appeared to be a couple of pilots waiting outside his room. Then Haven turned toward him, and with a sick, sinking feeling he realized the man with her was John Hyatt. Aren came to an abrupt halt; then, finally giving vent to his furious anger, he came forward with a fierce, menacing stride.

"Do you have any idea what you've done to the team? Why are you dressed in that strange garb? Is it supposed to be a disguise? I don't blame you. If I'd betrayed the Flames as maliciously as you have, I wouldn't want to be recognized around here either."

As soon as Aren came within reach, Ian grabbed him by the front of his blue Flames jacket, lifting him clear off his feet and slamming him into the wall. "You are never to use such an insulting tone with Haven again," he hissed. "Now open your door and invite us in."

Aren choked as Ian tightened his hold. His mouth opened and closed in soundless, fishlike gulps. He nodded frantically and, apparently satisfied that he would obey, Ian released him. As his feet touched down, Aren stumbled, bumped against the wall, and then straightened up and tried to look as though he had not just suffered the worst humiliation of his life. Unable to glance toward Haven, he keyed in the security code for his door and gestured for her and Ian to precede him into his room.

Ian removed his helmet, tossed it on Aren's bed, and then turned to Haven. "You take the first shower. I'll tell Aren everything he needs to know."

Haven had not been surprised by the rude way Aren had greeted her, but it had hurt all the same. Relieved to escape him, she went into the bathroom before removing her helmet. She yanked off her borrowed boots, peeled off the flight suit and Ian's tunic, and stepped into the shower. The warm, soapy spray came on to caress her weary muscles, but it stung the new cuts on her legs.

Turning her back to the spray, she shampooed her hair, then slid down the wall of the stall and sat in the corner. She watched the water swirl down the drain and, knowing it would be reclaimed, let it run. She wanted to go to sleep and wake up to find everything had been set right, but the brief time she had spent with Ian would leave her irrevocably changed. He would go on to another adventure and she would train for the next season, but nothing would ever be the same.

Ashamed to be indulging in self-pity when the miners who had abused them were still at large, Haven straightened up, left the shower, and donned the blue Flames robe hanging on the back of the door. A size larger than her own, it was even more comfortably roomy. She tied the belt and cast a quick glance in the mirror. Her face looked thin, her eyes hollow, but at least she had washed off all the astronium dust, and her hair was finally clean.

She left the bathroom and went straight to the bed. She put Ian's helmet aside and sat down. Aren was regarding her now with an incredulous stare, and she at last appreciated Ian's comment about being believed. "What day is this? Have we missed much of the games?"

"We've been gone more than a week," Ian told her. "The Flames will play the Satin Spikes in the championship game tonight. You and Aren can talk about what you want to do. All I want is a shower."

Haven waited until Ian had closed the bathroom door to speak. "I'd hoped there was a good chance you'd know I would never leave the team willingly. Obviously it didn't occur to you that we might have been kidnapped."

Aren doubted anything he said now would make up for the insensitive way he had greeted her. "You'd been restless. He's an attractive man. Even without knowing he's Ian St. Ives, I thought an elopement made sense. My God, Haven—how would any of us have guessed you'd been abducted when there was no ransom demand?"

Haven shrugged slightly. "I didn't realize you had so little faith in me. How did you find out about the elopement? Who announced it?"

"Egon Rascon read a message he said you'd sent from Ian's ship after you'd left 317. Of course he called him John Hyatt, but that didn't change the content. We all felt betrayed."

Aren's reaction was still mirrored in his anguished frown, but Haven wondered how many of her teammates had shared his sorrow. "Somehow I doubt Elida was all that distraught to have me out of her way," she mused aloud. Haven folded her hands in her lap. "Will Tory let me play tonight? I suppose if the team has gotten this far without me, they can go all the way, but I'd still like to play a few minutes at least."

Aren ran his hand through his hair and paced in front of her. "Of course Tory will let you play. The question is, do you feel up to it? You've obviously lost weight. Are you strong enough to compete?"

Haven doubted she could fool him, and knew it would be foolish to try. She felt completely drained but was confident that Aren could remedy her physical complaints. "Not now I'm not, but after one of your vitamin tonics and a nap I'll be in top form."

Aren halted in front of her. "It will take more than vitamins to repair whatever physical damage you've incurred. A transfusion would probably be more efficacious."

"Whatever it takes."

"You're sure you want to play?"

Haven was positive Rocketball would provide the focus she so desperately needed. Otherwise telling Ian good-bye would cause unbearable pain. "I wouldn't miss it. In fact, I'm sure Ian is tired of hearing how much I wanted to get back in time to play."

"I knew I'd seen him somewhere. It doesn't

make losing you any easier, but at least I know he's worthy of you."

Haven had no idea what Ian might have told Aren, but she couldn't imagine him making a vow of undying devotion. Had he really been John Hyatt, a conscientious insurance investigator, he surely would have, but not Ian. "We're still in danger," she replied. "Please don't tell anyone who he is."

"Don't worry, he's already sworn me to secrecy." Aren didn't look pleased about it, either. "You can stay here until the game tonight; they can't touch you on the court."

Ian came out of the bathroom in time to hear a mention of the game. "You're going to play?" he asked.

"Yes," Haven assured him. "If not the whole game, then a quarter or two."

Ian was wearing the khaki flight suit but was barefoot. Still wet, his hair dripped down on his collar. "Fine. I'll be there to see you play." He directed his next comment to Aren. "We'd no idea how long we'd been in the maze. Time as we're used to it doesn't exist there. It's possible other agents have had time to arrive on 317. You may have met them. They'd be relentless in their attempts to get information about my whereabouts."

Aren responded with a rueful laugh. "The reporters covering the tournament have featured you and Haven all week. That one of the most famous women in the galaxy chose to run off with one of the least-known men has made sensational news. Several reporters have gone for the 'princess and the pauper' angle, but that obviously isn't the case."

Ian hadn't considered that complication but quickly adjusted to the unwanted publicity. His cover story was so well imbedded in Alado's files, it would never arouse even the most inquisitive reporter's suspicions. "Do you know most of the reporters who usually cover the Rocketball games?"

"Yes. Most of them have been following the Rocketball circuit for longer than I have."

"Is there anyone new? Anyone about my size, my age, with dark brown hair and green eyes?"

Aren thought a moment. "Yeah. That sounds like Rick Nash. He flashed the proper credentials, but I've never seen him before."

Ian sat down beside Haven and took her hand. "I want you to page him, Aren. Tell him you have an exclusive story, and ask him to meet you here. If he's who I think he is, you'll let him in. If he isn't, just tell him you've had a change of heart and can't see him after all."

Aren did not want to appear a fool in front of a reporter, but when his hesitation caused Ian's gaze to darken, he swiftly thought better of crossing him. He stepped up to the communications panel above the desk and paged Rick Nash. While he awaited the response, Aren jammed his hands in his pockets and tried to find a place to fix his gaze. He had had more than a week to adjust to the fact that Haven was with John Hyatt—or Ian, he corrected himself—but that did not make seeing them together any less of a torment. When Rick Nash answered the page he gave him Ian's message.

"He'll be right over," Aren announced.

Ian gave Haven's hand a squeeze before leaving the bed and going to the door. He switched on the viewing screen on the security panel, then leaned back against the wall and crossed his arms over his chest. "If Rick Nash is who I think he is, we'll go to his room to plan our next move, but I'll be there tonight, Haven. Don't bother looking for me. Just know I'm there."

"Thank you, but it's just another game. Don't put yourself in any danger to attend."

Ian laughed at her warning. "My mission will be complete by tonight. After the game we'll celebrate both our victories."

"I'll look forward to it," Haven replied, but she doubted she could do more than sob when this would surely be their last night together.

There was a light knock at the door, and Ian turned to find Yale Lincoln, one of his fellow operatives, standing outside. Yale wore an impatient frown that vanished as soon as he stepped into Aren's room. "My God," he gasped. "I was just hoping for a lead. I never expected to find you here." He glanced toward the bed and immediately recognized Haven Wray. "I'd intended to rescue you, Ms. Wray. Looks like Ian has already taken care of it."

Haven smiled. "Yes, he has."

Ian came back to the bed. "Don't leave here until you absolutely have to to get ready for the game. Then try not to be recognized. I'll need a couple of hours to wrap up here, and I don't want you wandering around where you might be taken hostage."

That was a threat Haven didn't even want to consider. "You needn't worry that I'll jeopardize your mission. I'm not going to do anything more reckless than take a nap."

Ian leaned down to brush her lips lightly with a hasty kiss. With Aren and Yale in the room, he didn't want to offer any promises that might embarrass her. He quickly picked up his borrowed helmet, got his boots from the bathroom, and left with Yale.

Aren had never been so glad to see anyone leave. He had known Ian St. Ives only by his reputation, but now that he had met him he understood exactly why he had owned the Artic Warrior competition for so many years. "Isn't that man ever afraid?" he asked.

"No, I don't believe so, but it was a comfort in the situation in which we found ourselves. Now what can we do to get me ready for tonight's game?"

"I meant what I said about the transfusion. Go to sleep and I'll get the blood. When I get back I'll try to do it without waking you."

The Flames all banked their own blood in case of injuries, and Haven wasn't afraid of his needles. She stretched out on Aren's bed and covered a yawn. "As tired as I am, I could sleep through anything, but don't you dare let me miss the game."

There wasn't anything Aren wouldn't have done for her, and he left to gather everything he would need. As long as Haven played Rocketball, they would be together, and while it was small consolation, it gave him hope that he had not lost her completely.

Ian waited until they reached Yale's room to begin plotting strategy. "How many men did you bring with you?" He tossed the helmet aside and raked his hair off his forehead in a quick swipe.

Yale leaned back against the desk. "Fifty. A private firm was contracted to handle security for the games. Control replaced them with Alado's men. We knew you couldn't possibly have eloped in the middle of a mission, but we'd had no success in discovering just what did happen to you."

Ian gave Yale a quick summary of the time he and Haven had spent in the maze. "I think Egon Rascon is involved. If he thinks the others who were in on it have named him, he should be more than willing to talk. I want you to find a miner named T. L. Rainey and bring him here."

"You got it. The mine's closing down at the end of this shift so the miners can all either attend or watch the final game, but if Rainey is in the mine, it might take a while to locate him."

"He should have worked the night shift and be off. Page him, and offer him a ticket for tonight's game. Even if he already has one, he'll be sure to want another for a friend."

"Right. I'm looking forward to it myself. Not

that I wasn't worried sick about you, you understand."

The rivalry between Ian and Yale had gone on for years, and as usual Yale wore a cocky smirk that belied his words of concern. "Get out of here," Ian ordered and, still chuckling, Yale went after Rainey.

As soon as he was alone, Ian began to miss Haven. He walked over to the communications panel but decided against calling her. She needed her rest, and he didn't want to disturb her if she had already fallen asleep. He was worried about her playing that evening, but she was a thorough professional and he trusted her to call a time-out and leave the game if it became a strain. Watching her would certainly be a strain on him, but he was glad they had gotten back in time for her to participate.

He sat down at the desk and began making notes for his report, but the fact that they had lost more than a week in the maze still amazed him. Alado's scientists would study the puzzling structure for years and still might not find any clues as to its origin or enigmatic attributes. He made a few sketches, but trying to recall details of the fountain and cabinet full of rations was surprisingly difficult. He had completed only vague outlines of each before Yale Lincoln returned with T. L. Rainey. Ian stood and greeted the young miner with a relaxed smile, but at the same time he was studying his reaction closely.

It took a moment for T. L. to recognize Ian without his gray uniform. Then he broke into a wide grin and exclaimed, "Hey, I thought you were off on your honeymoon with Haven Wray."

T. L's expression was one of such exuberant enthusiasm that Ian was readily convinced that he had had nothing to do with abandoning Haven and himself in the maze. He reached out to shake his hand. "The report of our elopement was a hoax. Haven and I have been right here on 317 the whole time. I hope you can help me prevent the same people from carrying out any more dangerous jokes at other people's expense."

Confused, T. L. cast an anxious glance over his shoulder. "You said I'd won a ticket for tonight's game. Was that just a trick to get me here, Mr. Nash?"

Yale leaned back against the door and folded his arms across his chest. "You'll get to see the game," he promised smoothly, "in exchange for a little information."

Growing exquisitely uncomfortable, T. L. whipped his head back around to face Ian. "What's going on here?"

Ian gestured toward the chair at the desk. "Sit down, T. L."

T. L. started to back away, but Yale moved up to block his path. "Sit down or I'll put you in that chair, and I won't do it gently."

T. L. wiped his hands on his pants. Working in the mine had made him lean and fit, but he knew he was no match for either of these men. They had a toughness it took years to build, and he didn't want to risk infuriating either of them. "I thought you said your field was insurance, Mr.

Hyatt. Are you trying to sell me a policy?"

Had the miner not looked so terrified, Ian would have laughed out loud. He again gestured toward the chair and waited until T. L. had taken an uneasy perch on the edge. "No, this isn't a sales pitch," he assured him. "I appreciated your warning about the mine, and I intend to see you get a proper reward, should you expand on it a little."

"Expand?" T. L. echoed nervously.

Ian nodded. "Egon Rascon has an unusual tattoo on the inside of his left arm. Can you describe it?" Ian watched the color drain from T. L.'s face. With his spiked hair forming a halo, his ghostly pallor gave him the look of an anemic angel. "I see that you can. Mr. Nash hasn't had an opportunity to see it. Tell him how beautiful it is."

T. L. stared up at Ian, his eyes wide with fright. Ian waited a long moment; then, with a well-placed kick, he knocked the chair right out from under him. In the same agile motion, he sprang forward and caught T. L.'s arm before he fell. "Be careful," he warned. "Neither Mr. Nash nor I want to see you get hurt in some silly accident, do we, Mr. Nash?"

"Certainly not. I've been thinking of getting another tattoo. Is Egon's something I might like, T. L.?"

T. L. could scarcely draw breath to speak and his voice was hoarse when he finally replied. "I don't know anything about Rascon, but I've seen other tattoos. The men who have them will kill me if I tell. You know they will."

Ian shook his head. He picked up the over-
turned chair and again gestured invitingly. His
voice was low, soothing. "Sit down, T. L., and
relax. We're not violent, regardless of how badly
we might treat the furniture. I asked you to describe Egon's tattoo. If you'd prefer to give us a
verbal sketch of someone else's, go ahead. Just
don't make us wait. Neither of us has a bit of
patience."

T. L. swallowed with an audible gulp. "Rascon
doesn't shower with the miners, so I've no way
of knowing what kind of tattoos he has, but I
have seen several men with one that might interest you." He brought up shaking hands to gesture. "Well, I guess you could call it a mandala.
It's about this big, round, and looks like interlac-
ing vines, or knotted ribbon. The colors are iridescent."

"Have you ever seen a Celtic knot?" Ian asked.

"No, sir. Is that what it is?"

Ian shrugged, as though the point was unim-
portant. "What you told us is fine. Now we need
the names of all the men here with that tattoo."
He laid paper and a pen on the desk. "Go on.
Tell us their names. We don't want to miss any
of tonight's game."

T. L. crackled his knuckles; then, seeing Ian
straighten up, he grabbed hold of his chair. "I
don't want any part of this."

"Roll up your sleeves," Ian ordered.

T. L. quickly obeyed. His forearms were bare.
"See. I'm not one of them."

"I didn't say that you were," Ian replied.

347

"There's something very strange going on here, T. L., and we need your help to end it. Fifteen men are dead, and I don't want to see any others lost. Do you want more deaths on your conscience?"

T. L. squirmed unhappily, and his eyes began to fill with tears. "I'm the only one who's likely to end up dead, and that will be for talking to you."

"The mine is shutting down for tonight's game," Ian reminded him, "and it won't reopen. As I said, Haven Wray and I didn't elope. We were taken prisoner and held not in the mine, but in a labyrinth that predates the mine by what might be a thousand years. You could be a part of the most significant archaeological discovery of all time, or you could be just another kid who made the wrong choice and ended up in a penal colony. It's your call."

T. L. cast an anxious glance between Ian and Yale. They wore such serious expressions, he knew they weren't bluffing. "I'll talk, but only if you first agree to get me out of here. I've seen a few of the circle tattoos, but there might be more men wearing them and if only part of the group is arrested, the rest are sure to come after me."

Ian handed him the pen. "Your safety will be guaranteed. The men providing security for the games are our men. You can sleep on board one of their ships, and leave with them. We'll announce that you've been arrested for harrassing one of the Flames and are being transported for trial. Alado will provide you with another job, and you'll never have to spend another day in a mine."

T. L. licked his lips as he considered Ian's offer. "Can you really promise that?" he asked.

Yale took a step closer. "We never offer anything we can't provide. Why would you want to cover for murderers? Do you think they deserve your loyalty just because they work here on 317? You obviously know they're dangerous or you wouldn't be in fear for your life. You're the brave one, T. L.; don't sacrifice your future for cowards."

T. L. rolled the pen between his palms, then handed it back to Ian. "Would you put the promise you made to me in writing?"

"Are you saying my word isn't good enough for you?" Ian challenged.

Ian's golden stare made T. L. wish he had worded his request more diplomatically. "No, sir. I just thought I'd better have some proof I can take with me in case I really do get arrested for harrassing the Flames."

"It was only one of them," Yale reminded him, "not the whole team."

"Whatever. I don't want to have to defend myself with nothing but air."

Ian took the pen. "I knew the first time I talked with you that you were a smart man, T. L." He used the first sheet of paper and wrote a brief guarantee of armed guards to provide security, passage from 317 on a secure vessel, and a job that paid as well, or better than, being a miner did. He added a generous cash award; then, after a moment's hesitation, signed his real name and handed the page to T. L.

T. L. read the neatly penned words and appeared satisfied, but his mouth dropped open when he came to the signature. "You can't really be Ian St. Ives!" he cried, thinking he had been tricked.

"Oh yes, he is," Yale swore, "and he has the medals to prove it. You've got your promises in writing; now give us the names or I'll start squeezing them out of you like frosting from a pastry tube. Have you ever watched a chef decorate a cake? They don't like to waste a drop of frosting and they'll pull and twist and press with their thumbs to get the last sticky glob."

T. L. understood that was precisely what Yale intended to do to him and gagged just thinking about it. He pinned his hopes on Ian. Growing up, Ian had been one of his heroes, but he had never seen a photograph of him where he wasn't competing dressed in a sleek gold suit and a helmet. "It really is you, isn't it?"

Ian nodded. "Give us the names, T. L. I don't want to miss even a minute of tonight's game."

Even horrified by Yale's threats, T. L. was still wrestling with his conscience. "I had two older brothers, and as soon as I learned to talk, they taught me it was wrong to tattle. They weren't murderers though, and the men you want are, aren't they?"

"Every last one," Ian assured him. "If you can't do this for yourself, do it for Haven Wray. They dropped her into the maze to die. They knew I was after them, but there was no reason to harm her. What kind of men would kill a treasure like Haven?"

"I'm no snitch," T. L. exclaimed, "but you're right. They ought not to have endangered her life. Is she safe?" He seemed really concerned, and then his eyes took on a bright glow. "Is she going to play tonight? The Satin Spikes are favored to win, but if Haven's going to play, we ought to get our bets in quick before everyone finds out and the odds swing back in the Flames' favor."

Ian caught Yale's eye. He was providing Rainey with a generous cash reward, but clearly he was more excited about the possibility of winning even more. Ian used it. "We'll place a bet for you, but only after we have the names."

T. L. opened his mouth to argue, then thought better of it. He wouldn't have trusted another man, but he knew Ian St. Ives's word was good. Finally fully motivated to cooperate, he folded up the promises Ian had given him, shoved them into his pocket, and began to write. He wrote a name, Marshall Stone, then looked up. "All I know is that several of the miners have the same tattoo. If anyone asks about it, the answer is always the same: Curosity has killed more miners than rock bursts and cave-ins. That's enough to silence most of us."

"But not all?" Yale asked.

"I've not been here long enough to say." T. L. wrote the next name, Bill Tyler, then paused a minute to think. "You've talked with some of these men, so you'll recognize them when you see them. Just keep my name out of it."

Ian nodded. "Keep writing." He was really looking forward to interrogating the men whose names were listed. He wondered which ones they would be—the friendly ones, or the distant crowd who had regarded him with undisguised disdain. He glanced up at Yale. "Let's host a party before the game."

Yale liked the idea. "Perfect. I'm covering the games for the *Colony Sun,* and what my editor wants is the miners' view. Do they love the sport, or the women?"

"The women," T. L. answered without looking up. He had written two more names: Jeff Goodman and Renny Walker.

"You'll select the miners at random, of course," Ian suggested.

"Of course," Yale replied. "I want a fair sampling of opinion, and naturally I'll provide tickets so everyone I interview can attend tonight's game."

T. L. added another man, Mel Davis, then laid down the pen. "Am I going to get to see the game or not?" he asked.

"You can watch it with me from the Flames' bench if you like," Ian offered. "Unless you think that might be too dangerous."

T. L. thought about the risk and shuddered slightly. "Could I wear a disguise? Give me a trainer's jacket and a fake beard and I should be all right."

Ian rolled his eyes. "Did you bring a bag of disguises with you?"

"Damn, I forgot them again," Yale replied. "Don't worry, kid. I'll find something. Maybe we can make a robe out of a sheet, wind a turban around your head, and pass you off as the team's spiritual adviser."

"Are you making fun of me?"

Ian pointed to the list. "Of course not. Write."

T. L. re-read the list and pursed his lips thoughtfully. "I'm pretty sure Juan Gonzales has the circle tattoo." He wrote his name. "But if he doesn't, you won't give him any trouble, will you?"

"Absolutely none," Ian vowed. "You've only come up with six names. Is that it?"

T. L. turned around in his chair. "Look, I'm no undercover agent. I'm just a miner, and I don't make it a habit to eye the other men in the shower. Plenty of them have tattoos all over their bodies, so there's a good chance I've missed a few." He slapped his pocket. "You didn't say I had to provide you with any set number of names. Won't six be enough to start?"

Ian appeared to consider that question before he gave a reluctant nod. "It will have to be. I want you to wait right here, T. L., and help Mr. Nash set up the party." He quickly copied the list of names, gave it to Yale, and kept the original for himself. "Here's the guest list. I'll be back before you've opened the first bottle of wine."

"With me here?" T. L. howled. "I thought you were going to protect me."

353

"I am, but you'll make a great decoy for the time being." He grabbed his helmet, and pulled it on. "I'm going to pay Egon a little visit, and give him a personal invitation to our party."

"Oh my God," T. L. began to moan, but Yale slapped him on the back to silence him. "Stop that or I'll tie you up and toss you in the closet."

Leaving T. L. in capable hands, Ian strode out the door. Believing shutting down the mine would take a great deal of work, he thought he would find Egon Rascon at his desk. If he wasn't—well, Ian wasn't worried. The superintendent might believe he was still running things on 317, but wherever he was, he was about to learn he had just been demoted and replaced.

Chapter Eighteen

Ian lowered the visor on his helmet before he entered Egon Rascon's office and stood at attention as the electronic secretary's metallic voice greeted him from the communications panel. The name, Miles Keeton, appeared over his breast pocket, and the secretary's scanners read the identification and quickly compared it to the roster of transport personnel visiting 317. Once verified, the secretary greeted him warmly.

"Good afternoon, Lieutenant Keeton. If you wish an appointment with Mr. Rascon, state your problem and one will be made."

"I need to see Rascon immediately," Ian replied. "We've got a serious problem in the docking bay, and it can't wait. Tell him it's an emergency."

Ian waited as his message was transmitted to

Egon, and he rushed inside as the door to the inner office slid open. Egon looked up, obviously perplexed by the report of an emergency, but before he could speak Ian had circled his desk and yanked him out of his chair. Egon's dark eyes filled with confused terror, and Ian thoroughly enjoyed his discomfort before he flipped up his visor and spoke.

"I know you weren't expecting me this afternoon, or any other day, for that matter, but it's surprising how easily people can come back from the dead when they're highly motivated."

Panicked by the confrontation, Egon struggled to break free, but Ian slammed him back against the detailed maps of the mine hanging along the wall. He could actually see the collision of strong emotion and well-rehearsed alibis brighten the superintendent's gaze, and laughed. "Not even an avalanche could keep Haven and me trapped in the maze. How does it feel to be outsmarted, Rascon?" To emphasize his point, Ian bounced Egon off the wall with a force that nearly snapped his neck.

"Marshall Stone gave me the whole story. Renny Walker corroborated it in exchange for a reduced sentence. I've arrested the whole crowd, Rascon. Anyone who ever had anything to do with the maze is going down. Did you actually believe you could get away with abandoning Haven Wray and me to die underground?"

Egon had been so certain he was rid of John Hyatt, he couldn't even think, let alone defend himself. Terrified to have been caught, he just stared, hovering on the verge of hysteria as he saw his successful career turn to ashes around him. The members of the Circle had all sworn never to reveal the secrets of the maze. How could any of them have betrayed him?

Ian gave Egon time to become truly desperate, then offered a slim ray of hope. "I actually liked you, Rascon," he lied. "Jeff Goodman doesn't have a kind word to say about you. Neither does Bill Tyler, but I would have defended you had it not been for the avalanche. I don't recommend being buried alive. Would you like to discover firsthand how it feels?"

Egon shook his head emphatically. He would have died rather than implicate the others, but now, knowing that he had been betrayed, he was completely demoralized. He went limp, but Ian caught him and shoved him back against the maps.

"Everyone's talking," Ian swore, "and the story is even worse than I imagined." Ian would never have used such a transparent ruse on a seasoned criminal, but Egon was unfamiliar with the workings of the true criminal's mind and so was much easier to torment as a result.

"You're all more twisted than the swirling design of your tattoos, and nothing you can tell me will save you from multiple murder charges. Your whole evil pack will live out its days in penal colonies where the only magical maze will be what's left of your brain after a couple of years at hard labor. Working in a mine is light aerobic exercise compared to what a penal colony demands in exchange for subsistence rations."

"Please," Egon sputtered pathetically. "I know more than Renny. You ought to have offered me a deal rather than him."

Ian scoffed. "Do you honestly believe I'll fall for that? You couldn't possibly know more."

Terrified of a life sentence in a penal colony, Egon would have traded away his children for clemency, and he quickly elaborated on his plea. "Please. Let me give you a statement. You can compare it to Renny's, and you'll see at a glance that mine is much more valuable."

Ian scowled, appearing to be totally bored by Egon's suggestion. "I've already made the deal with Renny, and I won't go back on my word. Now we're going out to the docking bay where the security forces' ships are waiting. You'll be formally charged there." He kept hold of Egon's arm and forced him around the end of the desk. Ian waited until they were out in the hallway before issuing his next order.

"I meant what I said; I actually liked you, Rascon, so I'm going to let you walk out to the docking bay under your own power. But if you so much as break stride to sneeze, I'll put you in chains and drag you there." He released Egon with a shove that nearly knocked the devastated man off his feet.

Near tears, Egon shuffled down the corridor and through the wide double doors leading to the entrance of the mine. He veered to the right, rather than the left, and kept up a slow, docile pace until they entered the central docking bay, where the transport ships were loaded. On either side of the main launch area there were several additional bays, so that smaller commercial and private craft did not compete with the huge transport ships for docking space.

Without prodding, Egon led Ian into the bay where the ships belonging to the troops providing security for the games were docked. They climbed the ramp of the first vessel in line, and Ian was pleased to recognize the guard standing just inside the hatch. "I've a prisoner for you, Jackson. He claims to have vital information. Bring us a recorder and I'll interrogate him myself."

Yale Lincoln had just transmitted the message that Ian St. Ives had been found alive, and Jackson was eager to do whatever he could to assist him. He promptly furnished a recorder, and a private cabin for the interview. "Is there anything else you require, sir?"

Until that instant, Ian had had too much on his mind to remember how hungry he was. "Yes; bring me something to eat. I don't care what. Just make it quick."

As Jackson left to attend to the request, Ian pointed to the bunk. "I don't have much patience when I'm hungry. Sit down and start talking. Let's check to make certain the recorder is operating before you get too far along. State your name, the date, and give me the names of your group, starting with Stone."

Egon slumped down on the bed, his knees splayed wide. A man who usually took great pride in maintaining an immaculate appearance, he made no effort to look professional now. He stumbled over his name and the date. "Marshall Stone," he breathed out on a long sigh. "Renny Walker, Don Barnes, Bill Tyler, Jeff Goodman, Mel Davis, Juan Gonzales, Luis Moreno, Alan Packer, Ruben Flores." He paused, then couldn't bring himself to add the last name. When Ian didn't force the issue he looked up. Dispirited, his eyes held a wounded glaze.

"And you," Ian said. When Egon nodded Ian replayed the list, and was satisfied that the recorder was in perfect working order. "Eleven is an odd number in more ways than one," he prompted, wondering if there weren't more.

"There were usually twelve. The last man, the one whose death brought you here, was the twelfth."

"Twelve," Ian repeated. "The exact number of your crews."

Egon nodded. "It was a crew working on the third level that discovered the existence of the maze."

Ian remembered when the miners had first begun to disappear. "That was in the mine's second year of operation," he stated with convincing certainty. "Even if you believe Renny has already told me something, be sure to include it in your statement as well."

Egon wiped the threat of tears from his eyes. He was so badly frightened that he had great difficulty organizing his thoughts. "The original group knew their discovery was worth more than gold and didn't report it to the mine's owners. They swore themselves to secrecy, and the Circle was born."

"The Circle," Ian commented, as though this were nothing new, "sealed the oath with the Celtic tattoo."

Again he nodded. "They could not have found a more appropriate symbol. The Celts believed the winding of the knots traced a mystic path. You've been in the maze. It provides a glimpse into the mystery of life as no other experience ever has, or will. It allows one to walk the halls of eternity."

"Three men died that first year," Ian reminded him, "and their bodies were never found."

Egon shrugged helplessly. "The spirit of the maze can turn from sublime to cruel in an instant. You may have experienced that tendency yourself. Rather than see their numbers diminish and risk losing their fabulous secret, the survivors of the original Circle brought in new members to keep the size of the group constant at twelve. I was the first administrator invited to join, and because of their respect for Ruben Flores's work, he was also asked to become a member. It was agreed, though, that the miners would always be in the majority."

"What was the Circle's policy when a prospective member refused your invitation?" Ian asked.

"No one has ever refused!" Egon claimed. "Why would anyone reject the opportunity to experience what has to be the marvel of the universe? The current members follow the same pattern the first Circle set in the beginning. We draw lots for chances to run the maze, sneaking into the mine through the ventilation system. Sometimes a member doesn't come out, but that's a small risk considering what we've gained."

Ian removed the chair from the desk and sat down facing Egon. "Are you actually going to maintain that they just disappear?"

Egon's woebegone expression mirrored his distress. "Oh, I know how preposterous it sounds. They couldn't have simply vanished. They must have fallen into a pit hidden in a narrow hallway, or become trapped when the alignment of the walls shifted suddenly. There has to be a reasonable explanation, but the truth is, despite extensive searches, no evidence of the victims' fate has ever been found."

"Nothing?" Ian pried. "Not so much as a lost shoe or a pool of blood?"

Egon shook his head. "The maze presents a great many mysteries, and the fate of the missing men is among them."

"Convenient theory," Ian countered. "It's far more likely that whenever a miner threatened to leave the Circle he was the next one to 'disappear.'"

Even with his world collapsing around him, Egon wouldn't accept that accusation. "Absolutely not. We still have some of the original members of the Circle, and there's no reason to believe they've lied to the rest of us. I've only been a member for two years, but in that time the men who vanished hadn't made any threats. They hadn't caused any problems at all, and why would they, when the maze offers so much? It provides an endless challenge of adventure, but also the ultimate in tranquillity, and bliss for those who simply choose to meditate at its core."

Egon dared to meet Ian's gaze. "Why don't you join us? Isn't what you've experienced enough to make you long to return to the maze? Become one of us, and protect the Circle. What can you possibly gain by destroying us?"

Astounded by Egon's invitation, Ian sat back and regarded him with a skeptical gaze. "I don't find being lost and hungry all that enjoyable, nor did Haven Wray. But we're not miners. Perhaps after spending so much time burrowing underground the maze holds more appeal for them."

Seizing the chance to win Ian to his side, Egon grew positively inspired. "Dismiss all the charges against us for lack of evidence. Without our testimony, you've nothing whatsoever to implicate us in the deaths of the missing men. The simple truth is that we're not reponsible. All entered the maze willingly, and after the first few had vanished the risk was well known. We took it on eagerly, for the chance to confront the maze on its own terms. Join us, and you'll never regret the decision."

Ian wasn't even tempted. He was about to say so when Jackson returned with a thick sandwich and a tankard of Martian ale. He thanked him and took a bite of the sandwich, washing it down with ale. The potent beverage was chilled rather than warm, as he preferred it, but he was too thirsty to complain. He wiped his mouth and refused Egon's offer.

"I wouldn't join the Circle no matter what the compensation, but you're forgetting that you're the superintendent here, as well as a member of the Circle. You're responsible for the health and welfare of the men under your supervision. That you allowed them to continue entering the maze once the risk was known, makes you guilty of not merely abdicating your responsibility, but of participating in a conspiracy of silence as well. Had you handed the men an antique revolver to play Russian Roulette you would be no less responsible for their deaths."

Disappointed that the significance of his invitation had not been appreciated, Egon grew sullen. "What the men did in their free time was their own business, not mine. Besides, the majority of the deaths occurred before I was posted here, so you can't blame them on me."

"In addition to complicity in the deaths of the missing men, I'm charging you with attempted murder. Had Haven and I not been such well-trained athletes we'd never have survived the maze."

Egon didn't respond to Ian's mention of his athletic ability, and he saw no reason to admit who he really was. Regardless of what name he had used, Egon had wanted him dead.

"There was never any intention of allowing us to survive, was there? I know we were being tracked, because as soon as we escaped the maze, we came within inches of being buried beneath an avalanche you set in a deliberate attempt to kill us. Alado will continue to support your ex-wives and children, Egon, but a conviction is assured. You're going to live out your days in a penal colony."

Having heard enough, Ian switched off the recorder and stood. He slipped the recorder under his arm and picked up what was left of his sandwich and ale. "You'll have to excuse me; I'm hosting a pre-game party for your friends." He went to the door, then appeared to have just recalled an important point and turned back. "By the way, Marshall Stone hasn't told me a thing, and neither has Renny Walker. What do you suppose the Circle will do to you when they discover just how swiftly you betrayed them all?"

Egon Rascon's expression filled with such pitiful horror, Ian almost felt sorry for him. "If you think that's bad, wait until you get to the penal colony and the inmates learn you're a snitch. I'll bet you don't last a month."

Ian went out the door and handed the recorder to Jackson. "This contains testimony we'll need for the trial. Lock it up, and then take Mr. Rascon into custody. Separate him from the others I'll send over or they're likely to tear him to pieces."

"Yes, sir. I'll take good care of all the prisoners."

Ian finished eating before he left the ship. He had intended to go straight to Yale's room, but he wanted to be certain Haven was resting comfortably. He stopped by Aren's to check on her.

Rather than open his door, Aren gave him a whispered message. "She's asleep, and I don't think I ought to wake her."

"No, I don't want you to," Ian assured him. "I'll see her at the game." As Ian turned away, he was filled with a longing he scarcely recognized, but he missed Haven, and very badly. There were women he had bid good-bye with regret, but it had been such a fleeting emotion that it hadn't troubled him for more than a few moments. Being separated from Haven brought on an entirely different feeling, however—an aching need that signaled the deepest form of loneliness. He turned back toward Aren's door, but then, putting Haven's need for rest above his own need for her company, he went on to Yale's room as he had first intended.

Yale welcomed him, but T. L. begged him for the chance to leave. In an expansive mood, Ian took pity on him. "Rascon's already under arrest, but there won't be any announcement of the charges until after tonight's game, so don't go bragging to your friends that you've been part of an undercover operation. In fact, don't ever mention your part in this. Did you place your bet?"

"Yes, sir," T. L. assured him with an anxious nod. "Mr. Nash called it in just after you left, and he gave me a ticket too." He began inching toward the door. "Can I at least tell my friends that I've met you?"

Ian had never revealed his identity on another job, but this one had presented challenges unlike any he had ever faced. He couldn't continue to be a mystery figure at Haven's side, but revealing his identity would change his life so completely, he would no longer reconize it. It was no wonder T. L. was confused. So was he.

"That would be the same as admitting you were part of this operation, T. L., and you can't do that," Ian warned again.

Disgusted with himself for not understanding such an important detail, T. L. went to the door. "Right. Well, good luck with your party, and I'll check with you later about my new job."

Ian smiled as the young man hurried out. "Can you remember being that young, Yale?"

"Dimly. I was fresh out of Alado's flight academy and thought I knew it all."

"That's just because there was so much less to know way back then. How's the party coming? I have four more names for you."

Yale provided a quick overview of what he had accomplished. "I gave each of the men a slightly different time so they won't all be on the same tram and become suspicious. And I threw in a few men we've no reason to suspect, just to keep things interesting. Once everyone is here, I'll dismiss them and arrest the others. We can't let them see you until then."

"Unless, of course, I wear a disguise," Ian teased.

Yale laughed with him. "What did you have in mind?"

When the first of the men arrived to pick up his ticket for the game he was welcomed by Yale and served a plate of steaming hors d' oeuvres by a solicitous steward dressed in a starched white coat and tall chef's hat pulled low over his brow. A carelessly knotted neckerchief obscured his chin and muffled his words, but his graceful gestures kept the guest's attention focused on the food. The desktop had been turned into a buffet and bar, and with a drink in one hand and a plate in the other, each guest was soon engaged in a heated debate over which team would win that night. The efficient steward kept his back to the room as it began to fill, but he provided everyone passing by with a generous supply of both food and drink and won many a slap on the back for his hospitality.

The miners' deep voices echoed off the walls as the room became more crowded. After downing several drinks apiece they were a relaxed lot who lounged against the walls and sprawled back on the bed. Yale moved among them, refilling glasses and asking the questions necessary for his article on the popularity of Rocketball for the *Colony Sun*. While several men swore they simply loved the fast-paced sport, most admitted to a great fondness for the long-legged women who played the game.

Once everyone had arrived Yale quietly suggested to one of the miners who wouldn't be charged that he was in danger of missing the game if he didn't leave immediately. He slapped a ticket into the startled man's palm, relieved him of his plate and glass, and showed him to the door. He waited a few minutes before weeding out the next innocent man, but did it with an understated ease that escaped the others' notice.

Ian stiffened the drinks and replenished all he could as Yale thinned the ranks of the guests. While he had yet to attach the proper name to anyone other than Ruben Flores, the robotics expert, he recognized the faces of the rest. Without exception, like Ruben, they had been the friendly, charming men who had wished him luck on his mission. There wasn't one of the surly brutes who had shunned him among them.

As soon as the last man who would be excused was gone, Yale caught Ian's eye. Knowing the remaining ten men would soon notice something peculiar about the gathering, the agents did not waste another second. Yale raised the tablecloth slung over the desk, pulled a laser pistol from the drawer, and tossed it to Ian. Then he grabbed his own and wheeled around to face his guests. Well on the way to being drunk, several failed to notice that Yale had armed himself until he called their attention to the fact by waving the weapon dramatically.

"I must admit to inviting you all here under false pretenses, gentleman," Yale offered apologetically. "I didn't actually plan to hand out free tickets, but to arrest the whole lot of you for murder."

Yale had their full attention now, but as Ian removed his hat and tossed away his neckerchief it swiftly shifted to him. As the Circle recognized him with anguished gasps, he raised his pistol menacingly. "Should any of you make the mistake of thinking we're bluffing, I'll be happy to save Alado the cost of your trial. If that's not enough to make you behave yourselves, there are security forces right outside the door, waiting to back us up and take you into custody."

Only now did eyes blurred by alcohol notice that the membership of the Circle was gathered there. Ian waited for their plight to sink in before he added the next shock. "Haven and I escaped the maze this morning. In addition to being charged with complicity in the deaths of the missing men, you'll also face trial for attempting to murder us. With the convincing descriptions of the hazards of the maze we intend to give, to say nothing of the avalanche you set, you'll all be convicted."

Carefully separating himself from the miners, Ruben stepped to one side. "There's been a mistake," he insisted with a disarming smile. "I don't belong here. I'm an engineer, not a miner."

Ian gestured with his laser. "Roll up your left sleeve, Ruben. Then we'll see just how innocent you look."

Ruben's expression froze in a frenzied mask of horror. "You can't search us without warrants," he cried.

"We have them," Yale assured him.

"As well as a confession implicating all of you," Ian added. He watched the men scanning each other's faces to identify the missing man. "That's right: Egon Rascon has proven to be a wonderfully helpful source on the inner workings of the

Circle. For our side, at least. His testimony will seal your fate. I'll recommend that you're all placed on the same work detail at whatever penal colony you serve out your terms. That way you'll be able to maintain your splendid sense of camaraderie."

Because security forces really were waiting outside his door, Yale began to back up to let them in. He had taken only half a step before Ruben hurled his glass at him and, with a strangled cry, rushed Ian. Caught by surprise, the miners hesitated a moment too long, for as they began to surge forward, they tripped over Ruben's body. Ian had fired before anyone had had time to react. Glasses fell all around them as the miners threw up their hands to surrender peacefully.

"Oh damn," Yale howled. "It will take the rest of the afternoon to clean up this mess." He opened his door and, as promised, uniformed members of the security force entered the room. They plucked the men from the group one by one, secured their hands behind their backs, and marched them out. Several spit on Ian as they walked by.

"When's Control coming in?" he asked Yale.

"Tomorrow. It's a shame he'll miss the game, but he's never been a sports fan." Yale moved aside as two of the security troops slid a body bag under Ruben Flores and quickly zipped him up in it. "That was quite a shot."

Ian wasn't proud. "He as much as committed suicide and you know it. It didn't surprise me at all. In every operation there's one who prefers death to imprisonment."

Yale watched the security troops carry out Ruben's body. "I guess he didn't have anything to live for. What about you? Would you make the same choice?"

Ian sampled one of the pastry-wrapped hors d' oeuvres. He wasn't really hungry, but it was surprisingly good, and he ate another before responding. "No. I'm no coward. Besides, I've got good friends like you who'd find a way to break me out."

Yale laughed out loud at that boast, then punched Ian on the shoulder. "You might have a long wait, but it's nice to know you think so highly of my abilities."

"Let's just hope you never have to prove them on my behalf." Ian helped Yale pick up the glasses and plates littering the floor, but they carefully avoided stepping in the pool of blood. "Criminals always make mistakes," he mused aloud. "The Circle was so proud of the maze that they tattooed its design on their arms. What incredible arrogance."

Yale went to the communications panel to summon a maintenance detail to remove the gory stain from the carpet. "Want to give me a tour of the maze before Control arrives? I'd really like to see it."

Ian shot him a threatening glance. "I won't ever go back into the maze, and I wouldn't advise you to go in alone. Control will surely shut down the mine to allow experts to study it, but it's far more than a labyrinth made of stone. It has an extraordinary life to it, Yale, and I've got to work on my report before my memories grow any more faint."

"You're welcome to stay here."

"No thanks. I'm going back to Egon's office. It's sure to be quiet." Ian had the notes he had made earlier in his pocket, but he thought he might find some useful evidence in Egon's files that he would want to include. He paused at the door. "Thanks for your help. I know Control expects us to work together whenever the opportunity arises, but I don't want you to think I'm not grateful. You're a fine agent."

Surprised by that unexpected tribute, Yale stared at Ian. He had lost weight since he last saw him, and his features were sharper, if no less handsome, but there was an additional difference about him that he couldn't name. "This case has changed you," Yale commented softly.

"They all have," Ian replied on his way out, and for the first time it occurred to him that it might be time to make a change while there was still enough left of him to salvage.

Chapter Nineteen

Haven slept until an hour before the game. Aren had brought her uniform, boots, and helmet to his room, but she felt an unaccustomed reluctance to don them. She remembered her first game with the Flames. At seventeen, she had been so eager to get on the court, she had been dressed two hours before the rest of the team. Then she had had to endure a frustrating wait until the last few minutes of the final quarter, when she had finally been sent in as a substitute. She had seized the opportunity to prove her value to the team as though she might never have another; those were still some of the finest minutes she had ever played.

That game was as clear in her mind as the day it had been played. There were so many others, whole seasons perhaps, that she could not separate into distinct memories, but her first game existed in sparkling clarity. She had had a fabulous career, but as she sat in Aren's room her prospects for the future seemed as undistinguished as the bland beige decor. After ten years she had nothing left to prove on the Rocketball court, but not a single significant achievement of it.

That stunning lack was what ate at her now as she rose with a weary stretch and carried the colorful uniform into the bathroom to dress. There would be time enough to weep tomorrow, but tonight she would give the fans their money's worth, and lead the Flames to another championship.

Ian dressed in the white jacket, pants, and helmet of the arena security guards to watch the game. He would have preferred to simply go as himself but feared he might create a frenzy among the reporters should a miner point him out as Haven's "husband," John Hyatt. He waited until the spectators had all filed in and taken their seats before he entered. He took up a position in the aisle at the rear of the court nearest the players' cage, and hoped the Flames would have a good game.

The odds displayed above the court still favored the Satin Spikes, but he didn't feel any need to back Haven's team with a bet. He had promised her that he would be there, but he found it difficult to listen to the raucous hoots and shouts coming from the fans without wanting to turn around and demand a respectful silence. He did not understand how the players concentrated on the game with such a distracting racket echoing off the court's high walls. At least in the Artic Warrior competition the fans had been gathered at the finish line rather than strung out along the course.

With time-outs and a halftime break, the game could last two hours, and Ian was as anxious for it to be over as the noisy crowd was for it to begin. He clasped his hands behind his back and attempted to look as though he were really patrolling the arena, but he was far more worried about what might happen on the court than off. Though this was the first live game he had ever attended, he knew the sport's reputation for being brutal was well deserved. It pained him to think that women's lives would be at risk.

A slow smile played across his lips as he remembered the delicious feel of Haven's fair skin. She did not have a single scar, and there was no reason to expect her to gain any that night. Still, he wished she had been content to wave to her fans and sit out the game. During the final minutes before the opening ceremony, he grew increasingly apprehensive, fearing they were going to have a real problem if he couldn't stand to watch her play.

When Aren Manzari walked up beside him Ian didn't mask his anxiety. "Is Haven still going to play?" he asked.

"Yes, but probably only in a token appearance near the end of the game. You needn't worry about her. She's a superb player."

Ian did not understand how Aren could even suggest he adopt such a detached attitude. The arena was vibrating with the force of the crowd's stomps and cheers and the teams had yet to appear. "This is barbaric," he complained.

Aren nodded. "It certainly lacks the gentlemanly calm of your sport, but you can't beat it for excitement. Look, here they come." Eagerly awaiting the contest, the doctor began to applaud with the fans.

Ian would have recognized the entrance of the teams from the swelling volume of the noise alone, but standing in the front, he had a clear view. The Satin Spikes marched out onto the court first with the snappy precision of a military drill team. Lyne Lee, the team captain, moved with a bounce and verve the other eight members of the Spikes did their best to imitate. Dressed in silver suits with bright pink piping, pink boots, and pink helmets held clasped under their right arms, they were a well-coordinated unit.

When they reached center court they broke ranks and, in a move that delighted the spectators, began to wave and blow kisses. Several pointed up at the odds board and cheered. A nimble young woman, Lyne Lee tossed her helmet to a teammate and did three backflips, achieving amazing height on each leap.

"Do they ever get around to playing the game?" Ian asked.

Rather than being impressed, Aren laughed at the Spikes' antics. "Yes, but this serves to warm up the team as well as the crowd. We've used a number of routines this year ourselves. I missed part of the last meeting so I can't tell you what to expect from the Flames, but I can guarantee it will be spectacular."

"Great," Ian moaned under his breath. Positive the whole evening was going to be torture from beginning to end, he would gladly have dispensed with the pre-game entertainment. He enjoyed looking at pretty young women as much as any man, but when the one woman he wanted to see wasn't on the court, it was more of a chore than a treat.

Finally the Satin Spikes moved to the rear of the court to line up for introductions, and the Flames marched out. During the practice session he had attended the players had been wearing red and blue suits, but seeing them all dressed in the vibrant hues of living flames was breathtaking.

The Flames were wearing their helmets and carrying their racquets. They marched in three rows of three, their formation a tight cube until they reached center court. They spread their ranks then and, twirling their racquets, went through a complex rhythmic routine that quickly had the fans on their feet. Even above the wild cheers, Ian could hear men whispering Haven's name. No one had expected to see her play, but despite the surprise, a familiar chant quickly began to rock the arena with pulse-pounding intensity.

"Ha-ven! Ha-ven! Ha-ven!"

Aren looked up at Ian. "Can you stand that kind of competition everywhere she goes?"

Ian didn't disguise his sneer. "Haven and I just came out of a maze that swallowed fifteen men whole and you think I lack courage?"

Not having meant to insult him, Aren shrugged and glanced back toward the team. They performed with a sparkling finesse the Satin Spikes, for all their exuberance, couldn't match. Their right arms outstretched, the Flames formed a wheel they wound and unwound before tossing their racquets high into the air. The lightweight racquets spun, sparkling like pinwheels, before falling into their owners' hands. Then the team formed a single line and with a cocky strut moved to the rear of the court, where they would also be introduced. As Haven went by, Ian caught her eye and waved. She nodded, and he felt a gush of pleasure that warmed him clear through.

Aren left to join the coaching staff on the court, and Ian moved aside so he wouldn't block anyone's view. The game hadn't even started and his heart was pounding in his chest. The lights on the odds board began to flash, signaling the final odds, and a rolling moan washed through the crowd as the men who had bet on the Satin Spikes realized that now that Haven Wray had appeared, they would probably lose all they had wagered. The low, mournful sound was closely followed by cheers from those who had backed the Flames even without their star player.

Blake Ellis waved as the Spikes' coaching staff was introduced. Dressed in silver, he was a handsome figure, but Ian felt the same rage toward him that he had felt in the maze. He willed Blake to look his way, and when he did Ian sent him the most dangerously hostile glance he could affect. Had he been able to mimic his pet snow leopard's menacing growl, he would have. Blake quickly broke eye contact, and Ian gloated for a brief moment, then turned his attention to the game. After the coaches and substitutes filed off the court only the four starters for each team remained. Haven wasn't among her teammates, and Ian, enormously relieved, focused on the play to pick up the finer points of the game.

Only the team serving could score, and as the Satin Spikes had the first service, they fought hard to make good use of that advantage. They had walked onto the court expecting to win easily and played with a ferocious vigor that the Flames were sorely pressed to match. Elida Rivard was sent in to substitute when the Spikes had a five-point lead, and she quickly put an end to their streak. She began to serve for the Flames and soon had the score tied.

Ian had watched contests of every imaginable sort, but he had never seen any teams as competitive as these. The women leapt to great heights, seemingly able to fly, but could just as easily dive low to return a banked shot. They also kept up a running game so swift that Ian was shocked to discover that fifteen minutes had gone by when the buzzer sounded at the end of the first quarter. He expected several players to simply collapse where they stood, but Lyne Lee managed another back flip before leading the Satin Spikes off the court. As for the Flames, they left with the same syncopated strut he had seen earlier. The score now stood Flames twelve, Satin Spikes ten.

Yale Lincoln walked up behind Ian, but rather than tap his shoulder he waited for him to sense his presence and turn around. "Egon Rascon complained of chest pains, so I called the doctor to make certain he wasn't about to die on us. She's a cute little thing, isn't she?" When Ian shot him a bored glance, Yale hurried his report. "Anyway, Dr. Bergh said it was merely an anxiety attack, which is understandable. I told Jackson to allow the prisoners to view the game on the screens in their cells. It's more consideration than they deserve, but I hoped you wouldn't mind."

Ian thought for a moment and then shook his head. "Actually, I see it as more a form of elegant torture than a treat. After all, none of them will ever attend another live sporting event. Did you place a bet along with T. L.?"

Yale widened his eyes in a ludicrous attempt to appear innocent. "Seeing as how I had information that wasn't readily available to everyone, that wouldn't have been ethical."

"No, but it would have been extremely profitable."

"Only if the Flames win."

"They will," Ian assured him.

Yale moved close to whisper, "I placed a bet, but only a small one, so my winnings won't outrage anyone who loses with the Spikes." He winked and moved on, and Ian made another pass down the aisle in his security guard pose.

During the second quarter the competition continued at the same fierce pace, and Ian's mood vacillated between terrified fascination and rapt horror. Blake Ellis had apparently used the break between quarters to inspire the Satin Spikes to play with increased vigor, and despite the Flames' skill at defense, the second quarter ended with the Spikes leading, twenty-three points to twenty.

Rather than providing a respite from the tension, for Ian the half only brought Haven's entry into the game that much closer. Filled with dread, he viewed the season's highlights being flashed across the courts' three high walls. The spectators who didn't leave their seats to buy refreshments kept up a steady roar of exuberant cheers, but each time the play featured Haven, Ian held his breath. Even knowing she had survived the season uninjured, watching her play caused him nearly unbearable pain; the risk of grievous harm was constant.

Ian could not have swallowed a bite had he tried and, not wanting a second of the game to be blurred by alcohol, he remained sober. Fistfights were not uncommon between such partisan fans, and he sent appropriately menacing scowls whenever the behavior of the miners near him became too unruly. Not daring to risk being forcibly ejected from the championship game, the miners either settled back in their seats or left the arena to cool their tempers outside. Ian had never actually worked as a security guard, and in the few moments that he relaxed enough to enjoy himself, he was pleased by the effectiveness of his dark glances. He would have hated to have missed any of the play had he had to drag an obstreperous spectator outside.

At the close of halftime, the teams returned to the court without the theatrical choreography that had accompanied their first entrance, setting a more serious tone for the remainder of the game. Haven would serve as captain of the Flames, while the Spikes would again be led by Lyne Lee. The Flames were behind, so Ian could understand why the coaches had called on Haven so early, but he hoped she could swiftly run up the score and be replaced by a substitute.

Haven had the first serve, but before she let loose with the spectacular acrobatic technique that had made her famous she paused for a split second and nodded at Ian. He hadn't expected such a tribute, and he broke into a wicked grin despite his apprehension. He did not know how he was going to survive the tension of watching Haven play on a regular basis, but now he was so proud of her that he swallowed a plea for caution he knew she would never heed.

Haven's first serve rocketed into the front wall. Though Lyne Lee and her three teammates made a well-coordinated attempt to return it, the ball skidded so close to the side wall that none could. Ian's mouth was so dry he had to peel his tongue off the roof to take up the cheer for Haven, but his enthusiasm was wild and sincere. She sent her next serve low and into the corner. Again the sheer speed of the ball, and its unlikely direction, made the serve impossible to return.

Anticipating a similar serve, the Spikes shifted position, but this time Haven sent the ball straight down the middle to tie the score. Ian wondered how many points the Flames would consider a comfortable margin, and hoped the coaches would remove Haven the instant she reached it. She didn't appear to be tiring, but he knew superb technique could carry her only so far when her endurance could not possibly be at its peak.

Haven's next serve was another blistering attack that slammed into the corner, then zinged across the court at a wicked angle. The Flames now led by one point, but Rocketball was too fast a game for such a narrow lead to be comfortable. Always a play behind, the Spikes moved back, but this time Haven checked her serve so that the ball hit the front wall, bounced past the fault line, and then dropped sharply to roll across the court before any of the Spikes could race close enough to get a shot at it.

It was plain to Ian Haven had not only agility and strength, but an almost magical control of the ball. Small and hard, it sliced the air with lethal speed. Again Haven scored an ace. The score stood Flames twenty-six, Satin Spikes twenty-three.

Confident he was watching the game that would be remembered as Haven's finest, Ian was filled with immense pride. He might have been the best Arctic Warrior of all time, but Haven's incredible talent transcended the limits of any one sport. She combined the beauty and grace of every athletic contest with an instinctive precision no amount of practice could instill. Talent at her extraordinary level was a gift from God, and she had not wasted a particle of it.

The third quarter ended without the Satin Spikes ever breaking Haven's service, and Ian fully expected her to leave the game. When both she and Elida Rivard returned for the fourth quarter he was dismayed, but she still moved with a light, springy step that convinced him she remained in top form. The Spike's Lyne Lee had the first serve, and while her service was adequate, it certainly wasn't the inspired performance the crowd had seen from Haven Wray. Elida sprang forward to return the ball, and after a brief volley Haven slammed a ferocious backhand shot into the corner that dropped the ball cold.

Anticipating another lengthy scoring streak, the crowd roared as Elida Rivard moved to the back of the court to serve. The Flames made the point easily and the score was Flames thirty-eight, Satin Spikes twenty-three. Ian checked the time, and prayed the final quarter would move even more swiftly than the third.

On the next play Elida not only served the ball, she also rushed forward to get into the following volley. She brazenly elbowed Haven aside, but her shot fell short of the front wall, and the

Flames lost control of the ball.

Disgusted by the stupidity of Elida's tactics, the fans sent up a hissing moan, but she strutted back into place without apologizing to Haven, her other two teammates, or the crowd. The referee looked perplexed, pointed toward her, and shook his head, but there was no penalty for a player who abused her own teammates, and he could not expel her from the game. Ian did not like what he had seen any more than the rest of Haven's fans, but knowing Haven had to be running on excitement rather than strength, he was a good deal more worried.

"Take Haven out of the game," he urged under his breath, but the coaches failed to send in a substitute.

Because Ian had suggested it, he could not fault Tory Norton and Christine Barry for playing Haven and Elida together, but he had warned them to curb Elida's destructive tendency for ambitious solo moves at the expense of her teammates. He shuddered as, on the next play, Elida's wildly aggressive manner brought out the worst in the Satin Spikes. From that point on the pace of the game swiftly escalated from fast to erratic, while adherence to the sport's few rules deteriorated markedly and Elida's dangerously unbridled approach posed a threat to everyone.

While Ian's chief concern was for Haven's safety, he didn't want to see any of the players on the brightly lit court hurt. He did not understand why the coaches were allowing Elida to demonstrate such a contemptuous disregard for sportsmanship, unless winning meant more to them than taking pride in how they went about it. Infuriated, he would have removed both Haven and Elida, but while the game was in progress he could not reach the coaches to demand that they send in substitutes.

Rita Blanco was the next to serve. Elida began the play in the backcourt with her, but as Rita served the ball, she again rushed forward, careening past the Satin Spikes in a ruthless bid to block their attempts to return the ball. She was warned again by the referee but shrugged it off, showing no sign of moderating her combative style as the next play began.

Ian had shared the crowd's exhilaration when Haven had run up the score, but now his fears were too strong for him to enjoy the widening margin between the Flames and the Satin Spikes. The tempo of the game grew increasingly frantic, feeding his sense of impending disaster, but all he could do was watch. Haven had controlled the play when it had been her turn to serve, but Rita could only set the ball in motion and get out of Elida's way. On the next volley the ball slammed into the net, rocking the spectators back in their seats, but Ian leapt forward.

Years spent in ice-cloaked silence had given him a calm few men possessed, but he lost all semblance of composure now. The play flew by him as the teams tore down the court. One of the Satin Spikes fell, and Elida leapt right over her to return a shot. Lyne Lee caught the edge of that ball, sending it spinning into the wall and flying out over the court at an odd angle. It would have been an easy shot for Haven to return had Elida not fought her for it.

Elida bumped into Haven in what the hoarse crowd shrieked was a deliberate foul. Nearly run down by another player, the referee missed seeing it, and the play continued wildly out of control. Sent wide, Haven tried to recover, but as Elida raised her racquet in a sweeping arc, the teammates' feet became entangled. Elida went sprawling one way as Haven fell the other, the ball striking the side of her helmet with shattering force.

Already off balance, Haven was unconscious before she hit the highly polished wood. The jarring thump sickened even the most courageous of miners. As one, the other players turned toward the fallen star. The crowd swallowed their cheers in that instant, leaving only the ragged cadence of the players' heavy breathing to disturb the deathly quiet of the arena. The referee blew his whistle but produced only a breathless wheeze. The emergency medical team present displayed the same stunned inertia as the crowd, and only Ian, who had seen death visit too many friends and foes alike, was able to move.

He raced down the front aisle and whipped through the door where the players entered the court. Elida was sitting up now, staring at her fallen teammate with a look of dazed wonder while the other players stood slumped about the court, too shocked by where their violence had led them to come forward to help Haven or to flee the scene. By the time Ian reached her blood was pooling beneath Haven's right cheek. He tore off his own helmet, then unfastened her chinstrap, but he hesitated to remove her crushed helmet for fear of adding to her injuries.

Aren stumbled and nearly fell as he knelt beside Haven. He was ghostly pale and trembling badly. "Don't touch her," he cautioned Ian. "Her neck might be broken."

Elida staggered to her feet as the medical team entered the court. She had torn the skin off her knees, and blood seeped through her uniform, staining the legs, but that was such a slight wound compared to Haven's that the medics went right by her without stopping. Obviously in pain, she limped along behind them.

"You bitch!" Rita screamed. Arms outstretched, she went for Elida in a wild, clawing fit. Shaken, Elida threw up her hands to protect her face, but Rita simply redirected her blows and punched her hard in the stomach. Finally taking decisive action, the referee locked his arms around Rita's waist to pull her away, and Elida, the wind knocked out of her, sank down on her bloody knees and gasped for air. Ignored by the rest of her teammates, she sat alone, crying for the lost glory that would never be hers.

Tory Norton and Christine Barry came up behind Ian, followed by the rest of the Flames, who fanned out around Haven and shielded her from the crowd. "Is she still breathing?" someone asked. "Oh, God, is she dead?" called another, but Aren was too dazed to answer.

Ian couldn't hear Rita's insults or the team's anxious comments above the horrible sound that kept echoing in his mind. Haven's highly polished helmet had cracked with the clean snap of broken glass, but the next sound had been the impact of the ball against her head. Even from where he had been standing he had heard her skull shatter. He shut his eyes against the terrifying image, but he still saw sharp needles of bone piercing her brain.

Startled by a familiar voice, Ian looked up and found Blake Ellis bending over Haven. He was calling her name in anguished sobs. "Get away from her," Ian ordered, "or I'll rip your head right off your neck and kick it out into the crowd."

Blake's vision was blurred by tears, and he couldn't see the evil glint in Ian's eyes, but the grisly nature of his threat clearly registered. "She's my wife," he protested weakly. "I've a right to be here." Ian's harshly voiced denial made Blake flinch, but he refused to leave.

Leaning between them, Aren felt for the pulse in Haven's neck. His hands were shaking so badly, it took him a long moment to find it. "Fight later," he barked, "or we'll risk losing her."

The medical team was used to handling burly miners injured in rock bursts, but with the utmost care they protected Haven's neck and gingerly placed her on their stretcher. Her right arm slipped off and dangled loose until Ian caught her hand and placed it over her chest.

"Be careful," Ian cried. "She fell so hard, she may have several broken bones." He felt sick to his stomach. He glanced out at the crowd and found no one had left his seat. They were all leaning forward, their expressions anxious as they tried to peer around the players to see Haven.

As soon as the medical technicians began carrying Haven toward the exit, Blake shouted to the crowd. "The game's over. The Satin Spikes concede to the Flames."

Unable to understand how anyone could even recall the game, let alone care who won, Ian swept Blake and the Flames' coaches with a single blistering glance. "That's all any of you cares about, isn't it? But no championship is worth a life."

He started past Blake; then, too angry not to give vent to his rage, he wheeled around and slammed his fist into the astonished man's chin. Blake folded in on himself and, with a graceful sway, fell facedown in Haven's blood. Looking as though they feared they were next, Tory and Christine shrank back, but Ian just shook his head in disgust. Aren was tagging along after Haven's stretcher, and he hurried to catch up.

Chella Bergh met the rescue team as they entered the medical unit. Coolly professional, she directed them into the proper room for the treatment of head trauma. "We have the latest equipment. You may be assured that Ms. Wray will receive the very ·best care. Dr. Manzari, please wait here with Mr. Hyatt; I'll give you a full report after I've surveyed the damage."

Aren looked ready to collapse, but Ian wasn't about to relinquish his role in Haven's treatment.

" 'Surveyed the damage?' " he repeated. "Haven's a person, not a piece of equipment you can weld back together."

In a conciliatory gesture, Chella reached out to touch Ian's sleeve, but he backed away to avoid the contact and she was left with her hand hanging awkwardly in midair. Embarrassed, she quickly slipped her hand into her coat pocket to cover the rebuff. "Please forgive me. I didn't mean to sound as though I regarded her as such. The injured miners we treat here have no families present, and I'm dreadfully out of practice in dealing sympathetically with relatives. Now, please, I must ask you to excuse me. Any further delay in initiating treatment could lead to serious complications later." The petite brunette smile warmly. "I'm sure you understand."

Aren cleared his throat with a forced swallow. "Dr. Bergh, as the Flames' physician, I must insist upon being in charge of Haven's care. I won't wait out here as though I were merely a friend."

Chella cocked her head slightly. "Excuse me, but I believe your specialty is sports medicine. Are you also fully qualified to treat such serious head injuries?"

While Aren struggled with his reply, Ian looked past Chella. The technicians had left the door open, and he could see them bending over Haven, inserting an IV in her arm. He didn't want her left alone with strangers. "It really doesn't matter who's in charge," he argued. "Haven needs intensive care now!"

"Yes, of course she does," Chella agreed, "but

I can't begin to design the most effective treatment without a proper diagnosis. Do you wish to assist me in making it, Dr. Manzari?"

"Yes, I most certainly do," Aren replied.

"I want to stay with her too," Ian insisted. "My wife and I are very close."

Aren swore under his breath. "You're not really married, Ian."

Apparently confused, Chella frowned slightly. "What are you two talking about? I thought you and Ms. Wray had eloped, and isn't your name John?"

The tightening in Ian's chest that had begun before the game ratcheted up another notch, but he was no longer trapped outside the action and helpless to intervene. "Dr. Bergh, I do not want my wife to die while we argue technicalities. I insist that you begin her treatment immediately."

Chella gestured helplessly. "That's what I've been attempting to do all along, Mr. Hyatt." Rather than request his—or Aren's—permission this time she simply turned away and entered the treatment room.

Ian followed close on her heels. The technicians had already removed Haven's shattered helmet. One was sealing a long gash in her scalp with a thin instrument that emitted a pale blue light and left a smoking trail. Ian felt dizzy and had to grab the edge of the counter to steady himself. He had seen plenty of blood spilled over the years, but this was the woman he adored, and watching her being treated with such precise indifference was almost too much to bear.

Chella reached up to set the scanner positioned above the treatment table. "You'll be far more comfortable outside, Mr. Hyatt."

"I won't leave her," Ian announced, challenging not only her, but the three men in the room. He watched the technicians exchange puzzled glances, but neither man suggested that he leave.

"Fine, but if you faint, we won't be able to stop to revive you." Chella complimented her technicians on their work, then turned to Ian. "Scalp wounds bleed profusely, but we've taken care of that problem. She's breathing on her own, so let's hope the scanners don't find anything more serious than a slight concussion."

The technicians stepped aside and the first of the scanner's images appeared on the overhead screen. Chella made an adjustment to sharpen the focus and, although Ian lacked medical training, the dark shadow at Haven's temple made it clear that her injury was severe. He took her hand in both of his and squeezed hard, but her fingers remained limp, and he doubted she could feel his presence.

He could read nothing in Chella's expression as she studied the screen, but Aren gave voice to his despair in a low wail. Ian felt the pulse in Haven's wrist growing increasingly faint and bent down to whisper in her ear. "You wouldn't leave me when I was hurt. Don't leave me now. Please, Haven. Don't leave me now."

He closed his eyes and tried to share her dreams as he had in the maze, but all that swept through him was a cold chill, and only Aren's sobs pierced the silent darkness.

Chapter Twenty

Chella was completely out of patience with Aren. "I apologize for my colleague, Mr. Hyatt, but Dr. Manzari has obviously lost all objectivity in your wife's case." She signaled to her technicians. "Please show Dr. Manzari to the lounge." She waited until the sobbing physician had been escorted out of the room, then continued in the same thoroughly professional manner.

"We frequently treat rock burst trauma more severe than this and have an excellent survival rate. In Ms. Wray's case, the impact of the Rocketball is what's causing bleeding within her brain. I'll transfer her into an operating room immediately, and program the robotic surgeon to repair the ruptured blood vessels before swelling and lack of oxygen cause irreparable damage. I can't allow you to remain with her for such delicate surgery, but please be assured that she would receive no finer medical care anywhere in the galaxy."

The technicians returned and, after kissing Haven lightly on the cheek, Ian reluctantly released her hand and backed away. "How long will it take?" he asked.

"No more than a few minutes," Chella assured him, "though it will be several hours, perhaps even days, before we can be confident of a satisfactory result. Normally I'd advise you to wait in the lounge, but I'm afraid Dr. Manzari will only upset you. Stay here if you like, and I'll speak with you as soon as we're finished."

Ian nodded, and Chella pressed the button to open the sliding doors at the end of the treatment room. The technicians rolled Haven into the next room, where she would be prepped for surgery. After a final encouraging smile, Chella hurried after them. As the doors slid closed, Ian slumped back against the counter. After what must have been an initial blinding pain, he was certain Haven had not suffered, but he wanted her to awaken from the surgery the same vibrant woman she had been before today's tragic injury.

He would love her regardless of whatever permanent impairment she might have, but when she had been so special in every way, he did not want her to have to adjust to being anything less. Hot tears stung his eyes, and he brushed them away as he heard someone approaching. He couldn't hide his sorrow from Yale Lincoln.

"Has Haven already gone into surgery?" Yale asked.

"Yes, but Dr. Bergh says it won't take long."

"I'll wait with you."

Ian and Yale had never been particularly close, but Ian was grateful for his company nonetheless. "Thanks. I've never been through anything even remotely like this. I've had friends who've been badly hurt, but never—"

"Your woman," Yale supplied.

Ian had a difficult time pushing the words over the knot of pain clogging his throat. "Yes. My woman." He had never thought of another woman with any sense of permanence. Now, with Haven so gravely injured, he feared they might never have the chance to plan for the future. Growing restless, he began to pace, but the treatment room was small and, despite a usually adequate ventilation system, warm and airless.

His father had died in a medical facility similar to this one, but his death had been expected rather than the result of a sudden injury. Ian resembled him closely, and he recalled how often a cloud of sorrow had darkened his father's amber eyes. The man had never recovered from the loss of the only woman he had ever loved, and it had taken Ian this long to appreciate why.

Haven meant every bit as much to him as his mother must have meant to his father, and poignant memories of the lithe blonde brought back the magical visions they had shared. He lingered over the joyous wedding celebration and the precious child Haven had rocked so sweetly.

He hoped the little boy or girl had had a happy life. Then the bright flames of the first vision flashed across his mind's eye. He had assured Haven the funeral pyre had not been his without ever considering it might have been hers. Now the possibility had become terrifyingly real.

"I can't stand this," he said suddenly, and pressed the button to enter the next room. Used only briefly to prepare for surgery, it was empty now. As evidence of how quickly the technicians had worked, Haven's uniform had been slit open down the front and tossed aside, and now lay crumpled atop her discarded boots. Missing her terribly, Ian started toward the double doors leading into the operating room. There were large windows in the top half, and he approached them.

Yale reached out to stop him. "I don't think you ought to watch."

"I have to," Ian insisted, and quickly pushed past him to get a clear view from the windows. Chella and the technicians had changed into loose-fitting surgical garb, but even with hair covered and face masked, the doctor was recognizable by her petite size. She was standing at a console, programming the robotic surgeon.

Suspended directly above the operating table, the gleaming sphere bristled with multiple arms. It had a spider's fearsome appearance but could be expected to perform the most intricate of microscopic surgery without a single error. Following the diagnosis provided by the scan, it would complete the operation in only a few seconds, rather than the hours it had once required for human surgeons to treat such serious head wounds.

Ian recoiled slightly as a dozen blinking lights certified the robot as fully functional. Elbows jutting, it flexed its angular arms, and telescoping probes tipped with long thin needles appeared. Ian was confident that the robot would perform as expected, but the fact that it resembled a medieval instrument of torture made him ache with dread.

Chella was wearing short sleeves now and, as she reached up to initiate the robot's first sequence of procedures, Ian caught a glimpse of an iridescent blue-green tattoo on the inside of her left arm. "Oh my God," he moaned.

"I told you not to watch." Fearing Ian was about to faint, Yale reached out to grab his arm.

Ian brushed him aside. "Chella's part of the Circle!" he screamed. He slammed his palm against the button to open the operating-room doors, but access was denied from the control panel inside. Hoping the technicians would respond, he beat on the glass with his fists but was ignored. "She's going to kill Haven!"

Chella turned toward him, and though her mask hid her mouth, a taunting smile lit her eyes. The technicians finally glanced his way but obeyed an urgent command from Chella and quickly refocused their attention on their patient. An unconscious sacrifice, Haven was oblivious to the new threat to her life.

Ian had memorized the layout of 317, but even

if he sent Yale to cut the power at the main generators to stop the surgery, he knew he couldn't reach Haven in time. Its swollen metallic body gleaming with a menacing sparkle, the robot surgeon shifted its spindly arms. Then, sliding easily on its cables, it dropped a few inches closer to Haven.

"We've got to open these doors," Ian shouted to Yale.

Readily understanding Haven's plight, Yale turned with Ian to survey the equipment in the small room. The two men noted the bank of sinks at the same instant and ran to them. Prefabricated units, the three basins were bolted to the wall, but with Ian at one end and Yale at the other, they came loose with a jarring, splintering squeal. The men wrenched them from the drain pipes and used the sinks as a crude battering ram. On their second thrust, the wide automatic doors slid half open with a quivering jerk and remained ajar.

The first of the robot surgeon's probes was about to pierce Haven's scalp when the doors burst open. Dropping the sinks with a resounding clatter, Ian dashed into the operating room and with a flying leap swung the complex machine aside while Yale tackled Chella as she tried to flee. The astonished technicians raised their hands and moved back out of the way.

"This is my fault," Yale swore as he twisted Chella's arms behind her back. "I let her in to see Egon Rascon without even considering the possibility that she might be part of the Circle. That was a stupid mistake, and it might have cost Haven her life. I'll make it up to you, Ian."

"Just tie her up and throw her in the corner," Ian ordered, "then page the other team surgeons. There's got to be someone else who can program this ghastly device." Afraid the robot might go wild and injure Haven, Ian kept a firm hold on it. Although jarred when its sequence had been interrupted, it was still adjusting its probes, posing a very real danger to him as it searched for its patient.

Chella swore at Ian in a string of vile epithets but, muffled by her surgical mask, none was clear. "I should have known Egon was lying when he said there were only eleven of you," Ian responded. "Of course, with Ruben Flores dead, there are only eleven left."

Devastated by that news, Chella sagged back against Yale and, thinking she might be having difficulty breathing, he ripped away her mask. She looked up at him, her dark eyes glistening with tears. "Ruben's dead?" she sobbed. "When? How?"

Yale called to Ian. "Egon hasn't spoken to the others, so he didn't know about Flores and couldn't have told her."

"They can catch up on the casualty list later," Ian scolded. "What we need now is a competent surgeon."

Chella glowered at that insult, but when Yale hustled her over to the communications panel she kept quiet as he sent an urgent call for all available medical personnel. In a matter of minutes, 317's off-duty technicians and the surgeons from the Satin Spikes, Pagans, and Zephyrs arrived, along with Aren Manzari, who was still so badly shaken that he had to lean against the damaged doors to remain upright. Ian quickly described the problem, and the Satin Spikes' physician, an elegantly attired grayhaired woman, quickly came forward and introduced herself as Dr. Susan Meyers.

"Robotic surgery is one of my specialties," she announced confidently, but after checking the console she looked up in dismay. "The robot works in concert with the scan image, but what it's being fed is not the data on Ms. Wray's injury, but that from the file of a patient with a malignant brain tumor."

Chella returned the accusing glances sent her way with a sneer of disgust. "That's impossible. The robot must have malfunctioned."

"Get her out of here and charge her with attempted murder along with the rest of the Circle," Ian said. "Now my wife needs help, and fast."

"I've deactivated the robot," Dr. Meyers replied, and as soon as Ian had released it, she set to work reprogramming the highly skilled machine. "You may be assured the robot surgeon will now operate as it should. If the other team physicians will assist me, I won't need the technicians."

Yale hauled Chella toward the badly battered doors. "I'll hurry," he called to Ian, "and come right back."

Ian waved him away, but then took the precaution of checking the arms of the technicians who had been assisting Chella. Neither was tattooed. He took their names, and told them they would be questioned later.

Ian felt even more opposed to leaving Haven now than he had earlier, but knowing she was finally in good hands he took Aren's elbow and pulled him out through the doors.

"Show me where the lounge is," Ian urged, "and we'll wait together."

"I should never have left her," Aren argued. "Haven's health is my responsibility."

Ian looked back at Dr. Meyers. She was relaying orders to the other team physicians in a supremely confident manner; but then, Chella had been equally self-assured. He was used to assessing a situation and then making major decisions quickly, but not when he had as little information as this. "Is Dr. Meyers any good?" he asked Aren.

Aren's voice cracked as he replied, "Yes. She's the best."

Trusting Aren's judgment, Ian walked with him to the lounge, which was now filled with Haven's teammates, both Flames coaches, and several of the Satin Spikes. Blake Ellis was also there, and he came forward before Ian could demand that he leave. His chin was badly bruised, but he looked a whole lot better than he had after their first fight.

"The decision as to who can visit Haven and who's excluded ought to be hers alone," Blake stated forcefully. "Until she refuses to see me, I'm staying."

For a moment Ian was severely provoked, but then it dawned on him that even if Blake's show of concern was tragically late, he did care for Haven and ought to be allowed to remain. "Just stay on the other side of the room," Ian replied. He turned his back on Blake and found a vacant chair along the wall. He sank down into it, and though he was positive he did not look as though he wanted company, one of the Satin Spikes approached him. Still wearing her silver uniform, she looked no more than eighteen.

"Excuse me," she whispered, "but is it true that you're really Ian St. Ives?"

With short black curls and hazel eyes, she didn't bear the slightest resemblance to Haven, and yet that was who Ian saw in his mind. "I was," he answered, "but that was a long time ago."

Blake Ellis came over and took the girl's hand to lead her away. "I'm sorry, but she's just not thinking. I'll see the others don't bother you."

Ian was surprised by that show of courtesy, then realized that Blake must feel very guilty over the way he had treated Haven. He looked away rather than thank him. This should have been a night for wild celebration, but the Flames gathered nearby were weeping softly. Elida Rivard wasn't among them.

He leaned forward and put his head in his hands. He didn't want to think about the surgery, but the image of the robotic surgeon danced in his mind with stubborn persistence. He could not shake the memory of the ghastly scene in the operating room. Every bizarre second had added to the delay before Haven had finally begun receiving the care she so desperately needed, and he blamed himself as much as Chella. Because she had flirted with him as women so often did, he had dismissed her as harmless. He knew better than to make such costly blunders.

As he reviewed his work on 317, Ian was appalled by how stupid he had been. Had he made similar mistakes on previous assignments, he would have been dead years ago. That Haven had been injured on the Rocketball court rather than in the maze didn't matter. He knew he was to blame. Deeply depressed, he barely nodded when Yale joined him. He felt sick clear through, and when Dr. Meyers finally appeared he couldn't even manage an optimistic smile.

Rather than discuss Haven's case in the crowded lounge, Susan took him into an empty treatment room to make her report. "The surgery went well, but I'm afraid the injury was more extensive than we originally anticipated. Damaged nerve and brain tissue doesn't regenerate, but with intensive therapy other parts of Ms. Wray's brain can be trained to take over whatever function she may have lost. She's going to need a great deal of support in the coming months. I know you're not the type of man who'd abandon her, but you should be prepared for some difficult times ahead."

"Can you be more specific?" Ian pressed. "Is

she going to be partially paralyzed, or have great difficulty speaking or remembering things?"

Clearly uncomfortable, Dr. Meyers glanced away. "You're placing me in a very awkward position. I never like to make predictions, but statistics indicate that patients who have had similar injuries generally do suffer both physical and mental impairment. Ms. Wray would not have made such remarkable accomplishments during her career without courage, however, and I expect her to make a good, if perhaps not a full, recovery."

Despite the vagueness of Dr. Meyers's response, Ian understood her warning, but he knew Haven would never settle for anything less than a complete recovery. "May I see her?"

Susan Meyers almost refused, but then, impressed by the intensity of Ian's gaze, gave in, nodding. "She won't know that you're there, but I can see that you need to be with her. Come with me."

The intensive care unit was a circle of patient pods clustered around a technician's station. Rather than beds, the individual pods resembled partially opened cocoons and not only supplied every patient need but continuously monitored the patient's condition as well. Ian had expected the softly beeping monitors, but not how small and helpless Haven would appear in the starkly functional pod. Her head was heavily bandaged and her face was bruised from the fall to the court, but she still looked exceptionally beautiful to him.

"How long will it be before she wakes?" he whispered.

"I can't say, but don't expect it to be anytime soon."

Ian took Haven's hand in a tender clasp. When Dr. Meyers left his side he could more easily look past the bandages and bruises to the dear woman he loved. Earlier in the evening he had been tortured by how difficult it was to watch her play. Now it seemed unlikely that she would ever play Rocketball again, and he would give anything to see her back on the court.

"Can you hear me, Haven? If we've been together before, we'll surely be together again, but I want this life to be the very best it can be. Whatever it takes to make you well, I'll make certain you have it. We'll be a team again. Always."

Unwilling to leave her even if she wasn't aware of his presence, he found a chair so he could sit beside her, but he was soon overcome with the need to do more than simply wait. If Haven required months or even years of rehabilitation, he knew he couldn't show the gnawing impatience that plagued him now, but he did not know where he would find the strength to hide it. Haven was a proud woman, and he knew how hard she would work to regain her strength and agility, but what if her progress was minimal, or painfully slow? How would he keep her spirits up when his own would also be dangerously low?

He knew if he had come out of the maze with the painful injuries he had suffered in the avalanche she would have stood by him during his recovery, but there was a very real danger his pride might have gotten in her way. He had just thanked God for allowing him to walk out of the maze healthy when he was filled with the shattering realization of how close he had come to making another costly error.

The answers he sought were within his grasp; all he needed was the courage to seize them. Knowing that for Haven's sake he could do no less, he got up and went to find Yale Lincoln.

Dr. Meyers was providing those gathered in the lounge with an update on Haven's condition, but Ian caught Yale's eye and motioned for him to follow him. He led him down the hall but stopped outside the intensive care unit and spoke softly to draw Yale near. "I need you to get the laser pistols we used earlier and meet me back here."

Yale shuddered. "You've found more members of the Circle?"

"No, but I think Haven will do much better down in the maze than here in the medical unit, and I'll need your help in opening up a wider corridor to take her back inside."

Appalled, Yale stepped back. "You refused to give me a tour, but you want to take Haven back into the maze?"

"Hush," Ian cautioned. "There are shrines all over the galaxy where people swear they've had miraculous cures. I had a cure there that can't be explained in terms familiar to traditional medicine. It may only be that the maze warps time and speeds the body's own ability to heal itself. I

don't care how it works; all I know is that it does.
Now can I count on you or not?"

In the face of such an unusual request, Yale
did not know what to say. "Won't it be dangerous
to move her?"

That question stopped Ian cold. The possibility
that he might compound Haven's injuries rather
than cure them made his choice more difficult,
but he still felt it was the only one he had. "We'll
be careful," he assured Yale. "If we try to take her
out now, Blake Ellis, Aren Manzari, and probably everyone else here will try to stop us, but if
we wait until after two a.m. we should be able to
do it safely."

Yale still couldn't believe what he was hearing.
"And if we don't try this?"

Ian stifled his growing irritation in favor of a
persuasive calm. "Then Haven will face months,
possibly years, of painful therapy that may shatter her spirit before it heals her body and mind.
I'd want her to take this risk for me. Now go get
the pistols and meet me here at two." When Yale
hesitated Ian had no choice but to remind him
that he had promised to make up for his mistake
in allowing Chella to see Egon.

Yale hadn't forgotten that vow, but Ian had a
reputation for courting danger, and he felt torn.
He wanted to do what was right, but it just wasn't
clear what that was. "If we take her into the maze
and she dies, I don't think I could stand it."

"Do you honestly believe that I could?" Ian
asked. He looked up and down the corridor to
make certain Dr. Meyers wasn't approaching. "I

can't just do nothing, Yale. It wouldn't be right. If you can't bear to have this on your conscience, just bring me a pistol and leave. I'll handle everything on my own and no one need ever know you were involved."

"I'd know," Yale argued.

Determined to have his way, Ian fixed Yale with a defiant stare. "There's no time to waste. The maze healed the gashes in my back and fused my cracked ribs, but I still have a scar on my side, so it can't erase old wounds. If we were to wait until Haven is stronger, we might miss her only chance for a cure. We have to take her down there tonight, Yale. I won't force you to help me, but I'll see you're repaid a thousand times over if you do."

Yale drew in a deep breath and released it slowly. As he saw it, he could either help Ian in a wild scheme that might just as easily result in Haven's death as her salvation, or he could back away and hope nothing went wrong. It was the force of Ian's belief that finally swayed him.

"Well, I've never been one to stand back and watch," he finally replied. "I'll help you, but only because I don't want to see Haven suffer, not because I need to be repaid."

Ian controlled his smile before it spread too wide. "Thank you. I'll see you at two."

Yale turned away and headed down the corridor with a long, purposeful stride. Helping Ian would give him a chance to enter the maze, but he did not believe curiosity, no matter how intense, justified his participation. He was doing this for Haven.

Ian could not recall the last time he had slept, but when he again sat down beside Haven's pod and stretched out his legs, he was far too anxious to relax. "I wish you could help me decide what to do," he whispered. He trusted his heart to know what was right, but that did not mean he wasn't worried. Dr. Meyers stopped by several times and appeared satisfied with Haven's condition but, trapped in the darkness of her dreams, the star athlete had not stirred.

A few minutes before two Yale returned to the intensive care unit, but he waited at the end of the corridor until Dr. Meyers had finished conferring with the supervising technician and had gone on her way. Then he quickly joined Ian. He had the pistols hidden in a backpack he swung over his shoulder.

"Haven's the only patient in this unit, and the technician on duty is reading rather than watching the bank of monitors at his station. When we take Haven out of this pod it's sure to sound an alarm that will immediately catch his attention. How will you handle him?" he asked.

Ian had already solved that problem. "Give me one of the pistols."

Yale clutched the backpack to his chest. "You're not going to shoot him!"

"No, of course not," Ian insisted. "I'm just going to introduce myself as the acting commander of 317 and insist upon his cooperation." Ian extended his hand, and while Yale looked far from pleased, he gave him one of the weapons. "Look, I won't even arm it." Ian carried the laser pistol at his side as he approached the center station. When the technician rose to greet him he smiled, then rested the pistol on the counter.

"I'm Ian St. Ives, and I've placed Egon Rascon under arrest for attempted murder. As the ranking Alado representative, I've taken command of 317 and closed the mine until further notice. You're to finish out your shift and then wait for further instructions."

The startled technician sent a frantic glance between Ian and the pistol and back again. "You're the real Ian St. Ives?" he gasped.

"There's only one," Ian assured him. "I'm taking Ms. Wray out of your unit. Don't worry about her. She'll receive even better care with me."

The technician's mouth dropped open. He quickly caught himself, then checked Haven's monitors. "So far, Ms. Wray's holding her own, but she ought not to be moved."

Ian picked up the laser pistol. "Do you really want to argue with me?"

The lightweight pistol looked huge in Ian's hand. The technician knew the awful damage it could do and shook his head emphatically. "No, sir, I do not."

Ian read the man's identification badge. "Wise choice, Stevens. When Dr. Meyers makes her next pass through here tell her what I've told you. She'll be equally concerned, but there's absolutely no reason for worry. Haven's going to be fine."

Ian turned away, then stopped after a few paces and returned to the technician's station. "Don't even think about sounding an alarm, because everyone on 317 works for me now, and I'll be real annoyed if I have to stop caring for Ms. Wray to deal with security troops."

The technician's eyes were focused solely on the deadly laser. "Yes, sir. I won't cause you a bit of trouble."

"Thank you, Stevens. I'll see you receive a commendation." Ian hurried down the aisle to Haven's pod, where Yale had already shut down the unit's sensors, and removed her IV line. Ian returned the laser to Yale's backpack, then quickly wrapped her in the pod's light blanket, scooped her up in his arms, and nodded toward the exit.

Yale peeked out to make certain the way was clear. "You know this is crazy."

"I sure hope not." Ian followed Yale out into the corridor, and they quickly left the medical unit by the service exit. Had the championship game not ended so tragically, the whole complex would still be rocking with wild parties. But, shocked and saddened, the miners had sought solace in sleep rather than companionship and without a swing shift all of 317 was silent and still.

Her weight a slight burden, Ian sat with Haven relaxed across his lap as they rode the tram to the mine entrance. The machinery that usually created a constant rattle and roar sat idle, and no guards challenged Ian as he carried Haven into the emergency elevator. "Hit the button for the third level," he told Yale.

Unlike the free-falling bucket, the elevator provided a smooth ride, but as soon as Ian stepped out into the tunnel, he was hit with a thick wave of doubt. Refusing to acknowledge it, he lengthened his stride. "I counted the scanners when Haven and I came out this way. I just hope the maze hasn't sealed off the exit we found."

"How could it?"

"I've no idea how the maze works, Yale, but it's a living structure and apparently shifts to suit itself whenever it chooses."

Yale found it impossible to visualize such a marvel. Hoping to actually experience it, he followed along closely. When Ian finally came to a halt beside a narrow crevice he removed one of the laser pistols from his backpack and set it on full charge. "Did you pick up any tips on how to go about this from the miners?" he asked.

"No, but I saw them sweep the laser canons across the surface of the rock. I'll get out of the way while you try it."

Yale peered into the narrow fissure he was expected to widen. He supposed there might be other ways into the maze, but he knew none of the Circle would be cooperative should they ask for directions. He aimed the laser and passed the powerful beam of light along the inside of the crevice. Rock chips flew every which way, and he had to duck to avoid getting hit.

"This may take a while," he warned.

"Just do it," Ian replied. Haven was snuggled against him, and he hugged her more tightly as he moved farther out of the way. He found a place to sit where he could watch Yale without being bathed in shattered stone and hoped Haven wasn't too uncomfortable. He knew he should have thought to dress Yale in a miner's protective garb, but there was simply no time to return to the surface for a white suit.

Yale did not waste his breath complaining about the constant jagged shards sent his way. He changed pistols whenever the one in use needed to be recharged and gradually gouged out a larger channel. He had to stop frequently to clear away the rubble with his hands, but though it took longer than he would have liked, he finally succeeded in cutting a path wide enough for Ian to carry Haven into the maze.

"Do you mind going in first?" Ian asked. "There are a couple of massive doors I'll need you to open."

Still not certain what to expect, Yale returned the pistols to the backpack and slung it over his shoulder. "If we're going to back out, we ought to do it now."

Ian shifted his hold on Haven slightly. "No. For me, there's no turning back." As Yale entered the newly widened corridor, Ian followed, eager to return to the bright ring of flame. He felt the last chill of the cool mine air brush his nape and shivered with exhilaration rather than dread.

Yale hauled opened the first door, and Ian started down the long flight of stairs. Haven felt so warm and alive in his arms. He prayed that when they left the maze a second time, she would again be walking by his side.

Chapter Twenty-one

Without the security of a handrail, Control had to follow Yale Lincoln down the steps with a choppy, one-footed gait. When he at last reached the bottom and looked out over the maze he could only stare in wonder. He had observed a great many curiosities over the years, but none as powerfully forbidding as this sprawling secret city. The high walls and domes gave only a hint of its hidden wonders, but he longed to explore them all.

"I never expected anything as wondrous as this," he exclaimed.

Yale had brought along a sack of supplies for Ian and shifted it from one hand to the other. "Ian could have died here, and Haven Wray still may."

Unused to criticism from his agents, Control's

mouth sank into a hostile downward turn. "No one could have foreseen this alien world."

Yale thought that a pitiful excuse. "Drew Jordan retired. If Haven dies, Ian won't work for you again. If she lives, she may very well be an invalid whom he won't leave. It looks as though I've just been promoted to your top man by default." He waited until Control wrenched his gaze from the maze and turned toward him. "If you ever send me into a deathtrap like this, I'll come back to get you, even if it has to be from beyond the grave."

Control's sparse brows shot upward. "Threats, Lincoln? That's extremely unwise."

Yale responded with a deliberately evil smirk. "You'll have terrifying nightmares, symptoms of diseases so rare they haven't even been named, bizarre accidents, and miserable luck in everything you do. It will all be my handiwork, Control. You'd better take very good care of me, or what's left of your future will be painfully bleak."

"That is enough!" Control sputtered. Deeply insulted by Yale's flagrant insubordination, he started off toward the maze with an uncharacteristically aggressive swagger. Silhouetted against a dancing ring of fire, Ian St. Ives was easy to locate, but when Control reached his side and observed the fragile stillness of the lovely young woman lying in his arms, he had a difficult time greeting him. He waited for Ian to sense his presence and look up.

"I hope you understand that when I sent you here to 317 I never expected you to discover anything as fabulous, or as sinister, as this."

That was as close to an apology as Control was likely to offer for sending an agent out on an assignment totally unprepared, but Ian did not care enough about that oversight to demand anything more. His legs were dangling over the edge of the fiery moat, filled with an enjoyable warmth that dissolved all need for a show of righteous anger. He simply nodded, as though the job had not nearly ended his career.

A sudden bright tongue of flame licked the air, and Control marveled at the fire's lack of blistering heat. "How is Ms. Wray?" he asked.

As Ian looked up, his amber eyes shone with the reflected glow of the flames. "She's doing much better, thank you."

Control knelt down beside them. He was too warm in his black suit, but he did not even consider removing his coat. Haven looked gravely ill to him, but as he watched her chest rise and fall in a steady if shallow rhythm, she stirred slightly, which he hoped was a good sign.

"My ship is standing by to transport her to Alado's finest medical facility. The physicians there can work miracles."

"I've already had a miracle here."

Yale had briefed Control on the activities of the Circle and, realizing that Ian would not accept his advice concerning Ms. Wray, he chose to discuss them instead. "I had absolutely no idea what you'd find here," he apologized again, "or I'd have closed the mine the instant you failed to report in. Instead I sent Yale and security troops. It's always been an effective strategy in the past."

Rather than appreciating Control's tardy concern, Ian simply found his presence an unnecessary distraction. "You'll receive my report as soon as Haven can spare me long enough to write it," he promised. "For now, please, just leave us alone."

Control glanced over his shoulder to where Yale was waiting. "Yale says you've not eaten; he's brought you some food."

"We're not hungry."

"You soon will be." Control rose and motioned for Yale to come close. He took the bag of provisions and set it down beside Ian. "I don't feel right about leaving you here. I'll station a man at the bottom of the steps. He'll provide whatever assistance you might need."

"We have all we'll ever need right here," Ian replied. He meant it too. He had not been able to share Haven's dreams as he had prior to their escape from the maze, but he felt a remarkable closeness to her all the same. He was at peace here, and Haven's relaxed expression convinced him that she wasn't in any pain.

He rocked her gently and stared into the flames. Time might have no significance here, but he knew she was healing. He could sense each flicker of improvement and would remain with her for as long as it took for her to be whole again.

"Leave us alone," he repeated more forcefully.

Control shifted his weight nervously from one foot to the other but stayed put. "We recovered your ship," he said. "The navigational computer had been programmed for deep space, but the Circle didn't realize that the ship would begin broadcasting a distress signal as soon as it was launched from here without you at the controls. It will remain in the docking bay here until you need it."

Ian had forgotten all about his ship, but he was pleased it hadn't been lost. "I'm going to take Haven home to Iceland as soon as she's able to travel. I'll let your office know when we leave."

"There will be no need," Control advised. "I'm staying here for the time being. There is a great deal to be learned, and I don't trust anyone else to supervise the work."

"Be careful," Ian warned, "or the maze will make a prisoner of you too."

"I will exercise the utmost care to avoid such a catastrophe," Control replied. He gave Ian an awkward pat on the shoulder, and then left with Yale Lincoln.

The flames lit Haven's face with a soft glow, and Ian again tried to enter her dreams. They had been younger than they were now in their visions, and he wondered if they were destined always to be parted rather than allowed to live out their lives together. He thought of the mother he had never known, and missed her now with a painful longing. She ought not to have died before leaving an indelible imprint of her love on his heart.

He closed his eyes and breathed deeply. "Stay with me, Haven," he begged softly. "I don't want to miss anything this time. I want the big wedding and the babies and, most of all, to grow old with you."

He called silently to the maze, pleading for it to heal Haven's wounds as quickly as it had his, but she continued to sleep without any sign of waking. It had been almost twenty-four hours since she had been hurt, and he hoped he had not waited too long to bring her into the maze. If he had, then the miracle might never come, but he would not give up until all hope was gone.

When they had been trapped inside the maze had been a mocking prison, but he knew it to be capable of bestowing blessings as well as pain. To distract himself, he forced his mind back to the moment they had awakened on the mossy floor of the octagon. Haven had watched over him then, and he wished he knew what her thoughts had been while she had waited for him to wake.

He longed to take her home to where the ice and snow never melted, but his starkly furnished house held a delicious warmth. "You'll like my house," he whispered. "Or at least I hope you will. If you don't, I'll build you another wherever you want to live. It can be on the scorched plains of a desert, or the paradise of a tropical lagoon. I don't care where we live as long as we're together, Haven. Please don't leave me."

Ian's tears splashed on Haven's face and rolled down her cheek, but she was unaware of his pain. She was lost in a distant world where the shimmering creatures she had once chased through her dreams danced again. Their touch was as light as the mist that heralds a spring rain, and they banished her sorrow with songs of celestial beauty.

Her limbs felt stiff, her motions awkward as she tried to join them. She feared they would laugh, or leave her behind, but they floated near, their thoughts adoring as they reached out to touch her. They drew her into their midst, embracing her ecstatically, as though she were a precious daughter who had long been lost. They lifted her up, filling her with their graceful elegance, and coaxed her into their dance. Her steps were light, her gestures fluid, and she again felt the joy she had known in Ian's arms.

Wanting him to share this bliss, she turned to look for him. No longer needed, the delicate creatures began to fade. Forgetting them, Haven called to Ian, softly at first and then with an urgency that pierced her dreams. He was her very heart and soul, and even as she searched the darkness for him, she felt him reaching out to her with a desperate longing. They were meant to be together, not trapped in separate worlds. She ran toward the only ray of light in the darkness, and when she recognized the bright ring of flame her steps did not falter.

Ian was the fire; bathed in a shower of glowing sparks, she plunged into his heat. She felt herself sinking down into him, and yet there was no fear of falling, only a heavenly sense that at last she was precisely where she was meant to be. She opened her eyes and found herself in Ian's arms.

His eyes were closed and his lips moved slowly,

as though he was reciting an ancient prayer. Captivated anew, she drank in the sight of him, and a long moment passed before she recognized the magical flames surrounding them and realized where they were. Her head hurt very badly, but she was positive they had escaped the maze and could not understand why they had returned. Trusting Ian to know the answer, she slid her hand inside his shirt and fanned her fingers over his ribs.

Ian had been trying so hard to reach Haven that when she touched him he was startled. He first sucked in his breath and then let out a wild whoop. "Dear God! I thought you might never wake. How do you feel?"

Haven covered a wide yawn and snuggled closer. His concern touched her, but she felt too ill to lie. "My head feels as though half of it is gone, and I'm sick to my stomach, but outside of that I'm fine." Overwhelmed with a desperate longing, her eyes filled with tears. "I don't understand what we're doing back down here. I want to go home, and I don't even have one anymore."

Ian leaned down to kiss away her tears. "Yes, you do. You have mine." That she was talking lucidly thrilled him. As her fingertips strayed across his ribs in a sweet caress, it was plain she had no difficulty controlling her emotions either. For a split second he was elated, and then he was disgusted with himself for harboring the hope that she might have some slight impairment that would make her dependent upon him forever. It was a wicked thought, and he was thoroughly ashamed of himself for having it.

Haven could read Ian's expressions so easily, she was certain she had glimpsed a flash of something akin to terror before he had caught it. "What's wrong?" she asked. "Why are you so frightened?"

Ian hugged her close. "I'm not frightened," he lied, for truly he could not think of anything worse than losing her. He wanted her to be strong but feared she would never stay with him if she was. He forced aside that selfish wave of doubt and brought her fingertips to his lips.

"We're here because you were hurt playing in the championship game and I thought you'd have the best chance to heal here. What do you remember?"

Puzzled by his explanation, Haven closed her eyes and tried to see past her dreadful headache to the game. "I remember the mine, and riding up in that bucketful of ore." She paused, waiting for the next memory to come into focus, but found only a darkness that was eventually drawn away by the winsome spirits they had seen in their dreams.

"I don't remember the game. Who won?"

Ian laughed in spite of himself. "The Flames, of course, so I owe you a vacation." There would be a tape of the game, but he hoped she would not want to watch it and see herself getting hurt. He used his left hand to open the sack of provisions Yale had brought and found a container of water. "Are you thirsty?"

"A little, I suppose."

Ian gave her a drink." "Do you feel well enough to go back up to your room? I promise you can ride in the elevator this time rather than a dusty bucket."

"I'm really too comfortable to move. Do we have to go?"

"No." Then Ian changed his mind. "Of course, you'll need lots of rest, and you can sleep on my ship as well as here. I meant what I said, Haven. I want you to come home with me."

Haven frowned slightly. "I can't recall exactly what you said, but didn't you tell me women were too noisy to have around?"

Embarrassed, Ian nodded. "I was talking about other women, not you."

Haven muffled a yawn against his chest. "I'd not want to disappoint you," she mumbled softly.

Ian opened his mouth to argue, then realized Haven had fallen asleep. He was angry with himself for not reacting quickly when she had told him her head hurt. He should have had Control's man send for Dr. Meyers and gotten her something to ease the pain. Now he was afraid to yell for help for fear of waking her. At least he would know what to do the next time she opened her beautiful green eyes. Suddenly hungry, he rummaged in the bag for one of the sandwiches Yale had been thoughtful enough to provide.

Dr. Meyers did not actually believe Haven could be awake and asking for her, but she went to Ian St. Ives's room as soon as she received his message. It was her intention to demand that he be placed under arrest for kidnapping her patient from the medical unit, but when she found Haven sitting up in bed, clad in one of Ian's shirts and sipping a bowl of soup, she was too astonished to berate Ian for anything.

"I believe we met at a Rocketball game several years ago," Haven began. "I want to thank you for what was obviously expert care."

Suspecting a trick, Susan Meyers came close but found no evidence of one. This was the same young woman she had warned Ian might need months of therapy to achieve even a partial recovery. Nonplussed, she shrugged. "I don't believe I deserve the credit for your recovery, Ms. Wray. And as for you, Mr. St. Ives, I wish I had known who you were from the beginning."

"Would you have thought my actions any less reprehensible?" Ian inquired.

"Probably not."

Haven lay her spoon on her tray. "I realize taking me into the maze must have sounded foolish, but since it was such an effective treatment, I won't complain." She was about to ask if she was bald beneath her bandages so it would not be a shock when she removed them, but before she could, Blake Ellis and Aren Manzari appeared at the partially open door.

"I'll get rid of them," Ian offered quickly.

"No. Let them come in." Looking at Blake caused Haven only a dim memory of the pain he had once caused. "Thank you for worrying about me. As you can see, I'm just fine."

Aren needed proof and came forward, reaching for her wrist and taking her pulse. "Do you mind?" he asked.

With no more than the touch of his fingertips, Aren made Haven feel smothered. She withdrew her hand. "Yes. I most certainly do."

"Please be careful," Dr. Meyers advised. "The Rocketball season is over, and you deserve a long rest. Despite this apparently miraculous cure, don't pretend that you haven't suffered a serious injury. Pamper yourself, and take plenty of time to recover before you resume training."

Seizing upon that suggestion, Blake took a step closer to the bed. "Could we speak privately, Haven? I want a chance to start over, and I don't want to have to beg for it in front of a roomful of witnesses."

A furious shadow of anger crossed Ian's face, but Haven raised her hand to stop him before he picked another fight with Blake. Her ex-husband's voice and expression were painfully sincere, but though she believed his intentions were good, she had no interest in encouraging him. "Thank you for wanting to try again, but I can't, Blake. The past is gone, and what we once shared can't be recaptured."

"Think of your career," Blake exclaimed, instantly taking a new tactic. "You know I can have you back on the Rocketball court faster than anyone else."

Aren refused to accept that boast. "A physician's care would be far more appropriate," he argued. "We can go anywhere you like, Haven, and train for the next season at a pace that won't be too taxing."

Haven was amazed that these two men who claimed to love her still saw her in such a narrow light. She was Haven Wray, the Flames' star to them, but she had outgrown that role long before she had been injured. Blake obviously hadn't learned a thing in the years they had been apart, and though Aren had seen her dissatisfaction with her life, he offered nothing beyond the sport they shared.

"Please excuse me," she told them, "but I'm really tired and need to rest."

Still hoping to change her mind, Blake did not hide his disappointment. But he gave in to Susan Meyers's softly voiced urging and strayed toward the door with her and Aren. "I'll come back later," he called.

Haven responded with a faint smile but did not relax until the door slid closed behind them. Ian came to the bed and set aside her tray. "I don't want any more visitors," she said. "Does that sound very rude of me?"

"No, not at all, although I expect Elida Rivard to ask to see you. It was her fault that you were hurt."

"Really?" Haven listened attentively as Ian described the play. "Yes, that sounds exactly like Elida, but she's not malicious and I don't blame her." Her thoughts difficult to express, she frowned slightly. She had showered, eaten, and felt deliciously relaxed, but she wasn't really eager for another nap.

Ian had had a difficult time keeping still while Blake and Aren had offered their care, but noting how quickly Haven had brushed aside their propositions, he had no intention of pressing her to make plans. He sat down on the edge of the bed and took her hands in his. "That's very generous of you, but I doubt the Flames will renew her contract."

"I don't want to talk about Rocketball," Haven confided softly. Their hands fit together so smoothly, like the perfect partners she believed them to be. She met Ian's gaze and hoped she would not sound as fearful as she felt. She did not want to have to coax loving promises from him, but oh, how she longed to hear them.

"You began a story in the maze about an agent who wanted to marry a pirate's daughter," she reminded him. "You said the official story was that she was dead, but you promised to tell me the truth if I told you about Blake and me."

"Right, I did, but then we got distracted somehow." He paused, wondering why she had recalled the story now. Because he would have done anything to please her, he smiled, and tried to give the tale the romantic ending it deserved. "First, I must have your promise that you'll not breathe a word of this to anyone, because it could have terrible consequences for those involved."

Haven's eyes widened slightly. "Really?"

"Yes, really. Not only had the woman's background made her an unsuitable choice as a wife for one of Alado's agents, she was also facing a lengthy prison sentence. But love has a way of finding its own path no matter how great the obstacles."

"Like the glorious fire in the maze," Haven whispered.

"Yes, precisely like that." Haven was giving him such rapt attention, Ian could think only of how much he loved her, and it took real effort to describe another couple's story. "The agent is almost as clever as I am," Ian teased, "and faked his love's death so that he could create a new identity for her, marry that 'new' woman, and live happily with her forever."

That was a far more romantic tale than he had first told, and Haven envied the pair. "That must have been an enormous risk."

Ian nodded. "Yes, the agent gambled everything on the scheme, but he pulled it off. I can't help but admire him."

"You do?" Haven held her breath, wishing Ian thought her worthy of such a desperate bid for happiness.

Thinking back, Ian had to rephrase his remark. "Well, I certainly do now. At the time I didn't really appreciate why a man would risk all that he had for a woman."

"Then you didn't understand anything about love," Haven observed sadly.

Ian thought he had told the story in the touching manner it deserved, but Haven merely looked depressed rather than entertained. He had tried so many times to reach her, and now he saw another chance slipping away. Sick of the caution that had gotten him nowhere, he gently raised her chin to force her gaze to meet his.

"That was before I met you, and learned what being in love really means." Ian paused, hoping she would offer him some slight encouragement, but what he saw in her expression was an anguished confusion that broke his heart. "I'm sorry if I'm rushing you. I suppose we have only known each other a little more than a week, but—"

"No," Haven rushed to argue. "We've known each other several lifetimes at least."

That thought brought a smile to Ian's lips. "Yes, I like to think so. Is there any chance that you might fall in love with me again?"

"I can't remember when I didn't love you."

Growing more confident, Ian leaned close to kiss her. "I don't think having a crush on me when you were twelve counts, Haven. How do you feel now?"

Haven let the warmth of his gaze flow clear through her. "Better than I have in years, thank you. Did you mean what you said about taking me home?"

Ian tried not to look so happy that he would scare her off, but it was a struggle to contain his smile. "Yes, of course, I did. I don't toss invitations about like confetti. We can leave as soon as you feel well enough to travel. I'm afraid you'll find my house a bit stark, but we can redecorate it any way you like. I'd like more color. Really I would."

Ian was not the first man to invite her to his

home, but Haven had refused all previous invitations. She supposed there was some protocol covering the length of such visits, but she doubted many men would invite a woman to redecorate. The intimate turn of their conversation had made her throat very dry, and she reached for the glass of water beside the bed and took a hasty sip before asking, "Do you always give your guests the freedom to change your decor?"

Ian had not meant to confuse her, but clearly he had by not offering a formal proposal. "You won't be a guest, Haven. I want you to marry me and make my home your own."

Ian's eyes shone with a loving sparkle, and Haven grinned. But rather than respond directly to his proposal, she reached up to touch her bandages. "What if I'm bald?" she cried. "How would that look at the wedding?"

"Is that your only objection?" Ian knew he shouldn't, but he had to laugh. "I don't think they cut your hair, but let's look and see."

Haven drew back. "It's not that I'm vain, you understand."

"No, of course not," Ian agreed. He moved closer, and slowly unwound her makeshift turban. Her temple had been shaved, but the long scar left by the surgery would be hidden when her hair grew out. He tossed the bandages aside and fluffed out her curls to cover the pale evidence of her injury. "There, you see? You may not be able to pull your hair back in a braid for a while, but with it combed forward you look fine. Better than fine. You're as beautiful as ever."

Haven bit her lip to hold back her tears. She had not really been worried about her hair, but about all the other things that might go wrong and kill Ian's love. "I've been with the Flames for ten years," she blurted out. "But I don't really want to play Rocketball anymore."

Ian was elated by her decision. "Fine. Do whatever you like, or nothing at all. I've more money than you could ever spend."

"Yes, so do I," Haven agreed.

Ian was confident their finances would never be a problem, and he did not want Haven to have any other worries either. "We've proven to be such a great team, maybe we can find something we'd like to do together," he offered. "I'm as tired of assuming other men's identities as you must be of playing Rocketball. I'd like to be myself from now on."

A smile quivered on Haven's lips as she finally realized there were no conditions attached to Ian's love. He truly loved her for who she was, not what she was. "That would be fine with me." She reached out to caress his cheek, and he placed a kiss on her palm. "Oh, Ian. I love you so."

Ian was afraid it was too soon for her to make love, but he stretched out beside her on the bed and wrapped her in an adoring embrace. "I love you too, Haven, and I can't wait to take you home. Did I ever tell you that I have a snow leopard named Samson?"

Haven raised herself up slightly. "Are you talking about a real leopard?"

Ian nodded. "He's a magnificent beast and I've been meaning to find him a mate."

Haven settled back down into his arms and said with a playful growl. "You're a magnificent beast yourself, Ian St. Ives."

A low chuckle filled Ian's throat before he kissed her. Exercising restraint, he did not deepen the kiss, but when Haven responded with unmistakable passion, he followed her lead. He removed the shirt he had lent her and nuzzled the tattooed flames licking her ample breasts. "I can't look at you now without remembering the ring of fire that saved us in the maze."

After leaning back just long enough to pull off Ian's shirt, Haven molded her breasts to his bare chest. "I won't complain. I saw those pretty creatures again—the ones we chased in our dreams." She slid her fingers through his thick blond hair and kissed him soundly. "When you took me back into the maze they came to dance with me; but I still wanted you. Again," she added. "Forever."

Ian responded with a flurry of tender kisses, and with an enticing touch, Haven lured him back into the enchanted world where their hearts were bound for all eternity. The rapture they shared was rich and deep, and their souls soared with the grace of living flame. Lost in each other, they would chase only their own dreams now. With the joy they had found together, they would make them all come true in this latest and most blissful of shared lifetimes.

Note To Readers

I hope that you enjoyed entering Ian and Haven's magical maze and sharing their adventuresome love story. Your comments are most welcome. Please write to me in care of Leisure Books, 276 Fifth Avenue, New York, NY 10001, and enclose a SASE for an autographed bookmark.

COMING IN JANUARY 1996!

Love's Legacy

**THE GREATEST ROMANCE STORIES
EVER TOLD BY ELEVEN OF THE MOST
POPULAR ROMANCE AUTHORS
IN THE WORLD!
MADELINE BAKER
MARY BALOGH
ELAINE BARBIERI
LORI COPELAND
CASSIE EDWARDS
HEATHER GRAHAM
CATHERINE HART
VIRGINIA HENLEY
PENELOPE NERI
DIANA PALMER
JANELLE TAYLOR**

*ALL PROFITS WILL BE DONATED
TO THE LITERACY PARTNERSHIP!*

LEGACY OF LOVE

From the Middle Ages to the present day, these stories follow the men and women whose lives are forever changed by a special book—a cherished volume that teaches the love of learning and the learning of love!

JOIN US—
AND CELEBRATE THE LEARNING OF LOVE AND THE LOVE OF LEARNING!

ALL PROFITS WILL BE DONATED TO THE LITERACY PARTNERSHIP!

COMING IN JANUARY 1996!

MADELINE BAKER
"To Love Again"
Madeline Baker is the author of eighteen romances for Leisure. Her novels have consistently appeared on the Walden and B. Dalton bestseller lists, and she is the winner of the *Romantic Times* Reviewers' Choice Award. Her newest historical romance is *Apache Runaway* (Leisure; March 1995).

MARY BALOGH
"The Betrothal Ball"
With more than forty romances to her credit, Mary Balogh is the winner of two *Romantic Times* Career Achievement Awards. She has been praised by *Publishers Weekly* for writing an "epic love story...absorbing reading right up until the end!" Her latest historical romance is *Longing* (NAL Topaz; December 1994).

ELAINE BARBIERI
"Loving Charity"

The author of twenty romances for Jove, Zebra, Harlequin, and Leisure, Elaine Barbieri has been called "an absolute master of her craft" by *Romantic Times*. She is the winner of several *Romantic Times* Reviewers' Choice Awards, including those for Storyteller Of The Year and Lifetime Achievement; and her historical romance *Wings Of The Dove* was a Doubleday Book Club selection. Her most recent title is *Dance Of The Flame* (Leisure; June 1995).

LORI COPELAND
"Kindred Hearts"

Lori Copeland is the author of more than forty romances for Harlequin, Bantam, Dell, Fawcett, and Love Spell. Her novels have consistently appeared on the Walden, B. Dalton, and *USA Today* bestseller lists. Her newest historical romance is *Someone To Love* (Fawcett; May 1995).

CASSIE EDWARDS
"Savage Fantasy"

The author of fifty romances for Jove, Zebra, Harlequin, NAL Topaz, and Leisure, Cassie Edwards has been called "a shining talent" by *Romantic Times*. She is the winner of the *Romantic Times* Lifetime Achievement Award for Best Indian Romance Series. Her most recent title is *Wild Bliss* (Topaz; June 1995).

HEATHER GRAHAM
"Fairy Tale"

The author of more than seventy novels for Dell, Harlequin, Silhouette, Avon, and Pinnacle, Heather Graham also publishes under the pseudonyms Heather Graham Pozzessere and Shannon Drake. She has been celebrated as "an incredible storyteller" by the *Los Angeles Times*. Her romances have been featured by the Doubleday Book Club and the Literary Guild; she has also had several titles on the *New York Times* bestseller list. Writing as Shannon Drake, she recently published *Branded Hearts* (Avon; February 1995).

CATHERINE HART
"Golden Treasures"

Catherine Hart is the author of fourteen historical romances for Leisure and Avon. Her novels have consistently appeared on the Walden and B. Dalton bestseller lists. Her newest historical romance is *Dazzled* (Avon; September 1994).

VIRGINIA HENLEY
"Letter Of Love"

The author of eleven titles for Avon and Dell, Virginia Henley has been awarded the *Affaire de Coeur* Silver Pen Award. Two of her historical romances—*Seduced* and *Desired*—have appeared on the *USA Today*, *Publishers Weekly*, and *New York Times* bestseller lists. Her latest historical romance is *Desired* (Dell Island; February 1995).

PENELOPE NERI
"Hidden Treasures"

Penelope Neri is the author of eighteen historical romances for Zebra. She is the winner of the *Romantic Times* Storyteller Of The Year Award and *Affaire de Coeur's* Golden Certificate Award. Her most recent title is *This Stolen Moment* (Zebra; October 1994).

DIANA PALMER
"Annabelle's Legacy"

With more than eighty novels to her credit, Diana Palmer has published with Fawcett, Warner, Silhouette, and Dell. Among her numerous writing awards are seven Walden Romance Bestseller Awards and four B. Dalton Bestseller Awards. Her latest romance is *That Burke Man* (Silhouette Desire; March 1995).

JANELLE TAYLOR
"Winds Of Change"

The author of thirty-four books, Janelle Taylor has had seven titles on the *New York Times* bestseller list, and eight of her novels have sold over a million copies each. Ms. Taylor has received much acclaim for her writing, including being inducted into the *Romantic Times* Writers Hall Of Fame. Her newest historical romance is *Destiny Mine* (Kensington; February 1995).

Love in another time, another place.

New York Times Bestselling Author
Phoebe Conn writing as Cinnamon Burke!

Lady Rogue. Sent to infiltrate Spider Diamond's pirate operation, Drew Jordan finds himself in an impossible situation. Handpicked by Spider as a suitable "pet" for his daughter, Drew has to win Ivory Diamond's love or lose his life. But once he's initiated Ivory into the delights of lovemaking, he knows he can never turn her over to the authorities. For he has found a vulnerable woman's heart within the formidable lady rogue.

__3558-8 $5.99 US/$6.99 CAN

Rapture's Mist. Dedicated to preserving the old ways, Tynan Thorn has led the austere life of a recluse. He has never even laid eyes on a woman until the ravishing Amara sweeps into his bedroom to change his life forever. Daring and uninhibited, Amara sets out to broaden Tynan's viewpoint, but she never expects that the area he will be most interested in exploring is her own sensitive body. As their bodies unite in explosive ecstasy, Tynan and Amara discover a whole new world, where together they can soar among the stars.

__3470-0 $5.99 US/$6.99 CAN

Dorchester Publishing Co., Inc.
65 Commerce Road
Stamford, CT 06902

Please add $1.75 for shipping and handling for the first book and $.50 for each book thereafter. NY, NYC, PA and CT residents, please add appropriate sales tax. No cash, stamps, or C.O.D.s. All orders shipped within 6 weeks via postal service book rate. Canadian orders require $2.00 extra postage and must be paid in U.S. dollars through a U.S. banking facility.

Name_____

Address_____

City _____ State_____Zip_____

I have enclosed $_____in payment for the checked book(s).
Payment <u>must</u> accompany all orders.☐ Please send a free catalog.